"A [illegible] h century . . . The figure of Elric often resembles many purely contemporary figureheads from Charles Manson to James Dean."
—*Time Out*

"Elric is back! Herald the event!"
—*Los Angeles Daily News* on *The Fortress of the Pearl*

"[The Elric] novels are totally enthralling."
—*Midwest Book Review*

"Among the most memorable characters in fantasy literature."
—*Science Fiction Chronicle*

"If you are at all interested in fantastic fiction, you must read Michael Moorcock. He changed the field single-handedly: He is a giant."
—Tad Williams

"A work of powerful and sustained imagination . . . The vast, tragic symbols by which Mr. Moorcock continually illuminates the metaphysical quest of his hero are a measure of the author's remarkable talents."
—J. G. Ballard, author of *Crash*

"A giant of fantasy."
—*Kirkus Reviews*

"A superb writer."
—*Locus*

ELRIC
In the Dream Realms

ELRIC
In the Dream Realms

CHRONICLES OF THE
LAST EMPEROR OF MELNIBONÉ

— VOLUME 5 —

Michael Moorcock

FULLY ILLUSTRATED BY MICHAEL WM. KALUTA

BALLANTINE BOOKS • NEW YORK

A Del Rey Trade Paperback Original

Published in the United States by Del Rey, an imprint of The Random House Publishing Group, a division of Random House, Inc., New York.

The stories contained in this work originally appeared in various science fiction magazines and books, as noted on the following acknowledgments page.

ISBN 978-0-345-49866-3

Printed in the United States of America

www.delreybooks.com

1 3 5 7 9 8 6 4 2

Book design by Julie Schroeder

The Fortress of the Pearl was first published
in the UK, by Victor Gollancz, in 1989.

Elric: The Making of a Sorcerer was first serialized in the U.S., by DC Comics, 2004–06, and was first collected as a single volume in 2007.

"A Portrait in Ivory" first appeared in *Logorrhea: Good Words Make Good Stories,* edited by John Klima, Bantam Books, 2007.

"Aspects of Fantasy" (part three) first appeared in *Science Fantasy* magazine (edited by John Carnell) No. 63, February 1964.

"Earl Aubec of Malador" appears here for the first time.

The introduction to the Taiwanese editions first appeared in *Elric of Melniboné,* Fantasy Foundation Publishing, 2007.

Grateful acknowledgment is made to the following for permission to reprint previously published material:

"One Life, Furnished in Early Moorcock," by Neil Gaiman, first appeared in *Elric: Tales of the White Wolf,* edited by Edward E. Kramer and Richard Gilliam, White Wolf, 1994.

The Fortress of the Pearl, Gollancz first edition, cover artwork © 1989 by Geoff Taylor. Reprinted by permission of Geoff Taylor, www.geofftaylor.btinternet.co.uk.

The Fortress of the Pearl, Gollancz first edition, Elric thumbnail illustration © 1989 by James Cawthorn. Reprinted by permission of James Cawthorn.

"The World of Elric" map © Hayakawa Publishing, Inc., appeared in *Elric of Melniboné/The Fortress of the Pearl,* 2006. Reprinted by permission of Hayakawa Publishing, Inc.

Cover artwork for *Elric of Melniboné* and *The Fortress of the Pearl* (Taiwanese editions) by "Hugo," and "Elric" map by Li-Chin Zhang, all © 2007 by Fantasy Foundation Publishing. Reprinted by permission of Fantasy Foundation Publishing.

La Fortaleza de la Perla cover artwork "Elric Stormbringer" by Frank Brunner, copyright 1982 © Frank Brunner. Reprinted by permission of Frank Brunner.

Cover artwork and interior pages from *Elric: The Making of a Sorcerer* by Walter Simonson, 2004–06. *Michael Moorcock's Elric: The Making of a Sorcerer* published by DC Comics. Reprinted by permission of DC Comics.

The Fortress of the Pearl cover artwork by Dawn Wilson, © 1990 by Berkley Publishing Group. Reprinted by permission of Berkley Books.

ALSO BY MICHAEL MOORCOCK

Behold the Man
Breakfast in the Ruins
Gloriana
The Metatemporal Detective

CHRONICLES OF THE LAST EMPEROR OF MELNIBONÉ

Elric: The Stealer of Souls
Elric: To Rescue Tanelorn
Elric: The Sleeping Sorceress
Duke Elric

THE CORNELIUS QUARTET

The Final Program
A Cure for Cancer
The English Assassin
The Condition of Muzak

BETWEEN THE WARS: THE PYAT QUARTET

Byzantium Endures
The Laughter of Carthage
Jerusalem Commands
The Vengeance of Rome

And many more

To Alex, Tom, and Bobby—
my grandsons

CONTENTS

FOREWORD

by Neil Gaiman

"Rolling . . . we're rolling in the ruins," sings Michael Moorcock on my iPod as I write this, thrown up by coincidence or the magic of the shuffle. Which seems like a good place to start.

When I was nine I read *Stormbringer* by Michael Moorcock and it changed my life. Elric of Melniboné entered my head and it seemed that he had been there forever.

I was determined to read every tale of the albino prince with the black sword. I was an Elric reader, and only an Elric reader, until I found a copy of *The Sleeping Sorceress* a year later and discovered that the other aspects of the Eternal Champion—the heroes and the protagonists of the other books by Moorcock—were also Elric. This was permission to read everything Moorcock had written, and over the next two years I enthusiastically discovered Jerry Cornelius and Karl Glogauer, Dorian Hawkmoon, Corum and the rest of them (the rest of him?). I was fortunate that my desire to read Moorcock coincided with the desire of the British publishing industry to bring everything Michael Moorcock had written back into print, and those books, with their hallucinatory covers, was what my pocket money went on. In a tiny bookshop in Brighton I found a small press Elric novella called "The Jade Man's Eyes" that no one in the world had heard of. I was twelve years old and I wondered if it had been put there just for me.

I internalized the books: they became part of me on a very deep level. I forget to talk about Mike Moorcock, sometimes, when people ask me about my influences, because Mike's work, gulped and read and reread and absorbed when I was still forming, was less of an influence on what I was and how I thought than it was the foundation of it. For all my adult life it has seemed natural and sensible that fictions should be huge and sprawling, should contain their own cosmologies, cover unimaginable spans of time, encompass every possible genre and medium and, if possible, feature thin and pale princes who had trouble with relationships—family and interpersonal, not to mention sexual. (It is worth noting that all these things were, without any conscious thought on my part, evident in *Sandman,* my own largest work of fiction.)

My debt to Michael Moorcock is unrepayable. It was from him that I learned—at an early enough age that the information sculpted the way that I thought—that a good writer should be able to do anything: that you could write heroic fantasy and mainstream fiction with the same typewriter, not to mention comics and movies and essays, political screeds and strange punk fantasies. Moorcock was the kind of editor who changed the field of speculative fiction simply by publishing the kind of stories he wanted to read. When I was too young to do anything more than dream that I wanted to be a writer, he was my model for what a writer was and what a real writer did; more than twenty years after I read *Stormbringer* I wrote a story called "One Life, Furnished in Early Moorcock" that was the nearest I've come to pure autobiography, trying to explain the part that Moorcock (and Elric) had in making me who I am and who I was.

The Elric stories are quintessential Moorcock, the pure stuff, uncut and straight from the street (as are their fraternal twins and reflections, the Jerry Cornelius sequence, a land bridge to the work of the other Moorcock, the one who wrote *Mother London*). They span the entirety of Moorcock's remarkable career to date. They swim with color, delirious and fantastic tales of heartbreak and loss and bittersweet victory, anchored always by the pale prince and his black, soul-eating sword. They are wise and painful and smart and if you read them right, they'll change you.

I wouldn't trade them for worlds.

Neil Gaiman
Carharrack, Cornwall
April 9, 2008

INTRODUCTION

In the middle 1970s, with a fair amount of literary success in both generic and non-generic fiction, and having completed the final Corum sequence, I decided to stop writing epic fantasy fiction. One of the reasons for this was because there was now an entire genre come into existence. Tolkien's and my names were no longer the only ones decorating the fantasy shelves and I felt I had done everything I could do with the form. Fantasy, as a recognizable genre, was coming into its own.

Originally identified with a certain small school—which included Morris, Dunsany and Cabell (and with one fine example by Poul Anderson)—as it became a genre, fantasy quite naturally swiftly incorporated all the methods and imagery created by those few writers, including myself, who wrote it. Reader expectations became more fixed. I had been attracted to epic fantasy as a form precisely because it contained so many unexplored possibilities and nobody knew or thought they knew what it "should" do. As with science fiction, I felt I had done pretty much all I could within the form, and now I wanted to write a different kind of fantasy and some more non-generic fiction (I regard Cornelius as non-generic). I completed the fourth book in the original Cornelius tetralogy and it won a literary prize I greatly valued,* so I felt as if most of my often experimental work had, one way or another, been accepted by the public.

With this in mind, I wrote what was intended to be a fantasy swan song, a novel that would be an homage to Mervyn Peake, who had proven such an encouraging friend and continuing inspiration. My first surviving novel (at that time unpublished) was the Peake-influenced

---

**The Condition of Muzak* won the Guardian Fiction Prize in 1977.

The Golden Barge. His work is unquestionably *sui generis.* It makes use of fantastic landscape, grotesque or at least exaggerated characters and rather melodramatic events, but it contains little or nothing of the supernatural.

Gormenghast has far more in common with Kafka than Kuttner and is closer to the absurdism found in other work by Peake, whether in his drawings, poems, plays or short fiction. *Gloriana; or, The Unfulfill'd Queen* was an homage to Peake as well as my bow to Jacobean melodrama (the most sympathetic critics realized the language was not Elizabethan but closer to Carolingian). The book was well reviewed as a literary novel and at the same time won the World Fantasy Award (the "Howie"). With the acceptance of the non-generic Cornelius tetralogy as literary (as opposed to generic) fiction, together with *Gloriana*'s success, by 1977 I had finished everything I had set out to do in 1960. However, as readers of *New Worlds* issues from that time knew, I was not really satisfied that publishing had changed enough; and it would take a little longer for the mingling of fantasy and contemporary reality to become as familiar to the public as Ballard and I had hoped when we began to talk of finding a new literary form that would be as valid to the year 2000 as Modernism was to 1900.

By 1978, thanks to a bit of self-revelation in the bar of a Russian passenger ship, which I've described elsewhere, I was ready to begin what became my attempt to "explain" the Nazi holocaust by looking at Europe, America and the Middle East through the eyes of "Colonel Pyat," a crazed, terrified Ukrainian Jew who believes engineering (including social engineering) will save the world and who will go to any lengths to deny his Jewish origins. He is what Goebbels described as "that sad fellow, the anti-Semitic Jew." When you take on such a psychic load, you have no choice other than to go mad, especially when you realize that this acknowledgement of your own survival guilt should also be a comedy. By the summer of 1979, having completed the first volume of what became the realistic Pyat quartet, I had been mad for about a year, researching night and day, learning to read the Cyrillic alphabet and then Russian and Ukrainian, occupying the mind of that terrible character for whom sympathy has to be maintained, creating

Byzantium Endures. When I look back, with more guilt, to the domestic carnage the novel helped create, I have to admit that I do so with few regrets. But writing the first Pyat book left me wiped out, and I found I rather enjoyed contemplating the writing of a fantasy novel as a break. My next book, some time after completing *Byzantium Endures* (which was so heavily edited in the United States it amounted to censorship, something that didn't happen in France, Germany and elsewhere) was *The War Hound and the World's Pain,* set in what I regard as the dawn of modern European anti-Semitism, in the Hundred Years War, which so devastated Europe as various forms of Christianity clashed, made alliances and clashed again, often resulting in co-religionists fighting (dirty) to the death.

War Hound was the first of the von Bek novels. The overall sequence was intended to take place at key times in European history from the emerging modern age in the seventeenth century to the coming of the Age of Enlightenment and the moving of the French Revolution from Enlightenment to Terror (and which introduced my vulpine Encyclopaedist Lord Renyard) to the final clash of systems represented by the Nazis and Communists in the twentieth century. That we are back to sectarian warfare between the People of the Book is a sad fact that Jerry Cornelius was revived to encounter in the stories collected in *The Lives and Times of Jerry Cornelius.* The second von Bek novel, *The City in the Autumn Stars,* also dealt with our transition from alchemy and magic to modern physics, and the third was incorporated into the first of the most recent Elric/Eternal Champion stories beginning with *The Dreamthief's Daughter* in which I was at last able to give Elric a contemporary persona.

With all this going on, I thought I had put Elric behind me for good. But, in fact, by the 1980s, when most of the planned work was done, I still had not lost my fascination for the crimson-eyed albino. I wrote my novel *Mother London* as a celebration of my home city and remained unready to tackle the third Pyat novel. While researching those previous books I had ideas I thought would suit an Elric story. And so it slowly dawned on me that I might restore my literary wellsprings with a couple of Elric books. The first of these would incorporate images that had come to me in my travels through Europe and the Middle East. While I had not yet learned how Elric might confront modern times without turning into Jerry Cornelius, I wondered if there was anything new I could bring to the fantasy genre. I am now reconciled to knowing I will never leave it behind and will continue to enjoy writing it, at least in shorter forms, as in the Elric story I did in 2005 for an anthology using the U.S. National Spelling Bee as its base. The editor asked contributors to pick a word, and when I saw "insouciant," a word I might have overused to describe the albino prince, I knew I was fated to complete "A Portrait in Ivory."

I had already brought Elric back in the nineties on his first recorded dream quest in graphic form, "Duke Elric," published in *Michael Moorcock's Multiverse.* There, Elric traveled from Ethelred's Dane-plagued England to Moorish Spain and on to discover a kind of dragon's graveyard deep in the Sahara. Working with Walter Simonson had become a pleasant habit, and we embarked on a four-part graphic novel, *Elric: The Making of a Sorcerer,* also for DC. I wanted to show the history of the Melnibonéans from the time they arrived at their island home and also develop relationships between Cymoril, Yyrkoon and especially Elric's father, Sadric, showing how Melnibonéans achieved their vast knowledge of sorcery via their long dreams. Walter, as usual, rose to the occasion, and readers might find it interesting to see a script addressed to an artist who is also a friend. As with everything in this series, the intention is to offer readers insights they might not find elsewhere, so the only editing is for clarity.

Commissioned by Ted Carnell, "Aspects of Fantasy" was my first attempt at introducing readers of *Science Fantasy* magazine to the roots of modern fantasy fiction and suggesting where I thought the forms might go. Of course, I didn't know then what I know now, and it should be remembered that this was how a critic might talk about such books and ideas before, say, Lin Carter's Adult Fantasy series of reprints for Ballantine Books reintroduced readers to the origins of the genre. My articles, together with Carter's selections and mass-market reprints of Edgar Rice Burroughs, J. R. R. Tolkien and Robert E.

Howard, were, it emerged, early signs of a great renaissance of the fantastic that succeeded in allowing the fantasy genre regularly to dominate popular bestseller lists today and helped introduce certain conventions (often as magic realism) into our literature. Sophisticated writers like Alan Moore, Neil Gaiman, Iain Sinclair, Michael Chabon, Walter Mosley and Thomas Pynchon have all produced wonderful work over the past decade or two and demonstrate how a good writer, frustrated by the old traditions of modernist realism, believing them to be constricting and clichéd, can approach contemporary life with a richer, more complex set of literary tools to produce work that discovers sympathetic recognition in today's general reader. To have been part of the lives of such writers fills me with humility as well as pride. It gives me enormous delight and optimism to read their work, admire their sophistication and celebrate their part in securing that future for literature which a few of us had anticipated over the years. They have reunited popular and complex literary fiction. I love non-generic absurdists like Zoran Živković or Sebastien Doubinsky. I love the work of the best young adult writers, such as Holly Black or my old friend Terry Pratchett, whose work I published when he was far younger than I had been when I began selling to the same magazines. Terry's considerable success, making him the modern equivalent of P. G. Wodehouse, is perhaps the most honorable of all. I think of Thomas M. Disch, Jonathan Carroll, M. John Harrison, Howard Waldrop and Paul Di Filippo, who raised the general level of urban fantasy in particular. Talented writers such as China Miéville, Jeffrey Ford or Jeff VanderMeer still find splendid possibilities in generic forms, equal the best we have, and produce work that is immediately identifiable as theirs. That they prefer to be published in genre does not make their work any less sophisticated than that of P. D. James or Margaret Atwood, who vehemently deny that work of theirs, oozing familiar generic traits at every punctilious pore, is fantasy or its child, science fiction. Indeed, the writers I most admire recognize that they are using methods identified with genre and, by showing respect for their predecessors, gain a keener sense of what they are doing when they use generic materials.

Today, we frequently find superior talent working with genre-inspired ideas. These are signs of lively times and the plethora of talent they have thrown up. Does anyone remember when critics were wondering if the novel was dead?

Earl Aubec is a character I had always intended to do more with, and for a while I was considering writing a sequence dealing with his adventures. All I have now, thanks to David Hill of Cornwall, who hung on to a copy and was able to let me have it back for this edition, is a proposal I must have written but never submitted. I later considered doing the synopsis as an RPG game, but somehow I never did produce it, even though I have a healthy admiration for games writers. I have included it since so much of the work here has something to do with origins and because my fantasy work has always had an intimate relationship with games, since D&D days. I felt that *The Fortress of the Pearl* also might have functioned fairly readily as a game, since it is probably the most formulaic of the books. I'm not sure if anyone else noticed this, but I found it strange to be working within a genre whose conventions I had helped form; and, while many readers have said this book is their favorite Elric story, I felt I had relearned enough in writing it to try to do something a little bit different in the next one.

Although I have had other work published in the People's Republic of China, Elric has never appeared there, but I was especially delighted when Taiwan began to publish the books and asked me for a special introduction. I was pleased to provide it and I reprint it here as another example of how I introduce non-Anglophone readers to the albino.

Lastly, when Edward Kramer had the idea of producing an anthology of Elric stories by other hands some fifteen years ago, I was impressed by the level of talent the project attracted. One of these was by the amazing Neil Gaiman, whose typically quirky and original story he has kindly allowed us to reprint here (it also appeared, in illustrated form, in P. Craig Russell's graphic novel version of *Stormbringer*!). I first met Neil as a bright teenager when he came to visit me at my London flat, and I have been delighted and encouraged to see his talent recognized by a huge audience. He remains as pleasant, courteous and intelligent as he was all those years ago and, of course, his taste remains impeccable. . . . We don't meet often enough.

Lastly, I must thank Michael Kaluta, whom Walter Simonson once described—to Michael's embarrassment—as his mentor, for his fine, fine work. I am, as so often in my life, complemented by the best illustrators around. Who said this isn't a golden age?

Michael Moorcock
The Old Circle Squared
Lost Pines, Texas
June 2008

ELRIC
In the Dream Realms

THE FORTRESS OF THE PEARL

THE FORTRESS OF THE PEARL

(1989)

For Dave Tate

And when Elric had told his three lies to Cymoril, his betrothed, and had set his ambitious cousin Yyrkoon as regent on the Ruby Throne of Melniboné, and when he had taken leave of Rackhir the Red Archer, he set off into lands unknown, to seek knowledge which he believed would help him rule Melniboné as she had never been ruled before.

But Elric had not reckoned with a destiny already determining that he should learn and experience certain things which would have a profound effect upon him. Even before he encountered the blind captain and the Ship Which Sailed the Seas of Fate he was to find his life, his soul and all his idealism in jeopardy.

In Ufych-Sormeer he was delayed over a matter involving a misunderstanding between four unworldly wizards who amiably and inadvertently threatened the destruction of the Young Kingdoms before they had served the Balance's ultimate purpose; and in Filkhar he experienced an affair of the heart which he would never again speak about; he was learning, at some cost, the power and the pain of bearing the Black Sword.

But it was in the desert city of Quarzhasaat that he began the adventure which was to help set the course of his weird for years to come . . .

—The Chronicle of the Black Sword

BOOK ONE

Is there a madman with a brain
To turn the stuff of nightmare sane
And demons crush and Chaos tame,
Who'll leave his realm, forsake his bride
And, tossed by contradictory tides,
Give up his pride for pain?

—*The Chronicle of the Black Sword*

Chapter One

A Doomed Lord Dying

IT WAS IN LONELY QUARZHASAAT, destination of many caravans but terminus of few, that Elric, hereditary emperor of Melniboné, last of a bloodline more than ten thousand years old, sometime conjuror of terrible resource, lay ready for death. The drugs and herbs which usually sustained him had been used in the final days of his long journey across the southern edge of the Sighing Desert and he had been able to acquire no replacements for them in this fortress city which was more famous for its treasure than for its sufficiency of life.

The albino prince stretched, slowly and feebly, his bone-coloured fingers to the light and brought to vividness the bloody jewel in the Ring of Kings, the last traditional symbol of his ancient responsibilities; then he let the hand fall. It was as if he had briefly hoped the Actorios would revive him, but the stone was useless while he lacked energy to command its powers. Besides, he had no great desire to summon demons here. His own folly had brought him to Quarzhasaat; he owed

her citizens no vengeance. They, indeed, had cause to hate him, had they but known his origins.

Once Quarzhasaat had ruled a land of rivers and lovely valleys, its forests verdant, its plains abundant with crops, but that had been before the casting of certain incautious spells in a war with threatening Melniboné more than two thousand years earlier. Quarzhasaat's empire had been lost to both sides. It had been engulfed by a vast mass of sand which swept over it like a tide, leaving only the capital and her traditions, which in time became the prime reason for her continuing existence. Because Quarzhasaat had always stood there she must be sustained, her citizens believed, at any cost throughout eternity. Though she had no purpose or function, still her masters felt a heavy obligation to continue her existence by whichever means they found expedient. Fourteen times had armies attempted to cross the Sighing Desert to loot fabulous Quarzhasaat. Fourteen times had the desert itself defeated them.

Meanwhile the city's chief obsessions (some would say her chief industry) were the elaborate intrigues amongst her rulers. A republic, albeit in name only, and hub of a vast inland empire, albeit entirely covered by sand, Quarzhasaat was ruled by her Council of Seven, whimsically known as The Six and One Other, who controlled the greater part of the city's wealth and most of her affairs. Certain other potent men and women, who chose not to serve in this Septocracy, wielded considerable influence while displaying none of the trappings of power. One of these, Elric had learned, was Narfis, Baroness of Kuwai'r, who dwelled in a simple yet beautiful villa at the city's southern extreme and gave most of her attention to her notorious rival, the old Duke Ral, patron of Quarzhasaat's finest artists, whose own palace on the northern heights was as unostentatious as it was lovely. These two, Elric was told, had elected three members each to the Council, while the seventh, always nameless and simply called the Sexocrat (who ruled the Six), maintained a balance, able to sway any vote one way or the other. The ear of the Sexocrat was most profoundly desired by all the many rivals in the city, even by Baroness Narfis and Duke Ral.

Uninterested in Quarzhasaat's ornate politics, as he was in his own, Elric's reason for being here was curiosity and the fact that Quarzhasaat was clearly the only haven in a great wasteland lying north of the nameless mountains dividing the Sighing Desert from the Weeping Waste.

Moving his exhausted bones on the thin straw of his pallet, Elric wondered sardonically if he would be buried here without the people ever knowing that the hereditary ruler of their nation's greatest enemies had died amongst them. He wondered if this had after all been the fate his gods had in store for him: nothing as grandiose as he had dreamed of and yet it had its attractions.

When he had left Filkhar in haste and some confusion, he had taken the first ship out of Raschil and it had brought him to Jadmar, where he had chosen willfully to trust an old Ilmioran drunkard who had sold him a map showing fabled Tanelorn. As the albino had half-guessed, the map proved a deception, leading him far from any kind of human habitation. He had considered crossing the mountains to make for Karlaak by the Weeping Waste but on consulting his own map, of more reliable Melnibonéan manufacture, he had discovered Quarzhasaat to be significantly closer. Riding north on a steed already half-dead from heat and starvation, he had found only dried river-beds and exhausted oases, for in his wisdom he had chosen to cross the desert in a time of drought. He had failed to find fabled Tanelorn and, it seemed, would not even catch sight of a city which, in his people's histories, was almost as fabulous.

As was usual for them, Melnibonéan chroniclers showed only a passing interest in defeated rivals, but Elric remembered that Quarzhasaat's own sorcery was said to have contributed to her extinction as a threat to her half-human enemies: A misplaced rune, he understood, uttered by Fophean Dals, the Sorcerer Duke, ancestor to the present Duke Ral, in a spell meant to flood the Melnibonéan army with sand and build a bulwark about the entire nation. Elric had still to discover how this accident was explained in Quarzhasaat now. Had they created myths and legends to rationalize the city's ill-luck entirely as a result of evil emanating from the Dragon Isle?

Elric reflected how his own obsession with myth had brought him to almost inevitable destruction. "In my miscalculations," he murmured, turning dull crimson eyes again towards the Actorios, "I have shown that I share something in common with these people's ancestors." Some forty miles from his dead horse, Elric had been discovered by a boy out searching for the jewels and precious artifacts occasionally flung up by those sandstorms which constantly came and went over this part of the desert and were partially responsible for the city's survival, as well as for the astonishing height of Quarzhasaat's magnificent walls. They were also the origin of the desert's melancholy name.

In better health Elric would have relished the city's monumental beauty. It was a beauty derived from an aesthetic refined over centuries and bearing no signs of outside influence. Though so many of the curving ziggurats and palaces were of gigantic proportions there was nothing vulgar or ugly about them; they had an airy quality, a peculiar lightness of style which made them seem, in their terracotta reds and glittering silver granite, their whitewashed stucco, their rich blues and greens, as if they had been magicked out of the very air. Their luscious gardens filled marvelously complex terraces, their fountains and water courses, drawn from deep-sunk wells, gave tranquil sound and wonderful perfume to her old cobbled ways and wide tree-lined avenues; yet all this water, which might have been diverted to growing crops, was used to maintain the appearance of Quarzhasaat as she had been at the height of her imperial power and was more valuable than jewels, its use rationed and its theft punishable by the severest of laws.

Elric's own lodgings were in no way magnificent, consisting as they did of a truckle bed, straw-strewn flagstones, a single high window, a plain earthenware jug and a basin containing a little brackish water which had cost him his last emerald. Water permits were not available to foreigners and the only water on general sale was Quarzhasaat's single most expensive commodity. Elric's water had almost certainly been stolen from a public fountain. The statutory penalties for such thefts were rarely discussed, even in private.

Elric required rare herbs to sustain his deficient blood but their cost, even had they been available, would have proven far beyond his present means, which had been reduced to a few gold coins, a fortune in Karlaak but of virtually no worth in a city where gold was so common it was used to line the city's aqueducts and sewers. His expeditions into the streets had been exhausting and depressing.

Once a day the boy who had found Elric in the desert, and brought him to this room, paid the albino a visit, staring at him as if at a curious insect or captured rodent. The boy's name was Anigh and, though he spoke the Melnibonéan-derived *lingua franca* of the Young Kingdoms, his accent was so thick it was sometimes impossible to understand all he said.

Once more Elric tried to lift his arm only to let it fall. That morning he had reconciled himself to the fact that he would never again see his beloved Cymoril and would never sit upon the Ruby Throne. He knew regret, but it was of a distant kind, for his illness made him oddly euphoric.

"I had hoped to sell you."

Elric peered, blinking, into the shadows of the room on the far side of a single ray of sunlight. He recognized the voice but could make out little more than a silhouette near the door.

"But now it seems all I have to offer in next week's market will be your corpse and your remaining possessions." It was Anigh, almost as depressed as Elric at the prospect of his prize's death. "You are still a rarity, of course. Your features are those of our ancient enemies but whiter than bone and those I have never seen before in a man."

"I'm sorry to disappoint your expectations." Elric rose weakly on his elbow. He had deemed it imprudent to reveal his origins but instead had said he was a mercenary from Nadsokor, the Beggar City, which sheltered all manner of freakish inhabitants.

"Then I had hoped you might be a wizard and reward me with some bit of arcane lore which would set me on the path to becoming a wealthy man and perhaps a member of the Six. Or you might have been a desert spirit who would confer on me some useful power. But I have wasted my waters, it seems. You are merely an impoverished mercenary. Have you no wealth left at all? Some curio which might prove of value, for instance?" And the boy's eyes went towards a bundle which, long and slender, rested against the wall near Elric's head.

"That's no treasure, lad," Elric informed him grimly. "He who possesses it could be said to bear a curse impossible to exorcize." He smiled at the thought of the boy trying to find a buyer for the Black Sword which, wrapped in a torn cassock of red silk, occasionally gave out a murmur, like a senile man attempting to recall the power of speech.

"It's a weapon, is it not?" said Anigh, his thin, tanned features making his vivid blue eyes seem large.

"Aye," Elric agreed. "A sword."

"An antique?" The boy reached under his striped brown djellabah and picked at the scab on his shoulder.

"That's a fair description." Elric was amused but found even this brief conversation tiring.

"How old?" Now Anigh took a step forward so that he was entirely illuminated by the ray of sunlight. He had the perfect look of a creature adapted to dwell amongst the tawny rocks and the dusky sands of the Sighing Desert.

"Perhaps ten thousand years." Elric found that the boy's startled expression helped him forget, momentarily, his almost certain fate. "But probably more than that . . ."

"Then it's a rarity, indeed! Rarities are prized by Quarzhasaat's lords and ladies. There are those amongst the Six, even, who collect such things. His honour the Master of Unicht Shlur, for instance, has the armour of a whole Ilmioran army, each piece arranged on the mummified corpses of the original warriors. And my Lady Talith possesses a collection of war-instruments numbering several thousands, each one different. Let me take that, Sir Mercenary, and I'll discover a buyer. Then I'll seek the herbs you need."

"Whereupon I'll be fit enough for you to sell me, eh?" Elric's amusement increased.

Anigh's face became exquisitely innocent. "Oh, no, sir. Then you will be strong enough to resist me. I shall merely take a commission on your first engagement."

Elric felt affection for the boy. He paused, gathering strength before he spoke again. "You expect I'll interest an employer, here in Quarzhasaat?"

"Naturally." Anigh grinned. "You could become a bodyguard to one of the Six, perhaps, or at least one of their supporters. Your unusual appearance makes you immediately employable! I have already told you what great rivals and plotters our masters are."

"It is encouraging—" Elric paused for breath—"to know that I can look forward to a life of worth and fulfillment here in Quarzhasaat." He tried to stare directly into Anigh's brilliant eyes, but the boy's head turned out of the sunlight so that only part of his body was exposed. "However, I understood from you that the herbs I described grew only in distant Kwan, days from here—in the foothills of the Ragged Pillars.

I will be dead before even a fit messenger could be halfway to Kwan. Do you try to comfort me, boy? Or are your motives less noble?"

"I told you, sir, where the herbs grew. But what if there are some who have already gathered Kwan's harvest and returned?"

"You know of such an apothecary? But what would one charge me for such valuable medicines? And why did you not mention this before?"

"Because I did not know of it before." Anigh seated himself in the relative cool of the doorway. "I have made enquiries since our last conversation. I am a humble boy, your worship, not a learned man, nor yet an oracle. Yet I know how to banish my ignorance and replace it with knowledge. I am ignorant, good sir, but not a fool."

"I share your opinion of yourself, Master Anigh."

"Then shall I take the sword and find a buyer for you?" He came again into the light, hand reaching towards the bundle.

Elric fell back, shaking his head and smiling a little. "I, too, young Anigh, have much ignorance. But, unlike you, I think I might also be a fool."

"Knowledge brings power," said Anigh. "Power shall take me into the entourage of the Baroness Narfis, perhaps. I could become a captain in her guard. Maybe a noble!"

"Oh, one day you'll surely be more than either." Elric drew in stale air, his frame shuddering, his lungs enflamed. "Do what you will, though I doubt Stormbringer will go willingly."

"May I see it?"

"Aye." With painful awkward movements Elric rolled to the bed's edge and plucked the wrappings free of the huge sword. Carved with runes which seemed to flicker unsteadily upon the blade of black, glowing metal, decorated with ancient and elaborate work, some of mysterious design, some depicting dragons and demons intertwined as if in battle, Stormbringer was clearly no mundane weapon.

The boy gasped and drew back, almost as if regretting his suggested bargain. "Is it alive?"

Elric contemplated his sword with a mixture of loathing and something akin to sensuality. "Some would say it possessed both a mind and a will. Others would claim it to be a demon in disguise. Some believe it composed of the vestigial souls of all damned mortals, trapped within as once, in legend, a great dragon was said to dwell inside another pommel than that which the sword now bears." To his own faint distaste, he found that he was taking a certain pleasure in the boy's growing dismay. "Have you never looked upon an artifact of Chaos before, Master Anigh? Or one who is wedded to such a thing? Its slave perhaps?" He let his long, white hand descend into the dirty water and raised it to wet his lips. His red eyes flickered like dying embers. "During my travels I have heard this blade described as Arioch's own battlesword, able to slice down the walls between the very Realms. Others, as they die upon it, believe it to be a living creature. There is a theory that it is but one member of an entire race, living in our dimension but capable, should it desire, of summoning a million brothers. Can you hear it speaking, Master Anigh? Will that voice delight and charm the casual buyers in your market?" And a sound came from the pale lips that was not a laugh yet contained a desolate kind of humour.

Anigh withdrew hastily into the sunlight again. He cleared his throat. "You called the thing by a name?"

"I called the sword *Stormbringer* but the peoples of the Young Kingdoms sometimes have another name, both for myself and for the blade. The name is *Soulstealer.* It has drunk many souls."

"You're a dreamthief!" Anigh's eyes remained on the blade. "Why are you not employed?"

"I do not know the term and I do not know who would employ a 'dreamthief.' " Elric looked to the boy for further explanation.

But Anigh's gaze did not leave the sword. "Would it drink my soul, master?"

"If I chose. To restore my energy for a while, all I would have to do would be to let Stormbringer kill you and perhaps a few more and then she'd pass her energy on to me. Then, doubtless, I could find a steed and ride away from here. Possibly to Kwan."

Now the Black Sword's voice grew more tuneful, as if approving of this notion.

"Oh, Gamek Idianit!" Anigh got to his feet, ready to flee if necessary. "This is like that story on Mass'aboon's walls. This is what those who brought about our isolation were said to wield! Aye, the leaders bore identical swords to these. The teachers at the school tell of it. I was there. Oh, what did they say!" And he frowned deeply, an object lesson to anyone wishing to point a moral concerning the benefits of attending at classes.

Elric regretted frightening the boy. "I am not disposed, young Anigh, to maintain my own life at the expense of others who have offered me no harm. That is partly the reason why I find myself in this specific predicament. You saved my life, child. I would not kill you."

"Oh, master. Thou art dangerous!" In his panic he spoke a tongue more ancient than Melnibonéan and Elric, who had learned such things to aid his studies, recognized it.

"Where came you by that language, by that Opish?" the albino asked.

Even in his terror the boy was surprised. "They call it the gutter cant, here in Quarzhasaat. The thieves' secret. But I suppose it is common enough to hear it in Nadsokor."

"Aye, indeed. In Nadsokor, true." Elric was again intrigued by this minor turn of events. He reached towards the boy, to reassure him.

The motion caused Anigh to jerk up his head and make a noise in his throat. Clearly he set no store by Elric's attempt to regain his confidence. Without further remark, he left the room, his bare feet pattering down the long corridor and the steps into the narrow street.

Convinced that Anigh was now gone for good, Elric knew a sudden pang of sadness. He regretted only one thing now, that he would never be reunited with Cymoril and return to Melniboné to keep his promise to wed her. He understood that he had always been and probably would always be reluctant to ascend the Ruby Throne again, yet he knew it was his duty to do so. Had he deliberately chosen this fate for himself, to avoid that responsibility?

Elric knew that though his blood was tainted by his strange disease, it was still the blood of his ancestors and it would not have been easy to deny his birthright or his destiny. He had hoped he might, by his rule, turn Melniboné from the introverted, cruel and decadent vestige of a hated empire into a reinvigorated nation capable of bringing peace and justice to the world, of presenting an example of enlightenment which others might use to their own advantage.

For a chance to return to Cymoril he would more than willingly trade the Black Sword. Yet secretly he had little hope that this was possible. The Black Sword was more than a source of sustenance, a weapon against his enemies. The Black Sword bound him to his race's ancient loyalties, to Chaos, and he could not see Lord Arioch willingly allowing him to break that particular bond. When he considered these matters, these hints at a greater destiny, he found his mind growing confused and he preferred to ignore the questions whenever possible.

"Well, perhaps in folly and in death, I shall break that bond and thwart Melniboné's bad old friends."

The breath in his lungs seemed to grow thin and no longer burned. Indeed, it felt cool. His blood moved more sluggishly in his veins as he turned to rise and stagger to the rough wooden table where his few provisions lay. But he could only stare at the stale bread, the vinegary wine, the wizened pieces of dried meat whose origins were best not speculated upon. He could not get up; he could not summon the will to move. He had accepted his dying if not with equanimity then at least with a degree of dignity. Falling into a languorous reverie, he recalled his deciding to leave Melniboné, his cousin Cymoril's trepidation, his ambitious cousin Yyrkoon's secret glee, his pronouncements made to Rackhir the Warrior Priest of Phum, who had also sought Tanelorn.

Elric wondered if Rackhir the Red Archer had been any more successful in his quest or whether he lay somewhere in another part of this vast desert, his scarlet costume reduced to rags by the forever sighing wind, his flesh drying on his bones. Elric hoped with all his heart that Rackhir had succeeded in discovering the mythical city and the peace it promised. Then he found that his longing for Cymoril was growing and he believed that he wept.

Earlier he had considered calling upon Arioch, his patron Duke of Chaos, to save him, yet had continued to feel a deep reluctance even to contemplate the possibility. He feared that by employing Arioch's assistance once more he would lose far more than his life. Each time that powerful supernatural agreed to help, it further strengthened an agreement both implicit and mysterious. Not that the debate was anything more than notional, Elric reflected ironically. Of late Arioch had shown a distinct reluctance to come to his aid. Possibly Yyrkoon had superseded him in every way . . .

This thought brought Elric back to pain, to his longing for Cymoril. Again he tried to rise. The sun's position had changed. He thought he saw Cymoril standing before him. Then she became an aspect of Arioch. Was the Duke of Chaos playing with him, even now?

Elric moved his gaze to contemplate the sword, which seemed to shift in its loose silk wrappings and whisper some kind of warning, or possibly a threat.

Elric turned his head away. "Cymoril?" He peered into the shaft of sunlight, following it until he looked through the window at the intense desert sky. Now he believed he saw shapes moving there, shadows that were almost the forms of men, of beasts and demons. As these shapes grew more distinct they came to resemble his friends. Cymoril was there again. Elric moaned in despair. "My love!"

He saw Rackhir, Dyvim Tvar, even Yyrkoon. He called out to them all.

At the sound of his own cracked speech he realized he had grown feverish, that his remaining energy was being dissipated by his fantasies, that his body was feeding on itself and that death must be close.

Elric reached to touch his own brow, feeling the sweat pouring from it. He wondered how much each bead might fetch on the open market. He found it amusing to speculate on this. Could he sweat enough to buy himself more water, or at least a little wine? Or was this production of liquid in itself against Quarzhasaat's bizarre water laws?

He looked again beyond the sunlight, thinking he saw men there, perhaps the city's guard come to inspect his premises and demand to see his licence to perspire.

Now it seemed that the desert wind, which was never very far away, came sliding through the room, bringing with it some elemental gathering, perhaps a force which was to bear his soul to its ultimate destination. He felt relief. He smiled. He was glad in several ways that his struggle was over. Perhaps Cymoril would join him soon?

Soon? What could Time mean in that intemporal realm? Perhaps he must wait for Eternity before they could be together? Or a mere passing moment? Or would he never see her? Was all that lay ahead for him an absence, a nothingness? Or would his soul enter some other body, perhaps as sickly as his present one, and be faced again with the same impossible dilemmas, the same terrible moral and physical challenges which had plagued him since his emergence into adulthood?

Elric's mind drifted further and further from logic, like a drowning mouse swept away from the shore, spinning ever more crazily before death brought oblivion. He chuckled, he wept; he raved and occasionally slept as his life dissipated its last with the vapours now pouring from his strange, bone-white flesh. Any uninformed onlooker would have seen that some misborn diseased beast, not a man at all, lay in its final agonies upon that rough bed.

Darkness came and with it a brilliant panoply of people from the albino's past. He saw again the wizards who had educated him in all the arts of sorcery; he saw the strange mother he had never known and his stranger father; the cruel friends of his childhood with whom, bit by bit, he could no longer enjoy the luscious, terrible sports of Melniboné; the caverns and secret glades of the Dragon Isle, the slim towers and hauntingly intricate palaces of his unhuman people, whose ancestors were only partially of this world and who had arisen as beautiful monsters to conquer and rule before, with a deep weariness which he could appreciate all the better now, declining into self-examination and morbid fantasies. And he cried out, for in his mind he saw Cymoril, her body as wasted as his own while Yyrkoon, giggling with horrible pleasure, practised upon it the foulest of abominations. And then, again, he wanted to live, to return to Melniboné, to save the woman he loved so deeply that often he refused to let himself be conscious of the intensity of his passion. But he could not. He knew, as the visions passed and he saw only the dark blue sky through his window, that soon he would be dead and there would be nobody to save the woman he had sworn to marry.

By morning the fever was gone and Elric knew he was but a short hour or two from the end. He opened misted eyes to see the shaft of sunlight, soft and golden now, no longer glaring directly in as it had the previous day, but reflected from the glittering walls of the palace beside which his hovel had been built.

Feeling something suddenly cool upon his cracked lips he jerked his head away and tried to reach for his sword, for he feared that steel was being positioned against him, perhaps to cut his throat.

"Stormbringer . . ."

His voice was feeble and his hand was too weak to leave his side, let alone grip his murmuring blade. He coughed and realized that liquid was being dripped into his mouth. It was not the filthy stuff he had bought with his emerald but something fresh and clean. He drank, trying hard to focus his eyes. Immediately before him was an ornamental silver flask, a golden, soft hand, an arm clothed in exquisitely delicate brocade, a humorous face which he did not recognize. He coughed again. The liquid was more than ordinary water. Had the boy found some sympathetic apothecary? The potion was like one of his own sustaining distillations. He drew a ragged, grateful breath and stared in wary curiosity at the man who had resurrected him, however briefly. Smiling, his temporary saviour moved with studied elegance in his heavy, unseasonable robes.

"Good morning to you, Sir Thief. I trust I'm not insulting you. I gather you're a citizen of Nadsokor where all kinds of robbery are practised with pride?"

Elric, conscious of the delicacy of his situation, saw fit not to contradict him. The albino prince nodded slowly. His bones still ached.

The tall, clean-shaven man slipped a stopper into his flask. "The boy Anigh tells me you have a sword to sell?"

"Perhaps." Certain now that his recovery was only temporary Elric continued to exercise caution. "Though I would guess 'tis the kind of purchase most would regret making . . ."

"But your sword is not representative of your main trade, eh? You have lost your crooked staff, no doubt. Sold for water?" A knowing expression.

Elric chose to humour the man. He allowed himself to hope for life again. The liquid had revived him enough to bring back his wits, together with a proportion of his usual strength. "Aye," he said, appraising his visitor. "Maybe."

"So ho? What? Do you advertize your own incompetence? Is this the way of the Nadsokor Thieves' Company? Thou art a subtler felon than thy guise suggests, eh?" This last was delivered in the same canting tongue Anigh had used on the previous day.

Now Elric realized that this wealthy person had formed an opinion of his status and powers which, while at odds with any actuality, could provide him with a means of escape from his immediate predicament. Elric grew more alert. "You'd buy my services, is that it? My special prowess? That of myself and possibly my sword?"

The man affected carelessness. "If you like." But it was clear he suppressed some urgency. "I have been told to inform you that the Blood Moon must soon burn over the Bronze Tent."

"I see." Elric pretended to be impressed by what to him was pure gibberish. "Then we must move swiftly, I suppose."

"So my master believes. The words mean nothing to me, but they have significance for you. I was told to offer you a second draft if you appeared to respond positively to that knowledge. Here." And he held out, smiling more broadly, the silver flask, which Elric accepted, drank sparingly and feeling still more strength return, his aches gradually dissipating.

"Your master would commission a thief? What does he wish stolen that the thieves of Quarzhasaat cannot steal for him?"

"Aha, sir, you affect a literal-mindedness I cannot believe in now." He took back the flask. "I am Raafi as-Keeme and I serve a great man of this empire. He has, I believe, a commission for you. We have heard much of the Nadsokorian skills and for some while have been hoping one of your folk might wander this way. Did you plan to steal from us? None is ever successful. Better to steal *for* us, I think."

"Wise advice, I would guess." Elric rose in his bed and put his feet upon the flagging. Already the liquid's strength was ebbing. "Perhaps you would outline the nature of the task you have for me, sir?" He reached for the flask but it was withdrawn into Raafi as-Keeme's sleeve.

"By all means, sir," said the newcomer, "when we have discussed a little of your background. You steal more than jewels, the boy says. Souls, I hear."

Elric felt some alarm and looked suspiciously at the man whose expression remained bland. "In a manner of speaking . . ."

"Good. My master wishes to make use of your services. If you're successful you'll have a cask of this elixir to carry you back to the Young Kingdoms or anywhere else you desire to go."

"You are offering me my life, sir," said Elric slowly, "and I am willing to pay only so much for that."

"Ah, sir, you have a streak of the merchant's bartering instinct I see. I am sure a good bargain can be struck. Will you come with me now to a certain place?"

Smiling, Elric took Stormbringer in his two hands and flung himself back across the bed, his shoulders against the wall and the source of the sunlight. Placing the sword upon his lap he waved his hand in mockery of lordly hospitality. "Would you not prefer to stay and sample what I have to offer, Sir Raafi as-Keeme?"

The richly clad man shook his head deliberately. "I think not. You have doubtless become used to this stink and to the stink of your own body, but I can assure you it is not pleasant to one who is unfamiliar with it."

Elric laughed as he accepted this. He rose to his feet, hooking his scabbard to his belt and slipping the murmuring runesword into the black leather. "Then lead on, sir. I must admit I'm curious to discover what considerable risks I am to take that would make one of your own thieves refuse the kind of rewards a lord of Quarzhasaat can offer."

And in his mind he had already made a bargain: that he would not allow his life to slip away so easily a second time. He owed that much, he had decided, to Cymoril.

Chapter Two

"The Pearl at the Heart of the World"

In a room through which mellow sunlight slanted in dusty bands from a massive grille set deep into the ornately painted roof of a palace called Goshasiz whose complicated architecture was stained by something more sinister than time, Lord Gho Fhaazi entertained his guest to further draughts of the mysterious elixir and food which, in Quarzhasaat, was at least as valuable as the furnishings.

Bathed and wearing fresh robes, Elric possessed a new vitality, the dark blues and greens of his silks emphasizing the whiteness of his skin and long, fine hair. The scabbarded runesword leaned against the carved arm of his chair and he was prepared to draw it and use it should this audience prove an elaborate trap.

Lord Gho Fhaazi was modishly coiffed and clad. His black hair and beard were teased into symmetrical ringlets, the long moustachios were waxed and pointed, the heavy brows bleached blond above pale green eyes and a skin artificially whitened until it resembled Elric's own. The lips were painted a vivid red. He sat at the far end of a table which slanted down subtly towards his guest, his back to the light so that he almost resembled a magistrate sitting in judgment on a felon.

Elric recognized the deliberateness of the arrangement and was not put out by it. Lord Gho was still relatively young, in his early thirties, and had a pleasant, slightly high-pitched voice. He waved plump fingers at the plates of figs and dates in mint leaves, of honeyed locusts, which lay between them, pushed the silver flask of elixir in Elric's direction with an awkward display of hospitality, his movements revealing that he performed tasks he would usually have reserved for his servants.

"My dear fellow. More. Have more." He was unsure of Elric, almost wary of him, and it grew clear to the albino that there was some urgency involved in the matter, which Lord Gho had not yet proposed, nor revealed through the courier he had sent to the hovel. "Is there perhaps some favourite food we have not provided?"

Elric raised yellow linen to his lips. "I'm obliged to you, Lord Gho. I have not eaten so well since I left the lands of the Young Kingdoms."

"Aha, just so. Food is plentiful there, I hear."

"As plentiful as diamonds in Quarzhasaat. You have visited the Young Kingdoms?"

"We of Quarzhasaat have no need to travel." Lord Gho spoke in some surprise. "What is there abroad that we could possibly desire?"

Elric reflected that Lord Gho's people had a good deal in common with his own. He reached and took another fig from the nearest dish and as he chewed it slowly, savouring its sweet succulence, he stared frankly at Lord Gho. "How came you to learn of Nadsokor?"

"We do not travel ourselves—but, naturally, travelers come to us. Some of them have taken caravans to Karlaak and elsewhere. They bring back the occasional slave. They tell us such astonishing lies!" He laughed tolerantly. "But there's a grain of truth, no doubt, in some of what they say. While dreamthieves, for instance, are secretive and circumspect about their origins, we have heard that thieves of every kind are welcomed in Nadsokor. It takes little intelligence to draw the obvious conclusion . . ."

"Especially if one is blessed with only the barest information concerning other lands and peoples." Elric smiled.

Lord Gho Fhaazi did not recognize the albino's sarcasm, or perhaps he ignored it. "Is Nadsokor your home city or did you adopt it?" he asked.

"A temporary home at best," Elric told him truthfully.

"You have superficial looks in common with the people of Melniboné, whose greed led us to our present situation." Lord Gho informed him. "Is there Melnibonéan blood in your ancestry, perhaps?"

"I have no doubt of it." Elric wondered why Lord Gho failed to draw the most obvious conclusion. "Are the folk of the Dragon Isle still hated for what they did?"

"Their attempt upon our empire, you mean? I suppose so. But the Dragon Isle has long-since sunk beneath the waves, a victim of our sorcerous revenge, and her puny empire with her. Why should we give much thought to a dead race which was duly punished for its infamy?"

"Indeed." Elric realized that so thoroughly had Quarzhasaat explained away her defeat and provided herself with a reason for taking no action, that she had consigned his entire people to oblivion in her legends. He could not therefore be a Melnibonéan, for Melniboné no longer existed. On that score, at least, he could know some peace of mind. Moreover, so uninterested were these people in the rest of the world and its denizens that Lord Gho Fhaazi had no further curiosity about him. The Quarzhasaatim had decided who and what Elric was and were satisfied. The albino reflected on the power of the human mind to build a fantasy and then defend it with complete determination as a reality.

Elric's chief dilemma now lay in the fact that he had no clear notion at all of the profession he was thought to practise or of the task Lord Gho wished him to perform.

The Quarzhasaati nobleman lowered his hands into a bowl of scented water and washed his beard, ostentatiously letting the liquid fall upon the geometrical mosaics of the floor.

"My servant tells me you understood his references," he said, drying himself upon a gauzy towel. Again it was clear he usually employed slaves for this task but had chosen to dine alone with Elric, perhaps for fear of his secrets being overhead. "The actual words of the prophecy are a little different. You know them?"

"No," said Elric with immediate frankness. He wondered what would happen if Lord Gho realized that he was here under false pretenses.

"When the Blood Moon makes fire of the Bronze Tent, then the Path to the Pearl will be opened."

"Aha," said Elric. "Just so."

"And the nomads tell us that the Blood Moon will appear over the mountains in little less than a week. And will shine upon the Waters of the Pearl."

"Exactly," said Elric.

"And so the path to the Fortress shall, of course, be revealed."

Elric nodded with gravity and as if in confirmation.

"And a man such as yourself, with a knowledge at once supernatural and not supernatural, who can tread between reality and unreality, who knows the ways along the borders of dreams and waking, may break through the defenses, overwhelm the guardians, and steal the Pearl!" Lord Gho's voice was a mixture both lascivious, venal and hotly excited.

"Indeed," said the Emperor of Melniboné.

Lord Gho took Elric's reticence for discretion. "Would you steal that pearl for me, Sir Thief?"

Elric gave the matter apparent consideration before he spoke. "There is considerable danger in the stealing, I would guess."

"Of course. Of course. Our people are now convinced that none but one of your craft is able even to enter the Fortress, let alone reach the Pearl itself!"

"And where lies this Fortress of the Pearl?"

"I suppose at the Heart of the World."

Elric frowned.

"After all," said Lord Gho with some impatience, "the jewel is known as the Pearl at the Heart of the World is it not?"

"I follow your reasoning," said Elric, and resisted an urge to scratch the back of his head. Instead he considered a further draught of the marvelous elixir, although he was growing increasingly disturbed, both by Lord Gho's conversation and the fact that the pale liquid was so delicious to him. "But surely there is some other clue . . . ?"

"I had thought such things your sphere, Sir Thief. You must go, of course, to the Silver Flower Oasis. It is the time when the nomads hold one of their gatherings. Some significance, no doubt, concerning the Blood Moon. It is most likely that at the Silver Flower Oasis the path will be opened to you. You have heard of the oasis, naturally."

"I have no map, I fear," Elric informed him, a little lamely.

"That will be provided. You have never traveled the Red Road?"

"As I've explained, I'm a stranger to your empire, Lord Gho."

"But your geographies and histories must concern themselves with us!"

"I fear we are a little ignorant, my lord. We of the Young Kingdoms, so long in the shadow of wicked Melniboné, had not the opportunity to discover the joys of learning."

Lord Gho raised his unnatural eyebrows. "Yes," he said, "that would be the case, of course. Well, well, Sir Thief, we'll provide you with a map. But the Red Road's easy enough to follow since it leads from Quarzhasaat to the Silver Flower Oasis and beyond are only the mountains the nomads call the Ragged Pillars. They're of no interest to you, I think. Unless the Path of the Pearl takes you through them. That's a mysterious road and not, you'll appreciate, marked on any conventional map. At least none that we possess. And our libraries are the most sophisticated in the world."

So determined was Elric to get the best from his reprieve that he was prepared to continue with this farce until he was clear of Quarzhasaat and riding for the Young Kingdoms again. "And a steed, I hope. You'll give me a mount?"

"The finest. Will you need to redeem your crooked staff? Or is that merely a kind of sign of your calling?"

"I can find another."

Lord Gho put his hand to his peculiar beard. "Just as you say, Sir Thief."

Elric determined to change the subject. "You have said little about the nature of my fee." He drained his goblet and clumsily Lord Gho filled it again.

"What would you usually ask?" said the Quarzhasaati.

"Well, this is an unusual commission." Elric grew amused again at the situation. "You understand that there are very few of my skill or indeed standing, even in the Young Kingdoms, and fewer still who come to Quarzhasaat . . ."

"If you bring me that specific pearl, Sir Thief, you will have all manner of wealth. At least enough to make you one of the most powerful men in the Young Kingdoms. I would furnish you with an entire nobleman's household. Clothes, jewels, a palace, slaves. Or, if you wished to continue your travels, a caravan capable of purchasing a whole nation in the Young Kingdoms. You could become a prince there, possibly even a king!"

"A heady prospect," said the albino sardonically.

"Add to that what I have already paid and shall be paying and I think you'll judge the reward handsome enough."

"Aye. Generous, no doubt." Elric frowned, glancing around the great room, with its hangings, its rich gem-work, its mosaics of precious stones, its elaborately ornamental cornices and pillars. He had it in mind to bargain further, because he guessed it was expected of him. "But if I have a notion of the Pearl's worth to you, Lord Gho—what it will purchase for you here—you'll admit that the price you offer is not necessarily a large one."

Lord Gho Fhaazi grew amused in turn. "The Pearl will buy me the place on the Council of Six which shall shortly be vacated. The Nameless Seventh has given the Pearl as her price. It is why I must have it so soon. It is already promised. You have guessed this. There are rivals, but none who has offered so much."

"And do these rivals know of your offer?"

"Doubtless there are rumours. But I would warn you to keep silent on the nature of your task . . ."

"You do not fear that I could look for a better bargain elsewhere in your city?"

"Oh, there will be those who would offer you more, if you were so greedy and so disloyal. But they could not offer you what I offer, Sir Thief." And Lord Gho Fhaazi let his mouth form a terrible grin.

"Why so?" Elric felt suddenly trapped and his instinct was to reach for Stormbringer.

"They do not possess it." Lord Gho pushed the flask towards the albino and Elric was a little surprised to see that he had already drunk another goblet of the elixir. He filled his cup once more and drank thoughtfully. Some of the truth was coming to him and he feared it.

"What can be as rare as the Pearl?" The albino put down his goblet. He believed he had an idea of the answer.

Lord Gho was staring at him intently. "You understand, I think." Lord Gho smiled again.

"Aye." Elric felt his spirits drop and he knew a frisson of deep terror mixed with a growing anger. "The elixir, I suppose . . ."

"Oh, that's relatively easy to make. It is, of course, a poison—a drug which feeds off its user, giving him only an appearance of vitality. Eventually there is nothing left for the drug to feed upon and the death which results is almost always unpleasant. What a wretch the stuff makes of men and women who only a week or so earlier believed themselves powerful enough to rule the world!" Lord Gho began to laugh, his little ringlets bobbing at his face and on his head. "Yet, dying, they will beg and beg for the thing which has killed them. Is that not an irony, Sir Thief? What's so rare as the Pearl? you ask. Why, the answer must be clear to you now, eh? An individual's life, is it not?"

"So I am dying. Why then should I serve you?"

"Because there is, of course, an antidote. Something which replaces everything the other drug steals, which does not cause a craving in the one who drinks it, which restores the user to full health in a matter of days and drives out the need for the original drug. So you see, Sir Thief, my offer to you was by no means an empty one. I can give you enough of the elixir to let you complete your task and, so long as you return here in good time, I can give you the antidote. You'll have gained much, eh?"

Elric straightened himself in his chair and put his hand upon the pommel of the Black Sword. "I have already informed your courier that my life has only limited worth to me. There are certain things I value more."

"I understood as much," said Lord Gho Fhaazi with cruel joviality, "and I respect you for your principles, Sir Thief. Your point's well put. But there's another life to consider, is there not? That of your accomplice?"

"I have no accomplice, sir."

"Have you not? Have you not, Sir Thief? Would you come with me?"

Elric, mistrustful of the man, still saw no reason not to follow him when he strode arrogantly through the huge, curving doorway of the hall. At his belt once more Stormbringer grumbled and stirred like a suspicious hound.

The passages of the palace, lined in green, brown and yellow marble to give the feeling of a cool forest, scented with the most exquisite flowering shrubs, led them past rooms of retainers, menageries, tanks of fish and reptiles, a seraglio and an armoury, until Lord Gho arrived at a wooden door guarded by two soldiers in the impractically baroque armour of Quarzhasaat, their own beards oiled and forked into fantastically exaggerated shapes. They presented their engraved halberds as Lord Gho approached.

"Open this," he ordered. And one took a massive key from within his breastplate, inserting it into the lock.

The door opened upon a small courtyard containing a defunct fountain, a little cloister and a set of living quarters on the far side.

"Where are you? Where are you, my little one? Show yourself! Quickly now!" Lord Gho was impatient.

There was a clink of metal and a figure emerged from the doorway. It had a piece of fruit in one hand, a loop or two of chain in the other and it walked with difficulty for the links were attached to a metal band riveted around its waist. "Ah, master," it said to Elric, "you have not served me as I would have hoped."

Elric's smile was grim. "But maybe as you deserve, eh, Anigh?" He let his anger show. "I did not imprison you, boy. I think the choice, in reality, was probably your own. You tried to deal with a power which clearly recognizes no decencies."

Lord Gho was unmoved. "He approached Raafi as-Keeme's manservant," he said, staring at the boy with a certain interest, "and offered your services. He said he was acting as your agent."

"Well, so he was," agreed Elric, his smile more sympathetic in view of Anigh's evident discomfiture. "But that surely is not against your laws?"

"Certainly not. He showed excellent enterprise."

"Then why is he imprisoned here?"

"That's a matter of expediency. You appreciate that, Sir Thief?"

"In other circumstances I would suspect some minor infamy," said Elric carefully. "But I know you, Lord Gho, to be a nobleman. You would not hold this boy in order to threaten me. It would be beneath you."

"I hope I am a nobleman, sir. Yet in such times as these not all nobles in this city are bound by the old codes of honour. Not when such stakes are played for. You appreciate that, even though you are not yourself a nobleman. Or even, I suppose, a gentleman."

"In Nadsokor I am thought one," said Elric quietly.

"Oh, but of course. In Nadsokor." Lord Gho pointed at Anigh, who smiled uncertainly from one to the other, not following this exchange at all. "And in Nadsokor, I am sure, they would hold a convenient hostage if they could."

"But this is unfair, sir." Elric's voice was trembling with rage and he had to control himself not to reach his right hand towards the Black Sword on his left hip. "If I am killed in pursuit of my goal, the boy dies, just as if I had made my escape."

"Well, yes, that is true, dear Thief. But I expect you to return, you see. If not—well, the boy will still be useful to me, both alive and dead."

Anigh no longer smiled. Terror came slowly into his eyes. "Oh, masters!"

"He'll not be harmed." Lord Gho placed a cold, powdered hand on Elric's shoulder. "For you will return with the Pearl at the Heart of the World, will you not?"

Elric breathed deeply, controlling himself. He felt a need deep within him, a need he could not readily identify. Was it bloodlust? Did he want to draw the Black Sword and suck the soul from this scheming degenerate? He spoke evenly. "My lord, if you would release the boy, I will assure you of my best efforts . . . I will swear . . ."

"Good Thief, Quarzhasaat is full of men and women who give the most fulsome reassurances and who, I am sure, are sincere when they do so. They will swear great, important oaths upon all that is most holy to them. Yet should circumstances change, they forget those oaths. Some security, I find, is always useful to remind them of obligations undertaken. We are, you will appreciate, playing for the very highest stakes. There are really none higher in the whole world. A seat upon the Council." This last sentence was emphasized without mockery. Clearly Lord Gho Fhaazi could see no greater goal.

Disgusted by the man's sophistry and contemptuous of his provincialism, Elric turned his back on Lord Gho. He addressed the lad. "You'll observe, Anigh, that little luck befalls those who league themselves with me. I warned you of this. Yet still I shall endeavour to return to save you." His next sentence was uttered in the thievish cant. "Meanwhile do not trust this filthy creature and make every sensible effort to escape on your own."

"No gutter patois here!" cried Lord Gho, suddenly alarmed, "or you both die at once!" Evidently he did not understand the cant as his courier had done.

"Best not to threaten me, Lord Gho." Elric returned his hand to the hilt of his sword.

The nobleman laughed. "What? Such belligerence! Understand you not, Sir Thief, that the elixir you drink is already killing you? You have three weeks before only the antidote will save you! Do you not feel the gnawing need for the drug? If such an elixir were harmless, why, sir, we should all use it and become gods!"

Elric could not be sure if it were his mind or his body which felt the pangs. He realized that even as his instincts drove him to kill the Quarzhasaati nobleman his craving for the drug threatened to dominate him. Even close to death when his own drugs failed him he had never craved anything so much. He stood with his whole body trembling as he sought to master it again. His voice was icy. "This is more than minor infamy, Lord Gho. I congratulate you. You are a man of the cruelest and most unpleasant cunning. Are all those who serve upon the Council as corrupt as yourself?"

Lord Gho grew still more genial. "This is unworthy of you, Sir Thief. All I am doing is assuring myself that you'll follow my interests for a while." Again he chuckled. "I have assured myself, in fact, that for this period of time your interests become mine. What is so wrong with that? I would not think it fitting in a self-confessed thief, to insult a noble of Quarzhasaat merely because he knows how to strike a good bargain!"

Elric's hatred for the man, whom originally he had only disliked, still threatened to consume him. But a new, colder mood took him as his hold over his own emotions returned. "So you are saying that I am your slave, Lord Gho."

"If you wish to put it so. At least until you bring me back the Pearl at the Heart of the World."

"And should I find this pearl for you, how do I know you will supply me with the poison's antidote?"

Lord Gho shrugged. "That is for you to determine. You are an intelligent man for an outlander, and have survived this long, I'm sure, on your wits. But make no mistake. This potion is brewed for me alone and you'll not find the identical recipe anywhere else. Best hold to our bargain, Sir Thief, and depart from here ultimately a rich man. With your little friend all in one piece."

Elric's mood had changed to one of grim humour. With his strength returned, no matter how artificially, he could wreak considerable destruction to Lord Gho and, indeed, the whole city if he chose. As if reading his mind, Stormbringer seemed to stir against his hip and Lord Gho permitted himself a small, nervous glance towards the great runesword.

Yet Elric did not want to die and neither did he desire Anigh's death. He decided to bide his time; to pretend, at least, to serve Lord Gho until he discovered more about the man and his ambitions, and found out more, if possible, of the nature of the drug he so longed for. Possibly the elixir did not kill. Possibly it was a potion common to Quarzhasaat and many possessed the antidote. But he had no friends here, other than Anigh, not even allies serving interests prepared to help him against Lord Gho as a common enemy.

"Perhaps," said Elric, "I do not care what becomes of the boy."

"Oh, I think I read your character well enough, Sir Thief. You are like the nomads. And the nomads are like the people of the Young Kingdoms. They place unnaturally high values on the lives of those with whom they associate. They have a weakness for sentimental loyalties."

Elric could not help considering the irony of this, for Melnibonéans thought themselves equally above such loyalties and he was one of the few who cared what happened to those not of his own immediate family. It was the reason he was here now. Fate, he reflected, was teaching him some strange lessons. He sighed. He hoped they did not kill him.

"If the boy is harmed when I return, Lord Gho—if he is harmed in any way—you will suffer a fate a thousand times worse than any you bestow on him. Or, I'll add, on me!" He turned blazing red eyes upon the aristocrat. It seemed that the fires of hell raged inside that skull.

Lord Gho shuddered, then smiled to hide his fear. "No, no, no!" His unnatural brow clouded. "It is not for you to threaten me! I have explained the terms. I am unused to this, Sir Thief, I warn you."

Elric laughed and the fire in his eyes did not fade. "I will make you used to everything you have accustomed others to, Lord Gho. Whatever happens. Do you follow me? This boy will not be harmed!"

"I have told you . . ."

"And I have warned you." Elric's lids fell over his terrible eyes, as if he closed a door on a realm of Chaos, yet still Lord Gho took a step backward. Elric's voice was a cold whisper. "By all the power I command, I will be revenged upon you. Nothing will stop that vengeance. Not all your wealth. Not death itself."

This time when Lord Gho made to smile he failed.

Anigh grinned suddenly, like the happy child he had been before these events. Evidently he believed Elric's words.

The albino prince moved like a hungry tiger towards Lord Gho. Then he staggered a little and drew a sharp breath. Clearly the elixir was losing its strength, or demanding more of him; he could not tell. He had experienced nothing like this before. He longed for another draught. He felt pains in his belly and chest, as if rats chewed him from within. He gasped.

Now Lord Gho found a vestige of his former humour. "Refuse to serve me and your death's inevitable. I would caution you to greater politeness, Sir Thief."

Elric drew himself up with some dignity. "You should know this, Lord Gho Fhaazi. If you betray any part of our bargain I will keep my oath and bring such destruction upon you and your city you will regret you ever heard my name. And you will only hear who I am, Lord Gho Fhaazi, before you die, your city and all its degenerate inhabitants dying with you."

The Quarzhasaati made to reply then bit back his words, saying only, "You have three weeks."

With his remaining strength, Elric dragged Stormbringer from its scabbard. The black metal pulsed, black light pouring from it while the runes carved upon the blade twisted and danced and a hideous, anticipatory song began to sound in that courtyard, echoing through all the old towers and minarets of Quarzhasaat. "This sword drinks souls, Lord Gho. It could drink yours now and give me more strength than any potion. But you have a minor advantage over me for the moment. I'll agree to your bargain. But if you lie . . ."

"I do not lie!" Lord Gho had retreated to the other side of the barren fountain. "No, Sir Thief, I do not lie! You must do as I say. Bring me the Pearl at the Heart of the World and I will repay you with all the wealth I promised, with your own life and that of the boy!"

The Black Sword growled, clearly demanding the nobleman's soul there and then.

With a yelp, Anigh disappeared into the little room.

"I'll leave in the morning." Reluctantly Elric sheathed the sword. "You must tell me which of the city's gates I must use to travel upon the Red Road to the Silver Flower Oasis. And I will want your honest advice on how best to ration that poisoned elixir."

"Come." Lord Gho spoke with nervous eagerness. "There is more in the hall. It awaits you. I had no wish to spoil our encounter with bad manners . . ."

Elric licked lips already growing unpleasantly dry. He paused, looking towards the doorway from which the boy's face could just be seen.

"Come, Sir Thief." Lord Gho's hand again went to Elric's arm. "In the hall, more elixir. Even now. You long for it, do you not?"

He spoke the truth, but Elric let his hatred control his lust for the potion. He called: "Anigh! Young Anigh!"

Slowly the boy emerged. "Aye, master."

"I swear you'll suffer no harm from any action of mine. And this foul degenerate now understands that if he hurts you in any way while I am gone he will die in the most terrible torment. And yet, boy, you must remember all I've said, for I know not where this adventure will lead me." And Elric added in the cant, "Perhaps to death."

"I hear you," said Anigh in the same tongue. "But I would beg you, master, not to die yourself. I have some interest in your remaining alive."

"No more!" Lord Gho strode across the courtyard signaling for Elric to accompany him. "Come. I'll supply you with all you need to find the Fortress of the Pearl."

"And I would be most grateful if you did not let me die. I would be a most grateful boy, master," said Anigh from behind them as the door closed.

Chapter Three

On the Red Road

So it was that next morning Elric of Melniboné left ancient Quarzhasaat not knowing what he sought or where to find it; knowing only that he must take the Red Road to the Silver Flower Oasis and there find the Bronze Tent where he would learn how he might continue on the path to the Pearl at the Heart of the World. And if he failed in this numinous quest, his own life at very least would be forfeit.

Lord Gho Fhaazi had offered no further illumination and it was evident the ambitious politician knew no more than he had repeated.

"The Blood Moon must make fire of the Bronze Tent before the Pathway to the Pearl shall be revealed."

Knowing nothing of Quarzhasaat's legends or history and very little of her geography, Elric had decided to follow the map he had been given. It was simple enough. It showed a trail stretching for at least a hundred miles between Quarzhasaat and the oddly named oasis. Beyond this were the Ragged Pillars, a range of low mountains. The Bronze Tent was not named and neither was there any reference to the Pearl.

Lord Gho believed the nomads to be better informed but had not been able to guarantee that they would be prepared to talk to Elric. He hoped that, once they understood who he was, and with a little of Lord Gho's gold to reassure them, they would be friendly, but he knew nothing of the Sighing Desert's hinterland, nor its people. He knew only that Lord Gho despised the nomads as primitives and resented occasionally admitting them into the city to trade. Elric hoped the nomads would be better mannered than those who still believed this whole continent to be under their rule.

The Red Road was well-named, dark as half-dried blood, cutting through the desert between high banks which suggested it had once been the river on whose sides Quarzhasaat had originally been built. Every few miles the banks descended to reveal the great desert in all directions—a sea of rolling dunes which stirred in a breeze whose voice was faint here but still resembled the sighing of some imprisoned lover.

The sun climbed slowly into a glaring indigo sky as still as an actor's backdrop and Elric was grateful for the local costume provided him by Raafi as-Keeme before he left, a white cowl, loose white jerkin and britches, white linen shoes to the knee and a visor which protected his eyes. His horse, a bulky, graceful beast capable of great speed and endurance, was similarly clothed in linen, to protect it from both the sun and the sand which blew in constant gentle drifts across the landscape. Clearly some effort was made to keep the Red Road free of the drifts which gathered against its banks and gradually built them into walls.

Elric had lost none of his hatred either of his situation or of Lord Gho Fhaazi; neither had he lost his determination to remain alive and rescue Anigh, return to Melniboné and be reunited with Cymoril. Lord Gho's elixir had proved as addictive as he had claimed and Elric carried two flasks of it in his saddle-bags. Now he truly believed it must indeed kill him eventually and that only Lord Gho possessed an antidote. This belief reinforced his determination to be revenged upon that nobleman at the earliest possible opportunity.

The Red Road seemed endless. The sky shivered with heat as the sun climbed higher. And Elric, who disapproved of useless regret, found himself wishing he had never been foolish enough to buy the map from the Ilmioran sailor or to venture so badly prepared into the desert.

"To summon supernaturals to aid me now would compound the folly," he said aloud to the wilderness. "What's more I might need that aid when I reach the Fortress of the Pearl." He knew that his self-disgust had not merely caused him to commit further foolishness, but still dictated his actions. Without .it, his thoughts might have been clearer and he might better have anticipated Lord Gho's trickery.

Even now he doubted his own instincts. For the past hour he had guessed that he was being followed but had seen no-one behind him on the Red Road. He had taken to glancing back suddenly, to stopping without warning, to riding back a few yards. But he was apparently as alone now as he had been when he began the journey.

"Perhaps that damned elixir addles my senses also," he said, patting the dusty cloth of his horse's neck. The great bulwarks of the road were falling away here, becoming little more than mounds on either side of him. He reined in the horse, for he fancied he could see movement that was more than drifting sand. Little figures ran here and there on long legs, upright like so many tiny manikins. He peered hard at them but then they were gone. Other, larger, creatures moving with far slower speeds, seemed to creep just below the surface of the sand while a cloud of something black hovered over them, following them as they made their ponderous way across the desert.

Elric was learning that, in this part of the Sighing Desert at least, what appeared to be a lifeless wilderness was actually no such thing. He hoped that the large creatures he detected did not regard Man as a worthwhile prey.

Again he received a sense of something behind him and turning suddenly thought he glimpsed a flash of yellow, perhaps a cloak, but it had disappeared in a slight bend behind him. His temptation was to stop, to rest for an hour or two before continuing, but he was anxious to reach the Silver Flower Oasis as soon as possible. There was little time to achieve his goal and return with the Pearl to Quarzhasaat.

He sniffed the air. The breeze brought a new smell. If he had not known better he would have thought someone was burning kitchen waste; it was the same acrid stink. Then he peered into the middle-distance and detected a faint plume of smoke. Were there nomads so close to Quarzhasaat? He had understood that they did not like coming within a hundred miles or more of the city unless they had specific reasons to do so. And if people were camped here, why did they not set their tents closer to the road? Nothing had been said of bandits, so he did not fear attack, but he remained curious, continuing his journey with a certain caution.

The walls rose up again and blocked his view of the desert, but the stink of burning grew stronger and stronger until it was almost unbearable. He felt the stuff clogging his lungs. His eyes began to stream. It was a most noxious smell, almost as if someone were burning putrefying corpses.

Again the walls sank a little until he could see over them. Less than a mile away, as best he could judge, he saw about twenty plumes of smoke, darker now, while other clouds danced and zig-zagged about them. He began to suspect that he had come upon a tribe who kept their cooking fires alight as they traveled in wagons of some kind. Yet it was hard to know what kind of wagons would easily cross the deep drifts. And again he wondered why they were not on the Red Road.

Tempted to investigate he knew he would be a fool to leave the road. He might again become lost and be in even worse condition than when Anigh had found him all those days ago on the far side of Quarzhasaat.

He was about to dismount and rest his mind and eyes, if not his body, for an hour, when the wall nearest him began to heave and quake and large cracks appeared in it. The terrible smell of burning was even closer now and he cleared his throat, coughing to rid himself of the stench while his horse began to whinny and refuse the rein as Elric tried to drive him forward.

Suddenly a flock of creatures ran directly across his path, bursting from the newly made holes in the walls. These were what he had mistaken for tiny men. Now that he saw them more closely he realized they were some kind of rat, but a rat which ran on long hind-legs, its forelegs short and held up high against its chest, its long, grey face full of sharp little teeth, its huge ears making it seem like some flying creature attempting to leave the ground.

There came a great rumbling and cracking. Black smoke blinded Elric and his horse reared. He saw a shape moving out of the broken banks—a massive, flesh-coloured body on a dozen legs, its mandibles clattering as it chased the rats, which were clearly its natural prey. Elric let the horse have its head and looked back to get a clearer view of a creature he had thought existed only in ancient times. He had read of such beasts but had believed them extinct. They were called firebeetles. By some trick of biology the gigantic beetles secreted oily pools in their heavy carapaces. These pools, exposed to the sunlight and the flames already burning on other backs, would catch fire so that sometimes as many as twenty spots on the beetles' impervious backs would be burning at any one time and would only be extinguished when a beast dug its way deep underground during its breeding season. This was what he had seen in the distance.

The firebeetles were hunting.

They moved with awful speed now. At least a dozen of the gigantic insects were closing in on the road and Elric realized to his horror that he and his horse were about to be trapped in a sweep designed to catch the man-rats. He knew that the firebeetles would not discriminate where flesh was concerned and he could well be eaten by purest accident by a beast which was not known for making prey of men. The horse continued to rear and snort and only put all hoofs on the ground when Elric forced it under his control, drawing Stormbringer and considering how useless even that sorcerous sword would be against the pink-grey carapaces from which flames now leapt and guttered. Stormbringer drew scant energy from natural creatures like these. He could only hope for a lucky blow splitting a back, perhaps, and breaking through the tightening circle before he was completely trapped.

He swung the great black battle-blade down and severed a waving appendage. The beetle hardly noticed and did not pause for a second in its progress. Elric yelled and swung again and fire scattered. Hot oil was flung into the air as he struck the firebeetle's back and again failed to do it any significant harm. The shrieking of the horse and the wailing of the blade now mingled and Elric found himself yelling as he turned the horse this way and that in search of escape while all around his horse's feet the man-rats scurried in terror, unable to burrow easily into the hard clay of that much-traveled road. Blood spattered against Elric's legs and arms, against the linen which clad his horse to below its knees. Little spots of flaming oil flared on cloth and burned holes. The beetles were feasting, moving more slowly as they ate. There was nowhere in the circle a gap large enough for horse and rider to escape.

Elric considered trying to ride the horse over the backs of the great beetles, though it seemed their shells would be too slippery for purchase. There was no other hope. He was about to force the horse forward when he heard a peculiar humming in the air around him, saw the air suddenly fill with flies and knew that these were the scavengers which always followed the firebeetles, feeding off whatever scraps they left and upon the dung they scattered as they traveled. Now they were beginning to settle on him and his horse, adding to his horror. He slapped at the things, but they formed a thick coat, crawling on every part of him, their noise both sickening and deafening, their bodies half-blinding him.

The horse cried out again and stumbled. Elric desperately tried to see ahead. The smoke and the flies were too much for either himself or his horse. Flies filled his mouth and nostrils. He gagged, trying to brush them from him, spitting them down to where the little man-rats squealed and died.

Another sound came dimly to him and miraculously the flies began to rise. Through watering eyes he saw the beetles start to move all in one direction, leaving a space through which he might ride. Without another thought he spurred his horse towards the gap, dragging great gasps of air into his lungs, as yet unsure if he had escaped or whether he had merely moved into a wider circle of firebeetles, for the smoke and the noise were still confusing him.

Spitting more flies from his mouth, he adjusted his visor and peered ahead. The beetles were no longer in sight, though he could hear them behind him. There were new shapes in the dust and smoke.

They were riders, moving on either side of the Red Road, driving the beetles back with long spears which they hooked under the carapaces and used as goads, doing the creatures no real harm but giving them enough pain to make them move, where Elric's blade had failed. The riders wore flowing yellow robes which were caught by the breeze of their own movement and lifted about them like wings as, systematically, they herded the firebeetles away from the road and out into the desert while the remainder of the man-rats, perhaps grateful for this unexpected salvation, scattered and found burrows in the sand.

Elric did not sheath Stormbringer. He knew enough to understand that these warriors might well be saving him only incidentally and might even blame him for being in their way. The other possibility, which was stronger, was that these men had been following him for some time and did not wish the firebeetles to cheat them of their prey.

Now one of the yellow-clad riders detached himself from the throng and galloped up to Elric, hailing him with spear raised.

"I thank you mightily," the albino said. "You have saved my life, sir. I trust I did not disrupt your hunt too much."

The rider was taller than Elric, very thin, with a gaunt dark face and black eyes. His head was shaved and both his lips were decorated, apparently with tiny tattoos, as if he wore a mask of fine, multicoloured lace across his mouth. The spear was not sheathed and Elric prepared to defend himself, knowing that his chances against even so many human beings were greater than they had been against the firebeetles.

The man frowned at Elric's statement, puzzled for a moment. Then his brow cleared. "We did not hunt the firebeetles. We saw what was happening and realized that you did not know enough to get out of the creatures' way. We came as quickly as we could. I am Manag Iss of the Yellow Sect, kinsman to Councilor Iss. I am of the Sorcerer Adventurers."

Elric had heard of these sects, who had been the chief warrior caste of Quarzhasaat and had been largely responsible for the spells which inundated the empire with sand. Had Lord Gho, not trusting him completely, set them to following him? Or were they assassins instructed to kill him?

"I thank you, nonetheless, Manag Iss, for your intervention. I owe you my life. I am honoured to meet one of your sect. I am Elric of Nadsokor in the Young Kingdoms."

"Aye, we know of you. We were trailing you, waiting until we were far enough from the city to speak to you safely."

"Safely? You're in no danger from me, Master Sorcerer Adventurer."

Manag Iss was evidently not a man who smiled often and when he smiled now it was a strange contortion of the face. Behind them, other members of the sect were beginning to ride back, rehousing their long spears in the scabbards attached to their saddles. "I did not think we were, Master Elric. We come to you in peace and we are your friends, if you will have us. My kinswoman sends her greetings. She is the wife of Councilor Iss. Iss remains, however, our family name. We all tend to marry the same blood, our clan."

"I am glad to make your acquaintance." Elric waited for the man to speak further.

Manag Iss waved a long, brown hand whose nails had been removed and replaced with the same tattoos as those on his mouth. "Would you dismount and talk, for we come with messages and the offer of gifts."

Elric slipped Stormbringer back into the scabbard and swung his leg over his saddle, sliding to the dust of the Red Road. He watched as the beetles lurched slowly away, perhaps in search of more man-rats, their smoking backs reminding him of the fires of the leper camps on the outskirts of Jadmar.

"My kinswoman wishes you to know that she, as well as the Yellow Sect, are all at your service, Master Elric. We are prepared to give you whatever aid you require in seeking out the Pearl at the Heart of the World."

Now Elric felt a certain amusement. "I fear you have me at a disadvantage, Sir Manag Iss. Do you journey in quest of treasure?"

Manag Iss let an expression of mild impatience cross his strange face. "It is known that your patron Lord Gho Fhaazi has promised the Pearl at the Heart of the World to the Nameless Seventh and she, in turn, has promised him the new place on the Council in return. We have discovered enough to know that only an exceptional thief could have been commissioned to this task. And Nadsokor is famous for her exceptional thieves. It is a task which, I am sure you know, all Sorcerer Adventurers have failed in completing. For centuries members of every sect have tried to find the Pearl at the Heart of the World, whenever the Blood Moon rises. Those few who ever survived to return to Quarzhasaat were raving mad and died soon after. Only recently have we received some little knowledge and evidence that the Pearl does actually exist. We know, therefore, that you are a dreamthief, though you disguise your profession by not carrying your hooked staff, for we do know that only a dreamthief of the greatest skill could reach the Pearl and bring it back."

"You tell me more than I knew, Manag Iss," said Elric seriously. "And it is true that I am commissioned by Lord Gho Fhaazi. But know you this also—I go upon this journey reluctantly." And Elric trusted his instincts enough to reveal to Manag Iss the hold that Lord Gho had over him.

Manag Iss plainly believed him. His tattooed fingertips brushed lightly over the tattoos of his lips as he considered this information. "That elixir is well-known to the Sorcerer Adventurers. We have distilled it for millennia. It is true that it feeds the very substance of the user back to him. The antidote is much harder to prepare. I am surprised that Lord Gho claims to possess it. Only certain sects of the Sorcerer Adventurers own small quantities. If you would return with us to Quarzhasaat we shall, I know, be able to administer the antidote to you within a day at the most."

Elric considered this carefully. Manag Iss was employed by one of Lord Gho's rivals. This made him suspicious of any offer, no matter how generous it seemed. Councilor Iss, or the Lady Iss, or whoever it was desired to place their own candidate upon the Council, would no doubt be prepared to stop at nothing to achieve that end. For all Elric knew, Manag Iss's offer might merely be a means of lulling him out of his wariness so that he might be the more easily murdered.

"You'll forgive me if I am blunt," said the albino, "but I have no means of trusting you, Manag Iss. I know already that Quarzhasaat is a city whose chief sport is intrigue and I have no wish to be involved in that game of plots and counterplots which your fellow citizens seem to enjoy so thoroughly. If the antidote to the elixir exists, as you say, I would be better disposed to consider your claims if, for instance, you were to meet me at the Silver Flower Oasis in, say, six days from today. I have enough elixir to last me three weeks, which is the time of the Blood Moon plus the time of my journey from and to your city. This will convince me of your altruism."

"I shall also be frank," said Manag Iss, his voice cool. "I am commissioned and bound both by my blood oath, my sect contract and my honour as a member of our holy guild. That commission is to convince you, by any means, either to relinquish your quest or to sell the Pearl. If you will not relinquish the quest, then I will agree to purchase the Pearl from you at any price save, of course, a position on our Council. Therefore I will match Lord Gho's offer and add to it anything else you desire."

Elric spoke with some regret. "You cannot match his offer, Manag Iss. There is the matter of the boy whom he will kill."

"The boy is of little importance, surely."

"Little, doubtless, in the great scheme of things as they are played out in Quarzhasaat." Elric grew weary.

Realizing he had made a tactical mistake, Manag Iss said hastily: "We'll rescue the boy. Tell us how to find him."

"I think I'll keep to my original bargain," said Elric. "There seems little to choose between the offers."

"What if Lord Gho were assassinated?"

Elric shrugged and made to remount. "I'm grateful for your intervention, Manag Iss. I'll consider your offer as I ride. You'll appreciate I have little time to find the Fortress of the Pearl."

"Master Thief, I would warn you—" At this Manag Iss broke off. He looked behind him, along the Red Road. There was a faint cloud of dust to be seen. Out of it emerged dim shapes, their robes pale green and flowing behind them as they rode. Manag Iss cursed. But he was smiling his peculiar smile as the leaders galloped up.

It was clear to Elric, from their garb, that these men were also members of the Sorcerer Adventurers. They, too, had tattoos, but upon the eyelids and the wrists, and their billowing surcoats, which reached to their ankles, bore an embroidered flower upon them while the trimming of sleeves had the same design in miniature. The leader of these newcomers jumped from his horse and approached Manag Iss. He was a short man, handsome and clean-shaven save for a tiny goatee which was oiled in the fashion of Quarzhasaat and drawn to an exaggerated point. Unlike the Yellow Sect members, he carried a sword, unscabbarded in a simple leather harness. He made a sign which Manag Iss imitated.

"Greetings, Oled Alesham and peace upon you. The Yellow Sect wishes great successes to the Foxglove Sect and is curious as to why you travel so far along the Red Road." All this was spoken rapidly, a formality. Manag Iss doubtless was as aware as Elric why Oled Alesham and his men followed.

"We ride to give protection to this thief," said the leader of the Foxglove Sect with a nod of acknowledgment to Elric. "He is a stranger to our land and we would offer him help, as is our ancient custom."

Elric himself smiled openly at this. "And are you, Master Oled Alesham, related, by any chance, to some member of the Six and One Other?"

Oled Alesham's sense of humour was better developed than that of Manag Iss. "Oh, we are all related to everyone in Quarzhasaat, Sir Thief. We are on our way to the Silver Flower Oasis and thought you might require assistance with your quest."

"He has no quest," said Manag Iss, then instantly regretted the stupidity of the lie. "No quest, that is, save the one he shares with his friends of the Yellow Sect."

"Since we are bound by our guild loyalties not to fight, we are not,

I hope, going to quarrel over who is to escort our guest to the Silver Flower Oasis," said Oled Alesham with a chuckle. He was greatly amused by the situation. "Are we all to journey together, perhaps? And each receive a little piece of the Pearl?"

"There is no Pearl," said Elric, "and shall not be if I am further hindered in my journey. I thank you, gentlemen, for your concern, and I bid you all good afternoon."

This caused some consternation amongst the two rival sects and they were attempting to decide what to do when over the rubble created by the firebeetles there rode about half-a-dozen black-clad, heavily veiled and cowled warriors, their swords already drawn.

Elric, guessing these to mean him no good, withdrew so that Manag Iss and Oled Alesham and their men were surrounding him. "More of your kind, gentlemen?" he asked, his hand on the hilt of his own sword.

"They are the Moth Brotherhood," said Oled Alesham, "and they are assassins. They do nothing but kill, Sir Thief. You would best throw in with us. Evidently someone has determined that you should be murdered before you even see the Blood Moon rising."

"Will you help me defend myself?" asked the albino, mounting and getting ready to fight.

"We cannot," said Manag Iss and he sounded genuinely regretful. "We cannot do battle with our own kind. But they will not kill us if we surround you. You would be best advised to accept our offer, Sir Thief."

Then the impatient rage which was a mark of his ancient blood took hold of Elric and he drew Stormbringer without further ado. "I am tired of these little bargains," he said. "I would ask you to stand aside from me, Manag Iss, for I mean to do battle."

"There are too many!" Oled Alesham was shocked. "You'll be butchered. These are skilled killers!"

"Oh, so am I, master Sorcerer Adventurer. So am I." And with that Elric drove his horse forward, through the startled ranks of Yellow and Foxglove Sects, directly at the leader of the Moth Brotherhood.

The runesword began to howl in unison with its master and the white face glowed with the energy of the damned while the red eyes blazed and the Sorcerer Adventurers realized for the first time that an extraordinary creature had come amongst them and that they had underestimated him.

Stormbringer rose in Elric's gloved hand, its black metal catching the rays of the glaring sun and seeming to absorb them. The black blade fell, almost as if by accident, and split the skull of the Moth Brotherhood's leader, clove him to his breastbone and howled as it sucked the man's soul from him in the very split second of his dying. Elric turned in his saddle, the sword swinging to bury its edge in the side of the assassin riding up on his left. The man shrieked. "It has me! Ah, no!" And he, too, died.

Now the other veiled riders were warier, circling the albino at some distance while they determined their strategy. They had thought they would need none, that all they must do was ride a Young Kingdom thief down and destroy him. There were five of the black riders left. They were calling on their fellow guild members for aid, but neither Manag Iss nor Oled Alesham was ready to give orders to his own people which could result in the unholy death they had already witnessed.

Elric showed no such prudence. He rode directly at the next assassin, who parried with great cleverness and even struck under Elric's guard for a second before his arm was severed and he fell back in his saddle, blood gouting from the stump. Another graceful movement, half Elric's, half his sword's, and that man, too, had his soul drawn from him. Now the others fell back amongst the yellow and green robes of their brothers. There was panic in their eyes. They recognized sorcery, even if this was something more powerful than they had ever anticipated.

"Hold! Hold!" cried Manag Iss. "There is no need for any more of us to die! We are here to make the thief an offer. Did old Duke Ral send you here?"

"He wants no more intrigue around the Pearl," growled one of the veiled men. "He said clean death was the best solution. But these deaths are not clean for us."

"Those who commission us have set the pattern," said Oled Alesham. "Thief! Put up your sword. We do not wish to fight you!"

"I believe that." Elric was grim. The blood-lust was still upon him and he fought to control it. "I believe you merely wish to slay me without a fight. You are fools all. I have already warned Lord Gho of this. I have the power to destroy you. It is your good fortune that I am sworn to myself not to use my power merely to make others perform my will to my own selfish ends. But I am not sworn to let myself die at the hands of hired slaughterers! Go back! Go back to Quarzhasaat!"

This last was almost screamed and the sword echoed it as he lifted the great black blade into the sky, to warn them of what would befall them if they did not obey.

Manag Iss said softly to Elric, "We cannot, Sir Thief. We can only pursue our commissions. It is the way of our guild, of all the Sorcerer Adventurers. Once we have agreed to perform a task, then the task must be performed. Death is the only excuse for failure."

"Then I must kill you all," said Elric simply. "Or you must kill me."

"We can still make the bargain I spoke of," said Manag Iss. "I was not deceiving you, Sir Thief."

"My offer, too, is sound," said Oled Alesham.

"But the Moth Brotherhood is sworn to kill me," Elric pointed out, almost amused, "and you cannot defend me against them. Nor, I would guess, can you do anything but aid them against me."

Manag Iss was trying to draw back from the black-robed assassins but it was clear they were determined to retain the safety of their guild ranks.

Then Oled Alesham murmured something to the leader of the Yellow Sect which made Manag Iss thoughtful. He nodded and signed to the remaining members of the Moth Brotherhood. For a few moments they were in conference, then Manag Iss looked up and addressed Elric.

"Sir Thief, we have found a formula which will leave you in peace and allow us to return with honour to Quarzhasaat. If we retreat now, will you promise not to follow us?"

"If I have your word you'll not let those Moths attack me again." Elric was calmer now. He laid the crooning runeblade across his arm.

"Put away your swords, brothers!" cried Oled Alesham and the Moths obeyed at once.

Next Elric sheathed Stormbringer. The unholy energy which he had drawn from those who sought to slay him was filling him now and he felt all the old heightened sensibility of his race, all the arrogance and all the power of his ancient blood. He laughed at his enemies. "Know you not whom you would kill, gentlemen?"

Oled Alesham scowled a little. "I am beginning to guess a little of your origins, Sir Thief. 'Tis said that the lords of the Bright Empire carried such blades as yours once, in a time before this time. In a time before history. 'Tis said those blades are living things, a race allied to your own. You have the look of our long-lost enemies. Does this mean that Melniboné did not drown?"

"I'll leave that for you to think on, Master Oled Alesham." Elric suspected that they plotted some trick but was almost careless. "If your people spent less time maintaining their own devalued myths about themselves and more upon studying the world as it is I think your city would have a greater chance of surviving. As it is, the place is crumbling beneath the weight of its own degraded fictions. The legends which offer a race their sense of pride and history eventually become putrid. If Melniboné drowns, Master Sorcerer Adventurer, it will be as Quarzhasaat drowns now . . ."

"We are unconcerned with matters of philosophy," Manag Iss said with evident poor temper. "We do not question the motives or the ideas of those who employ us. That is written in our charters."

"And must therefore be obeyed!" Elric smiled. "Thus you celebrate your decadence and resist reality."

"Go now," said Oled Alesham. "It is not your business to instruct us in moral matters and not ours to listen. We have left our student days behind."

Elric accepted this mild rebuke and turned his tiring horse again towards the Silver Flower Oasis. He did not look back once at the Sorcerer Adventurers but guessed them to be deeper than ever in conversation.

He began to whistle as the Red Road stretched before him and the stolen energy of his enemies filled him with euphoria. His thoughts were on Cymoril and his return to Melniboné where he hoped to ensure his nation's survival by bringing about in her the very changes he had spoken of to the Sorcerer Adventurers. At this moment, his goal seemed a little closer, his mind clearer than it had been for several months.

Night seemed to come swiftly and with it a rapid descent in temperature which left the albino shivering and robbed him of some of his good humour. He drew heavier robes from his saddle-bags and donned them as he tethered his horse and prepared to build a fire. The elixir on which he had depended had not been touched since his encounter with the Sorcerer Adventurers and he was beginning to understand its nature a little better. The craving had faded, although he was still conscious of it, and he could now hope to free himself of his dependency without need of further bargaining with Lord Gho.

"All I have to do," he said to himself as he ate sparingly of the food provided him, "is to make sure that I am attacked at least once a day by members of the Moth Brotherhood . . ." And with that he put away his figs and bread, wrapped himself in the night-cloak and prepared to sleep.

His dreams were formal and familiar. He was in Imrryr, the Dreaming City, and Cymoril sat beside him as he lay back upon the Ruby Throne, contemplating his court. Yet this was not the court which the emperors of Melniboné had kept for the thousands of years of their rule. This was a court to which had come men and women of all nations, from each of the Young Kingdoms, from Elwher and the Unmapped East, from Phum, from Quarzhasaat even. Here information and philosophies were exchanged, together with all manner of goods. This was a court whose energies were not devoted to maintaining itself unchanged for eternity, but to every kind of new idea and lively, humane discussion, which welcomed fresh thought not as a threat to its existence but as a very necessity to its continued well-being, whose wealth was devoted to experiment in the arts and sciences, to supporting those who were needy, to aiding thinkers and scholars. The

Bright Empire's brightness would come no longer from the glow of putrefaction but from the light of reason and good will.

This was Elric's dream, more coherent now than it had ever been. This was his dream and it was why he traveled the world, why he refused the power which was his, why he risked his life, his mind, his love and everything else he valued, for he believed that there was no life worth living that was not risked in pursuit of knowledge and justice. And this was why his fellow countrymen feared him. Justice was not obtained, he believed, by administration but by experience. One must know what it was to suffer humiliation and powerlessness; at least to some degree, before one could entirely appreciate its effect. One must give up power if one was to achieve true justice. This was not the logic of Empire, but it was the logic of one who truly loved the world and desired to see an age dawn when all people would be free to pursue their ambitions in dignity and self-respect.

"Ah, Elric," said Yyrkoon, crawling like a serpent from behind the Ruby Throne, "thou art an enemy of your own race, an enemy of her gods and an enemy of all I worship and desire. That is why you must be destroyed and why I must possess all you own. All . . ."

At this, Elric woke up. His skin was clammy. He reached for his sword. He had dreamed of Yyrkoon as a serpent and now he could swear he heard something slithering over the sand not far off. The horse smelled it and grunted, displaying increasing agitation. Elric rose, the night-cloak falling from him. The horse's breath was steaming in the air. There was a moon overhead, casting a faintly blue light over the desert.

The slithering came closer. Elric peered at the high banks of the road but could make out nothing. He was sure that the firebeetles had not returned. And what he heard next confirmed this certainty. It was a great outpouring of foetid breath, a rushing sound, almost a shriek, and he knew some gigantic beast was nearby.

Elric knew also that the beast was not of this desert, nor indeed of this world. He could sniff the stink of something supernatural, something which had been raised from the pits of hell, summoned to serve his enemies, and he knew suddenly why the Sorcerer Adventurers had called off their attack so readily, what they had planned when they had let him go.

Cursing his own euphoria, Elric drew Stormbringer and crept back into the darkness, away from the horse.

The roar came from behind him. He whirled and there it was!

It was a huge catlike thing, save that its body resembled that of a baboon with an arching tail and there were spines along its back. Its claws were extended and it reared up, reaching for him as he yelled and jumped to one side, slashing at it. The thing flickered with peculiar colours and lights, as if not quite of the material world. He was in no doubt of its origin. Such things had been summoned more than once by the sorcerers of Melniboné to help them against those they sought to destroy. He searched his mind for some spell, something which would drive it back to the regions from which it had been summoned, but it had been too long since he had practised any kind of sorcery himself.

The thing had got his scent now and was moving in pursuit as he ran rapidly and erratically away from it across the desert, attempting to put as much space between himself and the creature as possible.

The beast screamed. It was hungry for more than Elric's flesh. Those who had summoned it had promised it his soul at very least. It was the usual reward to a supernatural beast of that kind. He felt its claws whistle in the air behind him as it again attempted to seize him and he turned, slashing at the creature's forepaws with his sword. Stormbringer caught one of the pads and drew something like blood. Elric felt a sickening wave of energy pour into him. He stabbed this time and the beast shrieked, opening a red mouth in which rainbow-coloured teeth glittered.

"By Arioch," gasped Elric, "you're an ugly creature. 'Tis almost a duty to send you back to hell . . ." And Stormbringer leapt out again, slashing at the same wounded paw. But this time the cat-thing saved itself and began to gather itself for a spring which Elric knew he had little chance of surviving. A supernatural beast was not as easily slain as the warriors of the Moth Brotherhood.

It was then he heard a yell and turning saw an apparition moving towards him in the moonlight. It was manlike, riding on an oddly humped animal which galloped more rapidly than any horse.

The cat-creature paused uncertainly and turned, spitting and growling, to deal with this distraction before finishing the albino.

Realizing that this was not a further threat but some passing traveler attempting to come to his assistance, Elric shouted: "Best save yourself, sir. That beast is supernatural and cannot easily be killed by familiar means!"

The voice which replied was deep and vibrant, full of good humour. "I'm aware of that, sir, and would be obliged if you would deal with the thing while I draw its attention to myself." Whereupon the rider turned his odd mount and began to ride at a reduced pace in the opposite direction. The supernatural creature was not, however, deceived. Clearly those who had raised it had instructed it as to its prey. It scented at the air, seeking out Elric again.

The albino lay behind a dune, gathering his strength. He remembered a minor spell which, given the extra energy he had drawn already from the demon, he might be able to employ. He began to sing in the old, beautiful, musical language they called High Melnibonéan, and as he did so he took up a handful of sand and passed it through the air with strange, graceful movements. Gradually, from the grains of the dunes, a spiral of sand began to move upwards, whistling as it spun faster and faster in the oddly coloured moonlight.

The cat-beast growled and rushed forward. But Elric stood between it and the whirling spiral. Then, at the last moment, he moved aside. The spiral's voice rose still higher. It was no more than a simple trick taught to young sorcerers by way of encouragement, but it had the effect of blinding the cat-thing long enough for Elric to charge and with his sword duck under the claws to plunge the blade deep into the beast's vitals.

At once the energy began to drain into the blade and from the blade into Elric. The albino screamed and raved as the stuff filled him. Demon-energy was not unfamiliar to him, but it threatened to make a demon of him, too, for it was all but impossible to control.

"Aah! It is too much. Too much!" He writhed in agony while the demonic life-essence poured into him and the cat-thing roared and died.

Then it was gone and Elric lay gasping on the sand as the beast's corpse gradually faded into nothingness, returning to the realm from which it had been summoned. For a few seconds Elric wanted to follow the thing into its home regions, for the stolen energy threatened to spill out of his body, burst its way from his blood and his bones; but old habits fought to control this lust until at last he once again had a rein upon himself. He began slowly to rise from the ground only to hear the approach of hoofs.

He whirled, the sword ready, but saw it was the traveler who had earlier sought to help him. Stormbringer felt no sentiment in the matter and stirred in his hand, ready to take the soul of this friend as readily as it had stolen the souls of Elric's enemies.

"No!" The albino forced the blade back into its scabbard. He felt almost sick with the energy leeched from the demon but he made himself take a grave bow as the rider joined him. "I thank you for your help, stranger. I had not expected to find a friend this close to Quarzhasaat."

The young man regarded him with some sympathy and good will. He had startlingly handsome features with dark, humorous eyes in his gleaming black flesh. On his short, curly hair he wore a skull-cap decorated with peacock feathers and his jacket and breeches seemed to be of black velvet stitched with gold thread, over which was thrown a pale-coloured hooded cloak of the pattern usually worn by desert peoples in these parts. He rode up slowly on the loping, bovine mount which had cloven hoofs and a broad head, a massive hump above its shoulders, like that of certain cattle Elric had seen in scrolls depicting the Southern Continent.

At the young man's belt was a richly carved stick of some kind with a crooked handle, about half his height, and on his other hip he wore a simple flat-hilted sword.

"I had not expected to find an emperor of Melniboné in these parts, either!" said the man with some amusement. "Greetings, Prince Elric. I am honoured to make your acquaintance."

"We have not met? How do you know my name?"

"Oh, such tricks are nothing to one of my craft, Prince Elric. My name is Alnac Kreb and I am making my way to the oasis they call the Silver Flower. Shall we return to your camp and your horse? I am glad to say he is unharmed. What powerful enemies you have, to send such a foul demon against you! Have you given offense to the Sorcerer Adventurers of Quarzhasaat?"

"It would seem so." Elric walked beside the newcomer as they made their way back towards the Red Road. "I am grateful to you, Master Alnac Kreb. Without your help, I should now be absorbed body and soul in that creature and borne back to whatever hell gave birth to it. But I must warn you, there is some danger that I shall be attacked again by those who sent it."

"I think not, Prince Elric. They were doubtless confident of their success and, what's more, wanted no further business with you, once they realized that you were no ordinary mortal. I saw a pack of them—from three separate sects of that unpleasant guild—riding rapidly back to Quarzhasaat not an hour since. Curious as to what they fled from, I came this way. And so found you. I was glad to be of some minor service."

"I, too, am riding for the Silver Flower Oasis, though I know not what to expect there." Elric had taken a strong liking to this young man. "I would be glad of your company on the journey."

"Honoured, sir. Honoured!" Smiling, Alnac Kreb dismounted from his odd beast and tethered it close to Elric's horse which was yet to recover from its terror, though it was now quieter.

"I will not ask you to weary yourself further tonight, sir," Elric added, "but I'm mightily curious to know how you guessed my name and my race. You spoke of a trick of your craft. What would that trade be, may I ask?"

"Why, sir," said Alnac Kreb, dusting sand from his velvet breeches, "I'd thought you guessed. I am a dreamthief."

Chapter Four

A Funeral at the Oasis

"The Silver Flower Oasis is rather more than a simple clearing in the desert as you'll discover," said Alnac Kreb, dabbing delicately at his beautiful face with a kerchief trimmed with glittering lace. "It is a great meeting place for all the nomad nations and much wealth comes to it to be traded. It is frequented by kings and princes. Marriages are arranged and often take place there, as do other ceremonies. Great political decisions are made. Alliances are maintained and fresh ones struck. News is exchanged. Every manner of thing is bartered. Not everything is conventional, not everything—material. It is a vital place, unlike Quarzhasaat, which the nomads visit reluctantly only when necessity—or greed—demands."

"Why have we seen none of these nomads, friend Alnac?" Elric asked.

"They avoid Quarzhasaat. For them the place and its people are the equivalent of hell. Some even believe that the souls of the damned are sent to Quarzhasaat. The city represents everything they fear and everything that is at odds with what they most value."

"I'd be inclined to see eye to eye with those nomads." Elric allowed himself a smile. Still free of the elixir, his body was again craving it. The energy his sword had given him would normally have sustained him for a considerably longer time. This was further proof that the elixir, as explained by Manag Iss, fed off his very life-force to give him temporary physical strength. He was beginning to suspect that as well as feeding his own vitality he was also feeding the elixir. The distillation had come almost to represent a sentient creature, like the sword. Yet the Black Sword had never given him the same sense of being invaded. He kept his mind free of such thoughts as much as he could. "I feel a certain kinship with them already," he added.

"Your hope, Prince Elric, is that they find you acceptable!" And Alnac laughed. "Though an ancient enemy of the lords of Quarzhasaat must have certain credentials. I have acquaintances amongst some of the clans. You must let me introduce you, when the time comes."

"Willingly," said Elric, "though you have yet to explain how you came to know me."

Alnac nodded as if he had forgotten the matter. "It is not complicated and yet it is remarkably complex, if you do not understand the fundamental workings of the multiverse. As I told you, I'm a dreamthief. I know more than most because I am familiar with so many dreams. Let's merely say that I heard of you in a dream and that it is sometimes my destiny to be your companion—though not for long, I'd guess, in my present guise."

"In a dream? You have yet to tell me what a dreamthief does."

"Why, steal dreams, of course. Twice a year we take our booty to a certain market to trade, just as the nomads trade."

"You trade in dreams?" Elric was disbelieving.

Alnac enjoyed his astonishment. "There are dealers at the market who'll pay for certain dreams. In turn they sell them to those unfortunates who either cannot dream or who have such banal dreams they desire something better."

Elric shook his head. "You speak in parables, surely?"

"No, Prince Elric, I speak the exact truth." He dragged the oddly hooked staff from his belt. It reminded Elric of a shepherd's crook, though it was shorter. "One does not acquire this without having studied the basic skills of the dreamthief's craft. I am not the best in my trade, nor am I likely ever to be, but in this realm, in this time, this is my destiny. There are few in this realm, for reasons you shall no doubt learn, and only the nomads and the folk of Elwher recognize our craft. We are not known, save to a few wise people, in the Young Kingdoms."

"Why do you not venture there?"

"We are not asked to do so. Have you ever heard of anyone seeking the services of a dreamthief in the Young Kingdoms?"

"Never. But why should that be?"

"Perhaps because Chaos has so much influence in the West and South. There, the most terrible nightmares can readily become reality."

"You fear Chaos?"

"What rational being does not? I fear the dreams of those who serve her." Alnac Kreb looked away towards the desert. "Elwher and what you call 'the Unmapped East' have in the main less complicated inhabitants, Melniboné's influence was never so strong. Nor was it, of course, in the Sighing Desert."

"So it is my folk whom you fear?"

"I fear any race which gives itself over to Chaos, which makes pacts with the most powerful of supernaturals, with the very Dukes of Chaos, with the Sword Rulers themselves! I do not regard such dealings as wholesome or sane. I am opposed to Chaos."

"You serve Law?"

"I serve myself. I serve, I suppose, the Balance. I believe that one can live and let live and celebrate the world's variety."

"Such philosophy is enviable, Master Alnac. I aspire to it myself, though I suppose you do not believe me."

"Aye, I believe you, Prince Elric. I am party to many dreams and you occur in some of them. And dreams are reality and vice versa in other realms." The dreamthief glanced sympathetically at the albino. "It must be hard for one who has known millennia of power to attempt a relinquishing of such power."

"You understand me well, Sir Dreamthief."

"Oh, my understanding is only ever of the broadest kind in such matters." Alnac Kreb shrugged and made a self-deprecating gesture.

"I have spent much time in seeking the meaning of justice, in visiting lands where it is said to exist, in trying to discover how best it may be accomplished, how it may be established so that all the world shall benefit. Have you heard of Tanelorn, Alnac Kreb? There justice is said to rule. There the Grey Lords, those who keep charge of the world's equilibrium, are said to have their greatest influence."

"Tanelorn exists," said the dreamthief quietly. "And it has many names. Yet in some realms, I fear, it is no more than an idea of perfection. Such ideas are what maintain us in hope and fuel our urge to make reality of dreams. Sometimes we are successful."

"Justice exists?"

"Of course it does. But it is not an abstraction. It must be worked for. Justice is your demon, I think, Prince Elric, more than any Lord of Chaos. You have chosen a cruel and an unhappy road." He smiled delicately as he stared ahead of them at the long, red trail stretching out to the horizon. "Crueler, I think, than the Red Road to the Silver Flower Oasis."

"You're not encouraging, Master Alnac."

"You must know yourself that there's precious little justice in the world that is not hard fought for, hard won and hard held. It is in our mortal nature to give that responsibility to others. Yet poor creatures like yourself continue to try to relinquish power while acquiring more and more responsibility. Some would say that it is admirable to do as you do, that it builds character and strength of purpose, that it reaches towards a higher form of sanity . . ."

"Aye. And some would say it is the purest form of madness, at odds with all natural impulses. I do not know what it is I long for, Sir Dreamthief, but I know I hope for a world where the strong do not prey on the weak like mindless insects, where mortal creatures may attain their greatest possible fulfillment, where all are dignified and healthy, never victims of a few stronger than themselves . . ."

"Then you serve the wrong masters in Chaos, prince. For the only justice recognized by the Dukes of Hell is the justice of their own unchallenged existence. They are like fresh-born babes in this. They are opposed to your every ideal."

Elric grew disturbed and spoke softly when he replied. "But can one not use such forces to defeat them—or at least challenge their power and adjust the Balance?"

"Only the Balance gives you the power you desire. And it is a subtle, sometimes exceptionally delicate power."

"Not strong enough in my world, I fear."

"Strong only when sufficient numbers believe in it. Then it is stronger than Chaos and Law combined."

"Well, I shall work for that day when the power of the Balance holds sway, Master Alnac Kreb, but I am not sure I will live to see it."

"If you live," said Alnac quietly, "I suspect it will not come. But it will be many years before you are called upon to blow Roland's horn."

"A horn? What horn is that?" But Elric's question was casual. He believed that the dreamthief was making another allegorical allusion.

"Look!" Alnac pointed ahead. "See in the far distance? There is the first sign of the Silver Flower Oasis."

To their left the sun was going down. It cast deep shadows across the dunes and the high banks of the Red Road while the sky was darkening to a deep amber on the horizon. Yet almost at the limit of his vision Elric made out another shape, something that was neither a shadow nor a sand-dune but which might have been a group of rocks.

"What is it? What do you recognize?"

"The nomads call it 'kashbeh.' In our common tongue we would say it was a castle, perhaps, or a fortified village. We have no exact word for such a place, for we have no need of them. Here, in the desert, it is a necessity. The Kashbeh Moulor Ka Riiz was built long before the extinction of the Quarzhasaatim Empire and is named for a wise king, founder of the Aloum'rit dynasty which still holds the place in charge for the nomad clans and is respected above all other peoples of the desert. It is a kashbeh sheltering anyone in need. Anyone who is a fugitive may seek shelter there and there may be assured of a fair trial."

"So justice exists in this desert, if nowhere else?"

"Such places exist, as I said, throughout the realms of the multiverse. They are maintained by men and women of the purest and most humane principle . . ."

"Then is this kashbeh not Tanelorn, whose legend brought me to the Sighing Desert?"

"It is not Tanelorn, for Tanelorn is eternal. The Kashbeh Moulor Ka Riiz must be maintained through constant vigilance. It is the antithesis of Quarzhasaat and that city's lords have made many attempts to destroy it."

Elric felt the pangs of craving and he resisted reaching for one of his silver flasks. "Is that also called The Fortress of the Pearl?"

At this, Alnac Kreb laughed suddenly. "Oh, my good prince, clearly you have only the haziest notion of the place and the thing you seek. Let me now say that the Fortress of the Pearl may well exist within that kashbeh and that the kashbeh could also have an existence within the Fortress. But they are in no way the same!"

"Please, Master Alnac, do not confuse me further! I pretended to know something of this, first because I wished to extend my own life and then because I needed to purchase the life of another. I would be grateful for some illumination. Lord Gho Fhaazi thought me a dreamthief, after all, which supposes that a dreamthief would know of the Blood Moon, the Bronze Tent and the location of the Place of the Pearl."

"Aye, well. Some dreamthieves are better informed than others. And if a dreamthief is required for this task, prince, if, as you've told me, Quarzhasaat's Sorcerer Adventurers cannot achieve it, then I would guess the Fortress of the Pearl is more than mere stones and mortar. It has to do with realms familiar only to a trained dreamthief—but one probably more sophisticated than myself."

"Know you, Master Alnac, that I have already traveled to strange realms in pursuit of my various goals. I am not completely unsophisticated in such matters . . ."

"These realms are denied to most." Alnac seemed reluctant to say more but Elric pressed him.

"Where lie these realms?" He stared ahead, straining his eyes to see more of the Kashbeh Moulor Ka Riiz but failing, for the sun was now almost below the horizon. "In the East? Beyond Elwher? Or in another part of the multiverse altogether?"

Alnac Kreb was regretful. "We are sworn to speak as little as we can of our knowledge, save in the most crucial and specific of circumstances. But I should inform you that those realms are at once closer and more distant than Elwher. I promise you that I will not mystify you any more than I have done so already. And if I can illuminate you and help you in your quest, that I will do also." He made to laugh, to lighten his own mood. "Best ready yourself for company, prince. We shall have a great deal of it by nightfall, if I'm not mistaken."

The moon had risen before the last rays of the sun had vanished and its silver bore a pinkish sheen, like that of a rare pearl itself, as they reached a rise in the Red Road and looked down now upon a thousand fires. Silhouetted against them were as many tall tents, settled on the sand so as to resemble gigantic winged insects stretched out to catch the warmth from above. Within these tents burned lamps while men, women and children wandered in and out. A delicious smell of mingled herbs, spices, vegetables and meats drifted up towards them and the soft smoke of the fires rose and curled into the sky above the great rocks on which perched the Kashbeh Moulor Ka Riiz, a massive tower about which had grown a collection of buildings, some of wonderfully imaginative architecture, the whole surrounded by a crenelated wall of irregular but equally monumental proportions, all of the same red rock so that it seemed to grow out of the very earth and sand that surrounded it.

At intervals around those battlements great torches blazed, revealing men who were evidently guards patrolling the walls and roofs, while through tall gates a steady stream of traffic came and went across a bridge carved from the living rock.

This was, as Alnac Kreb had warned him, not the simple resting place of primitive caravans Elric had expected to find on the Red Road.

They were not challenged as they descended towards the wide sheet of water around which blossomed a rich variety of palms, cypresses, poplars, fig trees and cactus, but many looked at them with open curiosity. And not all the curious eyes were friendly.

Their horses were of a similar build to Elric's own, while others of the nomads rode the bovine creatures favoured by Alnac. The sounds of bellowing, grunting and spitting rose from every quarter and Elric could see that beyond the field of tents lay corrals in which riding beasts as well as sheep, goats and other creatures were penned.

But the sight which dominated this extraordinary scene was that of some hundred or more torches blazing in a semi-circle at the water's edge.

Each torch was held by a cloaked and cowled figure and each burned with a bright, white steady flame which cast the same strong light upon a dais of carved wood at the very centre of the gathering.

Elric and his companion reined in their mounts to watch, as fascinated by this vision as the scores of other nomads who walked slowly to the edge of the semi-circle to witness what was clearly a ceremony of some magnitude. The witnesses stood in attitudes of respect, their various robes and costumes identifying their clan. The nomads were of a variety of colours, some as black as Alnac Kreb, some almost as white-skinned as Elric, with every shade in between, yet in features they were similar, with strong-boned faces and deep-set eyes. Both men and women were tall and bore themselves with considerable grace. Elric had never seen so many handsome people and he was as impressed by their natural dignity as he had been disgusted by the extremes of arrogance and degradation he had witnessed in Quarzhasaat.

Now a procession approached down the hill and Elric saw that six men bore a large, domed chest on their shoulders, proceeding with grave slowness until they came to the dais.

The white light showed every detail of the scene. The men were drawn from different clans, though all of the same height and all of middle age. A single drum began to sound, its beat sharp and clear in the night air. Then another joined it, then another, until at least twenty drums were echoing across the waters of the oasis and the rooftops of Kashbeh Moulor Ka Riiz, their voices at once slow and obeying complicated rhythmic patterns whose subtlety Elric gradually came to marvel at.

"Is it a funeral?" the albino asked his new friend.

Alnac nodded. "But I know not who they bury." He pointed to a series of symmetrical mounds in the distance beyond the trees. "Those are the nomad burial grounds."

Now another, older man, his beard and brows grey beneath his cowl, stepped forward and began to read from a scroll he produced from his sleeve, while two others opened the lid of the elaborate coffin and, to Elric's astonishment, spat into it.

Now Alnac gasped. He stood on his toes and peered, for the brands clearly illuminated the coffin's contents. He turned, still more mystified, to Elric. "'Tis empty, Prince Elric. Or else the corpse is invisible."

The rhythm of the drums increased in tempo and complexity. Voices began to chant, rising and falling like waves in an ocean. Elric had never heard such music before. He found that it was moving him to obscure emotions. He felt rage. He felt sorrow. He found that he was close to weeping. And still the music continued, growing in intensity. He longed to join in, but could understand nothing of the language they used. It seemed to him that the words were older by far than the speech of Melniboné, which was the oldest in the Young Kingdoms.

And then, suddenly, the singing and the drumming ended.

The six men took the coffin from the dais and began to march away with it, towards the mounds, and the men with the torches followed, the light casting strange shadows amongst the trees, illuminating sudden patches of shining whiteness which Elric could not identify.

As suddenly as they had stopped the drumming, the chanting began again, but this time they had a celebratory, triumphant note to them. Slowly the crowd lifted their heads and from several hundred throats came a high-pitched ululation, clearly a traditional response.

Then the nomads began to drift back towards their tents. Alnac stopped one, a woman wearing richly decorated green and gold robes, and pointed to the disappearing procession. "What is this funeral, sister? I saw no corpse."

"The corpse is not here," she said, and she was smiling at his confusion. "It is a ceremony of revenge, taken by all our clans at the instigation of Raik Na Seem. The corpse is not present because its owner will not know he is dead, perhaps for several months. We bury him now because we cannot reach him. He is not one of us, not of the desert. He is dead, however, but merely unaware of that fact. There is no mistake, though. We lack only the physical body."

"He is an enemy of your people, sister?"

"Aye, indeed. He is an enemy. He sent men to steal our greatest treasure. They failed, but they have done us profound harm in their failing. I know you, do I not? You are the one Raik Na Seem hoped would return. He sent for a dreamthief." And she looked back to the dais where, beneath the light of a single torch, a huge figure stood,

bowed as if in prayer. "You are our friend, Alnac Kreb, who aided us once before."

"I have been privileged to do your people a trifling service in the past, aye." Alnac Kreb acknowledged her recognition with his habitual grace.

"Raik Na Seem waits upon you," she said. "Go in peace and peace be with your family and friends."

Puzzled, Alnac Kreb turned to Elric. "I know not why Raik Na Seem should have sent for me but I feel obliged to find out. Will you stay here or accompany me, Prince Elric?"

"I am growing curious about this whole affair," said Elric, "and would know more, if that's possible."

They made their way through the trees until they stood on the banks of the great oasis, waiting respectfully while the old man remained in the position he had assumed since the coffin had been carried off. Eventually he turned and it was clear that he had been weeping. When he saw them he straightened up and, as he recognized Alnac Kreb, he smiled, making a gesture of welcome. "My dear friend!"

"Peace be upon you, Raik Na Seem." Alnac stepped forward and embraced the old man, who was at least a head and shoulders taller than himself. "I bring with me a friend. His name is Elric of Melniboné, of that same people who were the great enemies of the Quarzhasaatim."

"The name has substance in my heart," said Raik Na Seem. "Peace be upon you, Elric of Melniboné. You are welcome here."

"Raik Na Seem is First Elder to the Bauradi Clan," Alnac said, "and a father to me."

"I am blessed by a good, brave son." Raik Na Seem gestured back towards the tents. "Come. Take refreshment in my tent."

"Willingly," said Alnac. "I would learn why you are burying an empty casket and who your enemy is that he should merit such elaborate ceremony."

"Oh, he is the worst of villains, make no mistake of that." A deep sigh escaped the old man as he led them through the throngs of tents until he reached a massive pavilion into which they followed him, their feet treading on richly patterned carpets. The pavilion was actually a series of compartments, one leading into another, each occupied by members of Raik Na Seem's family, which seemed vast enough to be almost a tribe in itself. The smell of delicious food came through to them as they were seated on cushions and offered bowls of scented water with which to wash themselves.

Eventually, as they ate, the old man told his story and, while it unfolded, Elric came to realize that fate had brought him to the Silver Flower Oasis at an auspicious time, for he slowly recognized the significance of what was being said. At the time of the last Blood Moon, said Raik Na Seem, a group of men had come to the Silver Flower Oasis asking after the road to the Place of the Pearl. The Bauradim had recognized the name, for it was in their literature, but they understood the references to be poetic metaphor, something for scholars and other poets to discuss and interpret. They had told the newcomers this and hoped that they would leave, for they were Quarzhasaatim, members of the Sparrow Sect of Sorcerer Adventurers and as such notorious for their murky wizardry and cruelty. The Bauradim wanted no quarrel, however, with any Quarzhasaatim, with whom they traded. The men of the Sparrow Sect did not leave, though, but continued to ask anyone they could about the Place of the Pearl, which was how they came to learn of Raik Na Seem's daughter.

"Varadia?" Alnac Kreb knew alarm. "They surely did not think she knew anything of this jewel?"

"They heard that she was our Holy Girl, the one we believe will grow to be our spiritual leader and bring wisdom and honour to our clan. They believed that, because we say that our Holy Girl is the receptacle of all our knowledge, she must know where this pearl was to be found. They attempted to steal her."

Alnac Kreb growled with sudden anger. "What did they do, father?"

"They drugged her, then made to ride away with her. We learned of their crime and followed them. We caught them before they had completed half the length of the Red Road back to Quarzhasaat and in their terror they threatened us with the power of their master, the man who had commissioned them to seek out the Pearl and use any means to bring it back to him."

"Was his name Lord Gho Fhaazi?" asked Elric softly.

"Aye, prince, it was." Raik Na Seem looked at him with new curiosity. "Do you know him?"

"I know him. And I know him for what he is. Is that the man you buried?"

"It is."

"When do you plan his death?"

"We do not plan it. We have been promised it. The Sorcerer Adventurers attempted to use their arts against us, but we have such people of our own and they were easily countered. It is not something we like to use, that power, but sometimes it is necessary. A certain creature was summoned from the netherworld. It devoured the men of the Sparrow Sect and before it left it granted us a prophecy, that their master would die within the year, before the next Blood Moon had faded."

"But Varadia?" said Alnac Kreb urgently. "What became of your daughter, your Holy Girl?"

"She had been drugged, as I said, but she lived. We brought her back."

"And she recovered?"

"She half-wakes, perhaps once a month," said Raik Na Seem, controlling his sadness. "But the sleep will not lift from her. Shortly after we found her she opened her eyes and told us to take her to the Bronze Tent. There she sleeps, as she has slept for almost a year, and we know that only a dreamthief may save her. That was why I have sent word by every traveler and caravan we have encountered, asking for a dreamthief. We are fortunate, Alnac Kreb, that a friend heard our prayer."

The dreamthief shook his handsome head. "It was not your message which brought me hither, Raik Na Seem."

"Still," said the old man philosophically, "you are here. You can help us."

Alnac Kreb seemed disturbed, but disguised his emotions quickly. "I will do my best, that I swear. In the morning we shall visit the Bronze Tent."

"It is well guarded now, for more Quarzhasaatim have come since those first evil ones, and we have been forced to defend our Holy Girl against them. That has been a simple enough matter. But you spoke of the enemy we have buried, Prince Elric. What do you know of him?"

Elric paused for only a few seconds before he spoke. He told Raik Na Seem everything which had happened: how he had been tricked by Lord Gho, what he had been told to find, the hold which Lord Gho had over him. He refused to lie to the old man and the respect he showed Raik Na Seem was apparently reciprocated, for though the First Elder's face darkened with anger at the tale he reached out with a firm hand when it was finished and gripped Elric's arm in a gesture of sympathy.

"The irony is, my friend, that the Place of the Pearl exists only in our poetry and we have never heard of the Fortress of the Pearl."

"You must know that I would do your Holy Girl no further harm," said Elric, "and that if I can help you and yours in any way that is what I shall do. My quest is ended here and now."

"But Lord Gho's potion will kill you unless you can find the antidote. Then he'll kill your friend, too. No, no. Let us look more positively at these problems, Prince Elric. We have them in common, I think, for we are all victims of that soon-dead lord. We must consider how to defeat his schemes. It is possible that my daughter does indeed know something about this fabulous pearl, for she is the vessel of all our wisdom and has already learned more than ever my poor head could hold . . ."

"Her knowledge and her intelligence are as breathtaking as her beauty and her amiability," said Alnac Kreb, still fuming at the story of what the Quarzhasaatim had done to Varadia. "If you had known her, Elric . . ." He broke off, his voice shaking.

"We are all in need of rest, I think," said the First Elder of the Bauradim. "You shall be our guests and in the morning I shall take you to the Bronze Tent, there to look upon my sleeping daughter and hope, perhaps with the sum of all our wisdom, to find a means of bringing her waking mind back to this realm."

That night, sleeping in the luxury only a wealthy nomad tent could provide, Elric dreamed again of Cymoril, trapped in a drugged slumber by his cousin Yyrkoon, and it seemed that he slept beside her, that they were one and the same, as he had always felt when they lay together. But now he saw the dignified figure of Raik Na Seem standing over him and he knew that this was his father, not the neurotic tyrant, the distant figure of his childhood, and he understood why he was obsessed with questions of morality and justice, for it was this Bauradi who was his true ancestor. He knew a kind of peace, then, as well as some kind of new, disturbing emotion, and when he awoke in the morning he was reconciled to the fact that he was craving the elixir which at once brought him life and death, and he reached for his flask and took a small sip before rising, washing himself and joining Alnac and Raik Na Seem at the morning meal.

When this was done, the old man called for the fleet, sturdy mounts for which the Bauradim were famous, and the three of them rode away from the Silver Flower Oasis, which bustled with every kind of activity, where comedians, jugglers and snake-charmers were already performing their skills and story-tellers had gathered groups of children whose parents had sent them there while they went about their business, and they rode towards the Ragged Pillars seen faintly on the morning horizon. These mountains had been eroded by the winds of the Sighing Desert until they did, indeed, resemble huge columns of ragged red stone, as if they should have supported the roof of the sky itself. Elric had thought at first he observed the ruins of some ancient city. But Alnac Kreb had told him the truth.

"There are, indeed, many ruins in these parts. Farms, small villages, whole towns, which the desert sometimes reveals, all engulfed by the sand summoned by the foolish wizards of Quarzhasaat. Many built here, even after the sands came, in the belief that they would disperse after a while. Forlorn dreams, I fear, like so many of the things built by men."

Raik Na Seem continued to lead them across the desert, though he used no map or compass. Apparently he knew the way by habit and instinct alone.

They stopped once at a spot where a tiny growth of cacti had been all but covered by the sand and here Raik Na Seem took his long knife and sliced the plants close to their roots, peeling them swiftly and handing the juicy parts to his friends. "There was once a river here," he said, "and a memory of it remains, far below the surface. The cactus remembers."

The sun had reached the zenith. Elric began to feel the heat sapping him and was forced again to drink a little of the elixir, merely in order to keep pace with the other two. And it was not until evening, when the Ragged Pillars were considerably closer, that Raik pointed to something which flashed and glittered in the last rays of the sun. "There is the Bronze Tent, where the peoples of the desert go when they must meditate."

"It is your temple?" said Elric.

"It is the nearest thing we have to a temple. And there we debate with our inner selves. It is also the nearest thing we have to the religions of the West. And it is there we keep our Holy Girl, the symbol of all our ideals, the vessel of our race's wisdom."

Alnac was surprised. "You keep her there always?"

Raik Na Seem shook his head, almost amused. "Only while she sleeps in this unnatural slumber, my friend. As you know, before this she was a normal little child, a joy to all who met her. Perhaps with your help she will be that child again."

Alnac's brow clouded. "You must not expect too much of me, Raik Na Seem. I am an inexpert dreamthief at best. There are those with whom I learned my craft who would tell you so."

"But you are our dreamthief." Raik Na Seem smiled sadly and put his hand on Alnac Kreb's shoulder. "And our good friend."

The sun had set by the time they approached the great tent, which resembled those Elric had seen at the Silver Flower Oasis but was several times the size, its walls of pure bronze.

Now the moon made its appearance in the sky almost directly overhead. It seemed that the sun's rays reached for it even as they began to sink beneath the horizon, touching it with their colour, for it glowed with a richness Elric had never seen in Melniboné or the lands of the Young Kingdoms. He gasped in surprise, realizing the specific nature of the prophecy.

A Blood Moon had risen over the Bronze Tent. Here he would find the path to the Fortress of the Pearl.

Though it meant that his own life might now be saved, the Prince of Melniboné discovered that he was only disturbed by this revelation.

Chapter Five

The Dreamthief's Pledge

"Here is our treasure," said Raik Na Seem. "Here is what greedy Quarzhasaat would steal from us." And there was sorrow as well as anger in his voice.

At the very centre of the Bronze Tent's cool interior, in which tiny lamps burned over hundreds of heaped cushions and carpets occupied by men and women in attitudes of deep contemplation, was a raised level and on this a bed carved with intricate designs of exquisite delicacy, set with mother-of-pearl and pale turquoise, with milky jade and silver filigree and blond gold. Upon this, her little hands folded on her chest, which rose and fell with profound regularity, lay a young girl of about thirteen years. She had the strong beauty of her people and her hair was the colour of honey against her tawny skin. She might have been sleeping as naturally as any child of her age save for the single startling fact that her eyes, blue as the wonderful Vilmirian sea, stared upwards towards the roof of the Bronze Tent and were unblinking.

"My people believed that Quarzhasaat destroyed herself for ever," said Elric. "Would that they had or that Melniboné had shown less arrogance and completed what their wizards began!" He rarely betrayed such ferocious emotions towards those his race had defeated but now he knew only loathing for Lord Gho, whose men, he was sure, had done this terrible thing. He recognized the nature of the sorcery, for it was not unlike that he had learned himself, though his cousin Yyrkoon had shown more interest in those specific arts and cared to practise them where Elric did not.

"But who can save her now?" said Raik Na Seem softly, perhaps a little embarrassed by Elric's outburst in this place of meditation.

The albino recovered himself and made a gesture of apology. "Are there no potions which will rouse her from this slumber?" he asked.

Raik Na Seem shook his head. "We have consulted everyone and everything. The spell was cast by the leader of the Sparrow Sect and he was killed when we took our premature revenge."

In deference to those who sat within the Bronze Tent, Raik Na Seem now led them out into the desert again. Here guards stood, their lamps and torches casting great shadows across the sand, while the rays of the ruby moon drenched everything with crimson, so it was almost as if they drowned in a tide of blood. Elric was reminded how, as a youth, he had peered into the depths of his Actorios, imagining the gem as a gateway into other lands, each facet representing a different realm, for by then he had already read much of the multiverse and how it was thought to be constituted.

"Steal the dream which entraps her," Raik Na Seem was saying, "and you know that all we have will be yours, Alnac Kreb."

The handsome black man shook his head. "To save her would be all the reward I wanted, father. Yet I fear I have not the skills . . . Has no other tried?"

"We have been deceived more than once. Sorcerer Adventurers from Quarzhasaat, either believing themselves possessed of your knowledge or thinking they could accomplish what only a dreamthief can accomplish, have come to us, pretending to be members of your craft. We have seen them all go mad before our eyes. Several died. Some we let run back to Quarzhasaat in the hope they would be a warning to others not to waste their lives and our time."

"You sound very patient, Raik Na Seem," said Elric, remembering what he had already heard and clearer now as to why Lord Gho so desperately sought a dreamthief for this work. The news brought back to Quarzhasaat by the maddened Sorcerer Adventurers had been garbled. What little Lord Gho had made of it, he had passed on to Elric. But now the albino saw that it was the child herself who possessed the secret of the path to the Pearl at the Heart of the World. Doubtless, as the recipient of all her people's wisdom, she had learned of its location. Perhaps it was a secret she must keep to herself. Whatever the reason, it was obvious that the girl, Varadia, must wake from her sorcerous sleep before any further progress could be made. And Elric knew that even if she did wake it was not in his nature to question her, to beg for a secret which was not his to know. His only hope would be if she offered the knowledge freely to him but he knew that no matter what occurred he would never be able to ask.

Raik Na Seem seemed to understand a little of the albino's dilemma. "My son, you are a friend of my son," he said in the formal manner of his people. "We know that you are not our enemy and that you did not come here willingly to steal what was ours. We know, too, that you had no intention of taking from us any treasure to which we are guardian. Know this, Elric of Melniboné, that if Alnac Kreb can save our Holy Girl, we shall do all we can to put you on the path to the Fortress of the Pearl. The only reason for hindering you would be if Varadia, awakened, warned us against giving this aid. Then, at least, you will be told as much."

"There could be no fairer promise," said Elric gratefully. "Meanwhile, I pledge myself to you, Raik Na Seem, to help guard your daughter against all those who would harm her and to watch over her until Alnac should bring her back to you."

Alnac had moved a little away from the other two and was standing in deep thought on the edge of the torchlight, his white night-cloak drenched a dark pinkish hue by the rays of the Blood Moon. From his belt he had drawn his hooked staff and was holding it in his two hands, looking at it and murmuring to it, much as Elric might speak to his own runesword.

At length the dreamthief turned back to them, his face full of great seriousness. "I will do my best," he said. "I will call upon every resource within myself and upon everything I have been taught, but I should warn you that I have weaknesses of character I have not yet overcome. These are weaknesses which I can control if called upon to exorcize an old merchant's nightmares or a boy's love-trance. What I see here, however, might defeat the cleverest dreamthief, the most experienced of my calling. There can be no partial success. I succeed or I fail. I am willing, because of the circumstances, because of our old friendship, because I loathe everything that the Sorcerer Adventurers represent, to attempt the task."

"It is all I would hope," said Raik Na Seem sombrely. He was impressed by Alnac's tone.

"If you succeed you bring the child's soul back to the world where it belongs," said Elric. "What do you lose if you fail, Master Dreamthief?"

Alnac shrugged. "Nothing of any great value, I suppose."

Elric, looking hard into his new friend's face, saw that he lied. But he saw, too, that he wished to be questioned no further in the matter.

"I must rest," said Alnac. "And eat." He wrapped himself in the folds of his night-cloak, his dark eyes staring back at Elric as if he wished for all the world to share some secret which he felt in his heart should never be shared. Then he turned away suddenly, laughing. "If Varadia should wake as a result of my efforts and if she knows the whereabouts of your terrible pearl, why then, Prince Elric, I'll have done most of your work for you. I'll expect part of your reward, you know."

"My reward will be the slaying of Lord Gho," said Elric quietly.

"Aye," said Alnac, moving towards the Bronze Tent, which shifted and shimmered like some half-materialized artifact of Chaos, "that is exactly what I hope to share!"

The Bronze Tent consisted of the great central chamber and then a series of smaller chambers, where travelers could rest and revive themselves, and it was to one of these that the three men went to lay themselves down and, still wakeful, consider the work which must begin the next day. They did not talk, but it was several hours before all were eventually asleep.

In the morning, while Elric, Raik Na Seem and Alnac Kreb approached the place where the Holy Girl still lay, those who still remained in the Bronze Tent drew back respectfully. Alnac Kreb held his dreamwand gently in his right hand, balancing it rather than gripping it, as he stared down into the face of the child he loved almost as his own daughter. A long sigh escaped him and Elric saw that his sleep had not apparently refreshed him. He looked drawn and unhappy. He turned, smiling to the albino. "When I saw you partaking of the contents of that silver flask earlier, I had half a mind to ask you for a little . . ."

"The drug's poison and it's addictive," said Elric, shocked. "I thought I had explained as much."

"You had." Alnac Kreb again revealed by his expression that he possessed thoughts he felt unable to share. "I had merely thought that, in the circumstances, there would be little point in fearing its power."

"That is because you do not know it," said Elric forcefully. "Believe me, Alnac, if there was any way in which I could help you in this task I would do so. But to offer you poison would not, I think, be an act of friendship . . ."

Alnac Kreb smiled a little. "Indeed. Indeed." He slid his dreamwand from hand to hand. "But you said that you would watch over me?"

"I promise that, aye. And as you asked, the moment you tell me to carry the dreamwand from the Bronze Tent, I shall do so."

"That is all you can do and I thank you for that," said the dreamthief. "Now I'll begin. Farewell for the moment, Elric. I think we are fated to meet again, but perhaps not in this existence."

And with those mysterious words Alnac Kreb approached the sleeping girl, placing his dreamwand over her unblinking eyes, laying his ear against her heart, his own gaze growing distant and strange, as if he entered a trance himself. He straightened, swaying, then took the girl in his arms and lowered her gently to the carpets. Next he lay down beside her, putting her lifeless hand within his own, his dreamwand in the other. His breathing grew slower and deeper and Elric almost thought he heard a faint song coming from within the dreamthief's throat.

Raik Na Seem bent forward, peering into Alnac's face, but Alnac did not see him. With his other hand he brought up the dreamwand so that the hook passed over their clasped hands, as if to secure them, to bind them together.

To his surprise, Elric saw that the dreamwand was beginning to glow faintly and to pulse a little. Alnac's breathing grew deeper still, his lips opening, his eyes staring directly above him, just as Varadia's stared.

Elric thought he heard the child murmur and it was no illusion that a tremor passed between Alnac and the Holy Girl while the dreamwand pulsed in tempo with their mutual breathing and glowed brighter.

Then suddenly the dreamwand was curling and writhing, moving with astonishing speed between the two, as if it had entered their very veins and was following the blood itself. Elric had the impression of a tangle of arteries and nerves, all touched by the strange light from the dreamwand, then Alnac gave a single cry and his breathing was no longer the steady movement it had been. Instead it had become shallow, almost non-existent, while the child continued to breathe with the same slow, deep, steady rhythm.

The dreamwand had returned to Alnac. It seemed to burn from within his body, almost as if it had become fused with his spine and cortex. The hook end appeared to glow from within his brain, flooding his flesh with indescribable luminance, displaying every bone, every organ, every vein.

The child herself seemed unchanged until Elric looked at her more closely, seeing almost with horror that her eyes had turned from vibrant blue to jet black. Reluctantly he looked from Varadia's face to Alnac's and saw what he had not wished to see. The dreamthief's own eyes were now bright blue. It was as if the two of them had exchanged souls.

The albino, with all his experience of sorcery, had never witnessed anything like this and he found it disturbing. Gradually he was beginning to understand the strange nature of a dreamthief's calling, why it could be so dangerous, why there were so few who could practise the trade and why fewer still would wish to.

Now a further change began to take place. The crooked staff seemed to writhe again and begin to absorb the dreamthief's very substance, taking the blood and the vitality of flesh and bones and brain into itself.

Raik Na Seem groaned with terror. He stepped backwards, unable to control himself. "Ah, my son! What have I asked of thee!"

Soon all that remained of Alnac's splendid body seemed little more than a husk, like the discarded skin of some transmuted dragonfly. But the dreamwand lay where Alnac had first placed it upon his own hand and Varadia's, though it seemed larger and glowed with an impossible brilliance, its colours constantly moving through a spectrum part natural, part supernatural.

"I think he is giving much in his attempt to save my daughter," said Raik Na Seem. "Perhaps more than anyone should give."

"He would give everything," Elric said. "I think that it is in his nature. That is why you call him your son and why you trust him."

"Aye," said Raik Na Seem, "but now I fear that I lose a son as well as a daughter." And he sighed and was troubled, perhaps wondering if, after all, he had been wise in begging this service of Alnac Kreb.

For more than a day and a night Elric sat with Raik Na Seem and the men and women of the Bauradim within the shelter of the Bronze Tent, their eyes fixed upon the strangely wizened body of Alnac the

Dreamthief, which occasionally stirred and murmured yet still seemed as lifeless as the mummified goats which the sand-dunes sometimes revealed. Once Elric thought he heard the Holy Girl make a sound and once Raik Na Seem rose to put his hand on his daughter's brow, then returned shaking his head.

"This is not the time to despair, father of my friend," said Elric.

"Aye." The First Elder of the Bauradim drew himself up, then settled down again beside Elric. "We set high store by prophecies here in the desert. It seems that our longing for help might have coloured our reason."

They looked out of the tent into the morning. Smoke from the still-burning brands drifted across the lilac-coloured sky, borne upward and to the north by the light breeze. Elric found the smell almost sickening now, but his concern for his new friend made him forgetful of his own health. Occasionally he drank sparingly of Lord Gho's elixir, unable to do more than control his craving, and when Raik Na Seem offered him water from his own flask Elric shook his head. Within him there were still many conflicts. He felt a strong comradeship with these people, a liking for Raik Na Seem which he valued. He had grown to care for Alnac Kreb, who had helped save his life in an action clearly as generous as the man's general character. Elric was grateful for the Bauradim's trust of him. Having heard his tale they would have been within their rights to banish him at the very least from the Silver Flower Oasis. Rather they had taken him to the Bronze Tent when the Blood Moon burned, allowing him to follow Lord Gho's instructions, trusting him not to abuse their action. He was bound to them now by a loyalty he could never break. Perhaps they knew this. Perhaps they read his character as easily as they read Alnac's. This sense of their trust heartened him, though it made his task all the more difficult, and he was determined in no way, however inadvertently, to betray it.

Raik Na Seem sniffed the wind and looked back towards the distant oasis. A column of black smoke marched into the sky, growing taller and taller, mingling with the smoke closer at hand: some released afrit joining its fellows. Elric would not have been surprised if it had taken shape before his eyes, so familiar had he become with strange events in the past days.

"There has been another attack," said Raik Na Seem. He spoke unconcernedly. "Let us hope it is the last. They are burning the bodies."

"Who attacks you?"

"More men of the Sorcerer Adventurer societies. I suspect their decisions have something to do with the internal politics of the city. Dozens of them are battling for some favour or other—perhaps the seat on the Council you mentioned. From time to time their machinations involve us. This is familiar to us. But I suppose the Pearl at the Heart of the World has become the only price which will pay for the seat, eh? So as the story spreads, more and more of those warriors are sent here to find it!" Raik Na Seem spoke with fierce humour. "Let us hope they must soon run out of inhabitants and eventually only the scheming lords themselves will be left, squabbling for non-existent power over a non-existent people!"

Elric watched as a whole tribe of nomads rode past, keeping some distance away from the Bronze Tent in order to show their respect. These tanned, white-skinned people had burning blue eyes as bright as those which stared into nothing within the tent and when their hoods were thrown back, startlingly blond hair, also like Varadia's. Their clothing distinguished them, however, from the Bauradim. It was predominantly of a rich lavender shade with gold and dark green trimming. They were heading towards the Silver Flower Oasis, driving herds of sheep and riding the odd humped bull-like beasts which, as Alnac had declared, were so well-adapted to the desert.

"The Waued Nii," said Raik Na Seem. "They are amongst the last at any gathering. They come from the very edge of the desert and they trade with Elwher, bringing that lapis lazuli and jade carving we all value so much. In the winter, when the storms grow too intense for them, they even raid across the plains and into the cities. Once, they boast, they looted Phum, but we believe it was some other, smaller place which they mistook for Phum." This was clearly a joke the desert peoples enjoyed at the expense of the Waued Nii.

"I had a friend who was once of Phum," said Elric. "His name was Rackhir and he sought Tanelorn."

"Rackhir I know. A good bowman. He traveled with us for a few weeks last year."

Elric was strangely pleased by this news. "He was well?"

"In excellent health." Raik Na Seem was glad of a subject to draw his mind away from the fate of his daughter and his adoptive son. "He was a welcome guest and hunted for us when we went close to the Ragged Pillars, for there's game there which we lack the skill to find. He spoke of his friend. A friend who has many thoughts and whose thoughts led him to many quandaries. That was you, no doubt. I remember now. He must have been joking. He said that you were a little on the pale side. He wondered what had become of you. He cared for you, I think."

"And I for him. We had something in common. As I feel a bond with your folk and with Alnac Kreb."

"You shared dangers together, I gather."

"We had many strange experiences. He, however, was tired of the quest for such things and hoped to retire, to find peace. Know you where he went from here?"

"Aye. As you say, he was searching for legendary Tanelorn. When he had learned all he could from us, he bade us farewell and rode on to the West. We counseled him not to waste himself in pursuit of a myth, but he believed he knew enough to continue. Did you not wish to journey with your friend?"

"I have other duties which call me, though I, too, have sought Tanelorn." He would have added more but thought better of it. Any further explanation would have led him into memories and problems he had no wish to contemplate at present. His main concern was for Alnac Kreb and the girl.

"Ah, yes. Now I recall. You are a king in your own country, of course. But a reluctant one, eh? The duties are hard for a young man. Much is expected of you and you bear upon your shoulders the weight of the past, the ideals and loyalties of an entire people. It is difficult to rule well, to make good judgments, to dispense justice fairly. We have no kings here amongst the Bauradim, merely a group of men and women elected to speak for the whole clan, and I think it is better to share those burdens. If all share the burden, if all are responsible for themselves, then no single individual has to carry a weight that is too much for them."

"The reason I travel is to learn more of such means of administering justice," said Elric. "But I will tell you this, Raik Na Seem, my people are as cruel as any in Quarzhasaat, and have more real power. We have a scanty notion of justice and the obligations of rule involve little more than inventing new terrors by which we may cow and control others. Power, I think, is a habit as terrible as the potion I must now sip in order to sustain myself. It feeds upon itself. It is a hungry beast, devouring those who would possess it and those who hate it—devouring even those who own it."

"The hungry beast is not power itself," said the old man. "Power is neither good nor evil. It is the use one makes of it which is good or evil. I know that Melniboné once ruled the world, or that part of it she could find and the part she did not destroy."

"You seem to know more of my nation than my nation knows of you!" The albino smiled.

"It is said by our folk that we all came to the desert because we fled first Melniboné and then Quarzhasaat. Each was as cruel as the other, each as corrupting, and it did not matter to us which destroyed which. We had hoped they would extinguish each other of course, but that was not to be. The second-best thing occurred—Quarzhasaat almost destroyed herself and Melniboné forgot all about her—and us! I believe that soon after their war, Melniboné became bored with expansion and withdrew to rule only the Young Kingdoms. Now I hear she rules even less."

"Only the Dragon Isle now." Elric found that his thoughts were going back to Cymoril and he tried to stop himself thinking of her. "But many a reaver's sought to sail against her and loot her wealth. They discover, however, that she remains too powerful for them. They must continue to trade with her instead."

"Trade was ever War's superior," said Raik Na Seem and looked suddenly back over his shoulder at Alnac's withered body. The golden outline of the dreamwand was glowing again and throbbing, as it had done from time to time since Alnac had first lain down beside the girl.

"'Tis a strange organ," said Raik Na Seem softly. "Almost a second spine."

He was about to say more when there was a faint movement in Alnac's features and a dreadful, desolate groan escaped the bloodless lips.

They turned and went to kneel beside him. Alnac's eyes still blazed blue and Varadia's were still black.

"He is dying," whispered the First Elder. "Is it so, Prince Elric?"

Elric knew no more than the Bauradi.

"What can we do for him?" asked Raik Na Seem.

Elric touched the cold, leathery carcass. He lifted an almost weightless wrist and could feel no pulse beating. It was at this moment, startlingly, that Alnac's eyes turned from blue to black and looked at Elric with all their old intelligence. "Ah, you have come to help me. I have learned where the Pearl lies. But it is too well protected."

The voice was a whisper from the dusty-dry mouth.

Elric cradled the dreamthief in his arms. "I will help you, Alnac. Tell me how."

"You cannot. There are caverns . . . These dreams are defeating me. They are drowning me. They are drawing me in. I am doomed to join those already doomed. Poor company for one such as me, Prince Elric. Poor company . . ."

The dreamwand pulsed and glowed white as bleached bones. The dreamthief's eyes turned to blue again, then back to black. The thin air stirred in the leathery remains of his throat. Suddenly there was horror in his face. "Ah, no! I must find the will!"

The dreamwand moved like a snake through his body, then slithered into Varadia, then returned. "Oh, Elric," said the tiny voice, "help me if you can. Oh, I am trapped. This is the worst I have ever known . . ."

His words seemed to Elric to call to him directly from the grave, as if his friend was already dead. "Elric, if there is some way . . ."

Then the body shuddered, filled as if with a single huge breath while the dreamwand flickered and writhed again and then grew still, lying as it had first done with the crook upon the two clasped hands.

"Ah, my friend, I was a fool even to consider myself able to survive this . . ." The tiny voice faded. "Would that I had understood the nature of her mind. It is so strong! So strong!"

"Who does he speak of?" asked Raik Na Seem. "My child? That which holds her? My daughter is of the Sarangli women. Her grandmother could charm whole tribes to believe they died of disease. I told him as much. What does he not understand?"

"Oh, Elric, she has destroyed me!" There was a tremor in the frail hand as it reached towards the albino.

Then, suddenly, all the colour and life came flooding back into Alnac's body. It seemed to expand to its former size and vitality. The hooked staff became nothing more than the artifact Elric had originally seen at Alnac's belt.

The handsome dreamthief grinned. He was surprised. "I live! Elric, I live!"

He took a firmer grip on his staff and made to rise. Then he coughed and something disgusting oozed from his lips, like a gigantic, half-digested worm. It was as if he regurgitated his own rotten organs. He wiped the stuff away. For a moment he was bewildered, the terror returning to his eyes.

"No." Alnac seemed reconciled suddenly. "I was too proud. I die, of course." He collapsed backward onto the sheet as Elric again tried to hold him. With his old irony the dreamthief shook his head. "A little too late, I think. It's not my fate, after all, to be your companion, Sir Champion, in this plane."

Elric, to whom the words made no sense, believed Alnac to be raving and sought to quieten him.

Then the staff fell from the dreamthief's grasp and he rolled onto his side before a wavering, sickly scream came out of him, then a stink which threatened to drive Elric and Raik Na Seem from the Bronze Tent. It was as if his body putrefied before their eyes even as the dreamthief tried to speak again and failed.

And then Alnac Kreb was dead.

Elric, mourning a brave, good man, felt then that his own doom and that of Anigh had been determined. The dreamthief's death suggested forces at work of which the albino understood nothing, for all his sorcerous wisdom. He had come across no grimoire which even hinted of such a fate. He had seen worse befall those who meddled with sorcery, but here was a sorcery which he could not begin to interpret.

"He is gone, then," said Raik Na Seem.

"Aye." Elric's own breath shuddered in his throat. "Aye. His courage was greater than any of us suspected. Including, I think, himself."

The First Elder walked slowly to where his child still slept in her terrible trance. He looked down into her blue eyes as if he almost hoped to see the black eyes somewhere there within her.

"Varadia?"

She did not respond.

Solemnly, Raik Na Seem took the Holy Girl and placed her back upon the raised block, settling her into the cushions as if she merely slept a natural sleep and he, her father, laid her down for her nightly rest.

Elric stared at the remains of the dreamthief. He had doubtless understood the cost of failure and perhaps that was the secret he had refused to share.

"It is over," said Raik Na Seem gently. "Now I can think of nothing to do for her. He gave too much." He was fighting not to lose himself either in self-mortification or despair. "We must try to think what to do. Will you help me in this, friend of my son?"

"If I can."

As Elric rose, shaking, to his feet he heard a sound behind him. He thought at first it was some Bauradi woman come to mourn. He looked back at the light which streamed in through the tent and saw only her outline.

It was a young woman, but she was not of the Bauradim. She entered the tent slowly and there were tears in her eyes as she stared down at Alnac Kreb's ruined body.

"I am too late, then?"

Her musical voice was full of the most intense sorrow. She reached a hand to her face. "He should not have attempted such a task. They told me at the Silver Flower Oasis that you had come here. Why could you not have waited a little longer? Just a day more?"

It was with great effort that she controlled her grief and Elric felt a sudden, obscure kinship with her.

She took another step towards the body. She was an inch or so shorter than Elric, with a heart-shaped face framed by thick brown hair. Slender and well-muscled, she wore a padded jerkin slashed to show its red silk lining. She had soft velvet breeches, embroidered felt riding boots and over all this an almost transparent cotton dust-coat pushed back from her shoulders. At her belt was a sword while cradled above her left shoulder was a hooked staff of gold and ebony, a more elaborate version of the one which lay on the carpet beside Alnac's corpse.

"I taught him all he knew of this craft," she said. "But it was not enough for this. How could he ever have thought that it would be! He could never have achieved such a goal. He had not the character for it." She turned away, brushing at her face. When she looked back her tears had gone and she stared directly back into Elric's eyes.

"I am Oone," she said. She bowed briefly to Raik Na Seem. "I am the dreamthief you sent for."

BOOK TWO

Is there a daughter born in dreams
Whose flesh is snow, whose ruby eyes
Stare into realms whose substance seems
Strong as agony, soft as lies?
Is there a girlchild born of dreams
Who carries blood as old as Time,
Destined one day to blend with mine
And give new lands a newer queen?

—The Chronicle of the Black Sword

Chapter One

How a Thief May Instruct an Emperor

ONE REMOVED a date stone from her mouth and dropped it into the sand of the Silver Flower Oasis. She reached her hand towards one of the brilliant cactus flowers which gave the place its name. She stroked the petals with long, delicate fingers. She sang to herself and it seemed to Elric that her words were a lament.

Respectfully he remained silent, sitting with his back to a palm tree looking to the distant camp and its continuing activity. She had asked him to accompany her but had said little to him. He heard a calling from the kashbeh high above but when he peered in that direction he saw nothing. The breeze blew over the desert and red dust raced like water towards the Ragged Pillars on the horizon.

It was almost noon. They had returned to the Silver Flower Oasis that morning and the few remains of Alnac Kreb were to be burned with honour according to the customs of the Bauradim that night.

Oone's staff was no longer slung on her back. Now she held the dreamwand in both hands, turning it over and over, watching the light on its burnish and polish as if she had only now seen it for the first time. The other wand, Alnac's, she had tucked into her belt.

"It would have made my task a little easier," she said suddenly, "if Alnac had not acted so precipitously. He did not realize I was coming and was doing his best to save the child, I know. But a few more hours and I could have used his help, perhaps successfully. Certainly, I might have saved him."

"I do not understand what happened to him," said Elric.

"Even I do not know the exact cause of his fall," she said. "But I will explain what I can. That is why I asked you to come with me. I would not wish to be overheard. And I must demand your word that you will be discreet."

"I am ever that, madam."

"For ever," she said.

"For ever?"

"You must promise never to tell another soul what I tell you today, nor recount any event which results from the telling. You must agree to be bound by a dreamthief's code even though you are not of our kind."

Elric was baffled. "For what reason?"

"Would you save their Holy Girl? Avenge Alnac? Free yourself from the drug's slavery? Adjust certain wrongs in Quarzhasaat?"

"You know I would."

"Then we may reach an agreement, for it is certain that, unless we help each other, you and the girl and perhaps myself, too, will all be dead before the Blood Moon fades."

"Certain?" Elric was grimly amused. "Are you an oracle, too, then, madam?"

"All dreamthieves are that, to some degree." She was almost impatient, as if she spoke to a slow child. She caught herself. "Forgive me. I forget that our craft is unknown in the Young Kingdoms. Indeed, it's rarely that we travel to this plane at all."

"I have met many supernaturals in my life, my lady, but few who seem so human as yourself."

"Human? Of course I am human!" She seemed puzzled. Then her brow cleared. "Ah. I forget that you are at once more sophisticated and less learned than those of my own persuasion." She smiled at him. "I am still not recovered from Alnac's unnecessary dissolution."

"He need not have died." Elric's tone was flat, unquestioning. He had known Alnac long enough to care for him as a friend. He understood something of Oone's loss. "And there is no way to revive him?"

"He lost all essence," said Oone. "Instead of stealing a dream he was robbed of his own." She paused, then spoke quickly, as if she feared she would regret her words. "Will you help me, Prince Elric?"

"Yes." He spoke without hesitation. "If it is to avenge Alnac and save the child."

"Even if you risk Alnac's fate? The fate which you witnessed?"

"Even that. Can it be worse than dying in Lord Gho's power?"

"Yes," she said simply.

Elric laughed aloud at her frankness. "Ah, well. Just so, madam! Just so! What's your bargain?"

She moved her hand again towards the silver petals, balancing her wand between her fingers. She was frowning, still not wholly certain of the rightness of her decision. "I think that you are one of the few mortals on this earth who could understand the nature of my profession, who'll know what I mean when I speak of the nature of dreams and reality and how they intersect. I think, too, that you have habits of mind which would make you if not a perfect ally then an ally on whom I could to some extent depend. We dreamthieves have made something of a science of a trade which logically can tolerate no consistent laws. It has enabled us to pursue our craft with some success largely, I suspect, because we are able, to a degree, to impose our own wills upon the chaos we encounter. Does this make sense to you, prince?"

"I think so. There are philosophers of my own people who claim that much of our magic is actually the imposition of a powerful will upon the fundamental stuff of reality, an ability, if you like, to make dreams come true. Some claim our whole world was created thus."

Oone seemed pleased. "Good. I knew there were certain ideas I would not have to explain."

"But what would you have me do, lady?"

"I want you to help me. Together we can find a way to what the Sorcerer Adventurers call the Fortress of the Pearl and by so doing one or both of us might steal the dream which binds the child to perpetual sleep and free her to wakefulness, return her to her people to be their seeress and their pride."

"The two are linked then?" Elric began to rise to his feet, ignoring the call of his ever-present craving. "The child and the Pearl?"

"I think so."

"What is the link?"

"In discovering that we shall doubtless discover how to free her."

"Forgive me, Lady Oone," said Elric gently, "but you sound almost as ignorant as I!"

"In some ways it is true that I am. Before I go further, I must ask you to swear to abide by the Dreamthief's Code."

"I swear," said Elric, and he held up the hand on which his Actorios glowed to show that he swore by one of his people's most revered artifacts. "I swear by the Ring of Kings."

"Then I will tell you what I know and what I desire of you," said Oone. She linked her free hand in his arm and led him further into the groves of palms and cypress. Sensing the shuddering hunger in him which yearned for Lord Gho's terrible drug, she seemed to show some sympathy.

"A dreamthief," she began, "does exactly what the title implies. We steal dreams. Originally our guild were true thieves. We learned the trick of entering the worlds of other people's dreams and stealing those which were most magnificent or exotic. Gradually, however, people began to call upon us to steal unwanted dreams—or rather the dreams which entrapped or plagued friends or relatives. So we stole those. Frequently the dreams themselves were in no way harmful to another, only to the one who was in their power . . ."

Elric interrupted. "Are you saying that a dream has some material reality? That it can be seized, like a volume of verse, say, or a money purse, and slipped free of its owner?"

"Essentially, yes. Or, I should say, our guild learned the trick of making a dream sufficiently real for it to be handled thus!" She now laughed openly at his confusion and some of the care went away from her for a moment. "There is a certain talent needed and a great deal of training."

"But what do you do with these stolen dreams?"

"Why, Prince Elric, we sell them at the Dream Market, twice a year. There's a fine trade in almost any sort of dream, no matter how bizarre or terrifying. There are merchants who purchase them and customers who would buy them. We distill them, of course, into a form which can be transported and later translated. And because we make the dreams take substance, we are threatened by them. That substance can destroy us. You see what happened to Alnac. It takes a certain character, a certain cast of mind, a certain attitude of spirit, all combining, to protect oneself in the Dream Realms. But because we have codified these realms we have also to a degree made them our own to manipulate."

"You must explain more to me," said Elric, "if I am to follow you at all, madam!"

"Very well." She paused at the edge of the grove, where the earth grew dustier and formed a territory between oasis and desert that was a little of both and was neither. She studied the cracked earth as if the cracks were the outlines of a singularly complicated map, a geometry which only she could understand.

"We have made rules," she said. Her voice was distant, almost as if she spoke to herself. "And codified what we have discovered over the centuries. And yet we are still subject to the most unimaginable hazards . . ."

"Wait, madam. Are you suggesting that Alnac Kreb, by some wizardry known only to your guild, entered the world of the Holy Girl's dreams and there suffered adventures such as you or I might suffer in this material world?"

"Well put." She turned with a strange smile on her lips. "Aye. And his substance went into that world and was absorbed by it, strengthening the substance of her dreams . . ."

"The dreams he hoped to steal."

"He hoped to steal only one. The one which imprisons her in that perpetual slumber."

"And then he would sell it, you say, at your Dream Market?"

"Perhaps." She was clearly unwilling to discuss this aspect of the matter.

"Where is that market held?"

"In a realm beyond this one, in a place where only those of our profession, or those who attend upon us, may travel."

"You'd take me there?" Elric spoke from curiosity.

Her glance was a mixture of amusement and caution. "Possibly. But first we must be successful. We must steal a dream so that we may trade it there. Know you, Elric, I have every desire to inform you of all you wish to learn, but there are many things hard to explain to one who has not studied with our guild. They can only be demonstrated or experienced. I am not a native of your world, nor are most dreamthieves from this sphere. We are wanderers—nomads, you might say—between many times and many places. We have learned that a dream in one realm can be an undeniable reality in another, while what is utterly prosaic in that realm can elsewhere be the stuff of the most fantastic nightmare."

"Is all creation so malleable?" Elric asked with a shudder.

"What we create must ever be, lest it die," she said, her tone one of ironical finality.

"The struggle between Law and Chaos echoes that struggle within ourselves between unbridled emotion and too much caution, I suppose," Elric mused, aware that she did not wish to pursue this particular conversation.

With her foot Oone traced the cracks in the red earth. "To learn more you must become an apprentice dreamthief . . ."

"Willingly," said Elric. "I'm sufficiently curious now, madam. You spoke of your laws. What are they?"

"Some are instructive, some are descriptive. First I'll tell you that we have determined every Dream Realm shall have seven aspects, which we have named. By naming and describing we hope to shape that which has no shape and control that which few can begin to control. By such impositions we have learned to survive in worlds where others would be destroyed within minutes. Yet even when we perform such impositions, even that which our own wills define can become transmuted beyond our control. If you would accompany me and aid me in this adventure you must know that I have determined we shall pass through seven lands. The first land we call Sadanor, or the Land of Dreams-in-Common. The second land is Marador, which we call the Land of Old Desires, while the third is Paranor, the Land of Lost Beliefs. The fourth land is known to dreamthieves as Celador, which is the Land of Forgotten Love. The fifth is Imador, the Land of New Ambition, and the sixth is Falador, the Land of Madness . . ."

"Fanciful names indeed, madam. The Guild of Dreamthieves has a penchant for poetry, I think. And the seventh? What is that named?"

She paused before she replied. Her wonderful eyes peered into his, as if exploring the recesses of his own skull. "That has no name," she said quietly, "save any name the inhabitants shall give it. But there, if anywhere, you will find the Fortress of the Pearl."

Elric felt himself trapped by that gentle yet determined gaze. "And how may we enter these lands?" The albino forced himself to engage with these questions though by now his whole body was crying out for a draught of Lord Gho's elixir.

She sensed his tension and her hand on his arm was meant to calm and reassure him. "Through the child," said Oone.

Elric remembered what he had witnessed in the Bronze Tent and he shuddered. "How is such a thing achieved?"

Oone frowned and the pressure of her hand increased. "She is our gateway and the dreamwands are our keys. There is no way in which I will harm her, Elric. Once we have reached the seventh aspect, the Nameless Land, there we might in turn find the key to her particular prison."

"She is a medium, then? Is that what has happened to her? Did the Sorcerer Adventurers know something of her power and in attempting to use her put her into this trance?"

Again she hesitated, then she nodded. "Close enough, Prince Elric. It is written in our histories, of which we have many, though most are inaccessible to us in the libraries of Tanelorn, "*What lies within always has a form without and that which is without takes a shape within.*" Put another way, we sometimes say that what is visible must always have an invisible aspect, just as everything invisible must be represented by the visible."

Elric found this too cryptic for him, though he was familiar enough with such mysterious utterances from his own grimoires. He did not dismiss them, but he knew they frequently required much pondering and certain experience before they made complete sense. "You speak of supernatural realms, madam. The worlds inhabited by the Lords of Chaos and of Law, by the elementals, by immortals and the like. I know something of such realms and have even journeyed in them some little way. But I have never heard of leaving part of one's physical substance behind and traveling into those realms by means of a sleeping child!"

She looked at him for a long moment as if she thought he was deliberately disingenuous, then she shrugged. "You will find the realms of the dreamthief very similar. And you would do well to memorize and obey our code."

"You are a strict order, then, madam . . ."

"If we are to survive. Alnac had the instincts of a good dreamthief but he had not acquired the full discipline. That was one of the chief reasons for his dissolution. You on the other hand are familiar with the necessary disciplines, for they were how you came by your knowledge of sorcery. Without those disciplines you, too, would have perished."

"I have rejected much of that, Lady Oone."

"Aye. So I believe. But you have not lost the habit, I think. Or so I hope. The first law the dreamthief obeys says: 'Offers of guidance must always be accepted but never trusted.' The second says: 'Beware the familiar' and the third tells us: 'What is strange should be cautiously welcomed.' There are many others, but it is those three which encompass the fundamentals by which a dreamthief survives." She smiled. Her smile was oddly sweet and vulnerable and Elric realized she was weary. Perhaps her grief had exhausted her.

The Melnibonéan spoke gently, looking back to the great red rocks of the Silver Flower Oasis's protection and sanctuary. The voices were stilled now. Thin lines of smoke ascended the rich blue of the sky. "How long does it take to instruct and train one of your calling?"

She recognized his irony now. "Five years or more," she said. "Alnac had been a full member of the Guild for perhaps six years."

"And he failed to survive in the realm where the Holy Girl's spirit is held prisoner?"

"He was, for all his skills, only an ordinary mortal, Prince Elric."

"And you think I'm more than that?"

She laughed openly. "You are the last emperor of Melniboné. You are the most powerful of your race, which is a race whose familiarity with sorcery is legendary. True, you have left your bride-to-be waiting for you while you place your cousin Yyrkoon on the Ruby Throne to reign as regent until you return—a decision only an idealist would make—but nonetheless, my lord, you cannot pretend to me that you are in any way ordinary!"

In spite of his craving for the poisonous elixir, Elric found himself laughing back at her. "If I am such a man of qualities, madam, how is it that I find myself in this position, contemplating death from the tricks of a second-rate provincial politician?"

"I did not say you admired yourself, my lord. But it would be foolish to deny what you have been and what you could become."

"I prefer to consider the latter, my lady."

"Consider, if you will, the fate of Raik Na Seem's daughter. Consider the fate of his people deprived of their history and their oracle. Consider your own doom, to perish for no good reason in a distant land, your destiny unfulfilled."

Elric accepted this.

She continued. "It is probable, too, that you have no rival as a sorcerer in your world. While your specific skills might be of little use to you in the adventure I propose, your experience, knowledge and understanding might make the difference between success and failure."

Elric had become impatient as his body's demand for the drug grew unbearable. "Very well, Lady Oone. Whatever you decide, I shall agree to."

She took a step back from him and looked at him coolly. "You had best return to your tent and find your elixir," she said softly.

Familiar desperation filled the albino's mind. "I shall, madam. I shall." And he turned and strode swiftly back towards the gathered tents of the Bauradim.

He scarcely spoke to any of those who greeted him as he passed. Raik Na Seem had moved nothing from the tent Elric had last shared with Alnac Kreb and the albino hastily drew the flask from his saddle-bag and took a deep draught, feeling, for a short while at least, the relief, and resurgence of energy, the illusion of health which the Quarzhasaati's drug gave him. He sighed and turned towards the entrance of the tent as Raik Na Seem came up, his brow furrowed, his eyes full of pain which he tried to disguise. "Have you agreed to help the dreamthief, Elric? Will you attempt to achieve what the prophecy predicted? Bring our Holy Girl back to us? There is now less time than there ever was. Soon the Blood Moon will be gone."

Elric dropped the flask onto the carpet which covered the ground. He bent and picked up the Black Sword which he had unbuckled while he walked with Oone. The thing thrilled in his fingers and he felt vaguely nauseated. "I will do whatever is required of me," the albino said.

"Good." The older man gripped Elric by the shoulders. "Oone has told me that you are a great man with a great destiny and that this time is one of considerable moment in your life. We are honoured to be part of that destiny and grateful for your concern . . ."

Elric accepted Raik Na Seem's words with all his old grace. He bowed. "I believe that the health of your Holy Girl is more important than any fate of mine. I will do whatever is possible to bring her back to you."

Oone had entered behind the Bauradim's First Elder. She smiled at the albino. "You are ready now?"

Elric nodded and began to buckle on the Black Sword, but Oone stopped him with a gesture. "You'll find the weapons you need where we travel."

"But the sword is more than a weapon, Lady Oone!" the albino knew a kind of panic.

She held out Alnac's dreamwand to him. "This is all you need for our venture, my lord emperor."

Stormbringer murmured violently as Elric let the sword fall back to the cushions of the tent. It seemed almost to threaten him.

"I am dependent . . ." he began.

She shook her head gently. "You are not. You believe that sword to be part of your identity but it is not. It is your nemesis. It is the part of you which represents your weakness, not your strength."

Elric sighed. "I do not understand you, my lady, but if you do not wish me to bring the sword, I'll leave it."

Another sound, a peculiar growl, from the blade, but Elric ignored it. He left both flask and sword in the tent and strode to where horses awaited them to carry them from the Silver Flower Oasis back to the Bronze Tent.

As they rode a little distance behind Raik Na Seem, Oone told Elric something more of what the Holy Girl meant to the Bauradim.

"As you perhaps have already realized, the child holds in trust the history and the aspirations of the Bauradim—their collected wisdom. Everything they know to be true and of value is contained within her. She is the living representation of her people's learning—what is the essence of their history—of a time before they became desert dwellers even. If they lose her there is every chance, they believe, that they must begin their history all over again—relearn hard-won lessons, relive experience and make the mistakes and blunders which so painfully informed their people's understanding down the centuries. She is Time, if you like—their library, museum, religion and culture personified in a single human being. Can you imagine, Prince Elric, what her loss means to them? She is the very soul of the Bauradim. And that soul is imprisoned where only those of a certain skill can even find her, let alone free her."

Elric fingered the dreamwand which now replaced his runesword at his hip. "If she were only an ordinary child, bringing sorrow to her family through her condition, I would be inclined to help if I could," he said. "For I like this people and their leader."

"Her fate and yours are intertwined," said Oone. "Whatever your sentiments, my lord, you probably have little real choice in the matter."

He did not wish to hear this. "It seems to me, madam, that you dreamthieves are altogether too familiar with myself, my family, my people and my destiny. It makes me somewhat uncomfortable. Yet I cannot deny you know more than anyone, save my betrothed, about my inner conflicts. How come you by this power of divination and prophecy?"

She spoke almost casually. "There is a land all dreamthieves have visited. It is a place where all dreams intersect, where all that we have in common meets. And we call that land The Birthplace of the Bone, where mankind first assumed reality."

"This is legend! And primitive legend at that!"

"Legend to you. Truth to us. As one day you'll discover."

"If Alnac could foretell the future, why did he not wait for you to come to help him?"

"We rarely know our own destiny, only the general movements of the tides and of the figures who stand out in their world's histories. All dreamthieves, it is true, know the future, for half their lives are spent without Time. For us there is no past or future, only a changing present. We are free of those particular chains while bound as strongly by others."

"I have read of such ideas, but they mean very little to me."

"Because you lack experience to make sense of them."

"You have already spoken of the Land of Dreams-in-Common. Is that the same as the Birthplace of the Bone?"

"Perhaps. Our people are undecided on the point."

Temporarily invigorated by the drug, Elric began to enjoy the conversation, much of which he saw as mere pleasant abstraction. Free of his runesword he knew a kind of lightness of spirit which he had not experienced since the first months of his courtship of Cymoril in those relatively untroubled years before Yyrkoon's growing ambition had begun to contaminate life at the Melnibonéan court.

He recalled something from one of his own people's histories. "I have seen it said that the world is no more than what its denizens agree it is. I remember reading something to that effect in *The Gabbling Sphere* which said: 'For who is to say which is the inner world and which the outer? What we make reality may be what will alone decides and what we define as dreams may be the greater truth.' Is that a philosophy close to your own, Lady Oone?"

"Close enough," she said. "Though it seems a little airy."

They rode like this, almost like two children on a picnic until they reached the Bronze Tent when the sun was setting and were led, once more, into the place where men and women sat or lay around the great raised bed on which rested the little girl who symbolized their entire existence.

It seemed to Elric that the illuminating braziers and lamps were burning lower than when last he was here, and that the child looked even paler than before, but he forced an expression of confidence when he turned to Raik Na Seem. "This time we shall not fail her," he said.

Oone appeared to approve of Elric's words and watched carefully as, on her instructions, Varadia's frail body was lifted from the bed and placed this time upon a huge cushion which, in its turn, was set between two other cushions, also of great size. She signed to the albino to lay his body down on the far side of the child while she herself took up her position on the girl's left.

"Grasp her hand, my lord emperor," said Oone ironically, "and place the crook of the dreamwand over both yours and hers, as you saw Alnac do."

Elric felt some trepidation as he obeyed her, but he knew no fear for himself, only for the child and her people, for Cymoril waiting for him in Melniboné, for the boy who prayed in Quarzhasaat that he would return with the jewel his jailer had demanded. His hand locked to the girl's by the dreamwand, he knew a sense of fusion that was not unpleasant, yet seemed to burn as hot as any flame. He watched as Oone did the same thing.

Immediately Elric felt a power possess him and for a moment it was as if his body grew lighter and lighter until it threatened to drift away on the slightest breeze. His vision faded, yet dimly he could still see Oone. She seemed to be concentrating.

He looked into the face of the Holy Girl and for a second thought he saw her skin turn still whiter, her eyes glow as crimson as his own and a strange thought came and went in his mind: *If I had a daughter she would look thus . . .*

And then it was as if his bones were melting, his flesh dissolving, his whole mind and spirit dissipating. He gave himself up to this sensation as he had determined he must, since he now served Oone's purpose, and now the flesh became flowing water, the veins and blood were coloured strands of air, his skeleton flowed like molten silver, mingling with the Holy Child's, becoming hers, then flowing on beyond her, into caverns and tunnels and dark places, into places where whole worlds existed in hollowed rock, where voices called to him and knew him and sought to comfort him or frighten him or tell him truths he did not wish to learn; and then the air grew bright again and he felt Oone beside him, guiding him, her hand on his, her body almost his body, her voice confident and even cheerful, like one who moves towards familiar danger; danger which she had overcome many times. Yet there was an edge to her voice which made him believe she had never faced a danger as great as this one and that there was every chance neither of them would return to the Bronze Tent or the Silver Flower Oasis.

And there was music which he understood was the very soul of this child turned into sound. Sweet, sad, lonely music. Music so beautiful he would have wept had he anything more than the airiest substance.

Then he saw blue sky before him, a red desert stretching away towards red mountains on the horizon and he had the strangest of sensations, as if he were coming home to a land he had somehow lost in his childhood and then forgotten.

Chapter Two

In the Marches at the Heart's Edge

As Elric felt his bones reform and the flesh resume its familiar weight and contour he saw that the land they had entered seemed scarcely any different from that which they had left. Red desert stretched before them, red mountains lay beyond. So familiar was the landscape that Elric looked back, expecting to see the Bronze Tent, but immediately behind him now yawned a chasm so vast no further side could be seen. He knew sudden vertigo and checked his balance, somewhat to Oone's amusement.

The dreamthief was dressed in her same functional velvets and silks and seemed a little amused by his response. "Aye, Prince Elric! Now we are indeed at the very edge of the world! We have only certain choices here and they do not include retreat!"

"I had not considered it, madam." Looking more closely, he realized that the mountains were considerably taller and were all leaning in the same direction, as if bent by a tremendous wind.

"They are like the teeth of some ancient predator," said Oone with the shudder of one who might actually have stared into such a maw at some time in their career. "Doubtless the first stage of our journey takes us there. This is the land we dreamthieves always call Sadanor. The Land of Dreams-in-Common."

"Yet you seem unfamiliar with this scenery."

"The scenery varies. We know only the *nature* of the land. It may change in its details. But where we travel is frequently dangerous not because it is unfamiliar but because of its familiarity. That is the second rule of the dreamthief."

"Beware the familiar."

"You learn well." She seemed unduly pleased by his response, as if she had doubted her own description of his qualities and was glad to have them confirmed. Elric began to realize the degree of desperation involved in this adventure and was seized by that wild carelessness, that willingness to give himself up to the moment, to any experience, which so set him apart from the other lords of Melniboné, whose lives were ruled by tradition and a desire to maintain their power at any cost.

Smiling, his eyes alight with all their old vitality, he bowed ironically. "Then lead on, madam! Let us begin our journey towards the mountains."

Oone, a little startled by his mood, frowned. But she began to walk through sand so light it stirred like water around her feet. And the albino followed.

"I must admit," he said, after they had walked for perhaps an hour, without noting any shift in the position of the light, "this place begins to disturb me more the more I am in it. I thought the sun obscured, but now I realize there is no sun in the sky at all."

"Such abnormalities come and go in the Land of Dreams-in-Common," said Oone.

"I would feel more secure with my sword at my side."

"Swords are easily come by here," she said.

"Drinkers of souls?"

"Perhaps. But do you feel the need for that peculiar form of sustenance? Do you crave Lord Gho's drug?"

Elric admitted to his own surprise that he had lost no energy. For perhaps the first time in his adult life he had the sense that he was physically as other people, able to sustain himself without calling on any form of artifice. "It occurs to me," he said, "that I might be well-advised to make my home here."

"Ah, now you begin to fall into another of this realm's traps," she said, lightly enough. "First there is suspicion and maybe fear. Then there is relaxation, a feeling that you have always belonged here, that this is your natural home, or your spiritual home. These are all illusions common to the traveler, as I am sure you know. Here those illusions must be resisted, for they are more than sentiment. They may be traps set to snare you and destroy you. Be grateful that you have more apparent energy than that which you normally know, but remember another rule of the dreamthief—*Every gain is paid for, either before or after the event.* Every apparent benefit could well have its contrary disadvantage."

Privately Elric still thought the price of such a sense of well-being might be worth the paying.

It was at that moment that he saw the leaf.

It drifted down from over his head, a broad, red-gold oak leaf, falling gently as any ordinary autumn shedding, and landed upon the sand at his feet. Without at first finding this extraordinary, he bent to pick the leaf up.

Oone had seen it, too, and made as if to caution him, then changed her mind.

Elric laid the leaf on the palm of his hand. There was nothing unusual about it, save that there was not a tree visible in any direction. He was about to ask Oone to explain this phenomenon when he noticed that she was staring beyond him, over his shoulder.

"Good afternoon to you," said a jaunty voice. "This is luck indeed, to find some fellow mortals in such a miserable wilderness. What trick of the Wheel brought us here, do you think?"

"Greetings," said Oone, her smile growing broad. "You're ill-dressed, sir, for this desert."

"I was neither told of my destination nor the fact that I was leaving . . ."

Elric turned and to his surprise saw a small man whose sharp, merry features were shadowed by an enormous turban of yellow silk. This headdress, at least as wide as the man's shoulders, was decorated with a pin containing a great green gem and from it sprouted several peacock's feathers. He seemed to be wearing many layers of clothing, all highly coloured, of silk and linen, including an embroidered waistcoat and a long jacket of beautifully stitched blue patchwork, each shade subtly different from the one next to it. On his legs were baggy trousers of red silk and his feet sported curling slippers of green and yellow leather. The man was unarmed, but in his hands he held a startled black and white cat upon whose back were folded a pair of silky black wings.

The man bowed when he saw Elric. "Greetings, sir. You would be the incarnation of the Champion on this plane, I take it. I am—" he frowned as if he had for a second forgotten his own name. "I am something beginning with 'J' and something beginning with 'C'. It will return to me in a moment. Or another name or event will occur, I'm sure. I am your—what?—amanuensis, eh?" He peered up into the sky. "Is this one of those sunless worlds? Are we to have no night at all?"

Elric looked to Oone, who did not seem wary of this apparition. "I did not ask for a secretary, sir," he said to the small man. "Nor did I expect to be assigned one. My companion and I are on a quest in this world . . ."

"A quest, naturally. It is your role, as it is mine to accompany you. That's in order, sir. My name is—" But again his own name eluded him. "Yours is?"

"I am Elric of Melniboné and this is Oone the Dreamthief."

"Then this is the land the dreamthieves call Sadanor, I take it. Good, then I am called Jaspar Colinadous. And my cat's name is Whiskers, as always."

At this, the cat gave voice to a small, intelligent noise, to which its owner listened carefully and nodded.

"I recognize this land now," he said. "You'll be seeking the Marador Gate, eh? For the Land of Old Desires."

"You are a dreamthief yourself, Sir Jaspar?" Oone asked in some surprise.

"I have relatives who are."

"But how came you here?" Elric asked. "Through a medium? Did you use a mortal child, as we did?"

"Your words are mysterious to me, sir." Jaspar Colinadous adjusted his turban, the little cat tucked carefully under one voluminous silk sleeve. "I travel between the worlds, apparently at random, usually at the behest of some force I do not understand, frequently to find myself guiding or accompanying venturers such as yourselves. Not," he added feelingly, "always dressed appropriately for the realm or the moment of my arrival. I dreamed, I think, I was the sultan of some fabulous city, where I possessed the most astonishing variety of treasures. Where I was waited upon . . ." here he coloured and looked away from Oone. "Forgive me. It was a dream. I have awakened from it now. Unfortunately, the clothes followed me from the dream . . ."

Elric believed the man's words were close to nonsense, but Oone had no difficulty with them. "You know a road, then, to the Marador Gate?"

"Surely, I must, if this is the Land of Dreams-in-Common." Carefully, he placed his cat on his shoulder and then began to rummage in his sleeves, within his shirt, in the pockets of his several garments, producing all manner of scrolls and papers and little books, boxes, compacts, writing instruments, lengths of cord and reels of thread, until one of the rolled pieces of vellum caused him to cry out in relief. "Here it is, I think! Our map." He replaced all the other items in exactly the places he had drawn them from and unrolled the parchment. "Indeed, indeed! This shows us the road through yonder mountains."

"Offers of guidance . . ." began Elric.

"And beware the familiar," said Oone softly. Then she made a dismissive gesture. "Here we have conflict already, you see, for what is unfamiliar to you is highly familiar to me. That is part of the nature of this land." She turned to Jaspar Colinadous. "Sir? May I see your map?"

Without hesitation, the small man handed it to her. "A straight road. It's always a straightish road, eh? And only one. That's the joy of these dream realms. One can interpret and control them so simply. Unless, of course, they swallow one up completely. Which they are wont to do."

"You have the advantage of me," said Elric, "for I know nothing of this world. Neither was I aware that there are others like it."

"Aha! Then you have so much wonder to anticipate, sir! So many marvels yet to witness. I would tell you of them, but my own memory is not what it should be. I frequently have only the vaguest of recollections. But there is an infinity of worlds and some are yet unborn, some so old they have grown senile, some born of dreams, some destroyed by nightmares." Jaspar Colinadous paused apologetically. "I grow over-enthusiastic. I do not intend to confuse you, sir. Just know you that I am a little confused myself. I am ever that. Does my map make sense to you, Lady Dreamthief?"

"Aye." Oone was frowning over the parchment. "There is only one pass through those mountains, which are called the Shark's Jaws. If we assume that the mountains are lying to our north, then we must bear to the north-east and find the Shark's Gullet, as it's named here. We are much obliged to you, Master Jaspar Colinadous." She rolled up the map and returned it to him. It disappeared into one of his sleeves and the cat crept down to lie, purring, in the crook of his arm.

For a moment, Elric had the strongest instinct that this likable individual had been called up by Oone from her own imagination, though it was impossible to believe he did not exist in his own right, such a self-confident personality was he. Indeed, Elric had the passing fancy that perhaps he, himself, was the phantasy.

"You'll note there are dangers in that pass," said Jaspar Colinadous casually, as he fell in beside them. "I'll let Whiskers scout for us, if you like, when we get closer."

"We should be much obliged to you, sir," said Oone.

They continued their journey across the bleak landscape, with Jaspar Colinadous telling tales of previous adventures, most of which he could only half recall, of people he had known, whose names escaped him, and of great moments in the histories of a thousand worlds whose importance now eluded him. To hear him was like coming upon the old halls of Imrryr, on the Dragon Isle, where once huge series of windows had told in pictures the tales of the first Melnibonéans and how they had come to their present home. Now they were mere shards, small fragments of the story, brilliant details whose context was only barely imaginable and whose information was gone for ever. Elric ceased trying to follow Jaspar Colinadous's conversation but, as he had learned to do with the fragments of glass, let himself enjoy them for their texture and their colour instead.

The consistency of the light had begun to disturb him and eventually he interrupted the little man in his flow and asked him if he, too, were not made uncomfortable by it.

Jaspar Colinadous took this opportunity to stop and remove his slippers, shaking sand from them as Oone waited ahead of them, her stance impatient. "No, sir. Supernatural worlds are frequently sunless, for they obey none of the laws we are familiar with in our own. They may be flat, half-spheres, oval, circular, even shaped like cubes. They exist only as satellites to those realms we call 'real', and therefore are dependent not upon any sun or moon or planetary system for their ordering, but upon the demands—spiritual, imaginative, philosophical and so on—of worlds which do, in fact, require a sun to heat them and a moon to move their tides. There is even a theory that our worlds are the satellites and that these supernatural worlds are the birthplaces of all our realities." His shoes again free from sand, Jaspar Colinadous began to follow Oone, who was some distance on, having refused to wait upon them.

"Perhaps this is the land ruled by Arioch, my patron Duke of Hell," said Elric. "The land from which the Black Sword sprang."

"Oh, quite possibly, Prince Elric. For, see, there's a hellish sort of creature stooping on your friend at this moment and us without a weapon between us!"

The three-headed bird must have flown at such a great height it had not been seen to approach, but now it was dropping at terrifying speed from above and Oone, alerted by Elric's cry of warning, began to run, perhaps hoping to divert it in its descent upon her. It was like a gigantic crow, with two of its heads tucked deep into its neck, while the other stretched out to help its downward flight, its wings spread behind it, its claws extended, ready to seize the woman.

Elric began to run forward, screaming at the thing. He, too, hoped that this activity would disturb the creature enough and make it lose its momentum.

With a terrible cawing which seemed to fill the entire heavens, the monster slowed its descent a trifle in order to make a more accurate strike on the woman.

It was then that Jaspar Colinadous cried from behind Elric.

"Jack Three Beaks, thou naughty bird!"

The beast wavered in the air, turning all heads towards the turbaned figure who strode decisively towards it across the sand, his cat alert on his arm.

"What's this, Jack? I thought you were forbidden living meat!" Jaspar Colinadous's voice was contemptuous, familiar. Whiskers growled and gibbered at the thing, though it was many times larger than the little cat.

With a croak of defiance the bird flopped onto the sand and began to run at some considerable speed towards Oone, who had stopped to witness this bizarre event. Now she took to her heels again, the three-headed crow in pursuit.

"Jack! Jack! Remember the punishment."

The bird's cry was almost mocking. Elric began to stumble through the desert in its track, hoping to find a means of saving the dreamthief.

It was then that he felt something cut through the air above his head, fanning him with unexpected coolness, and a dark shape sped in pursuit of the thing Jaspar Colinadous had called Jack Three Beaks.

It was the black and white cat. The beast flung his little body at the bird's central neck and sank all four sets of claws into the feathers. With a shrill scream the gigantic three-headed crow whirled round, its other heads trying to peck at the tenacious cat and just failing to reach it.

To Elric's astonishment the cat seemed to swell larger and larger as if feeding on the lifestuff of the crow, while the crow appeared to grow smaller.

"Bad Jack Three Beaks! Wicked Jack!" The almost ridiculous figure of Jaspar Colinadous strutted up to the thing now, wagging a finger at which beaks snapped but dared not bite. "You were warned. And now you must perish. How came you here at all? You followed me, I suppose, when I left my palace." He scratched his head. "Not that I recall leaving the palace. Ah, well . . ."

Jack Three Beaks cawed again, glaring with mad, frightened eyes in the direction of his original prey. Oone was approaching again.

"This creature is your pet, Master Jaspar?"

"Certainly not, madam. It is my enemy. He knew he'd had his last warning. But I think he did not expect to find me here and believed he could attack living prey with impunity. Not so, Jack, eh?"

The answering croak was almost pathetic now. The little black and white cat resembled nothing so much as a feeding vampire bat as it sucked and sucked of the monster's lifestuff.

Oone watched in horror as gradually the crow shrank to a tiny, wizened thing and Whiskers at last sat back, huge and round, and began to clean himself, purring with considerable pleasure. Clearly pleased with his pet, Jaspar Colinadous reached up to pat his head. "Good lad, Whiskers. Now poor Jack's not even gravy for an old man's bread." He smiled proudly at his two new friends. "This cat has saved my life on many an occasion."

"How had you the name of that monster?" Oone wished to know. Her lovely features were flushed and she was out of breath. Elric was reminded suddenly of Cymoril, though he could not exactly identify the similarity.

"Why, it was Jack frightened the principality I visited before this." Jaspar Colinadous displayed his rich clothing. "And how I came to be so favoured by the folk of that place. Jack Three Beaks always knew the power of Whiskers and was afraid of him. He had been terrorizing the people when I arrived. I tamed Jack—or strictly speaking Whiskers did—but let him live, since he was a useful carrion eater and the province was given to terrible heat in the summer. When I fell through that particular rent in the fabric of the multiverse he must have come after me, without realizing I was already here with Whiskers. There's little mystery to it, Lady Oone."

She drew a deep breath. "Well, I'm grateful for your aid, sir."

He inclined his head. "Now had we better not move on towards the Marador Gate? There are more, if less unexpected, dangers ahead of us in the Shark's Gullet. The map marks 'em."

"Would that I had a weapon at my side," said Elric, feelingly. "I would be more confident, whether it were an illusion or no!" But he marched beside the others as they moved on towards the mountain.

The cat remained behind, licking his paws and cleaning himself, for all the world like an ordinary domestic creature which had killed a pantry-raiding mouse.

At last the ground began to rise as they reached the shallow foothills of the Shark's Jaws and saw ahead of them a great, dark fissure in the mountains, the Gullet which would lead them through to the next land of their journey. In the heat of the barren wilderness the pass looked cool and almost welcoming, though even from here Elric thought he could see shapes moving in it. White shadows flickered against the black.

"What manner of people live here?" he asked Oone, who had not shown him the map.

"Chiefly those who have either lost their way or become too fearful to continue the journey inwards. The other name for the pass is the Valley of Timid Souls." Oone shrugged. "But I suspect it is not from them that we shall be in danger. At least, not greatly. They'll ally themselves with whatever power rules the pass."

"And the map says nothing of its nature?"

"Only that we should be wary."

There came a noise from behind them and Elric turned, expecting threat, but it was only Whiskers, looking a little plumper, a little sleeker, but back to his normal size, who had at last caught up with them.

Jaspar Colinadous laughed and bent to let the cat leap onto his shoulder. "We have no need of weapons, eh? Not with such a handsome beast to defend us!"

The cat licked his face.

Elric was peering into the dark pass, trying to determine what he might find there. For a moment he thought he saw a rider at the entrance, a man mounted on a silvery-grey horse, wearing strange armour of different shades of white and grey and yellow. The warrior's horse reared as he turned it and rode back into the blackness and Elric knew a sensation of foreboding, though he had never seen the figure before.

Oone and Jaspar Colinadous were apparently unaware of the apparition and continued with untiring stride in the direction of the pass.

Elric said nothing of the rider but instead asked Oone how it was that they had all walked for hours and felt neither hungry nor weary.

"It is one of the advantages of this realm," she said. "The disadvantages are considerable, however, since a sense of time is easily lost and one can forget direction and goals. Moreover it's wise to bear in mind that while one does not appear to lose physical energy or experience hunger, other forms of energy are being expended. Psychic and spiritual they may be, but they are just as valuable, as I'm sure you appreciate. Conserve those particular resources, Prince Elric, for you'll have urgent need of them soon enough!"

Elric wondered if she, too, had caught sight of the pale warrior but, for a reason he could not understand, was reluctant to ask her.

The hills were growing ever taller around them as, subtly, they moved into the Shark's Gullet. The light was dimmer already, blocked by the mountains, and Elric felt a chill which was not altogether the result of the shade.

He became aware of a rushing sound and Jaspar Colinadous ran towards a high bank of rocks to peer over them and look down. He turned, a little baffled. "A deep chasm. A river. We must find a bridge before we can go on." He murmured to his winged cat, which immediately took flight over the abyss and was soon lost in the shadows beyond.

Forced to pause, Elric knew sudden gloom. Unable to gauge his physical needs, uncertain of what events took place in the world he had left, perturbed by the knowledge that their time was running short and that Lord Gho would certainly keep his word to torture young Anigh to death, he began to believe that he could well be on a fool's errand, embarked on an adventure which could only end in disaster for all. He wondered why he had trusted Oone so completely. Perhaps because he had been so desperate, so shocked by the death of Alnac Kreb . . .

She touched him on the shoulder. "Remember what I told you. Your weariness is not physical here, but it manifests itself in your moods. You must seek spiritual sustenance as assiduously as you would normally seek food and water."

He looked into her eyes, seeing warmth and kindness there. Immediately his despair began to dissipate. "I must admit I was beginning to know strong doubt . . ."

"When that feeling overwhelms you, try to tell me," she said. "I am familiar with it and might be able to help you . . ."

"So I am entirely in your hands, madam." He spoke without irony.

"I thought you understood that when you agreed to accompany me," she said softly.

"Aye." He turned in time to see the little cat coming back and alighting on Jaspar Colinadous's shoulder. The turbaned man listened carefully and intelligently and Elric was certain that the cat was speaking.

At last Jaspar Colinadous nodded. "There's a good bridge not a quarter of a mile from here and it leads to a trail winding directly into the pass. Whiskers tells me that the bridge is guarded by a single mounted warrior. We can hope, I suppose, that he will let us cross."

They followed the course of the river as the sky overhead grew darker and Elric wished that, together with his lack of hunger and tiredness, he did not feel the rapid drop in temperature which made his body shake. Only Jaspar Colinadous was unaffected by the cold.

The rough walls of rocks at the chasm's edge gradually fell away, curving inward towards the pass, and very soon they saw the bridge ahead of them, a narrow spur of natural stone pushing outwards over the foaming river below. And they heard the echo of the water as it plunged yet deeper down the gorge. Yet nowhere was there the guard which the little cat had reported.

Elric moved cautiously in the lead now, again wishing he had a weapon to give him reassurance. He reached the bridge and set a foot upon it. Far down at the base of the chasm's granite walls grey foam leapt and danced and the river gave voice to its own peculiar song, half triumph, half despair, almost as if it were a living thing.

Elric shivered and took another step. Still he saw no figure in that deepening gloom. Another step and he was high above the water, refusing to look down lest the water call him to it. He knew the fascination of such torrents and how one could be drawn into them, hypnotized by their rush and noise.

"See you any guard, Prince Elric?" called Jaspar Colinadous.

"Nothing," the albino cried back. And he took two more steps.

Oone was behind him now, moving as cautiously as he. He peered to the bridge's further side. Great slabs of dank rock, covered in lichen and oddly coloured creepers, rose up and disappeared into the dark air above. The sound of the river made him think he heard voices, little skittering sounds, the scuffle of threatening limbs, but still he saw nothing.

Elric was halfway across the bridge before he detected the suggestion of a horse in the shadows of the gorge, the barest hint of a rider, perhaps wearing armour which was the colour of his own bone-white skin.

"Who's that?" The albino raised his voice. "We come in peace. We mean no harm to anyone here."

Again it might have been that the water made him believe he heard a faint, unpleasant chuckle.

Then it seemed the rush of water grew louder and he realized he heard the sound of hoofs on rock. Formed as if by the spray, a figure suddenly appeared on the far side of the bridge, bearing down on him, its long, pale sword poised to strike.

There was nowhere to turn. The only way of avoiding the warrior was to jump from the bridge into the torrent below. Elric found his vision dimmed even as he prepared to spring forward, hoping to catch the horse's bridle and at least halt the rider in his tracks.

Then again there was a whirring of wings and something fixed itself on the attacker's helm, slashing at the face within. It was Whiskers, spitting and yowling like any ordinary alley cat engaged in a brawl over a piece of ripe fish.

The horse reared. The rider gave out a shriek of rage and pain and released the bridle in order to try to pull the little cat from him. Whiskers rushed upward into the air, out of reach. Elric glimpsed glaring, silvery eyes, a skin which glowed with the leper's mark, and then the horse, out of control, had slipped on the wet rock and fallen sideways. For a moment it tried to get back to its feet, the rider yelling and roaring as if demented, the long, white sword still in his hand. And then both had tumbled over the edge of the bridge and went falling, a chaotic mixture of arms and hoofs, down into the echoing chasm to be swallowed by the distant, murky waters.

Elric was gasping for breath. Jaspar Colinadous came to grip his arm and steady him, helping him and Oone cross to the far side of the rocky slab and stand upon the bank, still scarcely aware of what had happened to them.

"I'm grateful again to Whiskers," said Elric with an unstable grin. "That's a valuable pet you have, Master Colinadous."

"More valuable than you know," said the little man feelingly. "He has played a crucial part in more than one world's history!" He patted the cat as the beast returned to his arms, purring and pleased with himself. "I'm glad we were able to be of service to you."

"We're well rid of the bridge's guardian." Elric peered down into the foam. "Are we to encounter more such attacks, my lady?"

"Most certainly," she said. She was frowning as if lost in some conundrum only she perceived.

Jaspar Colinadous pursed his lips. "Here," he said. "Look how the gorge narrows. It becomes a tunnel."

It was true. They could now see how the rocks leaned in upon one another so that the pass was little more than a cave barely large enough to let Elric enter without bending his head. A set of crude steps led up to it and from time to time a little flicker of yellow fire appeared within, as if the place were lit by torches.

Jaspar Colinadous sighed. "I had hoped to journey with you further than this, but I must turn back now. I can go no further than the Marador Gate, which is what this seems to be. To do so would be to destroy me. I must find other companions now, in the Land of Dreams-in-Common." He seemed genuinely regretful. "Farewell, Prince Elric, Lady Oone. I wish you success in your adventure."

And suddenly the little man had turned and walked swiftly back over the bridge, not looking behind him. He left them almost as suddenly as he had arrived and was gone back into the darkness before either could speak, his cat with him.

Oone seemed to accept this and, at Elric's questioning glance, said: "Such people come and go here. Another rule the dreamthief learns is '*Hold on to nothing but your own soul.*' Do you understand?"

"I understand that it must be a lonely thing to be a dreamthief, madam."

And with that Elric began to climb the great rough-hewn steps which led into the Marador Gate.

Chapter Three

Of Beauty Found in Deep Caverns

The tunnel began to descend almost as soon as they had entered it. Where it had at first been cool now the air became hot and humid so that sometimes it seemed to Elric he was wading through water. The little lights which gave faint illumination were not, as he had at first thought, lamps or brands, but seemed naturally luminescent, delicate nodes of soft, glowing substance almost fleshlike in appearance. They found that they were whispering, as if unwilling to disturb any denizens of this place. Yet Elric did not feel afraid here. The tunnel had the atmosphere of a sanctuary and he noticed that Oone, too, had lost some of her normal caution, though her experience had taught her to be wary of anything as a potentially dangerous illusion.

There was no obvious transition from Sadanor to Marador, save perhaps a slight change of mood, and then the tunnel had opened up into a vast natural hall of richly glowing blues and greens and golden yellows and dark pinks, all flowing one to the other, like lava which had only recently cooled, more like exotic plants than the rock they were. Scents, like those of the loveliest, headiest flowers, made Elric feel he walked in a garden, not unlike the gardens he had known as a child, places of the greatest security and tranquility; yet there was no doubt that the place was a cavern and that they had traveled underground to reach it.

At first delighted by the sight, Elric began to feel a certain sadness, for until now he had not remembered those gardens of childhood, the innocent happiness which comes so rarely to a Melnibonéan, no matter what their age. He thought of his mother, dead in childbirth, of his infinitely mourning father, who had refused to acknowledge the son who, in his opinion, had killed his wife.

A movement from the depths of this natural hall and Elric again feared danger, but the people who began to emerge were unarmed and they had faces full of restrained melancholy.

"We have arrived in Marador," whispered Oone with certainty.

"You are here to join us?" A woman spoke. She wore flowing robes of myriad, glistening colours, mirroring the colours of the rock on walls and roof. She had long hair of faded gold and her eyes were the shade of old pewter. She reached to touch Elric—a greeting—and her hand was cold on his. He felt himself becoming infected with the same sad tranquility and it seemed to him that there could be worse fates than remaining here, recalling the desires and pleasures of his past, when life had been so much simpler and the world had seemed easily conquered, easily improved.

Behind him Oone said in a voice which sounded unduly harsh to his ear. "We are travelers in your land, my lady. We mean you no harm, but we cannot stay."

A man spoke. "Travelers? What do you seek?"

"We seek," said Elric, "the Fortress of the Pearl."

Oone was clearly displeased by his frankness. "We have no desire to tarry in Marador. We wish only to learn the location of the next gate, the Paranor Gate."

The man smiled wistfully. "It is lost, I fear. Lost to all of us. Yet there is no harm in loss. There is comfort in it, even, don't you feel?" He turned dreaming, distant eyes on them. "Better not to seek that which can only disappoint. Here we prefer to remember what we most wanted and how it was to want it . . ."

"Better, surely, to continue looking for it?" Elric was surprised by his own blunt tone.

"Why so, sir, when the reality can only prove inadequate when compared against the hope?"

"Think you so, sir?" Elric was prepared to consider this notion, but Oone's grip on his arm tightened.

"Remember the name that dreamthieves give this land," she murmured.

Elric reflected that it was truly the Land of Old Desires. All of his own forgotten yearnings were returning to him, bringing a sense of simplicity and peace. Now he remembered how those sensations had been replaced by anger as he began to realize that there was little likelihood of his dreams ever coming true. He had raged at the injustice of the world. He had flung himself into his sorcerous studies. He had become determined to change the balance of things and introduce greater liberty, greater justice by means of the power he had in the world. Yet his fellow Melnibonéans had refused to accept his logic. The early dreams had begun to fade and with them the hope which had at first lifted his heart. Now here was the hope offered him again. Perhaps there were realms where all he desired was true? Perhaps Marador was such a world.

"If I went back and found Cymoril and brought her here, we could live in harmony with these people, I think," he said to Oone.

The dreamthief was almost contemptuous.

"This is called the Land of Old Desires—not the Land of Fulfilled Desire! There is a difference. The emotions you feel are easy and easily maintained—while the reality remains out of your reach, while you merely long for the unattainable. When you set out to discover fulfillment, Elric of Melniboné, then you achieved stature in the world. Turn your back on that determination—your own determination to help build a world where justice reigns—and you'll lose my respect. You'll lose respect for yourself. You'll prove yourself a liar and you'll prove me a fool for believing you could help me save the Holy Girl!"

Elric was shocked by her outburst, which seemed offensive in that pleasant mood of serenity surrounding them. "But I think it is impossible to build such a world. Better to have the prospect, surely, than the knowledge of failure?"

"That is what all in this realm believe. Remain here, if you will, and believe what they believe for ever. But I think one must always make an attempt at justice, no matter how poor the prospect of success!"

Elric felt tired and wished to settle down and rest. He yawned and stretched. "These people seem to have a secret I would learn. I think I will talk to them for a while before continuing."

"Do so and Anigh dies. The Holy Girl dies. And everything of yourself that you value, that dies, also." Oone did not raise her voice. She spoke almost in a matter-of-fact tone. But her words had an urgency which broke Elric's mood. It was not for the first time that he had considered retreating into dreams. Had he done so, his people would now be ruled by him and Yyrkoon would be dead or exiled.

Thought of his cousin and his cousin's ambition, of Cymoril waiting for him to return so that they might be married, helped remind Elric of his purpose here and he shook off the mood of reconciliation, of retreat. He bowed to the people of the cavern. "I thank you for your generosity, but my own path lies forward, through the Paranor Gate."

Oone drew a deep breath, perhaps in relief. "Time's not measured in any familiar way here, Prince Elric, but be assured it's passing more rapidly than I would like . . ."

It was with a sense of deep regret that Elric left the melancholy people behind him and followed her further into the glowing caverns.

Oone added: "These lands are well-called. Be wary of the familiar."

"Perhaps we could have rested there? Restored our energies?" said Elric.

"Aye. And died full of sweet melancholy."

He looked at her in surprise and saw that she had not been unaffected by the atmosphere. "Is that what befell Alnac Kreb?"

"Of course not!" She recovered herself. "He was fully able to resist so obvious a trap."

Elric now felt ashamed. "I almost failed the first real test of my determination and my discipline."

"We dreamthieves have the advantage of having been tested thus many times," she told him. "It gets easier to confront, though the lure remains as strong."

"For you, too."

"Why not? You think I have no forgotten desires, nothing I would not wish to dream of? No childhood which had its sweet moments?"

"Forgive me, madam."

She shrugged. "There's an attraction to that aspect of the past. To the past in general, I suppose. But we forget the other aspects—those things which forced us into fantasy in the first place."

"You're a believer in the future, then, madam?" Elric tried to joke. The rock beneath their feet became slippery and they were forced to make the gentle descent with more caution. Ahead Elric thought he heard again the sound of the river, perhaps where it now raced underground.

"The future holds as many traps as the past," she said with a smile. "I am a believer in the present, my lord. In the eternal present." And there was an edge to her voice, as if she had not always held this view.

"Speculation and regret offer many temptations, I suppose," said Elric; then he gasped at what he saw ahead.

Molten gold was cascading down two well-worn channels in the rock, forming a gigantic V-shaped edifice. The metal flowed unchecked and yet as they approached it became obvious that it was not hot. Some other agent had caused the effect, perhaps a chemical in the rock itself. As the gold reached the floor of the cavern it spread into a pool and the pool in turn fed a brook which bubbled, brilliant with the precious stuff, down towards another stream which seemed at first to contain ordinary water. But when Elric looked more carefully he saw that that stream was, in turn, composed of silver and the two elements blended as they met. Following the course of this stream with his eyes he saw that it met, some distance away, with a further river, this one of glistening scarlet, which might be liquid rubies. In all his travels, in the Young Kingdoms and the realms of the supernatural, Elric had seen nothing like it. He made to move towards it, to inspect it further, but she checked him.

"We have reached the next gate, she said. "Ignore that particular wonder, my lord. Look."

She pointed between twin streams of gold and he could just make out something shadowy beyond. "There is Paranor. Are you ready to enter that land?"

Remembering the dreamthieves' term for it, Elric allowed himself an ironic smile. "As ready as I shall ever be, madam."

Then, just as he stepped towards the portal, there came the sound of galloping hoofs behind them. They rang sharply on the rock of the cavern. They echoed through the gloomy roof, through a thousand chambers, and Elric had no time to turn before something heavy struck his shoulder and he was flung to one side. He had the impression of a deathly white horse, of a rider wearing armour of ivory, mother-of-pearl and pale tortoiseshell, and then it was gone through the gate of molten gold and disappearing into the shadows beyond. But there was no doubt in Elric's mind that he had encountered one of the warriors who had already attacked him on the bridge. He had the impression of the same mocking chuckle as the hoofs faded and the sound was absorbed by whatever lay beyond the gate.

"We have an enemy," said Oone. Her face was grim and she clenched her hands to her sides, clearly taking a grip on herself. "We have been identified already. The Fortress of the Pearl does not merely defend. She attacks."

"You know those riders? You have seen them before?"

She shook her head. "I know their kind, that's all."

"And we've no means of avoiding them?"

"Very few." She was frowning to herself again, considering some problem she was not prepared to discuss. Then she seemed to dismiss it and taking his arm led him under the twin cascades of cool gold into a further cavern which this time suddenly filled with a gentle green glow, as if they walked beneath a canopy of leaves in autumn sunlight. And Elric was reminded of Old Melniboné, at the height of her power, when his people were proud enough to take the whole world for granted. When entire nations had been remoulded for their passing pleasure. As they emerged into a further cavern, so vast he did not at first realize they were still underground, he saw the spires and minarets of a city, glowing with the same warm green, which was as beautiful as his own beloved Imrryr, the Dreaming City, which he had explored throughout his boyhood.

"It is like Imrryr and yet it is not like Imrryr at all," he said in surprise.

"No," she said, "it is like London. It is like Tanelorn. It is like Ras-Paloom-Atai." And she did not speak sarcastically. She spoke as if she really did believe the city resembled those other cities, only one of which Elric recognized.

"But you have seen it before. What is it called?"

"It has no name," she said. "It has all names. It is called whatever you desire to call it." And she turned away, as if resting herself, before she led him onwards down the road past the city.

"Should we not visit it? There may be people there who can help us find our way."

Oone gestured. "And there may be those who would hamper us. It is now clear, Prince Elric, that our mission is suspected and that certain forces could well have the intention of stopping us at any cost."

"You think the Sorcerer Adventurers have followed us?"

"Or preceded us. Leaving at least something of themselves here." She was peering cautiously towards the city.

"It seems such a peaceful place," said Elric. The more he looked at the city the more he was impressed by the architecture, all of the same greenish stone but varying from yellow to blue. There were vast buttresses and curving bridges between one tower and another; there were spires as delicate as cobwebs yet so tall they almost disappeared into the roofs of the cavern. It seemed to reflect some part of him which he could not at once recall. He longed to go there. He grew resentful of

Oone's guidance, though he had sworn to follow it, and began to believe that she herself was lost, that she was not better suited to discover their goal than was he.

"We must continue," she said. She was speaking more urgently now.

"I know I would find something within that city which would make Imrryr great again. And in her greatness I could lead her to dominate the world. But this time, instead of bringing cruelty and terror, we could bring beauty and good will."

"You are more prone to illusion than I thought, Prince Elric," said Oone.

He turned on her angrily. "What's wrong with such ambitions?"

"They are unrealistic. As unreal as that city."

"The city looks solid enough to me."

"Solid? Aye, in its way. Once you enter its gate it will embrace you as thoroughly as any long-lost lover! Come then, sir. Come!" She seemed seized by an equally poor temper and strode on up an obsidian road which twisted along the hill towards the city.

Startled by her sudden change, Elric followed. But now his own anger was dissipating. "I'll abide, madam, by your judgment. I am sorry . . ."

She was not listening to him. Moment by moment the city came closer until soon they were overshadowed by it, looking up at walls and domes and towers whose size was so tremendous it was almost impossible to guess at their true extent.

"There's a gate," she said. "There! Go through and I'll say farewell. I'll try to save the child myself and you can give yourself up to lost beliefs and so lose the beliefs you currently hold!"

And now Elric looked closer at the walls, which were like jade, and he saw dark shapes within the walls and he saw that the dark shapes were the figures of men, women and children. He gasped as he stepped forward to peer at them, observing living faces, eyes which were undying, lips frozen in expressions of terror, of anguish, of misery. They were like so many flies in amber.

"That's the unchanging past, Prince Elric," said Oone. "That's the fate of those who seek to reclaim their lost beliefs without first experiencing the search for new ones. This city has another name. Dreamthieves call it the City of Inventive Cowardice. You would not understand the twists of logic which brought so many to this pass! Which made them force those they loved to share their fate. Would you stay with them, Prince Elric, and nurse your lost beliefs?"

The albino turned away with a shudder. "But if they could see what had happened to earlier travelers, why did they continue into the city?"

"They blinded themselves to the obvious. That is the great triumph of mindless need over intelligence and the human spirit."

Together the two returned to the path below the city and Elric was relieved when the beautiful towers were far behind and they had passed through several more great caverns, each with its own city, though none as magnificent as the first. These he had felt no desire to visit, though he had detected movement in some and Oone had said she suspected not all were as dangerous as the City of Inventive Cowardice.

"You called this world the Dream Realm," he said, "and indeed it's well-named, madam, for it seems to contain a catalogue of dreams, and not a few nightmares. It's almost as if the place was born of a poet's brain, so strange are some of the sights."

"I told you," she said, speaking more warmly now that he had acknowledged the danger, "much of what you witness here is the semiformed stuff of realities other worlds, such as yours and mine, are yet to witness. To what extent they will come to exist elsewhere I do not know. These places have been fashioned over centuries by a succession of dreamthieves, imposing form on what is otherwise formless."

Elric was now beginning to understand better what he had been told by Oone. "Rather than making a map of what exists, you impose your own map upon it!"

"To a degree. We do not invent. We merely describe in a particular way. By that means we can make pathways through each of the myriad Dream Realms for, in this alone, the realms comply one with the other."

"In reality there could be a thousand different lands in each realm?"

"If you would see it so. Or an infinity of lands. Or one with an infinity of aspects. Roads are made so that the traveler without a compass may not wander too far from their destination." She laughed almost gaily. "The fanciful names we give these places are not from any poetical impulse, nor from whim, but from a certain necessity. Our survival depends on accurate descriptions!"

"Your words have a profundity to them, madam. Though my survival has also tended to depend on a good, sharp blade!"

"While you depend upon your blade, Prince Elric, you condemn yourself to a singular fate."

"You predict my death, eh, madam?"

Oone shook her head, her beautiful lips forming an expression of utmost sympathy and tenderness. "Death is inevitable to almost all of us, in some shape or another. And I'll admit, if Chaos ever conquered Chaos, then you would be the instrument of that remarkable conquest. It would be sad indeed, Prince Elric, if in taming Chaos you destroyed yourself and all you loved into the bargain!"

"I promise you, Lady Oone, to do my best to avoid such a fate." And Elric wondered at the look in the dreamthief's eyes and then chose not to speculate further.

They walked through a forest of stalagmites and stalactites now, all of the same glowing colours, dark greens and dark blues and rich reds, and there was a musical sound as water splashed from roof to floor. Every so often a huge drop would fall on one or the other of them but such was the nature of the caverns that they were soon dry again. They had begun to relax and walked arm in arm, almost merry, and it was only then that they saw the figures flitting between the upward-thrusting fangs of rock.

"Swordsmen," murmured Elric. He added ironically, "This is when a weapon would be useful . . ." His mind was half with the situation, half feeling its way out through the worlds of the elementals, seeking some kind of spell, some supernatural aid, but he was baffled. It seemed that the mental paths he was used to following were blocked to him.

The warriors were veiled. They were dressed in heavy flowing

cloaks and their heads were protected by helms of metal and leather. Elric had the impression of cold, hard eyes with tattooed lids and knew at once that these were members of the Sorcerer Assassin Guild from Quarzhasaat, left behind when their fellows had retreated from the Dream Realms. Doubtless they were trapped here. It was clear, however, that they did not intend to parley with Elric and Oone, but were closing in, following a familiar pattern of attack.

Elric was struck by a strangeness about these men. They lacked a certain fluidity of movement and, the closer they came, the more he realized that it was almost possible to see past their eyes and into the hollows of their skulls. These were not ordinary mortals. He had seen men like them in Imrryr once, when he had gone with his father on one of those rare times when Sadric chose to take him upon some local expedition, out to an old arena whose high walls imprisoned certain Melnibonéans who had lost their souls in pursuit of sorcerous knowledge, but whose bodies still lived. They, too, had seemed to be possessed of a cold, raging hatred against any not like themselves.

Oone cried out and moved rapidly, dropping to one knee as a sword struck at her, then clattered against one of the great pointed pillars. So close together were the stalagmites that it was difficult for the swordsmen to swing or to stab and for a while both the albino and the dreamthief ducked and dodged the blades until one cut Elric's arm and he saw, almost in surprise, that the man had drawn blood.

The Prince of Melniboné knew that it was just a matter of time before they were both killed and, as he fell back against one of the great rocky teeth, he felt the stalagmite move behind him. Some trick of the cavern had weakened the rock and it was loose. He flung all of his weight forward against it. It began to topple. Quickly he got his body in front of it, supporting the thing on his shoulder, then, with all his energy he ran with the great rocky spear at his nearest assailant.

The point of the rock drove full into the veiled man's chest. The Sorcerer Assassin uttered a bleak, agonized shout, and strange, unnatural blood began to well up around the stone, gushing down and soaking into the warrior's bones, almost reabsorbed by him. Elric sprang forward and dragged the sabre and the poignard from his hands even as another of the attackers came upon him from the rear. All his battle cunning and his war skills returned to Elric. Long before he had come by Stormbringer he had learned the arts of the sword and the dagger, of the bow and the lance, and now he had no need of an enchanted blade to make short work of the second Sorcerer Assassin, then a third. Shouting to Oone to help herself to weapons, he darted from rock to rock, taking one of the warriors at a time. They moved sluggishly, uncertainly now, yet none ran from him.

Soon Oone had joined him, showing that she was as accomplished a fighter as he. He admired the delicacy of her technique, the sureness of her hands as she parried and thrust, striking with the utmost efficiency and piling up her corpses with all the economy of a cat in a nest of rats.

Elric took time to grin over his shoulder. "For one who so recently extolled the virtues of words over the sword, you show yourself well-accomplished with a blade, madam!"

"It is often as well to have the experience of both before one makes the choice," she said. She despatched another of their assailants. "And there are times, Prince Elric, I'll admit, when a decent piece of steel has a certain advantage over a neatly turned phrase!"

They fought together like two old friends. Their techniques were complementary but not dissimilar. Both fought as the best soldiers fight, with neither cruelty nor pleasure in the killing, but with the intention of winning as quickly as possible, while causing as little pain to their opponents.

These opponents appeared to suffer no pain, as such, but every time one died he offered up the same disturbing wail of anguish and the blood which poured from the wounds was strange stuff indeed.

At last the man and the woman were done and stood leaning on their borrowed blades panting and seeking to control that nausea which so often follows a battle.

Then, as Elric watched, the corpses around them swiftly faded, leaving only a few swords behind. The blood too disappeared. There was virtually nothing to say that a fight had taken place in that great cavern.

"Where have they gone?"

Oone picked up a sheath and fitted her new sabre into it. For all her words, she clearly had no intention of proceeding any further without arms. She placed two daggers in her belt. "Gone? Ah." She hesitated. "To whatever pool of half-living ectoplasm they came from." She shook her head. "They were almost phantasms, Prince Elric, but not quite. They were, as I told you, what the Sorcerer Adventurers left behind."

"You mean part of them returned to our own world, as part of Alnac returned?"

"Exactly." She drew a breath and made as if to continue.

"Then why shall we not find Alnac here? Still alive?"

"Because we do not seek him," she said. And she spoke with all her old firmness, enough to make Elric proceed only a degree further with the subject.

"And perhaps anyway we would not find him here, as we found the Sorcerer Adventurers, in the Land of Lost Beliefs," said the albino quietly.

"True," she said.

Then Elric took her in his arms for a moment and they remained, embracing, for a few seconds, until they were ready to continue forward, seeking the Celador Gate.

Later, as Elric helped his ally across another natural bridge, below which flowed a river of dull brown stuff, Oone said to him, "This is no ordinary adventure for me, Prince Elric. That is why I needed you to come with me."

A little puzzled as to why she should, after all, say something which they had both taken for granted, Elric did not reply.

When the snout-faced women attacked them, with nets and spikes, it did not take them long to cut their way free and drive the cowardly creatures off, and neither were they greatly inconvenienced by the vulpine things which loped on their hind-legs and had claws like birds. They even joked together as they despatched packs of snapping beasts which resembled nothing so much as horses the size of dogs and spoke a few words of a human tongue, though without any sense of the meaning.

Now at last they were reaching the borders of Paranor and saw looming ahead of them two enormous towers of carved rock, with little balconies and windows and terraces and crenelations, all covered in old ivy and climbing brambles bearing light yellow fruit.

"It is the Celador Gate," said Oone. She seemed reluctant to approach it. Her hand on the hilt of her sword, her other arm linked with Elric's, she stopped and drew a deep, slow breath. "It is the land of forests."

"You called it the Land of Forgotten Love," said Elric.

"Aye. That's the dreamthieves' name." She laughed a little sardonically.

Elric, uncertain of her mood and not wishing to intrude upon her, held back also, looking from her to the gate and back again.

She reached a hand to his bone-white features. Her own skin was golden, still full of enormous vitality. She stared into his face. Then, with a sigh, she turned away and stepped towards the gate, taking his hand and pulling him after her.

They passed between the towers and here Elric's nostrils immediately were filled with the rich smells of leaf and turf. All around them were massive oak-trees and elms and birches and every other kind of tree, yet all of them, though they formed a canopy, grew not beneath the light of the open sky but were nurtured by the oddly glowing rocks in the cavern ceilings. Elric had thought it impossible for trees to grow underground and he marveled at the health, the very ordinariness, of everything.

It was therefore with some astonishment that he observed a creature emerge from the wood and plant itself firmly on the path along which they must move.

"Halt! I must know your business!" His face was covered in brown fur and his teeth were so prominent, his ears so large, his eyes so large and doelike, he resembled nothing so much as an overgrown rabbit, though he was armoured solidly in battered brass, with a brass cap upon his head and his weapons, a sword and spear of workmanlike steel, were also bound in brass.

"We seek merely to pass through this land without doing harm or being harmed," said Oone.

The rabbit-warrior shook his head. "Too vague," he said, and suddenly he hefted his spear and plunged the point deep into the bole of an oak. The oak tree screamed. "That's what he told me. And many more of these."

"The trees were travelers?" said Elric.

"Your name, sir?"

"I am Elric of Melniboné and, like my lady Oone here, I mean you no disturbance. We travel on to Imador."

"I know no 'Elric' or 'Oone.' I am the Count of Magnes Doar and I hold this land as my own. By my conquest. By my ancient right. You must go back through the gate."

"We cannot," said Oone. "To retreat would mean our destruction."

"To proceed, madam, would mean the same thing. What? Shall you camp at the gates for ever?"

"No, sir," she said. She put her hand to the hilt of her sword. "We will hack our way through your forest if need be. We are on urgent business and will accept no halt."

The rabbit-warrior pulled the spear from the oak, which ceased to scream, and flung it into another tree. This, in turn, set up a swirling and a moaning until even the Count of Magnes Doar shook his head in irritation and drew his weapon out of the trunk. "You must fight me, I think," he said.

It was then that they heard a yell from the other side of the right pillar and something white and rearing appeared there. It was another of the pale riders in armour of bone, tortoiseshell and mother-of-pearl, his horrible eyes slitted with hatred, his horse's hoofs beating at a barrier which had not been there when Oone and Elric passed through.

Then it was down and the warrior was charging.

The albino and the dreamthief made to defend themselves, but it was the Count of Magnes Doar who moved ahead of them and jabbed his spear up at the warrior's body. Steel was deflected by an armour stronger than it looked and the sword rose and fell, almost contemptuously, slicing down through the brass helm into the brain of the rabbit-warrior. He staggered backwards, his hands clutching at his head, his sword and spear abandoned. His round brown eyes seemed to grow still wider and he began to squeal. He turned slowly, round and round, then fell to his knees.

Elric and Oone had positioned themselves behind the bole of one of the oaks, ready to defend themselves when the rider attacked.

The horse reared again, snorting with the same mindless fury as its master, and Elric darted from his cover, seized the dropped spear and stabbed up to where the breastplate and gorget joined, sliding the spearhead expertly into the warrior's throat.

There came a choking sound which in turn grew to a familiar chuckling and the rider had turned his horse and was riding ahead of them again, along the path through the forest, his body swaying and jerking as if in its death agonies, yet still borne on by the horse.

They watched it disappear.

Elric was trembling. "If I had not already seen him die on the bridge from Sadanor I would swear that was the same man who attacked me there. He has a puzzling familiarity."

"You did not see him die," said Oone. "You saw him plunge into the river."

"Well, I think he is dead now, after that stroke. I almost severed his head."

"I doubt if he is," she said. "It's my belief he is our most powerful enemy and we shall not have to deal with him in any serious way until we near the Fortress of the Pearl itself."

"He protects the Fortress?"

"Many do." She embraced him again, swiftly, then sank to one knee to inspect the dead Count of Magnes Doar. In death he more resembled a man, for already the hair on his face and hands was fading to grey and even his flesh seemed on the point of disappearance. The brass helm, too, had turned an ugly shade of silver. Elric was reminded of Alnac's dying. He averted his eyes.

Oone, too, stood up quickly and there were tears in her eyes. The tears were not for the Count of Magnes Doar. Elric took her in his arms. He was suddenly full of longing for someone he barely remembered from old dreams, the dreams of his youth, someone who, perhaps, had never existed.

He thought he felt a slight shudder run through Oone as he embraced her. He reached out for a memory of a little boat, of a fair-haired girl sleeping at the bottom of the vessel as it drifted out to open sea, of himself sailing a skiff towards her, full of pride that he might be her rescuer. Yet he had never known such a girl, he was sure, though Oone reminded him of that girl grown up.

With a gasp Oone moved away from him. "I thought you were . . . It's as if I'd always known you . . ." She put her hands to her face. "Oh, this damned land is well-called, Elric!"

"Yet what danger is there to us?" he asked.

She shook her head. "Who knows? Much or little. None? The dreamthieves say that it is in the Land of Forgotten Love that the most important decisions are made. Decisions which can have the most monumental consequences."

"So one should do nothing here? Make no decisions?"

She passed her fingers through her hair. "At least we should be aware that the consequences might not manifest themselves for a long while yet."

Together they left the dead rabbit-warrior behind them and continued down the tunnel of trees. Now from time to time Elric thought he saw faces peering at him from the green shadows. Once he was sure he saw the figure of his dead father, Sadric, mourning for Elric's mother, the only creature he had ever truly loved. So strong was the image that Elric called out.

"Sadric! Father! Is this your Limbo?"

At this Oone cried urgently. "No! Do not address him. Do not bring him to you. Do not make him real! It is a trap, Elric. Another trap."

"My father?"

"Did you love him?"

"Aye. Though it was an unhappy kind of love."

"Remember that. Do not bring him here. It would be obscene to recall him to this gallery of illusion."

Elric understood her and used all his habits of self-discipline to rid himself of his father's shade. "I tried to tell him, Oone, how much I grieved for him in his loss and his sorrow." He was weeping. His body was shaking with an emotion from which he believed he had long since freed himself. "Ah, Oone. I would have died myself to let him have his wife returned to him. Is there no way . . . ?"

"Such sacrifices are meaningless," she said, gripping him in both her hands and holding him to her. "Especially here. Remember your quest. We have already crossed three of the seven lands which will bring us to the Fortress of the Pearl. We have crossed half this. That means we have already accomplished more than most. Hold on to yourself, Prince of Melniboné. Remember who and what depends upon your success!"

"But if I have the opportunity to make something right that was so wrong . . . ?"

"That is to do with your own feelings, not what is and what can be. Would you invent shadows and make them play out your dreams? Would that bring happiness to your tragic mother and father?"

Elric looked over her shoulder into the forest. There was no sign of his father now. "He seemed so real. Of such solid flesh!"

"You must believe that you and I are the only solid flesh in this entire land. And even we are—" She stopped herself. She reached up to his face and kissed it. "We will rest for a little, if only to restore our psychic strength."

And Oone drew Elric down into the soft leaves at the side of the path. And she kissed him and she moved her lovely hands over his body and slowly she became all that he had lost in his love of women and he knew that he, in turn, became everything she had ever refused to allow herself to desire in a man. And he knew, without guilt or regret, that their love-making had no past and that its only future lay somewhere beyond their own lives, beyond any realm they would ever visit, and that neither would ever witness the consequences.

And in spite of this knowledge they were careless and they were happy and they gave each other the strength they would need if they ever hoped to fulfill their quest and reach the Fortress of the Pearl.

Chapter Four

The Intervention of a Navigator

Surprised by his own lack of confusion, filled with an apparent clarity, Elric stepped, side by side with Oone, through the shimmering silver gateway into Imador, called mysteriously by dreamthieves the Land of New Ambition, and found himself at the top of an heroic flight of steps which curved downward towards a plain which stretched towards an horizon turned a pale, misty blue and which he could almost have mistaken for the sky. For a moment he thought that he and Oone were alone on that vast stairway and then he saw that it was crowded with people. Some were engaged in hectic conversation, some bartering, some embracing, while others were gathered around holy men, speech makers, priestesses, story-tellers, either listening avidly or arguing.

The steps down to the plain were alive with every manner of human intercourse. Elric saw snake-charmers, bear-baiters, jugglers and acrobats. They were dressed in costumes typical of the desert lands—enormous silk pantaloons of green, blue, gold, vermilion and amber—coats of brocade or velvet—turbans, burnouses and caps of the most intricate needlework—and burnished metal and silver, gold, precious jewels of every kind—animals, stalls, baskets overflowing with produce, with fabrics, with goods of leather and copper and brass.

"How handsome they are!" he remarked. It was true that though they were of all shapes and sizes the people had a beauty which was not easily defined. Their skins were all healthy, their eyes bright, their movements dignified and easy. They bore themselves with confidence and good humour and while it was clear they noticed Oone and Elric walking down the steps, they acknowledged them without making any great effort to greet them or ask them their business. Dogs, cats and monkeys ran about in the crowd and children played the cryptic games all children play. The air was warm and balmy and full of scents of fruit, flowers and the other goods being sold. "Would that all worlds were like this," Elric added, smiling at a young woman who offered him embroidered cloth.

Oone bought oranges from a boy who ran up to her. She handed one to Elric. "This is a sweet realm indeed. I had not expected it to be so pleasant." But when she bit into the fruit she spat it into her hand. "It has no taste!"

Elric tried his own orange and he, too, found it a dry, flavourless thing.

The disappointment he felt at this was out of all proportion to the occurrence. He threw the orange from him. It struck a step below and bounced until it was out of sight.

The grey-green plain appeared unpopulated. There was a road sweeping across it, wide and well-paved, but there was not a single traveler visible, in spite of the great crowd. "I wonder why the road is empty," he said to Oone. "Do all these people sleep at nights on these steps? Or do they disappear into another realm when their business here is done?"

"Doubtless that question will be answered for us soon enough, my lord."

She linked her arm in his own. Since their love-making in the wood a sense of considerable comradeship and mutual liking had grown up between them. He knew no guilt; he knew in his heart that he had betrayed no-one and it was clear she was equally untroubled. In some strange way they had restored each other, making their combined energy something more than its sum. This was the kind of friendship he had never really known before and he was grateful for it. He believed that he had learned much from Oone and that the dreamthieves would teach him more that would be valuable to him when he returned to Melniboné to claim his throne back from Yyrkoon.

As they descended the steps it seemed to Elric that the costumes became more and more elaborate, the jewels and headdresses and weapons richer and more exotic, while the stature of the people increased and they grew still more handsome.

From curiosity he stopped to listen to a story-teller who held a crowd entranced, but the man spoke in an unfamiliar language—high and flat—which meant nothing to him. He and Oone paused again, beside a bead-seller, and he asked her politely if those gathered on the steps were all of the same nation.

The woman frowned at him and shook her head, replying in still another language. There seemed few words in it. She repeated much. Only when they were stopped by a sherbet-seller, a young boy, could they ask their question and be understood.

The lad frowned, as if translating their words in his head. "Aye, we are the people of the steps. Each of us has a place here, one below the other."

"You grow richer and more important as you descend, eh?" asked Oone.

He was puzzled by this. "Each of us has a place here," he said again and, as if alarmed by their questions, he ran off up into the dense crowd above. Here, too, there were fewer people and Elric could see that their numbers thinned increasingly as the steps neared the plain. "Is this an illusion?" he murmured at Oone. "It has the air of a dream."

"It is our sense of what should be that intrudes here," she said, "and it colours our perception of the place, I think."

"It is not an illusion?"

"It is not what you would call an illusion." She made an effort to find words but eventually shook her head. "The more it seems an illusion to us, the more it becomes one. Does that make sense?"

"I think so."

At last they were nearing the bottom of the stairway. They were on the last few steps when they looked up to see a horseman riding towards them across the plain, creating a huge pillar of dust as he came.

There was a cry from the people behind them. Elric looked back and saw them all rushing rapidly up the stairs and his impulse was to join them, but Oone stayed him. "Remember we cannot go back," she said. "We must meet this danger as best we can."

Gradually the figure on the horse became distinguishable. It was either the same warrior in the armour of mother-of-pearl, ivory and tortoiseshell, or one who was identical. He bore a white lance tipped with a point of sharpened bone and the thing was aimed directly at Elric's heart.

The albino jumped forward in a manoeuvre designed to confuse his attacker. He was almost under the horse's hoofs when he struck upwards with his swiftly drawn sword and cut at the lance. The force of the blow sent him reeling to one side while Oone, reacting with almost telepathic co-ordination, almost as if they were controlled by a single brain, leapt and thrust beneath the raised left arm, seeking their assailant's heart.

Her thrust was parried by a sudden movement of the rider's gauntleted right hand and he kicked out at her. Now, for the first time, Elric saw his face clearly. It was thin, bloodless, with eyes like the flesh of long-dead fish and a sneering gash of a mouth, opening now in a grimace of contempt. Yet with a shock he saw, too, something of Alnac Kreb! The lance swung to strike Oone's shoulder and send her to the ground.

Elric was up again before the lance could return, his sword slashing at the horse's girth-strap in an old trick learned from the Vilmirian bandits, but he was blocked by an armoured leg and the lance returned to thrust at him while he darted clear, giving Oone her opportunity.

Though Elric and Oone fought as a single entity, their attacker was almost prescient, seeming to guess their every move.

Elric began to believe the rider to be wholly supernatural in origin and even as he feinted again he sent his mind out into the realms of the elementals, seeking any aid which might possibly be available to him. But there was none. It was if every realm were deserted, as if, overnight, the entire world of elementals, demons and spirits had been banished to limbo. Arioch would not aid him. His sorcery was completely useless here.

Oone cried out sharply and Elric saw that she had been flung back against the lowest step. She tried to climb to her feet but something was paralyzed. She could hardly move her limbs.

Again the pale rider chuckled and began to advance for the kill.

Elric roared out his old battle-shout and raced towards their opponent, trying to distract him. The albino was horrified at the possibility of harm coming to the woman for whom he felt both profound love and comradeship and he was willing to die to save her.

"Arioch! Arioch! Blood and souls!"

But he had no runesword to aid him there. Nothing save his own wits and skills.

"Alnac Kreb. Is this what remains of you?"

The rider turned, almost impatiently, and flung the lance at the running man. His answer.

Elric had not anticipated this. He tried to throw his body aside but the haft of the lance struck his shoulder and he fell heavily into the dust, losing his grip on the unfamiliar sabre. He began to scrabble towards it even as he saw the rider draw his own long blade and continue towards the helpless Oone. He raised himself to one knee and threw his poignard with desperate accuracy. The blade went true, between the plates of the rider's back armour, and the lifted sword fell suddenly.

Elric reached his sabre, got to his feet and saw to his horror that the rider was rearing over Oone, the sword again raised, ignoring the wound in his shoulder.

"Alnac?"

Again Elric tried to appeal to whatever part of Alnac Kreb was there, but this time he was completely ignored. That same hideous, inhuman chuckling filled the air; the horse snorted, its hoofs pawing at the woman as she struggled on the step.

Scarcely aware of his own movement, Elric reached the rider and leapt forward, dragging at his back, trying to haul him from the horse. The rider growled and managed to turn. His whistling sword was parried by Elric's and the albino had unseated him. Together the pair fell to the sand, a few inches from where Oone lay. Elric's sword-hand was crushed under his attacker's armoured back, but he managed to tug the poignard free with his left hand and would have struck at those hideous dead eyes had not the man's fingers closed on his wrist.

"You'll kill me before you harm her!" Elric's normally melodic voice was a snarl of hatred. But the warrior merely laughed again, the ghost of Alnac fading from his eyes.

They fought thus for several moments, neither gaining any true advantage. Elric could hear his own breathing, the grunting of the armoured man, the whinnying of the horse and Oone's gasp as she tried to get to her feet.

"Pearl Warrior!"

It was another voice. Not Oone's, but a woman's; and it carried considerable authority.

"Pearl Warrior! You must do no further violence to these travelers!"

The warrior grunted but ignored the woman. His teeth snapped at Elric's throat. He tried to turn the poignard towards the albino's heart. There were drops of foaming saliva on his lips now—beads of white rimming his mouth.

"Pearl Warrior!"

Suddenly the warrior began to speak, whispering to Elric as if to a fellow conspirator. "Don't listen to her. I can aid thee. Why do you not come with us and learn to explore the Great Steppe, where all the hunting is rich? And there are melons, tasting like the most delicate cherries. I can give thee such wonderful clothing. Do not listen. Do not listen. Yes I am Alnac, thy friend. Yes!"

Elric was repelled by the insane babble, more than he had been by the creature's horrible appearance and his violence.

"Think of all the power there is. They fear thee. They fear me. Elric. I know thee. Let us not be rivals. Together we can succeed. I am not free, but thou couldst journey for us both. I am not free, but thou wouldst never bear responsibilities. I am not free, but, Elric, I have many slaves at my disposal. They are thine. I offer thee new wealth and new philosophies, new ways of fulfilling every desire. I fear thee and thou fearest me. So we will bind us together, one to the other. It is the only tie that ever means anything. They dream of thee, all of them. Even I, who do not dream. Thou art the only enemy . . ."

"Pearl Warrior!"

With a rattle of bone and ivory, of tortoiseshell and mother-of-pearl, the leprous-skinned warrior disentangled himself from Elric.

"Together we can defeat her," he mumbled urgently. "There would be no force to resist us. I will give thee my ferocity!"

Nauseated by all this, Elric climbed slowly to his feet, turning to stare in the same direction as Oone, who now sat on the step, nursing limbs to which life seemed to be restored.

A woman, taller either than Elric or Oone, stood there. She was veiled and hooded. Her eyes moved steadily from them to the one she called Pearl Warrior and then she raised the great staff she held in her right hand and struck at the ground with it.

"Pearl Warrior! You must obey me!"

The Pearl Warrior was furious. "I do not wish this!" he snarled and, clattering, brushed at his breastplate. "You anger me, Lady Sough."

"These are my charges and under my protection. Go, Pearl Warrior. Kill elsewhere. Kill the true enemies of the Pearl."

"I do not want you to order me!" He was surly, sulking like a child. "All are enemies of the Pearl. You, too, Lady Sough."

"You are a silly creature! Begone!" And she lifted the staff to point beyond the stairway, where hazy rock could be seen, rising up for ever.

He said again, warningly, "You make me angry, Lady Sough. I am the Pearl Warrior. I have the strength from the Fortress." He turned to Elric as if to a comrade. "Ally yourself with me and we'll kill her now. Then we shall rule—thou in thy freedom, me in my slavery. All of this and many other realms beside, unknown to dreamthieves. Safety is there for ever. Be mine. We shall be married. Yes, yes, yes . . ."

Elric shuddered and turned his back on the Pearl Warrior. He went to help Oone to her feet.

Oone was able to move all her limbs but she was still dazed. She looked back at the steps which disappeared above them. Not a single one of the people who had occupied that vast staircase was visible.

Troubled, Elric glanced at the newcomer. Her robes were of different shades of blue, with silver threads running through them, hemmed with gold and dark green. She carried herself with extraordinary grace and dignity and stared back at Oone and Elric with an air of amusement. Meanwhile the Pearl Warrior climbed to his feet and stood defiantly to one side, alternately glaring at Lady Sough and offering Elric a hideous conspiratorial smile.

"Where are all the folk of the steps gone?" Elric asked her.

"They have merely returned to their home, my lord," said Lady Sough. Her voice, when she addressed him, was warm and full, yet retained all the authority with which she had ordered the Pearl Warrior to stop his attack. "I am Lady Sough and I bid you welcome to this land."

"We are grateful for your intervention, my lady." Oone spoke for the first time, though with a degree of suspicion. "Are you the ruler here?"

"I am merely a guide and a navigator."

"That mad thing there accepts your command." Oone rose, rubbing at her arms and legs, glaring at the Pearl Warrior who sneered, becoming shifty as Lady Sough gave him her attention.

"He is incomplete." Lady Sough was dismissive. "He guards the Pearl. But he has such an insubstantial intelligence, he cannot understand the nature of his task, nor who is friend or who foe. He can make only the most limited choices, poor corrupt thing. The ones who put him to this work had, themselves, only the faintest understanding of what was required in such a warrior."

"Bad! I will not!" The Pearl Warrior began to utter his chuckle again. "Never! It is why! *It is why!*"

"Go!" cried Lady Sough, gesturing once more with her staff, her eyes glaring above her veil. "You have no business with these."

"Dying is unwise, madam," said the Pearl Warrior, lifting his shoulder in a gesture of defiant arrogance. "Beware thine own corruption. We may all dissolve if this achieves that resolution."

"Go, stupid brute!" She pointed at his horse. "And leave that spear behind you. Destructive, insensate grotesque that you are."

"Am I mistaken," said Elric, "or does he speak gibberish?"

"Possibly," murmured Oone. "But it could be he speaks more of the truth than those who would protect us."

"Anything will come and anything will have to be resisted!" said the Pearl Warrior darkly as he mounted. He began to ride to where his lance had fallen after he had thrown it at Elric. "This is why we are to be!"

"Begone! Begone!"

He leaned from his saddle, reaching towards the lance.

"No," she said firmly, as if to a silly child. "I told you that you should not have it. Look what you have done, Pearl Warrior! You are forbidden to attack these people again."

"No alliance, then. Not now! But soon this freedom will be exchanged and all shall come together!" Another appalling chuckle from the half-crazed rider and he was digging his spurs into his horse's flanks, going at a gallop in the direction he had come. "There shall be bonds! Oh, yes!"

"Do his words make sense to you, Lady Sough?" Elric asked politely, when the warrior had disappeared.

"Some of them," she said. It seemed that she was smiling behind her veil. "It is not his fault that his brain is malformed. There are few warriors in this world, you know. He is perhaps the best."

"Best?"

Oone's sardonic question went unanswered. Lady Sough reached out a hand on which delicately coloured jewels glowed and she beckoned to them. "I am a navigator here. I can bear you to sweet islands where two lovers could be happy for ever. I have a place that is hidden and safe. Can I take you there?"

Elric glanced at Oone, wondering if perhaps she was attracted by Lady Sough's invitation. For a second he forgot their purpose here. It would be wonderful to spend a short idyll in Oone's company.

"This is Imador, is it not, Lady Sough?"

"It is the place the dreamthieves call Imador, aye. We do not call it by that name." She seemed disapproving.

"We are grateful for your help in this matter, my lady," said Elric, thinking Oone a little brusque and seeking to apologize for his friend's manner. "I am Elric of Melniboné and this is Lady Oone of the Dreamthieves' Guild. Do you know that we seek the Fortress of the Pearl?"

"Aye. And this road is a straight one for you. It can lead you forward to the Fortress. But it might not lead you by the best route. I will guide you by whatever route you wish." She sounded a little distant, almost as if she were half-asleep herself. Her tone had become dreamy and Elric guessed she was offended.

"We owe you much, Lady Sough, and your advice is of value to us. What would you suggest?"

"That you raise an army first, I think. For your own safety. There are such terrible defenses at the Fortress of the Pearl. Why, and before that, too. You are brave, the both of you. There are several roads to success. Death lies at the end of many other paths. Of this, you are I am sure aware . . ."

"Where could we recruit such an army?" Elric ignored Oone's warning look. He felt that she was being obstinate, overly suspicious of this dignified woman.

"There is an ocean not far from here. There is an island in it. The people of that island long to fight. They will follow anyone who promises them danger. Will you come there? It is very good. There is warmth and secure walls. Gardens and much to eat."

"Your words have a strong degree of common sense," said Elric. "It would be worth, perhaps, pausing in our quest to recruit those soldiers. And I was offered alliance by the Pearl Warrior. Will he help us? Can he be trusted?"

"For what you wish to do? Yes, I think." Her forehead furrowed. "Yes, I think."

"No, Lady Sough." Oone spoke suddenly and with considerable force. "We are grateful for your guidance. Will you take us to the Falador Gate? Do you know it?"

"I know what you call the Falador Gate, young woman. And whatever your questions or your desires, they are mine to answer and fulfill."

"What is your own name for this land?"

"None." She seemed confused by Oone's question. "There is not one. It is this place. It is here. But I can guide you through it."

"I believe you, my lady." Oone's voice softened. She took Elric by the arm. "Our other name for this land is the Land of New Ambition.

But new ambitions can mislead. We invent them when the old ambition seems too hard to achieve, eh?"

Elric understood her. He felt foolish. "You offer a diversion, Lady Sough?"

"Not so." The veiled woman shook her head. The movement had all her gracefulness in it and she seemed a little wounded by the directness of his question. "A fresh goal is sometimes preferable when the road becomes impassable."

"But the road is not impassable, Lady Sough," said Oone. "Not yet."

"That is true." Lady Sough bowed her head a fraction. "I offer you all truth in this matter. Every aspect of it."

"We shall retain the aspect of which we are most sure," Oone continued softly, "and thank you greatly for your help."

"It is yours to take, Lady Oone. Come." The woman whirled, her draperies lifting like clouds in a gale, and led them away from the steps to a place where the ground dipped and revealed, when they were closer, a shallow river. There a boat was moored. The boat had a curling prow of gilded wood, not unlike the crook of Oone's dreamwand, and its sides were covered with a thin layer of beaten gold, and bronze, and silver. Brass gleamed on rails, on the single mast, and a sail, blue with threads of silver, like Lady Sough's robes, was furled upon the yardarm. There was no visible crew. Lady Sough pointed with her staff. "Here is the boat with which we shall find the gate you seek. I have a vocation, Lady Oone, Prince Elric, to protect you. Do not fear me."

"My lady, we do not," said Oone with great sincerity. Still, her voice was gentle. Elric was mystified by her manner but accepted that she had a clear notion of their situation.

"What does this mean?" Elric murmured as Lady Sough descended towards the boat.

"I think it means we are close to the Fortress of the Pearl," said Oone. "She tried to help us but is not altogether sure how best to do it."

"You trust her?"

"If we trust ourselves, we can trust her I think. We must know what are the right questions to ask her."

"I'll trust you, Oone, to trust her." Elric smiled.

At Lady Sough's insistent beckoning they clambered into the beautiful boat which rocked only slightly on the dark waters of what seemed to Elric an entirely artificial canal, straight and deep, moving in a sweeping curve until it disappeared from sight a mile or two from them. He peered upwards, still not sure if he looked upon a strange sky or the roof of the largest cavern of all. He could just see the stairs stretching away in the distance and wondered again what had happened to the inhabitants when they had fled at the Pearl Warrior's attack.

Lady Sough took the great tiller of the boat. With a single movement she guided the craft into the centre of the waterway. Almost at once the ground leveled out so that it was possible to see the grey desert on all sides, while ahead was foliage, greenery, the suggestion of hills. There was a quality about the light which reminded Elric of a September evening. He could almost smell the early autumn roses, the turning trees, the orchards of Imrryr. Seated near the front of the boat with Oone beside him, leaning on his shoulder, he sighed with pleasure, enjoying the moment. "If the rest of our quest is to be conducted in such a way, I shall be glad to accompany you on many such adventures, Lady Oone."

She, too, was in good humour. "Aye. Then all the world would desire to be dreamthieves."

The boat rounded a bend of the canal and they were alerted by figures standing on both banks. These sad, silent people, dressed in white and yellow, regarded the sailing barge with tear-filled eyes, as if they witnessed a funeral. Elric was sure they did not weep for himself or Oone. He called out to them, but they did not seem to hear him. They were gone almost at once and they passed by gently rising terraces, cultivated for vines and figs and almonds. The air was sweet with ripening harvests and once a small, foxlike creature ran along beside them for a while before veering off into a clump of shrubs. A little later naked, brown-skinned men prowled on all fours until they, too, grew bored and disappeared into the undergrowth. The canal began to twist more and more and Lady Sough was forced to throw all her weight upon the tiller to keep the boat on course.

"Why should a canal be built so?" Elric asked her when they were once more upon a straight stretch of water.

"What was above us is now ahead and what was below is now behind," she replied. "That is the nature of this. I am the navigator and I know. But ahead, where it grows darker, the river is unbending. This is made to help understanding, I think."

Her words were almost as confusing as the Pearl Warrior's and Elric tried to make sense by asking her further questions. "The river helps us understand what, Lady Sough?"

"Their nature—her nature—what you must encounter—ah, look!"

The river was widening rapidly into a lake. There were reeds growing on the banks now, silver herons flying against the soft sky.

"It is no great distance to the island I spoke of," said Lady Sough. "I fear for you."

"No," said Oone with determined kindness. "Take the boat across the lake towards the Falador Gate. I thank you."

"This thanks is . . ." Lady Sough shook her head. "I would not have you die."

"We shall not. We are here to save her."

"She is afraid."

"We know."

"Those others said they would save her. But they made her—they made it dark and she was trapped . . ."

"We know," said Oone, and laid a comforting hand on Lady Sough's arm as the veiled woman guided the boat out on to the open lake.

Elric said: "Do you speak of the Holy Girl and the Sorcerer Adventurers? What imprisons her, Lady Sough? How can we release her? Bring her back to her father and her people?"

"Oh, it is a lie!" Lady Sough almost shouted, pointing to where, swimming directly towards them, came a child. But the boy's skin was metallic, of glaring silver, and his silver eyes were begging them for help. Then the child grinned, reached to pull off its own head, and submerged.

"We near the Falador Gate," said Oone grimly.

"Those who would possess her also guard her," said Lady Sough suddenly. "But she is not theirs."

"I know," said Oone. Her gaze was fixed on what lay ahead of them. There was a mist on the lake. It was like the finest haze which forms on water in an autumn morning. There was an air of tranquility which clearly she mistrusted. Elric looked back at Lady Sough but the navigator's eyes were expressionless, offering no clue to what dangers they might soon be facing.

The boat turned a little and there was land just visible through the mist. Elric saw tall trees rising above a tumble of rocks. There were white pillars of limestone, shimmering faintly in that lovely light. He saw hummocks of grass and below them little coves. He wondered if Lady Sough had, after all, brought them to the island she had mentioned and was about to question her when he saw what appeared to be a massive door of carved stone and intricate mosaic bearing an air of considerable age.

"The Falador Gate," said Lady Sough, not without a hint of trepidation.

Then the gate had opened and a horrible wind rushed out of it, tearing at their hair and clothing, clawing at their skins, shrieking and wailing in their ears. The boat rocked and Elric feared it must capsize. He ran to the stern to help Lady Sough with the tiller. Her veil had been ripped from her face. She was not a young woman, but she bore an astonishing resemblance to the little girl they had left in the Bronze Tent, the Holy Child of the Bauradim. And Elric, taking the tiller while Lady Sough replaced her veil, remembered that no mention had ever been made of Varadia's mother.

Oone was lowering the sail. The wind's initial strength had died and it was possible to tack gradually towards the dark, strangely-smelling entrance which had been revealed as the mosaic door had blown down.

Three horses appeared there. Hoofs flailed at the air. Tails lashed. Then they were galloping across the water in the direction of the boat. Then they had passed it and vanished into the mist. Not one of the beasts had possessed a head.

Now Elric knew terror. But it was a familiar terror and within seconds he had regained control of himself. He knew that, whatever its name, he was about to enter a land where Chaos ruled.

It was only as the boat sailed under the carved rocks and into the grotto beyond that he recalled he had none of his familiar spells and enchantments; not one of his allies, nor his patron Duke of Hell, were available to him here. He had only experience and courage and his ordinary sensibilities. And at that moment he doubted if they were enough.

Chapter Five

The Sadness of a Queen Who Cannot Rule

The mighty barrier of obsidian rock suddenly started to flow. A mass of glassy green flooded down into the water which hissed and began to stink and mountains of steam rose ahead of them. As the steam gradually dissipated another river was revealed. This one, flowing through the narrow walls of a deep canyon, appeared of natural origin and Elric, his mind now keyed to interpretation, wondered if it were not the same river they had crossed earlier, when he had fought the Pearl Warrior on the bridge.

Then the barge, which had seemed so sturdy, appeared all at once fragile as the waters tossed it, roaring steadily downwards until Elric thought they must eventually reach the very core of the world.

Standing with Lady Sough in the prow of the boat, Oone and Elric helped her use the tiller to hold a course that was almost steady. And then, ahead, the river ended without warning and they had tipped over a waterfall and before they knew it were landing heavily in calmer water, the barge bobbing like a scrap of bread on a pond and overhead they could see a diseased sky like pewter in which dark, leathery things flew and communicated with desolate cries above palms whose leaves resembled nothing so much as viridian skins stretched out to await a sun which never rose. There was a rich, rotten smell about the place and the constant splashing and distant roaring of the water filled a silence broken only by the flying creatures above the rocks and the foliage which surrounded them.

It was warm, yet Elric shivered. Oone drew up the collar of her doublet and even Lady Sough gathered her robes more tightly about herself.

"Are you familiar with this land, Lady Oone?" Elric asked. "You have visited this realm before, I know, but you seem as surprised as I."

"There are always new aspects. It is in the nature of the realm. Perhaps Lady Sough can tell us more." And Oone turned courteously to their navigator.

Lady Sough had secured her veils more firmly. She seemed unhappy that Elric had seen her face. "I am the queen of this land," she said, exhibiting no pride or any other emotion.

"Then you have minions who can assist us?"

"It was a queen for me, so that I had no power over it, only the land's protection. This is the place you call Falador."

"And is it mad?"

"It has many defenses."

"They keep out what might also wish to leave," said Oone, almost to herself. "Are you afraid of those who protect Falador, Lady Sough?"

"I am Queen Sough now." A drawing up of the graceful body, but whether in parody or in earnest Elric could not tell. "I am protected. You are not. Even I am not able to guard you here."

The barge continued to float slowly along the water-course. The slime of the rocks appeared to shift and move as if alive and there were shapes in the water which disturbed Elric. He would have drawn his sword if it had not seemed ill-mannered.

"What must we fear here?" he asked the queen.

Now they floated below a great spur of rock on which a horseman had positioned himself. It was the Pearl Warrior, glaring down with the same mixture of mockery and mindlessness. He lifted a long stick to which he had tied some animal's sharp, twisted horn.

Queen Sough shook her hand at him. "Pearl Warrior shall not do this! Pearl Warrior cannot defy, even here!"

The warrior let out his hideous chuckle and turned his horse back from the rock. Then he was gone.

"Will he attack us?" Oone asked the queen.

Queen Sough was concentrating on her tiller, steering the boat subtly along a smaller water-course, away from the main river. Perhaps she already aimed to avoid any conflict. "He is unpermitted," she said. "Ah!"

The water had turned a ruby-red and there were now banks of glistening brown moss, gently rising towards the walls of rock. Elric was convinced he saw ancient faces staring at him both from the banks and from the cliffs, but he did not feel threatened. The red liquid looked like wine and there was a heady sweetness here. Did Queen Sough know all the secret, tranquil places of this world and was she guiding them through so as to avoid its dangers?

"Here my friend Edif has influence," she told them. "He is a ruler whose chief interest is poetry. Will it be now? I do not know."

They had quickly become used to her strange speech forms and were finding her more easily understood, though they had no idea who Edif might be and had passed through his land into a place where the desert appeared suddenly on both sides of them, beyond flanking lines of palms, as if they moved towards an oasis. Yet no oasis materialized.

Soon the sky was the colour of bad liver again and the rocky walls had risen around them and there was the sickly, oppressive odour, which reminded Elric of some decadent court's ante-rooms. Perfume which had once been sweet but had now grown stale; food which had once made the mouth water but which was now too old; flowers which no longer enhanced but reminded one only of death.

The walls on either side now had great jagged caves in them where the water echoed and tumbled. Queen Sough seemed nervous of these and kept the barge carefully in the centre of the river. Elric saw shadows moving within the caves, both above and below the water. He saw red mouths opening and closing and saw pale, unblinking eyes staring. They had the air of Chaos-born creatures and he wished mightily then for his runesword, for his patron Duke of Hell, for his repertoire of spells and incantations.

The albino was not altogether surprised when at last a voice spoke from one of the caverns.

"I am Balis Jamon, Lord of the Blood and I wish to have some kidneys."

"We sail on!" cried Queen Sough in response. "I am not your food nor shall I ever be."

"Their kidneys! Theirs!" the voice demanded implacably. "I have fed on no true grub for so long. Some kidneys! Some kidneys!"

Elric drew his sword and his dagger. Oone did the same.

"You'll not have mine, sir," said the albino.

"Nor mine," said Oone, seeking the source of the voice. They could not be sure which of the many caves sheltered the speaker.

"I am Balis Jamon, Lord of the Blood. You'll pay a toll here in my land. Two kidneys for me!"

"I'll take yours instead, sir, if you like!" said Elric defiantly.

"Will you now?"

There was a great movement from the furthest cave and water foamed in and out. Then something stooped and came wading into midstream, its fleshy body festooned with half-decayed plants and ruined blooms, its horned snout lifted so that it could stare at them from two tiny black eyes. The fangs in the snout were broken, yellow and black, and a red tongue licked at them, flicking little pieces of rotten meat into the water. It held one great paw over its chest and when the paw was lowered it revealed a dark, gaping hole where the heart would have been.

"I am Balis Jamon, Lord of the Blood. Look what I must fill for me to live! Have mercy, little creatures. A kidney or two and I'll let you pass. I have nothing here, while you are complete. You must make justice and share with me."

"This is my only justice for you, Lord Balis," said Elric, gesturing with a sword which seemed a feeble thing even to him.

"You will never be complete, Balis Jamon!" called out Queen Sough. "Not until you know more of mercy!"

"I am fair! One kidney will do!" The paw began to reach towards Elric who cut at it but missed, then cut again and felt the sword strike the creature's hide, which scarcely showed a mark. The paw grabbed at the sword. Elric withdrew it. Balis Jamon growled with a mixture of frustration and self-pity and reached both paws towards the albino.

"Stop! Here's your kidney!" Oone held up something which dripped. "Here it is, Balis Jamon. Now let us pass. We are agreed."

"Agreed." He turned, evidently mollified, delicately took what she handed up to him and popped it into the hole in his chest. "Good. Go!" And he waded passively back towards his cave, honour and hunger both satisfied.

Elric was baffled, though grateful that she had saved his life. "What did you do, Lady Oone?"

She smiled. "A large bean. Some of the provisions I still carried in my purse. It looked similar to a kidney, especially when dipped in water. And I doubt if he knows the difference. He seemed a simple creature."

Queen Sough's eyes were lifted upwards even as she steered the barge past the caves and into a wider stretch of water where buffalo lifted their heads from where they drank and stared at them with wary curiosity.

Elric followed the navigator's gaze but saw only the same lead-coloured sky. He sheathed his sword. "These creatures of Chaos seem simple enough. Less intelligent in some ways than others I've encountered."

"Aye." Oone was unsurprised. "That's likely, I think. She would be—"

The boat was lifted suddenly and for a second Elric thought Lord Balis had returned to take vengeance on them for tricking him. But they appeared to be on the crest of a huge wave. The water level rose rapidly between the slimy walls and now, on the cliffs' edges, figures appeared. They were of every kind of distorted shape and unlikely size and Elric was reminded a little of the beggar populace of Nadsokor, for these, too, were dressed in rags and bore the evidence of self-mutilation, as well as disease, wounding and ordinary neglect. They were filthy. They moaned. They looked greedily at the boat and they licked their lips.

Now, more than ever before, Elric wished he had Stormbringer with him. The runesword and a little elemental aid would have driven this rabble away in terror. But he had only the blades captured from the Sorcerer Adventurers. He must rely upon those, his alliance with Oone and their naturally complementary fighting skills. There came a juddering from the bottom of the barge and the wave receded as suddenly as it had risen, but now they were stranded on the very top of the cliff, with the misshapen horde all around them, panting and grunting and sniffing at their prey.

Elric wasted no time with parleying but jumped at once from the boat's prow and cut at the first two who grabbed for him. The blade, still sharp enough, severed their heads and he stood over their bodies grinning at them like the wolf he was sometimes called. "I want you all," he said. He used the battle bravado he had learned from the pirates of the Vilmirian Straits. He moved forward again and thrust, catching still another Chaos creature in the chest. "I must kill every one of you before I am satisfied!"

They had not expected this. They shuffled. They looked at each other. They turned their weapons in their hands, they adjusted their rags and tugged at their limbs.

Now Oone was beside Elric. "I want my fair share of these," she cried. "Save them for me, Elric." Then she, too, darted forward and cut down an ape-faced thing which carried a jeweled axe of beautiful workmanship, clearly stolen from an earlier victim.

Queen Sough called from behind them. "They have not attacked you. They only threaten. Is this the true thing you must do?"

"It's our only choice, Queen Sough!" cried Elric over his shoulder, and feinted at two more of the half-human things.

"No! No! It is not heroic. What can the guardian do, who is no longer a hero?"

Even Oone could not follow this and when Elric met her eye in a question she shook her head.

The rabble was gaining some confidence now, closing in. Snouts sniffed at them. Tongues licked saliva from slack lips. Hot, dirty eyes full of blood and pus squinted their hatred.

Then they had begun to close and Elric felt his blade meet resistance, for he had already blunted it on the first two creatures. Yet still the neck split and the head fell to one side, glaring the while, hands clutching. Oone had her back to his and together they moved so that they were protected from one side by the boat which the rabble did not seem to wish to touch. Queen Sough, in obvious distress, wept as she watched but clearly had no authority over the Chaos creatures. "No! No! This does not help her to sleep! No! No! She is in need of them, I know!"

It was at that point that Elric heard the sound of hoofs and saw, over the heads of the closing crowd, the white armour of the Pearl Warrior.

"They are his creatures!" he said in sudden understanding. "This is his own army and he is to be revenged on us!"

"No!" Queen Sough's voice was distant now, as if very far away. "This cannot be useful! It is your army. They'll be loyal. Yes."

Hearing her, Elric knew unexpected clarity. Was it that she was not really human? Were all of these creatures merely shape-changers of some kind, disguising themselves as humans? It would explain their strange cast of mind, the peculiar logic, the strange phrasing.

But there was no time for speculation, for now the creatures were hard about him and Oone, so that it was hardly possible to swing their blades to keep them back. Blood flowed, sticky and foetid, splashing on blades and arms and making them gag. Elric felt he might be overwhelmed by the stench before he was defeated by their weapons.

It was clear they could not resist the mob and Elric was bitter, feeling that they had come very close to the object of their quest only to be cut down by the most wretched of the denizens of Chaos.

Then more bodies fell at his feet and he realized that he had not killed them. Oone, too, was astonished by this turn of events.

They looked up. They could not understand what was happening.

The Pearl Warrior was riding through the ranks of the rabble cutting this way and that, jabbing with his makeshift spear, slicing with his sword, cackling and crowing at every fresh life he took. His horrible eyes were alight with some sort of amusement and even his horse was slashing at the rabble with its hoofs, nipping at them with its teeth.

"This is the proper thing!" Queen Sough clapped her hands. "This is true. This is to ensure honour for you!"

Gradually driven back by the Pearl Warrior, by Elric and Oone as they resumed their attack, the rabble began to break up.

Soon the whole awful mob was running for the cliff edge, leaping into the abyss rather than die by the Pearl Warrior's bone spear and his silver sword.

His laughter continued as he herded the remainder to their doom. He screamed his mockery at them. He raved at them for cowards and fools. "Ugly things. Ugly! Ugly! Go! Perish! Go! Go! Go! Banished now, they are. Banished to that! Yes!"

Elric and Oone leaned against the barge trying to catch their breaths.

"I am grateful to you, Pearl Warrior," said the albino as the armoured rider approached. "You have saved our lives."

"Yes." The Pearl Warrior nodded gravely, his eyes unusually thoughtful. "That is so. Now we shall be equal. Then we shall know the truth. I am not free, as you. You believe this?" His last question was addressed to Oone.

She nodded. "I believe that, Pearl Warrior. I, too, am glad you helped us."

"I am the one who protects. This must be done. You go on? I was your friend."

Oone looked back to where Queen Sough was nodding, her arms outstretched in some kind of offering.

"Here I am not your enemy," said the Pearl Warrior, as if instructing the simple-minded. "If I were complete, we three would be a trinity of greatness! Aye! Thou knowest it! I have not the personal. This words are hers, you see. I think."

And with that particularly mystifying pronouncement he wheeled his horse and rode away over the grassy limestone.

"Too many defenders, not enough protectors, perhaps." Oone sounded as odd as the others. Before Elric could quiz her on this she had given her attention back to Queen Sough. "My lady? Did you summon the Pearl Warrior to our aid?"

"She called him to you, I think." Queen Sough seemed almost in a trance. It was odd to hear her speaking of herself in the third person. Elric wondered if this were the normal mode here and again it occurred to him that all the people of this realm were not human but had assumed human shape.

They were now stranded high above the river. Going to the edge of the abyss, Elric stared down. He saw only some bodies which had been caught on the rocks, others drifting downstream. He was glad, then, that their boat was not having to negotiate waters clogged with so many corpses.

"How can we continue?" he asked Oone. He had a vision of himself and her in the Bronze Tent, of the child between them. All were dying. He knew a pang of need, as if the drug were calling to him, reminding him of his addiction. He remembered Anigh in Quarzhasaat and Cymoril, his betrothed, waiting in Imrryr. Had he been right to let Yyrkoon rule in his place? Every one of his decisions seemed now to be foolish. His self-esteem, never high, was lower than he could remember. His lack of forethought, his failures, his follies, all reminded him that not only was he physically deficient, he was also lacking in ordinary common sense.

"It is in the nature of the hero," said Queen Sough in relation to nothing. Then she looked at them and her eyes were maternal, kindly. "You are safe!"

"I think there is some urgency," said Oone. "I sense it. Do you?"

"Aye. Is there danger in the realm we left?"

"Perhaps. Queen Sough, are we far from the Nameless Gate? How can we continue?"

"By means of the moth-steeds," she said. "The waters always rise here and I have my moths. We have only to wait for them. They are on their way." Her tone was matter-of-fact. "It was that rabble which could have been yours. No more. But I cannot anticipate, you see. Every new trap is mysterious to me, as to you. I can navigate, as you navigate. This is together, you know."

Against the horizon there were rainbow lights winking and shimmering, like an aurora. Queen Sough sighed when she saw them. She was content.

"Good. Good. That is not late! Just the other."

The colours filled the sky now. As they came closer Elric realized that they belonged to huge, filmy wings supporting slender bodies, more butterfly than moth, of enormous size. Without hesitation the beasts began to descend until the three of them as well as the barge were engulfed by soft wings.

"Into the boat!" cried Queen Sough. "Quickly. We fly."

They hurried to obey her and at once the barge was rising into the air, apparently carried on the backs of the great moths, who flew beside the canyon for a while before plunging down into the abyss.

"I watched but there was nothing," said Queen Sough by way of explanation to Elric and Oone. "Now we shall resume."

With astonishing gentleness the creatures had deposited the barge on the river and were flying back up between the walls of the canyon again, filling the whole gloomy place with brilliant multicoloured light before they vanished. Elric rubbed at his brow. "This is truly the Land of Madness," he said. "I believe it is I who am mad, Lady Oone."

"You are losing confidence in yourself, Prince Elric." She spoke firmly. "That is the particular trap of this land. You come to believe that it is yourself, not what surrounds you, that has little logic. Already we have imposed our sanity on Falador. Do not despair. It cannot be much longer before we reach the final gate."

"And what is there?" He was sardonic. "Sublime reason?" He felt the same strange sense of exhaustion. Physically he was still capable of continuing, but his mind and his spirit were depleted.

"I cannot begin to anticipate what we shall find in the Nameless Land," she said. "Dreamthieves have little power over what occurs beyond the seventh gate."

"I've noticed your considerable influence here!" But he did not mean to hurt her. He smiled to show that he joked.

From ahead they heard a howling, so painful that even Queen Sough covered her ears. It was like the baying of some monstrous hound, echoing up and down the abyss and threatening to shake the very boulders loose from the walls. As the river bore them round the bend they saw the beast standing there, a great shaggy wolflike beast, its head lifted as it howled again. The water rushed around its huge legs, foamed against its body. As it turned its gaze upon them the beast vanished completely. They heard only the echo of its howling. The speed of the water increased. Queen Sough had removed her hands from the tiller to block her ears. The boat swung in the water and bounced as it struck a rock. She made no attempt to steer it. Elric seized the long arm but in spite of using all his strength he could do nothing with the boat. Eventually, he, too, gave up.

Down and down the river ran. Down into a gorge growing so deep that soon there was scarcely any light at all. They saw faces grinning at them. They felt hands reach out to touch them. Elric became convinced that every mortal creature who had ever died had come here to haunt him. In the dark rock he saw his own face many times, and those of Cymoril and Yyrkoon. Old battles were fought as he watched. And old, agonizing, emotions came back to him. He felt the loss of all he had ever loved, the despair of death and desertion, and soon his own voice joined the general babble and he howled as loudly as the hound had howled until Oone shook him and yelled at him and brought him back from the madness which had threatened to engulf him.

"Elric! The last gate! We are almost there! Hold on, Prince of Melniboné. You have been courageous and resourceful until now. This will require still more of you and you must be ready!"

And Elric began to laugh. He laughed at his own fate, at the fate of the Holy Child, at Anigh's fate and at Oone's. He laughed when he thought of Cymoril waiting for him on the Dragon Isle, not knowing even now if he lived or died, if he were free or a slave.

When Oone shouted at him again, he laughed in her face.

"Elric! You betray us all!"

He paused in his laughter long enough to say softly, almost in triumph, "Aye, madam, that is so. I betray you all. Have you not heard? It is my destiny to betray!"

"You shall not betray me, sir!" She slapped at his face. She punched him. She kicked his legs. "You shall not betray me and you shall not betray the Holy Girl!"

He knew intense pain, not from her blows but from his own mind. He cried out and then he began to sob. "Oh, Oone. What is happening to me?"

"This is Falador," she said simply. "Are you recovered, Prince Elric?"

The faces still gibbered at him from the rock. The air was still alive with all he feared, all he most misliked in himself.

He was trembling. He could not meet her gaze. He realized he was weeping. "I am Elric, last of Melniboné's royal line," he said. "I have looked upon horror and I have courted the Dukes of Hell. Why should I know fear now?"

She did not answer and he expected no answer from her.

The boat surged, swung again, lifted and dipped.

Suddenly he was calm. He took hold of Oone's hand in a gesture of simple affection.

"I am myself again I think," he said.

"There is the gateway," said Queen Sough from behind them. She had her grip on the tiller again and with her other hand was pointing ahead.

"There is the land you call the Nameless Land," she said. She spoke plainly now, not in the cryptic phrasing she had used since they had met her. "There you will find the Fortress of the Pearl. She cannot welcome you."

"Who?" said Elric. The waters were calm again. They ran slowly towards a great archway of alabaster, its edges trimmed by soft leaves and shrubs. "The Holy Girl?"

"She can be saved," said Queen Sough. "Only by you two, I think. I have helped her remain here, awaiting rescue. But it is all I can do. I am afraid, you see."

"We are all that, madam," said Elric feelingly.

The boat was caught by new currents and traveled still more slowly, as if reluctant to enter the last gate of the Dream Realm.

"But I am of no help," said Queen Sough. "I might even have conspired. It was those men. They came. Then more came. There was only retreat thereafter. I wish I could know such words. You would understand them if I had them. Ah, it is hard here!"

Elric, looking into her agonized eyes, realized that she was probably more of a prisoner in this world than he and Oone. It seemed to him that she longed to escape and was only kept here by her love of the Holy Girl, her protective emotions. Yet surely she had been here long before Varadia had come?

The boat had begun to pass under the alabaster arch now. There was a salty, pleasant taste to the air, as if they approached the ocean.

Elric decided he must ask the question which was on his mind.

"Queen Sough," he said. "Are you Varadia's mother?"

The pain in the eyes grew even more intense as the veiled woman turned away from him. Her voice was a sob of anguish and he was shocked by it.

"Oh, who knows?" she cried. "*Who knows*?"

BOOK THREE

Is there a brave lord birthed by Fate
To wield old weapons, win new estates
And tear down the walls Time sanctifies,
Raze ancient temples as hallowed lies,
His pride to break, his love to lose,
Destroying his race, his history, his muse,
And, relinquishing peace for a life of strife,
Leave only a corpse that the flies refuse?

—*The Chronicle of the Black Sword*

Chapter One

At the Court of the Pearl

AGAIN ELRIC EXPERIENCED that strange frisson of recognition at the landscape before him, though he could not remember ever seeing anything like it. Pale blue mist rose around cypresses, date palms, orange trees and poplars whose shades of green were equally pale; flowing meadows occasionally revealed the rounded white of boulders and in the far distance were snow-peaked mountains. It was as if an artist had painted the scenery with the most delicate of washes, the finest of brushstrokes. It was a vision of Paradise and completely unexpected after the insanity of Falador.

Queen Sough had remained silent since she had answered Elric's question, and a peculiar atmosphere had developed between the three of them. Yet all the uneasiness failed to affect Elric's delight at the world they had entered. The skies (if skies they were) were full of pearly cloud, tinged by pink and the faintest yellow, and a little white smoke rose up from the flat-roofed house some distance away. The barge had come to rest in a pool of still, sparkling water and Queen Sough gestured for them to disembark.

"You will come with us to the Fortress?" asked Oone.

"She does not know. I do not know if it is permitted," said the queen, her eyes hooded above her veil.

"Then I shall say farewell now." Elric bowed and kissed the woman's soft hand. "I thank you for your assistance, madam, and trust you will forgive me for the crudeness of my manners."

"Forgiven, yes." Elric, looking up, thought Queen Sough smiled.

"I thank you also, my lady." Oone spoke almost intimately, as to one with whom she might share a secret. "Know you how we shall find the Fortress of the Pearl?"

"That one will know." The queen pointed towards the distant cottage. "Farewell, as you say. You can save her. Only you."

"I am grateful for your confidence, also," said Elric. He stepped almost jauntily onto the turf and followed Oone as they made their way across the fields to the little house. "This is a great relief, my lady. A contrast, indeed to the Land of Madness!"

"Aye." She responded a trifle cautiously, and her hand went to the hilt of her sword. "But remember, Prince Elric, that madness takes many forms in all worlds."

He did not allow her wariness to let him lose his enjoyment. He was determined to restore himself to the peak of his energies, in preparation for whatever might lie ahead.

Oone was first to reach the door of the white house. Outside were two chickens scratching in the gravel, an old dog, tethered to a barrel, who looked up at them over a grey muzzle and grinned, a pair of short-coated cats cleaning their silvery fur on the roof over the lintel. Oone knocked and the door was opened almost immediately. A tall, handsome young man stood there, his head covered by an old burnouse, his body clad in a light brown robe with long sleeves. He seemed pleased to see visitors.

"Greetings to you," he said. "I am Chamog Borm, currently in exile. Have you come with good news from the Court?"

"We have no news at all, I fear," said Oone. "We are travelers and we seek the Fortress of the Pearl. Is it close by here?"

"At the heart and the centre of those mountains." He waved with his hand towards the peaks. "Will you join me for some refreshment?"

The name the young man had given, together with his extraordinary looks, caused Elric again to rack his brains, trying to recall why all this was so familiar to him. He knew that he had only recently heard the name.

Within the cool house, Chamog Borm brewed them an herbal drink. He seemed proud of his domestic skills and it was clear he was no simple farmer. In one corner of the room was heaped a pile of rich armour, steel chased with silver and gold, a helm decorated with a tall spike, that spike decorated with ornamental snakes and falcons locked in conflict. There were spears, a long, curved sword, daggers—weapons and accoutrements of every description.

"You are a warrior by trade?" said Elric as he sipped the hot liquid. "Your armour is very handsome."

"I was once a hero," said Chamog Borm sadly, "until I was dismissed from the Court of the Pearl."

"Dismissed?" Oone was thoughtful. "On what charge?"

Chamog Borm lowered his eyes. "I was charged with cowardice. Yet I believe that I was not guilty, that I was subject to an enchantment."

And now Elric recalled where he had heard the name. When he had arrived in Quarzhasaat he had in his fever wandered in the market places and listened to the story-tellers. At least three of the stories he had heard had concerned Chamog Borm, hero of legend, the last brave knight of the empire. His name was venerated everywhere, even in the camps of the nomads. Yet Elric was sure Chamog Borm had existed—if he had ever existed—at least a thousand years earlier!

"What was the action of which you were accused?" he asked.

"I failed to save the Pearl, which now lies under an enchantment, imprisoning us all in perpetual suffering."

"What was that enchantment?" Oone asked quickly.

"It became impossible for our monarch and many of the retainers to leave the Fortress. It was for me to free them. Instead I brought a worse enchantment upon us. And my punishment is contrary to theirs. They may not leave. I may not return." As he spoke he became increasingly melancholy.

Elric, still astonished at this conversation with a hero who should have been dead centuries before, could say little, but Oone seemed to understand completely. She made a sympathetic gesture.

"Can the Pearl be found there?" Elric asked, conscious of the bargain he had made with Lord Gho, of Anigh's impending torture and death, of Oone's predictions.

"Of course," Chamog Borm was surprised. "Some believe it rules the whole Court, perhaps the world."

"Was this always so?" Oone asked softly.

"I have told you that it was not." He looked at them both as if they were simpletons. Then he lowered his eyes, lost in his own dishonour and humiliation.

"We hope to free her," said Oone. "Would you come with us, to help us?"

"I cannot help. She no longer trusts me. I am banished," he said. "But I can let you have my armour and my weapons so that part of me, at least, can fight for her."

"Thank you," said Oone. "You are generous."

Chamog Borm grew more animated as he helped them choose from his store. Elric found that the breastplate and greaves fitted him perfectly, as did the helmet. Similar equipment was found for Oone and the straps tightened to adjust to her slightly smaller body. They looked almost identical in their new armour, and something in Elric was again struck, some deep sense of satisfaction that he could hardly understand but which he welcomed. The armour gave him not only a greater sense of security but a sense of deep recognition of his own inner strength, a strength which he knew he must call upon to the utmost in the encounter to come. Oone had warned him of subtler dangers at the Fortress of the Pearl.

Chamog Borm's gifts continued, in the shape of two grey horses which he led from their stable at the back of the house. "These are

Taron and Tadia. Brother and sister, they were twin foals. They have never been separated. Once I rode them into battle. Once I took up arms against the Bright Empire. Now the last emperor of Melniboné will ride in my place to fulfill my destiny and end the siege of the Fortress of the Pearl."

"You know me?" Elric looked hard at the handsome youth, seeking deception or even irony, but there was none in those steady eyes.

"A hero knows another, Prince Elric." And Chamog Borm reached out to grip Elric's forearm in the gesture of friendship of the desert peoples. "May you gain all you wish to gain and may you do so with honour. You, too, Lady Oone. Your courage is the greatest of all. Farewell."

The exile watched them from the roof of his little house until they were out of sight. Now the great mountains were close, almost embracing them, and they could see a wide, white road stretching through them. The light was like that of a late summer afternoon, though Elric could still not be sure if it was sky above them or the distant roof of a vast cavern, for the sun was still not in evidence. Was the Dream Realm a limitless series of such caverns or had the dreamthieves mapped the entire world? Could they cross the mountains, cross the nameless land beyond and begin again to travel through the seven gates, ultimately arriving back at the Land of Dreams-in-Common? And would they find Jaspar Colinadous waiting for them where they had left him?

The road, when they reached it, proved to be of pure marble, but the horses' hoofs were so well shod they did not slip once. The noise of their galloping began to echo through the wide pass and herds of gazelles and wild sheep looked up from their grazing to watch them pass, two silver riders on silver horses on their way to do battle with the forces who had seized power at the Fortress of the Pearl.

"You have understood these people better than I," he said to Oone, as the road began to twist upwards towards the centre of the range and the light had grown colder, the sky a bright, hard grey. "Do you know what we might expect to find at the Fortress of the Pearl?"

She shook her head in regret. "It is like understanding a code without knowing what the words actually relate to," she told him.

"The force is powerful enough to banish a hero as potent as Chamog Borm."

"I know only the legend, and that from a little I heard in the Slave Market at Quarzhasaat."

"He was summoned by the Holy Girl as soon as she realized that she was under further attack. That is what I believe, at any rate. She did not expect him to fail her. Somehow, indeed, he made matters worse. She felt betrayed by him and banished him to the edge of the Nameless Land, there perhaps to greet and assist others who might come to help her. That is no doubt why we are given all the appurtenances of the hero, so that we may be as much like heroes as he."

"Yet we know this world less well. How may we succeed where he failed?"

"Perhaps because of our ignorance," she said. "Perhaps not. I cannot answer you, Elric." She rode close to him, leaning from her saddle to kiss that part of his cheek exposed by the helmet. "Only know this. I will neither betray her nor, if I can help it, you. Yet if I must betray one of you, I suppose it will be you."

Elric looked at her in bafflement. "Is that likely to be an issue?"

She shrugged and then she sighed. "I do not know, Elric. Look. I think we have come to the Fortress of the Pearl!"

It was like a palace carved from the most delicate ivory. White against the silver sky it rose above the snows of the mountain, a great multitude of slender spires and turreted towers, of cupolas, of mysterious structures which seemed almost as if they had been arrested in mid-flight. There were bridges and stairways, curving walls and galleries, balconies and roof-gardens whose colours were a spectrum of pastel shades, a myriad of different plants, flowers, shrubs and trees. In all his travels Elric had only seen one place that was the equal to the Fortress of the Pearl and that was his own city, Imrryr. Yet the Dreaming City was exotic, rich, earthy in comparison, a romantic fancy compared to the complicated austerity of this palace.

As they approached on the marble road, Elric realized that the Fortress was not pure white, but contained shades of blue, silver, grey and pink, sometimes a little yellow or green, and he had the notion that

the entire thing had been carved from a single gigantic pearl. Soon they had reached the Fortress's only gate, a great circular opening protected by spiked grilles which came from above and below and both sides to meet at the centre. The Fortress was vast but even its gate dwarfed them.

Elric could think of nothing to do but cry out, "Open in the name of the Holy Girl! We come to do battle with those who imprison her spirit here!"

His words echoed through the towers of the Fortress and through the jagged peaks of the mountains beyond and seemed to lose themselves in the heights of a cavern's roof. In the shadows beyond the gateway he saw something scarlet move and then vanish again. There came the smell of delicious perfume, mixed with the same strange ocean scent they had noticed when they first reached the Nameless Land.

Then the gates had parted, so swiftly that they seemed to melt into the air, and a rider confronted them, his humourless chuckling by now all too familiar.

"This is what should be, I think," said the Pearl Warrior.

"League yourself with us again, Pearl Warrior," said Oone, with all her considerable authority. "It is what she desires!"

"No. It is so that she shall not be betrayed. You must dissolve. Now! Now! Now!" His head was flung back as he screamed these last words, for all the world like a dog gone rabid.

Elric drew a sword from its scabbard. It shone with the same silver light that poured from the Pearl Warrior's blade. Oone followed his example, though more reluctantly.

"We shall pass now, Pearl Warrior."

"Nothing will here! I want your freedom."

"She shall have it!" said Oone. "It is not yours, not unless she bestows it upon you herself."

"She says it is mine. I will be that. I will be *that*!"

Elric could not follow this strange conversation and he chose not to waste time with it. He urged his silver horse forward, the blade glaring in his hand. So balanced was this sword, so familiar to his grip, that he felt for a moment that it was somehow the natural counterpart to his runesword. Was this a sword forged by Law to serve its purposes, just as Stormbringer had, by all accounts, been forged by Chaos?

The Pearl Warrior guffawed and widened his awful eyes. Death was in them. The death of the world. He lowered the same misshapen lance he had brandished at them before and Elric saw it was encrusted with old blood. The warrior held his ground and the lance was suddenly threatening Elric's eyes so that the albino had to throw himself to one side to avoid its points, striking upwards as he did so and feeling a greater resistance to his blow than anything he had felt before. The Pearl Warrior seemed to have gained strength since their last encounter.

"Ordinary soul!" The lips twisted in this insult, clearly as disgusting as any the Pearl Warrior could conceive. And he began to chuckle again, this time because Oone was riding at him, her sword stretched out full before her, a spear held in her hand, her reins between her teeth. The sword drove forward, the spear swung back as she poised to throw. Then sword and spear struck the Pearl Warrior at the exact same moment so that his breastplate cracked like the shell of some great crustacean and was pierced by the sword.

Elric marveled at this strategy, which he had never witnessed before. Oone's strength and co-ordination were almost beyond credibility. It was a feat of arms warriors would speak of for a thousand years to come, which many would try to emulate and would die in the trying.

The spear had done its work in breaking open the Pearl Warrior's armour and the sword had completed the action. But the Pearl Warrior had not been killed.

He groaned. He cackled. He floundered. His sword came up as if to protect his chest from the blow already struck. His great horse reared and its nostrils flared with fury. Oone turned her own mount away. Her sword had left its tip in the Pearl Warrior's body. She was reaching for a second spear, for her dagger.

Elric drove forward again, his own spear aimed at the cracked armour, hoping to follow her example, but the blade struck the ivory and was turned. Elric lost balance long enough for the Pearl Warrior to take the advantage. The sword struck the steel of Elric's armour with a noise that made a cacophony in his helmet and brought bright sparks like a fire. He fell onto his horse's neck, barely able to block the next thrust. Then the Pearl Warrior had shrieked, the eyes growing still wider, the mouth gaping red and the foul breath steaming from it, while blood poured from under the gorget between his helmet and his breastplate. He fell towards Elric and the albino realized that the haft of a spear was sticking from his chest in exactly the same place where Oone had broken the creature's armour.

"This will not remain so!" cried the Pearl Warrior. It was a threat. "I cannot do that thing!"

Then he had tumbled in a heap from his horse and clattered like old bones onto the flagstones of the courtyard. From behind him an ornamental fountain, representing a fig tree in full fruit, began to spurt water, filling the surrounding trough and overflowing until it touched the body of the Pearl Warrior. The riderless horse began to scream, turning round and round, rearing, foaming, then it had galloped out through the gate and back down the marble road.

Elric turned the heavy corpse over to make sure that no life was left in the Pearl Warrior and to inspect the shattered armour. He remained admiring of Oone's manoeuvre. "I have never seen that done before," he said, "and I have fought beside and against famous warriors."

"A dreamthief must know many things," she said, by way of acknowledgment of his praise. "I learned such tactics from my mother, who was a greater battle-woman than I shall ever be."

"Your mother was a dreamthief?"

"No," said Oone absently as she inspected her ruined sword and then picked up the Pearl Warrior's, "she was a queen." She tested the weight of the dead creature's blade and discarded her own, trying it in her scabbard and finding that it was a little too wide. Carelessly she stuck it in her belt and unhooked the scabbard, throwing it upon the ground. The water from the fountain was around their ankles now and was disturbing their horses.

Leading the steeds they passed under a heart-shaped arch and into another courtyard. Here, too, fountains played, but these were not flooding. They seemed carved out of ivory, like so much of the Fortress, and represented stylized herons, their beaks meeting at a point above their heads. Elric was reminded vaguely of the architecture of Quarzhasaat, though this had none of the decadence of that place, none of the look of senile old age which characterized the city at its worst. Had the Fortress been built by the ancestors of the present Lords of Quarzhasaat, the Council of Six and One Other? Had some great king fled the city millennia before and journeyed here to the Dream Realm? Was that how the legend of the Pearl had come to Quarzhasaat?

Courtyard after courtyard, each in its own way of extraordinary beauty, followed until Elric began to wonder if this path were merely leading them through the Fortress to the other side.

"For such a large building it's somewhat underpopulated," he said to Oone.

"We shall find the inhabitants soon enough, I think," Oone murmured. Now they ascended a spiral causeway which led around a huge central dome. Although the palace had such a mood and look of austerity, Elric did not find its architecture cold and there was something almost organic about it, as if it had been formed from flesh, then petrified.

Their horses still with them, the sound now muffled by luxurious carpet, they moved through halls and corridors whose walls were hung with tapestries and decorated with mosaics, though they saw no pictures of living things, only geometrical designs.

"We near the heart of the Fortress, I think," Oone told him in a whisper. It was as if she feared to be overheard, yet they had seen no-one. She looked beyond tall columns, through a series of rooms seemingly lit by sunshine from without. Following her gaze, Elric had the impression of blue fabric wafting through a door and vanishing. "Who was that?"

"All the same," said Oone to herself. "All the same." Her sword was drawn again, however, and she signed to Elric to imitate her. They entered another courtyard. This one seemed to be open to the sky—the same grey sky they had first seen in the mountains. Gallery after gallery rose up all around them, many storeys to the top. Elric thought he saw faces peering back at him, then something liquid struck his face and he almost inhaled the sickly red stuff which covered his body. More of it was pouring down on them from every part of the gallery and already the courtyard was knee-deep in what seemed to Elric to be human blood. He heard a muttering overhead, soft laughter, a cry.

"Stop this!" he shouted, wading to the side of the chamber. "We are here to parley. All we want is the Holy Girl! Give her spirit back to us and we shall leave!"

He was answered by a further shower of blood and he hauled his horse towards the next door. There was a gate across it. He tried to lift it. He tried to bounce it free of its mountings. He looked to Oone who, wiping the red liquid from herself, joined him. She reached out her long fingers and found some kind of button. The gate opened slowly, almost reluctantly, but it opened. She grinned at him. "Like most men, you become a brute when you panic, my lord."

He was hurt by her joke. "I had no idea I should find such a means of opening the gate, my lady."

"Think of such things in future and you will stand a better chance of survival in this fortress," she said.

"Why will they not parley with us?"

"They probably do not believe that we are ready to bargain," she said. Then she added: "In reality, I can only guess at their logic. Each adventure of a dreamthief is different from the others, Prince Elric. Come." She led them on past a series of pools full of warm water from which a little steam rose. There were no bathers in the pools. Then Elric thought he saw creatures, perhaps fish, swimming in the depths. He leaned forward to look, but Oone pulled him back. "I warned you. Your curiosity could bring your destruction and mine."

Something threshed and bubbled in the pool and then was gone. All at once the rooms began to shake and the water foamed. Cracks appeared in the marble floors. Their horses snorted with fear and threatened to lose their footing. Elric himself almost toppled down into one of the fissures which had opened. It was as if an earthquake had suddenly struck the mountains. Yet as they dashed hastily for the next gallery, which opened on to a peaceful lawn, all signs of the earthquake had vanished.

A man approached them. In bearing, he resembled Queen Sough, but he was shorter and older. His white beard hung upon a surcoat of gold cloth and in his hand he held a salver on which were placed two leather bags. "Will you accept the authority of the Fortress of the Pearl?" he said. "I am the seneschal of this place."

"Who do you serve?" Elric asked brusquely. His sword was still in his hand and he made no effort to disguise his readiness to use it.

The seneschal looked bewildered. "I serve the Pearl, of course. This is the Fortress of the Pearl!"

"Who rules here, old man?" Oone asked him pointedly.

"The Pearl. I have said so."

"Does no-one rule the Pearl?" Elric was mystified.

"No longer, sir. Now, will you take this gold and go. We have no wish to expend more of our energies upon you. They flag, but they are not exhausted. I think you will be dissolved soon."

"We have defeated all your defenders," said Oone. "Why should we want gold?"

"Do you not desire the Pearl?"

Before Elric could answer, Oone silenced him with a warning gesture.

"We come only to secure the release of the Holy Girl."

The seneschal smiled. "They have all made that claim, but what they want is the Pearl. I cannot believe you, lady."

"How can we prove our words?"

"You cannot. We already know the truth."

"We have no interest in bargaining with you, Sir Seneschal. If you serve the Pearl, who does the Pearl serve?"

"The child, I think." His brow furrowed. Her question had confused him, yet to Elric it had seemed so simple. His admiration for the dreamthief's skill increased.

"You see, we can help you in this," said Oone. "The child's spirit is imprisoned. And while it is imprisoned, so are you held captive."

The old man offered the bags of gold again. "Take this and leave us."

"I do not think we shall," said Oone firmly and she led her horse forward, past the old man. "Come, Elric."

The albino hesitated. "We should question him more, Oone, surely?"

"He could not answer more."

The seneschal ran at her, swinging the heavy bags, the salver falling to the floor with a clang. "She is not! It will hurt! This is not to be. Pain will come! Pain!"

Elric felt sympathy for the old man. "Oone. We should listen to him."

She would not pause. "Come. You must."

He had learned to trust her judgment. He, too, pushed past the old man who beat at his body with the bags of gold and wailed, the tears pouring down his cheeks and into his beard. It took a different courage to perform that particular action.

There was another great curving doorway ahead of them, all elaborate lattice-work and mosaic, bordered by bands of jade, blue enamel and silver. Two large doors of dark wood, hinges and studs of brass, blocked their way.

Oone did not know. She reached gently towards the doors and placed her fingertips against them. Gradually, just as with the other gate, the doors began to part. They heard a faint noise from within, almost a whimper. The doors opened wider and wider until they were completely back on their hinges.

For a moment Elric was overwhelmed by what he saw.

A grey-gold glow filled the great chamber which had been revealed to them. The glow came from a column about the height of a tall man which was topped by a globe. At the centre of the globe shone a pearl of enormous size, almost as big as Elric's fist. Short flights of steps led up to the column from all sides and around these steps were what at first appeared to be ranks of statues. Then Elric realized that they were men, women, and children, dressed in all manner of costumes, though most of them in the styles favoured in Quarzhasaat and by the desert clans.

The old man came stumbling behind them. "Do not hurt this!"

"We defend ourselves, Sir Seneschal," Oone told him without turning to look at him. "That is all you need to know from us."

Slowly, still leading the silver horses, still with their silver swords in their hands, the light from the pearl touching their silver armour and their helmets and making these, too, glow with soft radiance, they made their way into the chamber.

"This is not to destroy. This is not to defeat. This is not to despoil."

Elric shivered when he heard the voice. He looked over towards the distant walls of the room and there was the Pearl Warrior, his armour all cracked and slimed with blood, his face a terrible bruise, the eyes seeming alternately to fade and take fire. And sometimes they were Alnac's eyes.

The warrior's next words were almost pathetic. "I cannot fight you. No more."

"We are not here to hurt," said Oone again. "We are here to free you."

There was a movement amongst the still figures. A blue-gowned veiled woman appeared. Queen Sough's own eyes had a suggestion of tears. "With these you come?" she indicated the swords, the horses, the armour. "But our enemies are not here."

"They will be here soon," said Oone. "Soon, I think, my lady."

Still baffled, Elric looked behind him, as if he would see their enemies. He made a movement towards the Pearl at the Heart of the World, merely to admire a marvel. At once all the figures came to life, blocking his path.

"You will steal!" The old man sounded even more wretched than before, even more impotent.

"No," said Oone. "It is not our purpose. You must understand that." She spoke urgently. "Raik Na Seem sent us to find her."

"She is safe. Tell him she is safe."

"She is not safe. Soon she will dissolve." Oone turned her gaze on the whispering throng. "She is separated, as we are separated. The Pearl is the cause."

"This is a trick," said Queen Sough.

"A trick," echoed the wounded Pearl Warrior and there was a faint chuckle from his spoiled throat.

"A trick," said the seneschal, and held out the bags of gold.

"We come to steal nothing. We come to defend. Look!" Oone made a circular movement with her sword to show them what they had evidently not yet seen.

Emerging through the walls of the chamber, their hands filled with every imaginable weapon, came the hooded, tattooed soldiers of Quarzhasaat. The Sorcerer Adventurers.

"We cannot fight them," said Elric quietly to his friend. "There are too many of them." And he prepared himself for death.

Chapter Two

The Destruction in the Fortress

Then Oone had mounted her silver horse and raised her silver sword. She called out: "Elric, do as I do!" and had urged the stallion into a canter so that its hoofs rattled like thunder in the chamber.

Prepared to die with courage, even at the moment of apparent triumph, Elric climbed into his saddle, took a spear in the hand that held the reins and with his sword already swinging charged against the invaders.

Only as they crowded around him, axes, maces, spears and swords lifted to attack, did Elric understand that Oone's action had not been one of mere desperation. These half-shades moved sluggishly, their eyes were misted, they stumbled and their blows were feeble.

The slaughter now became sickening to him. Following her example, he hacked and stabbed from side to side, almost mechanically. Heads came away from bodies like rotten fruit; limbs were sliced as easily as leaves from a stick; torsos collapsed under the thrust of a spear or sword. Their viscous blood, already the blood of the dead, clung to weapons and armour and their cries of pain were pathetic to Elric's ears. If he had not sworn to follow Oone, he would have ridden back and let her continue the work alone. There was little danger to them as the veiled men continued to pour through the walls and be met by sharp steel and cunning intelligence.

Behind them, around the column of the Pearl, the courtiers watched. These clearly did not know what a mediocre threat the two silver-armoured warriors confronted.

At last it was done. Decapitated, limbless bodies were piled all around the hall. Elric and Oone rode out of that slaughter and they were grim, unhappy, nauseated by their own actions.

"It is done," said Oone. "The Sorcerer Adventurers are slain."

"You truly are heroes!" Queen Sough came down the steps towards them, her eyes bright with admiration, her arms outstretched.

"We are who we are," said Oone. "We are mortal fighters and we have destroyed the threat to the Fortress of the Pearl." Her words had taken on a ritualistic tone and Elric, trusting her, was content to listen.

"You are the children of Chamog Borm, Brother and Sister to the Bone Moon, Children of Water and Cool Breezes, Parents of the Trees . . ." The seneschal had dropped his bags of gold and was shaken by his weeping. He wept with relief and with joy and Elric saw how much he resembled Raik Na Seem.

Oone, down from her horse again, was embraced by Queen Sough. Meanwhile, a shuffling and cackling announced the approach of the Pearl Warrior.

"There is no more for me," he said. Alnac's dead eyes had nothing but resignation in them. "This is for dissolution . . ." And he fell forward onto the marble floor, his armour all broken, his limbs sprawling, and there was no longer any flesh on him, only bone, so that what was left of the Pearl Warrior resembled little more than the inedible remains of a crab, the supper of some sea-giant.

Queen Sough came towards Elric, her arms outstretched, and she seemed much smaller than when he had first encountered her. Her head hardly reached to his lowered chin. Her embrace was warm and he knew she, too, was weeping. Then her veil fell away from her face and he saw that she had lost years, that she was little more than a girl.

Behind Queen Sough the Lady Oone was smiling at him as astonished understanding filled him. Gently he touched the girl's face, the familiar folds of her hair and he drew in a sudden breath.

She was Varadia. She was the Holy Girl of the Bauradim. She was the child whose spirit they had promised to free.

Oóne joined him, placing a protective hand upon Varadia's shoulder. "You know now that we are truly your friends."

Varadia nodded, looking about her at the courtiers who had assumed their earlier frozen stances. "The Pearl Warrior was the best there was," she said. "I could summon none better. Chamog Borm failed me. The Sorcerer Adventurers were too strong for him. Now I can release him from his exile."

"We combined his strength with our own," said Oone. "Your strength and our strength. That is how we succeeded."

"We three are not shadows," said Varadia smiling, as if at a revelation. "*That* is how we succeeded."

Oone nodded agreement. "That is how we succeeded, Holy Girl. Now we must consider how to bring you back to the Bronze Tent, to your people. You carry all their pride and history with you."

"I knew that. I had to protect it. I thought I had failed."

"You have not failed," said Oone.

"The Sorcerer Adventurers will not attack again?"

"Never," said Oone. "Not here, nor anywhere. Elric and I will make sure of it."

And then Elric realized in admiration that it had been Oone, in the end, who had summoned the Sorcerer Adventurers, summoned those shades for the last time, summoned them so that she might demonstrate their defeat.

Oone looked at him and warned him with her eyes not to say too much. But now he realized that all that they had fought, save perhaps a little of the Pearl Warrior and the Sorcerer Adventurers, had been a child's dreams. The hero of legend, Chamog Borm, could not save her because she knew he was not real. Similarly, the Pearl Warrior, chiefly her own invention, could not save her. But he and Oone were real. As real as the girl herself! In her deep dream, in which she had disguised herself as a queen, seeking power but failing to find it, just as she had described, she had known the truth. Unable to escape from the dream, she had yet recognized the difference between her own invention and that which she had not invented—herself, Oone and Elric. But Oone had had to show that she could defeat what remained of the original threat, and in demonstrating the defeat, she freed the child.

And yet they were still within the dream, all three of them. The great pearl pulsed as powerfully as before, the Fortress with all its mazes and intertwined passages and chambers was still their prison.

"You understood," Elric said to Oone. "You knew what they spoke of. The language was a child's language—a language seeking power and failing. A child's understanding of power."

But again Oone, with a glance, cautioned him to silence. "Varadia knows now that power is never discovered in retreat. All one can hope to do by retreating is to let one power destroy another or hide as one hides from a storm one cannot control, until the force has passed. One cannot gain anything, save one's own self. And ultimately one must always confront the evil that would destroy one." It was almost as if she herself were in a trance and Elric guessed that she repeated lessons learned in pursuit of her craft.

"You did not come to steal the Pearl but to save me from its prison," said Varadia as Oone took her young hands and held them tightly. "My father sent you to help me?"

"He asked our help and we gave it willingly," said Elric. At last he sheathed the silver sword. He felt slightly foolish in the armour of a fairy-tale hero.

Oone recognized his discomfort. "We shall give all this back to Chamog Borm, my lord. Is he permitted to return to the Fortress, Lady Varadia?"

The child grinned. "Of course!" She clapped her hands and through the doorway to the Court of the Pearl, walking proudly, still in the clothes of his banishment, came Chamog Borm, to kneel at the feet of his mistress.

"My queen," he said. There was strong emotion in his wonderful voice.

"I return to you your armour and your weapons, your twin horses Tadia and Taron and all your honour, Chamog Borm." Varadia spoke with warm pride.

Soon Elric and Oone had discarded the armour and again wore only their ordinary clothes. Chamog Borm was in his silver- and gold-chased breastplate and greaves, his helmet of gleaming silver, his swords and his spears in their sheaths at hip and on horse. His other armour he bound to the back of his Tadia. At last he was ready. Again he kneeled before his queen. "My lady. What task wouldst thou have me accomplish for thee?"

Varadia said deliberately, "You are free to travel where you will, great Chamog Borm. But know only this—you must continue to fight evil wherever you find it and you must never again allow the Sorcerer Adventurers to attack the Fortress of the Pearl."

"I swear."

With a bow to Oone and Elric, the legendary hero rode slowly from the Court, his head high with pride and noble purpose.

Varadia was content. "I have made him again what he was before I called him. I now know that legends in themselves have no power. The power comes from the uses that the living make of the legend. The legends merely represent an ideal."

"You are a wise child," said Oone admiringly.

"Should I not be, madam? I am the Holy Girl of the Bauradim." Varadia spoke with considerable irony and good humour. "Am I not the Oracle of the Bronze Tent?" She lowered her eyes, perhaps in sudden melancholy. "I shall be a child only a little longer. I think I shall miss my palace and all its kingdoms . . ."

"Something is always lost here." Oone placed a comforting hand on the child's shoulder. "But much is gained, also."

Varadia looked back at the Pearl. Following her gaze, Elric saw that the entire Court had now vanished, just as the crowds had vanished on the great staircase when they had been attacked by the Pearl Warrior just before they first met Lady Sough. He now realized that in that guise she herself had guided them to her own rescue, as best she could. She had reached out to them. She had shown them the way in which they could, with their wits and courage, accomplish her salvation.

Varadia was ascending the steps, her hands outstretched towards the Pearl. "This is the cause of all our misfortune," she said. "What can we do with it?"

"Destroy it, perhaps," said Elric.

But Oone shook her head. "While it remains an undiscovered treasure thieves will constantly seek it. This is the cause of Varadia's imprisonment in the Dream Realm. This is what brought the Sorcerer Adventurers to her. It is why they drugged and attempted to abduct her. All the evil comes not from the Pearl itself but what evil men have made of it."

"What shall you do?" asked Elric. "Trade it in the Dream Market when you next go?"

"Perhaps that is what I should do. But it would not be the means of ensuring Varadia's safety in the future. Do you understand?"

"While the Pearl is a legend, there will always be those who will pursue the legend?"

"Exactly, Prince Elric. So we shall not destroy it, I think. Not here."

Elric did not care. So absorbed had he become in the dream itself, the revealing of the levels of reality existing in the Dream Realm, that he had forgotten his original quest, the threat to his life and that of Anigh in Quarzhasaat.

It was for Oone to remind him. "Remember, there are those in Quarzhasaat who are not only your enemies, Elric of Melniboné. They are the enemies of this girl. The enemies of the Bauradim. You have still a further task to accomplish, even when we return to the Bronze Tent."

"Then you must advise me, Lady Oone," said Elric simply, "for I am a novice here."

"I cannot advise you with any great clarity." She turned her eyes away from him, almost in modesty, perhaps in pain. "But I can make a decision here. We must claim the Pearl."

"As I understand it, the Pearl did not exist before the Lords of Quarzhasaat conceived it, before someone discovered the legend, before the Sorcerer Adventurers came."

"But it exists now," said Oone. "Lady Varadia, would you give the Pearl to me?"

"Willingly," said the Holy Girl, and she ran up the remaining steps and took the globe from the plinth and threw it to the ground so that shards of milky glass shattered everywhere, mingling with the bones and the armour of the Pearl Warrior, and she took the Pearl in one hand, as an ordinary child might grasp a lost ball. And she tossed it from palm to palm in delight, fearing it no longer. "It is very beautiful. No wonder they sought it."

"They made it, then they used it to trap you." Oone reached up and caught it as Varadia threw it to her. "What a shame those who could conceive of such beauty would go to such evil lengths to own it . . ." She frowned, looking about her in sudden concern.

The light was fading in the Court of the Pearl.

From all around them came an appalling noise, an anguished groaning; a great creaking and keening, a tortured screaming, as if all the tormented souls in all the multiverse had suddenly given voice.

It pierced their brains. They covered their ears. They stared in terror, watching as the floor of the Court erupted and undulated, as the ivory walls with all their wonderful mosaics and carvings began to rot before their eyes, crumbling and falling, like the fabric in a tomb suddenly exposed to daylight.

And then, over all the other noises, they heard the laughter.

It was sweet laughter. It was the unaffected laughter of a child.

It was the laughter of a freed spirit. It was Varadia's.

"It is dissolving at last. It is all dissolving! Oh, my friends, I am a slave no longer!"

Through all the falling filthy stuff, through all the decay and dissolution which tumbled upon them, through the destroyed carcass of the Fortress of the Pearl, Oone came towards them. She was hasty but she was careful. She held one of Varadia's hands.

"Not yet! Too soon! We could all dissolve in this!"

She made Elric take the child's hand and they led her through the crashing, shrieking darkness, out of the chamber, down through the swaying corridors, out past the courtyards where fountains now gushed detritus and where the very walls were constructed of putrefying flesh which began to rot to nothing even as they went by. Then Oone made them run, until the final gateway lay ahead of them.

They reached the causeway and the marble road. There was a bridge ahead of them. Oone almost dragged the other two towards it, running as fast as she could possibly run, with the Fortress of the Pearl tumbling into nothing, roaring like a dying beast as it did so.

The bridge seemed infinite. Elric could not see to the further side. But at length Oone stopped running and allowed them to walk, for they had reached a gateway.

The gateway was carved of red sandstone. It was decorated with geometrical tiles and pictures of gazelles, leopards and wild camels. It had an almost prosaic appearance after so many monumental doorways, yet Elric felt some trepidation in passing through it.

"I am afraid, Oone," he said.

"You fear mortality, I think." She pressed on. "You have great courage, Prince Elric. Make use of it now, I beg you."

He quelled his terrors. His grip on the child's hand was firm and reassuring.

"We go home, do we not?" said the Holy Girl. "What is it you do not want to find there, Prince Elric?"

He smiled down at her, grateful for her question. "Nothing much, Lady Varadia. Perhaps nothing more than myself."

They stepped together into the gateway.

Chapter Three

Celebrations at the Silver Flower Oasis

Waking beside the still-sleeping child, Elric was surprised to feel so refreshed. The dreamwand, which had helped them attain substance in the Dream Realm, was still hooked over their clasped hands and, looking across the child, he saw Oone beginning to stir.

"You have failed, then?"

It was Raik Na Seem's voice, full of resigned sadness.

"What?" Oone glanced at Varadia. Even as they watched her skin began to shine with ordinary health and her eyes opened to see her anxious father staring down at her. She smiled. It was the easy, unaffected smile with which Oone and Elric were already familiar.

The First Elder of the Bauradi Clan began to weep. He wept as the seneschal of the Court of the Pearl had wept; he wept in relief and he wept in joy. He took up his daughter in his arms and he could not speak for the gladness in his heart. All he could do was reach one hand out towards his friends, the man and the woman who had entered the Dream Realm to free his child's spirit, where it had fled to escape the evil of Lord Gho's hirelings.

They touched his hand and they left the Bronze Tent. They

walked together into the desert and then they stood face to face, staring into one another's eyes.

"We have a dream in common now," said Elric. His voice was gentle, full of affection. "I think the memory will be a good one, Lady Oone."

She reached to hold his face in her hands. "You are wise, Prince Elric, and you are courageous, but there is a certain kind of ordinary experience you lack. I hope that you are successful in finding it."

"That is why I wander this world, my lady, and leave my cousin Yyrkoon as regent on the Ruby Throne. I am aware of more than one deficiency."

"I am glad we dreamed together," she said.

"You lost your true love, I think," Elric told her. "I am glad if I helped you ease the pain of that parting."

She was baffled for a moment, then her brow cleared. "You speak of Alnac Kreb? I was fond of him, my lord, but he was more a brother to me than a lover."

Elric became embarrassed. "Forgive my presumption, Lady Oone."

She looked up into the sky. The Blood Moon had not yet waned. It cast its red rays onto the sand, onto the gleaming bronze of the tent where Raik Na Seem welcomed his daughter back to him. "I do not love easily in the way you mean." Her voice was significant. She sighed. "Do you still plan to return to Melniboné and your betrothed?"

"I must," he said. "I love her. And my duty lies in Imrryr."

"Sweet duty!" Her tone was sarcastic and she took a step or two away from him, her head bowed, her hand on her belt. She kicked at dust the colour of old blood.

Elric had disciplined himself against his heart's pain for too long. He could only stand and wait until she walked back to him. And now she was smiling. "Well, Prince Elric, would you join the dreamthieves and make this your living for a while?"

Elric shook his head. "It is a calling which requires too much of me, my lady. Yet I am grateful for what this adventure has taught me, both about myself and about the world of dreams. I still understand only a little of it. I am still not wholly sure where we traveled or what we encountered. I do not know how much in the Dream Realm was the Lady Varadia's creation and how much was yours. It was as if I witnessed a battle of inventors! And did I contribute? I do not know."

"Oh, without you, believe me, Prince Elric, I think I would have failed. You have seen so much of other worlds! And you have read more. It does not do to analyze too closely the creatures and places one encounters in the Dream Realm, but be assured that you made your contribution. More, perhaps, than you'll ever know."

"Can reality ever be made from the fabric of those dreams?" he wondered.

"There was an adventurer of the Young Kingdoms called Earl Aubec," she said. "He knew how potent a creator of reality the human mind can be. Some say he and his kind helped make the world of the Young Kingdoms."

Elric nodded. "I've heard that legend. But I think it is as substantial as the story of Chamog Borm, my lady."

"You must think what you wish." She turned away from him to look at the Bronze Tent. The old man and his daughter were emerging. From somewhere within the tent drums began to beat. There came a wonderful chanting, a dozen melodies linked together, interwoven. Slowly all the people who had remained at the Bronze Tent keeping vigil over the body of the Holy Girl began to gather around Raik Na Seem and Varadia. Their songs were songs of immense joy. Their voices filled the desert with the most gorgeous life and made even the distant mountains echo.

Oone linked her arm in Elric's, a gesture of comradeship, of reconciliation. "Come," she said, "let us join the celebrations."

They had only walked a few more paces before they were lifted on the shoulders of the crowd and soon they were borne, laughing and infected by the general joyousness, over the desert towards the Silver Flower Oasis.

The celebrations began at once, as if the Bauradim and all the other desert clans had been preparing for this moment. Every kind of delicious food was prepared until the air was rich with an enormous variety of mouth-watering smells and it seemed all the great spice warehouses of the world had been made to release their contents. Cooking fires blazed everywhere, as did great brands and lamps and candles, and from out of the Kashbeh Moulor Ka Riiz, overlooking the great oasis, rode the Aloum'rit guardians in all the glory of their ancient armour, their red-gold helmets and breastplates, their weapons of bronze and brass and steel. They had huge forked beards and massive turbans wound around the spikes of their helms. They wore surcoats of elaborate brocade and cloth-of-silver and their high boots were embroidered with designs almost as intricate as those on their shirts. They were proud, good-humoured men who rode at the sides of their wives, who were also armoured and carried bows and slender spears. All had soon mingled with the enormous crowd who had erected a large platform and placed a carved chair upon it and sat the smiling Varadia in the chair so that all could see the Holy Girl of the Bauradim restored to her clan, bringing back their history, their pride and their future.

Raik Na Seem still wept. Whenever he saw Oone and Elric he grasped them and pulled them to him, thanking them, telling them, as best he could, what it meant to him to have such friends, such saviours, such heroes.

"Your names will be remembered by the Bauradim for all time. And whatever favour you shall ask of us, so long as it be honourable, as we know it shall, then we shall grant it to you. If you are in danger ten thousand miles away you will send a message to the Bauradim and they will come to your aid. Meanwhile you must know that you have freed the spirit of a good-hearted child from dark captivity."

"And that is our reward," said Oone, smiling.

"Our wealth is yours," said the old man.

"We have no need of wealth," Oone told him. "We have discovered better resources, I think."

Elric agreed with her. "Besides, there is a man in Quarzhasaat who has promised me half an empire if I but do him a small service."

Oone understood Elric's reference and laughed.

Raik Na Seem was a little disturbed. "You go to Quarzhasaat? You still have business there?"

"Aye," said Elric. "There is a boy who is anxiously awaiting my return."

"But you have time to celebrate with us, to talk with us, to feast with myself and Varadia? You have scarcely exchanged a word with the child!"

"I think we know her pretty well," said Elric. "Enough to think highly of her. She is indeed the greatest treasure of the Bauradim, my lord."

"You were able to hold conversations in that gloomy realm where she was held prisoner?"

Elric thought to enlighten the First Elder, but Oone was quick to interrupt, so familiar was she with such questions.

"Some, my lord. We were impressed by her intelligence and her courage."

Raik Na Seem's brow furrowed as another thought occurred to him. "My son," he said to Elric, "were you able to sustain yourself in that realm without pain?"

"Without pain, aye," said Elric. Then he realized what had been said. For the first time he understood what good had come about from his adventure. "Aye, sir. There are benefits to assisting a dreamthief. Great benefits which I had not until now appreciated!"

With relish now Elric joined in the feasting, treasuring these hours with Oone, the Bauradim and all the other nomad clans. Again he felt as if he had come home, so welcoming were the people, and he wished that he could spend his life here, learning their ways, their philosophies and enjoying their pastimes.

Later, as he lay beneath a great date-palm, rolling one of the silver flowers between his fingers, he looked up at Oone who sat beside him and he said: "Of all the temptations I faced in the Dream Realm, this temptation is perhaps the greatest, Oone. This is simple reality and I am reluctant to leave it. And you."

"We have no further destiny together, I think." She sighed. "Not in this life, at any rate, or this world, perhaps. You shall be first a legend, then there will be none left to remember you."

"My friends will all die? I shall be alone?"

"I believe so. While you serve Chaos."

"I serve myself and my people."

"If you would believe that, Elric, you must do more to achieve it. You have created a little reality and perhaps will create a little more. But Chaos cannot be a friend without it betraying you. In the end, we have only ourselves to look to. No cause, no force, no challenge, will ever replace that truth . . ."

"It is to be myself that I travel as I do, Lady Oone," he reminded her. He looked out over the desert, over the tranquil waters of the oasis. He breathed in the cool, scented desert air.

"And you will leave here soon?" she asked.

"Tomorrow," he said. "I must. But I am curious to know what reality I have created."

"Oh, I think a dream or two has come true," she said cryptically, kissing him on the cheek. "And another will come true soon enough."

He did not pursue the question, for she had taken the great pearl from the pouch at her belt and held it out to him.

"It exists! It was not the chimera we believed it to be! You still have it!"

"It is for you," she said. "Use it how you will. That is what brought you here to the Silver Flower Oasis. It is what brought you to me. I think I will not trade it at the Dream Market. I would like you to have it. I think it might be yours by right, Elric. Be that as it may, the Holy Girl gave it to me and now I give it to you. It is what Alnac Kreb died because of, what all those assassins died to possess . . ."

"I thought you said that the Pearl did not exist before the Sorcerer Assassins sought to find it."

"That is true. But it exists now. Here it is. The Pearl at the Heart of the World. The Great Pearl of legend. Have you no use for it?"

"You must explain to me . . ." he began, but she cut him short.

"Ask me not how dreams take substance, Prince Elric. That is a question that concerns philosophers in all ages and all places. I ask you again—have you no use for it?"

He hesitated, then reached out to take the lovely thing. He held it in his two palms, rolling it back and forth. He wondered at its richness, its pale beauty. "Aye," he said, "I think I have a use for it."

When he had placed the jewel in his own pouch, Oone said very softly: "I think it is an evil thing, that pearl."

He agreed with her. "I think so, too, but sometimes evil can be used to counter evil."

"I cannot accept that argument." She seemed troubled.

"I know," he said. "You have already said as much." And then it was his turn to reach towards her and kiss her tenderly upon the lips. "Fate is cruel, Oone. It would be better if it provided us with one unaltering path. Instead it forces us to make choices, never to know if those choices were for the best."

"We are mortals," she said with a shrug. "That is our particular doom."

She stroked his forehead. "You have a troubled mind, my lord. I think I will steal a few of the smaller dreams which make you uneasy."

"Can you steal pain, Oone, and turn it into something to sell in your market?"

"Oh, frequently," she said.

She took his head in her lap and began to massage his temples. Her look was tender.

He said sleepily: "I cannot betray Cymoril. I cannot . . ."

"I ask no more of you but that you sleep," she said. "One day you will have much to regret and you will know real remorse. Until then, I can take away a little of what is unimportant."

"Unimportant?" His voice was slurred as she gradually stroked him into slumber.

"To you, I think, my lord. Though not to me . . ."

And the dreamthief began to sing. She sang a lullaby. She sang of a sickly child and a grieving father. She sang of happiness found in simple things.

And Elric slept. And as he slept the dreamthief performed her easy magic and took away just a few of the half-forgotten memories which had spoiled his nights in the past and might spoil those yet to come.

And when Elric awoke that next morning, it was with a light heart and an easy conscience, only the faintest memories of his adventures in the Dream Realm, a continuing affection for Oone and a determination to reach Quarzhasaat as soon as possible and take to Lord Gho what Lord Gho most desired in all the world.

His farewells to the people of the Bauradim were sincere and his sadness in parting was reciprocated. They begged him to return, to join them on their travels, to hunt with them as Rackhir, his friend, had once hunted.

"I will try to return to you one day," he said. "But first I have more than one oath to fulfill."

A nervous boy brought him his great black battle-blade. As he buckled on Stormbringer the sword seemed to moan with considerable satisfaction at being reunited with him.

It was Varadia, clasping his hands and kissing them, who gave him the blessing of her clan. It was Raik Na Seem who told him that he was now Varadia's brother, his own son, and then Oone the Dreamthief stepped forward. She had decided to remain a while as a guest of the Bauradim.

"Farewell, Elric. I hope that we may meet again. In better circumstances."

He was amused. "Better circumstances?"

"For me, at any rate." She grinned, contemptuously tapping the pommel of his runesword. "And I wish you well with your attempts to become that thing's master."

"I am its master now, I think," he said.

She shrugged. "I'll ride with you a little way up the Red Road."

"I would welcome your company, my lady."

Side by side, as they had done in the Dream Realm, Elric and Oone rode together. And, although he did not remember how he had felt before, Elric knew a certain resonance of recognition, as if he had found his soul's satisfaction, so that it was with sadness that eventually he parted from her to go on alone towards Quarzhasaat.

"Farewell, good friend. I'll remember how you defeated the Pearl Warrior in the Fortress of the Pearl. That is one memory I do not think will ever fade."

"I am flattered." There was a touch of melancholy irony in her voice. "Farewell, Prince Elric. I trust you will find all that you need and that you will know peace when you return to Melniboné."

"It is my firm intention, madam." A wave to her, not wishing to prolong the sadness, and he spurred his horse forward.

With eyes which refused to weep she watched him ride away up the long Red Road to Quarzhasaat.

Chapter Four

Certain Matters Resolved in Quarzhasaat

When Elric of Melniboné rode into Quarzhasaat he was limp in his saddle, hardly controlling his horse at all, and the people who gathered around him asked him if he were ill, while some feared that he brought plague to their beautiful city and would have driven him out at once.

The albino lifted his strange head long enough to gasp out the name of his patron, Lord Gho Fhaazi, and to say that all he lacked was a certain elixir which that nobleman possessed. "I must have that elixir," he told them, "or I will be dead before I have accomplished my task . . ."

The old towers and minarets of Quarzhasaat were lovely in the fading rays of a huge red sun and there was a certain peace about the city which comes when the day's business is done and before it begins to take its pleasures.

A rich water-merchant, anxious to find favour with one who might soon be elected to the Council, personally led Elric's horse through the elegant alleys and impressive avenues until they came to the great palace, all golds and faded greens, of Lord Gho Fhaazi.

The merchant was rewarded by a steward's promise to mention his name to the nobleman and Elric, now mumbling and whimpering to himself, sometimes groaning a little and licking anxious lips, passed through into the lovely gardens surrounding the main palace.

Lord Gho himself came to meet the albino. He was laughing heartily at the sight of Elric in such poor condition.

"Greetings, greetings, Elric of Nadsokor! Greetings, white-faced clown-thief. Oh, you are not so proud today! You were profligate with the elixir I gave you and now you return to beg for more—in worse condition than when you first arrived here!"

"The boy . . ." whispered Elric, as servants helped him from the horse. His arms hung limply as they carried him on their shoulders. "Does he live?"

"In better health than yourself, sir!" Lord Gho Fhaazi's pale green eyes were full of exquisite malice. "And in perfect safety. You were most adamant about that before you set off. And I am a man of my word." The politician stroked the ringlets of his oily beard and chuckled to himself. "And you, Sir Thief, do you also keep your word?"

"To the letter," muttered the albino. His red eyes rolled back in his head and it appeared for a second that he died. Then he turned a painful gaze in Lord Gho's direction. "Will you give me the antidote and all that you've promised? The water? The wealth? The boy?"

"No doubt, no doubt. But you have a poor bargaining position at present, thief. What of the Pearl? Did you find it? Or are you here to report failure?"

"I found it. And I have it hidden," said Elric. "The elixir has . . ."

"Yes, yes. I know what the elixir does. You must have a fundamentally strong constitution even to be able to speak by now." The Quarzhasaati supervised the men and women who carried Elric into the cool interior of the palace and placed him on great tasseled cushions of scarlet and blue velvet and gave him water to drink and food to eat.

"The craving grows worse, does it not?" Lord Gho took considerable pleasure at Elric's discomfort. "The elixir must feed off you, just as you appear to feed off it. You are cunning, eh, Sir Thief. You have hidden the Pearl, you say? Do you not trust me? I am a nobleman of the greatest city in the world!"

Elric sprawled on the cushions, all dusty from his long ride, and wiped his hands slowly on a cloth. "The antidote, my lord . . ."

"You know I shall not let you have the antidote until the Pearl is in my hands . . ." Lord Gho was expansively condescending as he looked down on his victim. "To tell you the truth, thief, I had not expected you to be as coherent as you are! Would you care for another draft of my elixir?"

"Bring it if you will."

Elric appeared to be careless, but Lord Gho understood how desperate he must actually be. He turned to give instructions to his slaves.

Then Elric said: "But bring the boy. Bring the boy so that I may see he has come to no harm and hear from his own lips what has taken place while I have been gone . . ."

"It's a small request. Very well." Lord Gho Fhaazi signed to a slave. "Bring the boy Anigh."

The nobleman crossed to a great chair, placed on a small dais between brocaded awnings, and slumped himself down in it while they waited. "I had scarcely expected you to survive the journey, Sir Thief, let alone succeed in finding the Pearl. Our Sorcerer Adventurers are the bravest, most skillful of warriors, trained in all the arts of sorcery and incantation. Yet those I sent, and all their brothers, failed! Oh, this is a happy day for me. I will revive you, I promise, so that you can tell me all that happened. What of the Bauradim? Did you kill many? You will recount everything so that when I present the Pearl to obtain my position I can give the story that goes with it. This will add to its value, you see. When I am elected, I shall be asked to retell such a story many times, I am sure. The Council will be so envious . . ." He licked his painted red lips. "Did you have to kill that child? What was the first thing you witnessed, for instance when you reached the Silver Flower Oasis?"

"A funeral, as I recall . . ." Elric showed a little more animation. "Aye, that was it."

Two guards brought in a wriggling boy who did not seem greatly overjoyed when he saw Elric stretched upon the cushions. "Oh, master! You are more wretched than before." He stopped his struggling and tried to hide his disappointment. There were no marks of torture on him. He seemed not to have been harmed.

"Are you well, Anigh?"

"Aye. My chief problem has been in passing the time. Occasionally his lordship there has come to tell me what he will do if you fail to bring back the Pearl, but I have read such things on the walls of the lunatic stockades and they are nothing new to me."

Lord Gho scowled. "Be careful, boy . . ."

"You must have returned with the Pearl," said Anigh, glancing around him. "That is so, eh, my lord? Or you would not be here?" He was a little more relieved. "Are we to go now?"

"Not yet!" growled Lord Gho.

"The antidote," said Elric. "Do you have it here?"

"You are too impatient, Sir Thief. And your cunning is matched by mine." Lord Gho giggled and raised an admonishing finger. "I must have some proof that you possess the Pearl. Would you give me your sword as surety, perhaps? You are, after all, too weak to wield it. It is of no further use to you." He reached a greedy hand towards the albino's hip and Elric made a feeble movement away from him.

"Come, come, Sir Thief. Be not afraid of me. We are partners in this. Where is the Pearl? The Council congregates this evening at the Great Meeting House. If I can bring them the Pearl then . . . Oh, I shall be powerful by tonight!"

"The worm is so proud to be king of the dunghill," said Elric.

"Do not anger him, master!" cried Anigh in alarm. "You have still to learn where he hides the antidote!"

"I must have the Pearl!" Lord Gho grew petulant in his impatience. "Where have you hidden it, thief? In the desert? Somewhere in the city?"

Slowly Elric raised his body on the cushions. "The Pearl was a dream," he said. "It took your killers to make it real."

Lord Gho Fhaazi frowned, scratching at his whitened forehead and showing further nervousness. He looked suspiciously at Elric. "If you would have more elixir, you had best not insult me, thief. Nor play any game. The boy could die in an instant, and you with him, and I would be in no worse a position."

"But you would better yourself, my lord, I think. With the price of a place on the Council, I think." Elric seemed to gather strength and now he was upright on the luxurious velvet, signing for the boy to come towards him. The guards looked questioningly at their master, but he shrugged. Anigh walked, his brow furrowed with curiosity, towards the albino. "You are greedy, my lord, I think. You would own the whole of your world. This pathetic monument to your race's ruined pride!"

Lord Gho glared at him. "Thief, if you would recover yourself, if you would take the antidote to make you free of the drug I gave you, you will be more polite to me . . ."

"Ah, yes," said Elric thoughtfully, reaching into his jerkin. He pulled out a leather pouch. "The elixir which was to make me your slave!" He smiled. He opened the pouch.

Onto his extended palm now rolled the jewel for which Gho Fhaazi had offered half his fortune, for which he had sent a hundred men to their deaths, for which he had been prepared to abduct and kill one child and imprison another.

The Quarzhasaati began to tremble. His painted eyes rounded. He gasped and bent forward, almost fainting.

"It is true," he said. "You have found the Pearl at the Heart of the World . . ."

"Merely a gift from a friend," said Elric. The Pearl still displayed on his hand, he rose to his feet and put a protective arm around the boy. "In obtaining it I found that my body lost its demand for the elixir and therefore has no need for your antidote, Lord Gho."

Lord Gho hardly heard him. His eyes were fixed on the great pearl. "It is monstrous big . . . Even larger than I had heard . . . It is real. I can see it is real. The colour . . . Ah . . ." And he stretched towards it.

Elric drew his hand back. Lord Gho frowned and looked up at the albino with eyes that were hot with greed. "Did she die? Was it, as some said, in her body?"

Anigh shivered at Elric's side.

Full of loathing, Elric's voice was still soft. "No-one died at my hand who was not already dead. As you are already dead, my lord. It was your funeral I witnessed at the Silver Flower Oasis. I am now the agent of the Bauradi prophecy. I am to avenge all the grief you brought to them and their Holy Child."

"What! The others all sent their soldiers, too! The entire Council and half the candidates had sects of Sorcerer Adventurers seeking the Pearl. Every one. Most of these warriors failed or were killed. Or were executed for their failure. You killed no-one, you said. Well, so there's no blood on our hands, eh? All's for the best. I'll give you what I promised, Sir Thief . . ."

Trembling with lust Lord Gho extended his plump hand to take the Pearl.

Elric smiled and to Anigh's astonishment let the nobleman lift the Pearl from his palm.

Breathing heavily, Lord Gho caressed his prize. "Oh, it is lovely. Oh, it is so good . . ."

Elric spoke again, just as levelly as before. "And our reward, Lord Gho?"

"What?" He looked up absently. "Why yes, of course. Your lives. You no longer need the antidote, you say. Excellent. So you may go."

"I believed you also offered me a large fortune. All manner of wealth. Great stature amongst the lords of Quarzhasaat?"

Lord Gho dismissed this. "Nonsense. The antidote would have sufficed. You are not the type of person to enjoy such things. Breeding is required if they are to be used wisely and with appropriate discretion. No, no, I will let you and the boy go . . ."

"You will not keep your original bargain, my lord?"

"There was talk—but no bargain. The only bargain involved the boy's freedom and the antidote to the elixir. You were mistaken."

"You remember nothing of your promises . . . ?"

"Promises? Certainly not." The ringleted beard and hair quivered.

" . . . and mine?"

"No, no. You are irritating me." His eyes were still upon the Pearl.

He fondled it as another might fondle a beloved child. "Go, sir. While I am still pleased with you."

"I have many oaths to fulfill," said Elric, "and I do not break my word."

Lord Gho looked up, his expression hardening. "Very well. I am tired of this. By this evening I shall be a member of the Six and One Other. By threatening me you threaten the Council. You are therefore enemies of Quarzhasaat. You are traitors to the empire and must be disposed of accordingly! Guards!"

"Oh, you are a foolish fellow," said Elric. Then Anigh cried out, for unlike Lord Gho, he had not forgotten the power of the Black Sword.

"Do as he demands, Lord Gho!" shouted Anigh, fearing as much for himself as the nobleman. "I beg you, great lord! Do what he says!"

"This is not how a member of the Council is addressed." Lord Gho's tone was that of a baffled, reasonable individual. "Guards—take them from my hall at once. Have them strangled or cut their throats—I care not . . ."

The guards knew nothing of the runesword. They saw only a slender man who might have been a leper and they saw a young, defenseless boy. They grinned, as if at a joke of their master's, and they drew their blades, advancing almost casually.

Elric pressed Anigh behind him. His hand went to Stormbringer's hilt. "You are unwise to do this," he told the guards. "I have no particular wish to kill you."

Behind the soldiers one of the servants opened the door and slipped out into the corridor. Elric watched her go. "Best copy her," he said. "She has some idea, I think, of what will happen if you threaten us further . . ."

The guards laughed openly now. "This is a madman," said one. "Lord Gho is well rid of him!"

They came at Elric in a rush and then the runesword was howling in the cool air of that luxurious chamber—howling like a hungry wolf freed from a cage and longing only to kill and to feed.

Elric felt the power surge through him as the blade took the first guard, splitting him from crown to breastbone. The other tried to change direction from attack to flight, stumbled forward and was impaled on the blade's tip, his eyes horrified as he felt his soul being drawn from him into the runesword.

Lord Gho cringed in his great chair, too frightened to move. In one hand he clutched the great pearl. His other hand was held palm outwards as if he hoped to ward off Elric's blow.

But the albino, strengthened by his borrowed energy, sheathed the black blade and took five quick strides across the hall to mount the dais and stare down into Lord Gho's face which twisted in terror.

"Take the Pearl back. For my life . . ." whispered the Quarzhasaati. "For my life, thief . . ."

Elric accepted the offered jewel, but he did not move. He reached into the pouch at his belt and drew forth a flask of the elixir Lord Gho had given him. "Would you care for something to help you wash it down?"

Lord Gho trembled. Beneath the chalky substance on his skin his face had gone still paler. "I do not understand you, thief."

"I want you to eat the Pearl, my lord. If you can swallow it and live, well, it will be clear that the prophecy of your death was premature."

"Swallow it? It is too large. I could hardly get it into my mouth!" Lord Gho sniggered, hoping that the albino joked.

"No, my lord. I think you can. And I think you can swallow it. After all, how else would it have got into the body of a child?"

"It was—they say it was a—a dream . . ."

"Aye. Perhaps you can swallow a dream. Perhaps you can enter the Dream Realm and so escape your fate. You must try, my lord, or else my runesword drinks your soul. Which would you prefer?"

"Oh, Elric. Spare me. This is not fair. We made a bargain."

"Open your mouth, Lord Gho. Who knows if the Pearl might shrink or your throat expand like a snake's? A snake could easily swallow the Pearl, my lord. And you, surely, are superior to a snake?"

Anigh whispered from the window where he had been staring with studied gaze, unwilling to look upon a vengeance he regarded as just but distasteful. "The servant, Lord Elric. She has alarmed the city."

For a second a desperate hope came into Lord Gho's green eyes and then faded as Elric placed the flask on the arm of the great chair and drew the runesword part way from its scabbard. "Your soul will help me fight those new soldiers, Lord Gho."

Slowly, weeping and whimpering, the great Lord of Quarzhasaat began to open his mouth.

"Here is the Pearl again, my lord. Put it in. Do your best, my lord. You have some chance of life this way."

Lord Gho's hand shook. But eventually he began to force the lovely jewel between his reddened lips. Elric took the stopper from the elixir and poured some of the liquid into the nobleman's distorted cheeks. "Now swallow, Lord Gho. Swallow the Pearl you would have slain a child to own! And then I will tell you who I am . . ."

A few minutes later the doors crashed inward and Elric recognized the tattooed face of Manag Iss, leader of the Yellow Sect and kinsman to the Lady Iss. Manag Iss looked from Elric to the distorted features of Lord Gho. The nobleman had failed completely to swallow the Pearl.

Manag Iss shuddered. "Elric. I heard that you had returned. They said you were close to death. Clearly this was a trick to deceive Lord Gho."

"Aye," said Elric. "I had this boy to free."

Manag Iss gestured with his own drawn sword. "You found the Pearl?"

"I found it."

"My Lady Iss sent me to offer you anything you desired for it."

Elric smiled. "Tell her I shall be at the Council Meeting House in half-an-hour. I shall bring the Pearl with me."

"But the others will be there. She wishes to trade privately."

"Would it not be wise to auction so valuable a thing?" said Elric.

Manag Iss sheathed his sword and smiled a little. "You're a cunning one. I do not think they know how cunning you are. Nor who you are. I have yet to tell them that particular speculation."

"Oh, you may tell them what I have just told Lord Gho. That I am the hereditary emperor of Melniboné," said Elric casually. "For that is the truth of the matter. My empire has survived rather more successfully than yours, I think."

"That could incense them. I am willing to be your friend, Melnibonéan.

"Thanks, Manag Iss, but I need no more friends from Quarzhasaat. Please do as I say."

Manag Iss looked at the slaughtered guards, at the dead Lord Gho, who had turned a strange colour, at the nervous boy, and he saluted Elric.

"The Meeting House in half-an-hour, Emperor of Melniboné." He turned on his heel and left the chamber.

After issuing certain specific instructions to Anigh concerning travel and the products of Kwan, Elric went out into the courtyard. The sun had set and there were brands burning all over Quarzhasaat as if the city were expecting an attack.

Lord Gho's house was empty of servants. Elric went to the stables and found his horse and his saddle. He dressed the Bauradi stallion, carefully placing a heavy bundle over the pommel, then he had mounted and was riding through the streets, seeking the Meeting House where Anigh had told him it would be.

The city was unnaturally silent. Clearly some order had been given to uphold a curfew, for there was not even a city guard on the streets.

Elric rode at an easy canter along the wide Avenue of Military Success, along the Boulevard of Ancient Accomplishment and half-a-dozen other grandiosely named thoroughfares until he saw the long low building ahead of him which, in its simplicity, could only be the seat of Quarzhasaati power.

The albino paused. At his side the black runesword crooned a little, almost demanding a further letting of blood.

"You must be patient," said Elric. "Could be there will be no need for battle."

He thought he saw shadows moving in the trees and shrubberies around the Meeting House but he paid them no attention. He did not care what they plotted or who spied on him. He had a mission to fulfill.

At last he had reached the doors of the building and was not surprised to find them standing open. He dismounted, threw the bundle over his shoulder and walked heavily into a large, plain room, without decoration or ostentation, in which were placed seven tall-backed chairs and a lime-washed oak table. Standing in a semi-circle at one end of the table were six robed figures wearing veils not unlike certain sects of the Sorcerer Adventurers. The seventh figure wore a tall, conical hat which completely covered the face. It was this figure who spoke. Elric was not unsurprised to hear a woman's tones.

"I am the Other," she said. "I believe you have brought us a treasure to add to the glory of Quarzhasaat."

"If you believe this treasure to add to your glory then my journey has not been fruitless," said Elric. He dropped the bundle to the ground. "Did Manag Iss tell you all I asked him to tell you?"

One of the Councilors stirred and said, almost as an oath: "That you are the progeny of sunken Melniboné, aye!"

"Melniboné is not sunken. Nor does she cut herself off from the world's realities quite as much as do you." Elric was contemptuous. "You challenged our power long ago, and defeated yourselves by your own folly. Now through your greed you have brought me back to Quarzhasaat when I would as readily have passed through your city unnoticed."

"Do you accuse us!" A veiled woman was outraged. "You who have caused us so much trouble? You, who are of the blood of that degenerate unhuman race which couples with beasts for its pleasure and produces—" she pointed at Elric—"the likes of you!"

Elric was unmoved. "Did Manag Iss tell you to be wary of me?" he asked quietly.

"He said you had the Pearl and that you had a sorcerous sword. But he also said you were alone." The Other cleared her throat. "He said you brought the Pearl at the Heart of the World."

"I have brought it and that which contains it," said Elric. He bent down and tugged the velvet free of his bundle to reveal the corpse of

Lord Gho Fhaazi, his face still contorted, the great lump in his throat making it seem as if he had an enormously enlarged adam's apple. "Here is the one who first commissioned me to find the Pearl."

"We heard you had murdered him," said the Other with disapproval. "But that would be a normal enough action for a Melnibonéan."

Elric did not rise to this. "The Pearl is in Lord Gho Fhaazi's gullet. Would you have me cut it out for you, my nobles?"

He saw at least one of them shudder and he smiled. "You commission assassins to kill, to torture, to kidnap and to perform all other forms of evil in your name, but you would not see a little spilled blood? I gave Lord Gho a choice. He took this one. He talked so much and ate and drank so copiously I thought he might well have succeeded in getting the Pearl into his stomach. But he gagged a little and I fear that was the end of him."

"You are a cruel rogue!" One of the men came forward to look at his would-be colleague. "Aye, that's Gho. His colour has improved, I'd say."

This jest did not meet with the leader's approval.

"We are to bid for a corpse, then?"

"Unless you wish to cut the Pearl free, aye."

"Manag Iss," said one of the veiled women, lifting her head. "Step out, will you, sir?"

The Sorcerer Adventurer emerged from a door at the back of the hall. He looked at Elric almost apologetically. His hand went to his knife.

"We would not have a Melnibonéan spill more Quarzhasaati blood," said the Other. "Manag Iss will cut the Pearl free."

The leader of the Yellow Sect drew a deep breath and then approached the corpse. Swiftly he did what he had been ordered to do. Blood poured down his arm as he held up the Pearl at the Heart of the World.

The Council was impressed. Several of the members gasped and they murmured amongst themselves. Elric believed they had suspected him of lying to them, since lies and intrigues were second nature to them.

"Hold it high, Manag Iss," said the albino. "It is this that you all desired so greedily that you were prepared to pay for it with what was left of your honour."

"Be careful, sir!" cried the Other. "We are patient with you now. Name your price and then begone."

Elric laughed. It was not pleasant laughter. It was Melnibonéan laughter. At that moment he was a pure denizen of the Dragon Isle. "Very well," he said, "I desire this city. Not its citizens, not any of its treasure, nor its animals nor even its water. I would let you leave with everything you can carry. I desire only the city itself. It is, you see, mine by hereditary right."

"What? This is nonsense. How could we agree?"

"You must agree," said Elric, "or you must fight me."

"Fight you? There is only one of you."

"There is no question of it," said another Councilor. "He is mad. He must be put down like a crazed dog. Manag Iss, call in your brothers and their men."

"I do not believe it is advisable, cousin," said Manag Iss, clearly addressing Lady Iss. "I think it would be wise to parley."

"What? Have you turned coward? Has this rogue an army with him?"

Manag Iss rubbed at his nose. "My lady . . ."

"Call in your brothers, Manag Iss!"

The captain of the Yellow Sect scratched at one silk-clad arm and he frowned. "Prince Elric, I understand that you force us to a challenge. But we have not threatened you. The Council came here honestly to bid for the Pearl . . ."

"Manag Iss, you repeat their lies," said Elric, "and that is not an honourable thing to do. If they meant me no harm, why were you and all your brothers standing by? I saw almost two hundred warriors in the grounds."

"That was a precaution only," said the Other. She turned to her fellow councilors. "I told you I thought it was stupid to summon so many so soon."

Elric said evenly: "Everything you have done, my nobles, has been stupid. You have been cruel, greedy, careless of others' lives and wills. You have been blind, thoughtless, provincial and unimaginative. It seems to me that a government so careless of anything but its own gratification should be at very least replaced. When you have all left the city I will consider electing a governor who will know better how to serve Quarzhasaat. Then, later perhaps, I will let you back into the city . . ."

"Oh, slay him!" cried the Other. "Waste no more time on this. When that's done we can decide amongst ourselves who owns the Pearl."

Elric sighed almost regretfully and said: "Best parley with me now, madam, before I myself lose patience. I shall not, once I have drawn my blade, be a rational and merciful being . . ."

"Slay him!" she insisted. "And have done with it!"

Manag Iss had the face of a man condemned to more than death. "Madam . . ."

She strode forward, her conical hat swaying, and tugged the sword from his scabbard. She raised the blade to behead the albino.

He reached out swiftly. His arm was a striking snake. He gripped her wrist. "No, madam! I am, I swear, giving you fair warning . . ."

Stormbringer murmured at his side and stirred.

She dropped the sword and turned away, nursing her bruised wrist.

Now Manag Iss reached for his fallen blade, making as if to sheathe it, and then, with a subtle movement, tried to bring the weapon up and take Elric in the groin, an expression of resignation crossing his terrified features as the albino, anticipating him, sidestepped and in the same action drew the Black Sword which began to sing its strange demonic song and glow with a terrible black radiance.

Manag Iss gasped as his heart was pierced. The hand that still held the Pearl seemed to stretch out, offering it back to Elric. Then the jewel had rolled from his fingers and rattled on the floor. Three Councilors rushed forward, saw Manag Iss's dying eyes, and stepped backward.

"Now! Now! Now!" cried the Other and, as Elric had expected, from every cranny of the Meeting House, members of the various sects of Sorcerer Adventurers came, their weapons at the ready.

And the albino began to grin his horrible battle-grin, and his red eyes blazed and his face was the skull of Death and his sword was the vengeance of his own people, the vengeance of the Bauradim and all those who had suffered under the injustice of Quarzhasaat over the millennia.

And he offered up the souls he took to his patron Duke of Hell, the powerful Duke Arioch who had grown sleek on many lives dedicated to him by Elric and his black blade.

"Arioch! Arioch! Blood and souls for my lord Arioch!"

Then the true slaughter began.

It was a slaughter to make all other events pale into insignificance. It was a slaughter that would never be forgotten in all the annals of the desert peoples, who would learn of it from those who fled Quarzhasaat that night—flinging themselves into the waterless desert rather than face the white laughing demon on a Bauradi horse who galloped up and down their lovely streets and taught them what the price of complacency and unthinking cruelty could be.

"Arioch! Arioch! Blood and souls!"

They would speak of a white-faced creature from hell whose sword poured with unnatural radiance, whose crimson eyes blazed with hideous rage, who seemed possessed, himself, of some supernatural force, who was no more master of it than were his victims. He killed without mercy, without distinction, without cruelty. He killed as a mad wolf kills. And as he killed, he laughed.

That laughter would never leave Quarzhasaat. It would remain on the wind which came in from the Sighing Desert, in the music of the fountains, the clang of the metal-workers' and jewelers' hammers as they fashioned their wares. And so would the smell of blood remain, together with the memory of slaughter, that terrible loss of life which left the city without a Council and an army.

But never again would Quarzhasaat foster the legend of her own power. Never again would she treat the desert nomads as less than beasts. Never again would she know that self-destructive pride so familiar to all great empires in decline.

And when the slaughter was finished, Elric of Melniboné slumped in his saddle, sheathing a sated Stormbringer, and he gasped with the demon power which still pulsed through him and he took a great pearl from his belt and held it to the rising sun.

"They have paid a fair price now, I think."

He tossed the thing into a gutter where a little dog licked congealing blood.

Above, the vultures, called from a thousand miles around by the prospect of memorable feasting, were beginning to drop like a dark cloud upon the beautiful towers and gardens of Quarzhasaat.

Elric's face held no pride in his achievements as he spurred his horse for the west and the place on the road where he had told Anigh to await them with enough Kwani herbs, water, horses and food to cross the Sighing Desert and seek again the more familiar politics and sorceries of the Young Kingdoms.

He did not look back on the city which, in the name of his ancestors, had been conquered at last.

Chapter Five

An Epilogue at the Waning of the Blood Moon

The celebrations at the Silver Flower Oasis had continued long after the news came of Elric's vengeance-taking on those who would have harmed the Holy Girl of the Bauradim. The news was brought by Quarzhasaatim, fleeing from the city in an action which had no precedent in all their long history.

Oone the Dreamthief, who had stayed at the Silver Flower Oasis longer than was necessary and who was yet reluctant to leave and go about her proper business, learned of Elric's vengeance without joy. The news saddened her, for she had hoped for something else to happen.

"He serves Chaos as I serve Law," she said to herself. "And who is to say which of us is the worse enslaved?" But she sighed and threw herself into the festivities with a force which was less than spontaneous.

The Bauradim and the other nomad clans did not notice, for their own pleasure was intensified. They were rid of a tyrant, of the only thing in the desert lands that they had ever feared.

"The cactus tears our flesh so that we shall be shown where water is," said Raik Na Seem. "Our troubles were great but thanks to you, Oone, and Elric of Melniboné, our troubles turned to triumphs. Soon some of us will visit Quarzhasaat and set out the terms on which we intend to trade in future. There will be a welcome equality about the transaction, I think." He was greatly amused. "But we will wait until the dead are decently eaten."

Varadia took Oone's hand and they walked together beside the pools of the great oasis. The Blood Moon was waning and the silver petals of the flowers were shining brighter still. Soon the Blood Moon must wane and the flowers shed their petals and then it would be time for the people of the desert to go their different ways.

"You loved that white-faced man, did you not?" Varadia asked her friend.

"I hardly knew him, child."

"I knew you both very well, not so long ago." Varadia smiled. "And I am growing rapidly, am I not? You said as much yourself."

Oone was forced to agree. "But there was no hope for it, Varadia. We have such different destinies. And I have scant sympathy for the choices he makes."

"He is driven, that one. He has little in the way of ordinary volition." She pushed a strand of honey-coloured hair away from her dark features.

"Perhaps," said Oone. "Yet some of us can refuse the destiny that the Lords of Law and Chaos set out for us and still survive, still create something which the gods are forbidden to touch."

Varadia was sympathetic. "What we create remains a mystery," she said. "It is still hard for me to understand how I made that pearl, creating the very thing my enemies sought in order to escape them. And then it became real!"

"I have known this to happen," said Oone. "It is those creations that a dreamthief seeks and earns a living from." She laughed. "That pearl would bring me a good wage for a long time if I took it to market."

"How is it that reality is formed from dreams, Oone?"

Oone paused and looked down into the water which reflected the faint pink disc of the moon. "An oyster, threatened by intrusion from without, seeks to isolate that threat by forming the thing around it that eventually becomes a pearl. Sometimes this is how it happens. At other times the will of humanity is so strong, the desire for something so intense, that they will bring into existence that which was thought until then to be impossible. It is not unusual, Varadia, for a dream to be made reality. This knowledge is one of the reasons why my respect for humanity is maintained, in spite of all the cruelties and injustices I witness in my travels."

"I think I understand," said the Holy Girl.

"Oh, you will understand all this very well in time," Oone assured her. "For you are one of those capable of such creation."

A few days later Oone was ready to ride away from the Silver Flower Oasis, towards Elwher and the Unmapped East. Varadia spoke with her for the last time.

"I know you have a further secret," she said to the dreamthief. "Will you not share it with me?"

Oone was astonished. Her regard for the girl's sensitive intelligence increased. "Do you want to talk more about the nature of dreams and reality?"

"I think you carry a child, Oone," said Varadia directly. "Is that not so?"

Oone folded her arms and leaned against her horse. She shook her head in frank good humour. "It is true that all the wisdom of your people is accumulated in you, young woman?"

"The child of one you have loved and who is lost to you?"

"Aye," said Oone. "A daughter, I think. Maybe even a brother and a sister, if the omens are properly interpreted. More than pearls can be conceived in dreams, Varadia."

"And will the father ever know his offspring?" gently asked the Holy Girl.

Oone tried to speak and discovered that she could not. She looked away quickly towards distant Quarzhasaat. Then, after a few moments, she was able to force herself to answer.

"Never," she said.

ELRIC:
THE MAKING OF A SORCERER

ELRIC: THE MAKING OF A SORCERER

A graphic novel

drawn by Walter Simonson

(2004)

Note: The events in this story occur immediately before the opening of the novel *Elric of Melniboné*.

BOOK ONE

THE DREAM OF ONE YEAR:
THE DREAM OF EARTH

BARGAINS IN BLADES

Chapter One

Friends at Court

FOR TEN THOUSAND YEARS the Bright Empire of Melniboné ruled the world—drawing her power from terrifying compacts with the supernatural.

Some say she's invulnerable and will rule for another ten thousand . . .

Some say corruption already comes from within . . .

Some say her doom will fall from outside . . .

But, decidedly, doom is written in her future.

In mysterious realms of the multiverse ruled by the Lords of the Higher Worlds omens and portents proliferate.

Even in the corridors of dreaming Imrryr—capital of the empire—forbidden words are whispered.

They say the empire will live or die according to which of two youths becomes the next emperor.

Meanwhile, plots are hatched and abandoned.

Even the Tower of D'a'rputna, home to the emperor's own kin and court, festers and itches with hitherto unthinkable thoughts.

(Note on style: Make towers very elongated wigwams—cowled rather than roofed. The designs and dominant styles—braided hair or shaven scalp with

single lock—are Plains and forest Indian, as if these early Americans had risen to the skills of building a huge city like this and practising advanced metallurgy. No feathers, as such but some have crowns of metal feathers and so on. The colours are native American. Nothing too obvious, but that's the underlying style.)

Opening shot of Imrryr, the Dreaming City of ancient towers, rising up upon a volcanic mound like a choir of angels, a chord of music made into subtle, complex architecture. The characteristic architecture of Melniboné is tall towers, with a single large room at each level of each tower. They rise above the warehouses and trading sheds of the ancient harbour—itself surrounded by jagged cliffs, the same cliffs which guard the entrances to the sea-maze which leads to the port.

High above all this, in the tallest, perhaps even slenderist, tower, dwells the royal family of Melniboné—Sadric the emperor, Elric his son, a youth, his sister-in-law Ederin, mother to daughter Cymoril (on whom she dotes), son Yyrkoon (whom she mistrusts and dislikes) also certain members of the Tvar family, who are all expert Dragon Masters and are close kin to the emperor.

And there is also a human servant woman, Arisand, whose secret ambitions are not inconsiderable . . .

Arisand moves from floor to floor. We identify some of our characters in their various rooms of the Tower of D'a'rputna, The Emperor's Tower . . . She enters the highest chamber of the tower, flanked by what appear to be great buttresses, where looms the shadow of Sadric, the King Emperor . . . (Ivan the Terrible but with less charm).

But first, a few floors down, we are introduced to Yyrkoon (Olivier as Richard III, Walter? Sans *hump?) in his bed of concubines.*

He is dismissing certain officers of his acquaintance.

YYRKOON: "You may go, but consider carefully what I have said. All our fates depend on this moment!"

On the steps outside this room some soldierly types confer. A slave closes a door on them as they leave. Three captains pause for a moment on the top stair before it curves out of sight.

FIRST CAPTAIN: "Prince Yyrkoon doesn't persuade me. My loyalty's still to Elric."

SECOND CAPTAIN: "Elric's weak. He's sick. How many years can he live? Only sorcery sustains him. Ambitious and aggressive, Yyrkoon will claw us back to our former power."

THIRD CAPTAIN: "He'll defend and expand the old dragon fiefdoms. The Young Kingdoms shall be no more. Each captain shall rule a province!"

SECOND CAPTAIN: "Conquest will revive our blood. Our wives will again bear healthy children. The empire will rule with all her old arrogance . . . yet it's hard to turn against traditional loyalties . . ."

FIRST CAPTAIN: "Treachery doesn't taste too good, eh? Well I hope the rest of you have equally delicate palates. Think long and hard before you betray our rightful lord." *(He's emphatic, almost mocking them . . . He indicates a portrait which hangs below them on the curve*

of the stair, half-seen from above—another Melnibonéan albino . . .)
"Six thousand years ago, the silver kings brought our nation greatness and honour. Some 'silverskins' attract great fortune to the Ruby Throne. Think on that, my captains. Then dare treason . . ."

He throws this behind him as he disappears down the spiral staircase of the tower.

At this moment, Prince Elric, the only rightful inheritor of the mantle of empire, is oblivious to talk of treason.

He's oblivious to any talk. Or action. He's ignorant of where his own body lies. He is elsewhere . . .

The last face we'll see is young Elric, apparently dead, but actually sleeping on his dream couch, soon to be awakened by Doctor Tanglebones.

The black raven Sepiriz settles on Doctor Tanglebones's ungainly shoulder.

DOCTOR TANGLEBONES: "Wake now, my lord. Gently, my lord."

Elric blinks but is fairly blank still. Tanglebones is pleased. He realizes Elric is alive and safe from his dream-quest.

TANGLEBONES: "Aha! Back with us. Safe and sound from the inner landscapes of your common memory . . . You've learned much, though you won't remember how you learned it . . ."

TANGLEBONES: "Ha! Ha! Good lad! Brave, resourceful lad!"

Elric begins to rise on the couch. But he is weak. He falls back onto one elbow. Totally wiped out. Tanglebones, old as he is, has to assist him. A woman's hand extends into the picture, she is holding tongs holding a hanging brazier on which a copper dish cooks herbs into a single sticky sap . . .

TANGLEBONES: "There's never been a better dream-scholar—"

He reaches towards the copper dish . . . rapidly scooping the still-viscous sap into an earthenware cup to which he swiftly adds wine, which steams and bubbles. Stirring it, he hands this to Elric to drink.

TANGLEBONES: "—nor one stranger . . . Drink this down. All of it, mind! It will help you recover your strength."

Elric drinks the potion. He is immediately invigorated, handing the dish back to Tanglebones.

ELRIC: "Ugh! I'll suffer no more such fearful dream-quests, Doctor Tanglebones. Surely there are easier ways of earning my people's wisdom?"

Elric looks out of the picture to where the unseen woman no doubt still stands. He begins to smile.

TANGLEBONES: "None more effective. Rest for a few days. Ready yourself for the long dreams."

TANGLEBONES: "The first is the Dream of One Year. The Dream of Earth. I'll give you a week to prepare . . ."

ELRIC: "You delight to torture me, doctor. It's unseemly in a physician, especially a royal one!"

Elric is as outraged as any student being given an especially hard schedule. He wants to argue. Then that same female hand falls on his arm. He turns to see his beautiful, slender, dark-haired cousin Cymoril come to welcome him back to the world's reality. Again he smiles, immediately courteous, relaxed and friendly.

CYMORIL: "Hush, Elric, you mustn't tease Doctor Tanglebones. I waited with him to be sure you awakened . . ."

ELRIC: "Cousin, you're the best friend I have! For your sake and yours alone . . . I will forgive the old fraud."

He is invigorated by the drink but also rather flattered by Cymoril's attention. He has something of a swagger now. He wants to show his individualism.

ELRIC: "Besides, in all fairness, his vile decoction begins to improve my outlook."

In defiance, with an exaggerated gesture, Elric bows and shows Cymoril the way to the door . . .

ELRIC: "Come, sweet Cymoril. Let's ride to the wilder reaches of our island."

Cymoril looks to Doctor Tanglebones, who is grave.

TANGLEBONES: "You must prepare yourself mentally and bodily for your coming trials."

TANGLEBONES: "My lord, you must rest . . ."

ELRIC: "And so I shall, good doctor, so I shall."

He's determined to enjoy this sense of release, to get the most out of it. He is a boy overburdened with duty and destiny.

Cymoril goes with him when he leaves the chamber. She shares his grin as they head for the stables.

Shot of them riding hell for leather from the walls of Imrryr, into the craggy beauty of the island's interior.

But, of course, in Melniboné royal princes and princesses rarely go unwatched . . .

Wearing his crown of iron feathers, Old Sadric, gaunt and haunted, stares from a window at his departing son, then turns his mind to more important matters.

Sadric, the old Sorcerer Emperor, hated his son, blamed Elric for killing his mother in childbirth.

Sadric had read the portents, heard the omens.

Was there any other interpretation?

Elric must bring shame to his own blood and drag destruction down on all the world . . .

Watched by the human woman Arisand, who holds back in a gesture of supplication, Sadric pushes open the doors of the great Hall of Steel. Here are the weapons, banners and armour of his ancestors.

So Sadric cared little where his son rode or with whom. Sadric had a colder choice to make . . .

Sadric has come to stand before the traditional armour of a Melnibonéan Sorcerer Emperor. This is constituted pretty much how Whelan depicts it on the DAW covers. A breastplate decorated with dragon motif, backplate matching. The dragon helm—crowned by a slender dragon about to take flight, with pieces protecting nose, eyes, ears. Grieves and gauntlets of similar design. A great war-shield, also of similar design. He's reaching to take down the helmet . . .

SADRIC: "My old armour. The armour of all Melniboné's emperors."

As he removes it, the helmet falls from his ancient, palsied hands and rolls on the stone slabs at his feet.

Proudly, Sadric peers down at the helm.

SADRIC: "Not a dent. Not a scratch. Sorcery or science? I once knew what it was. But I forget everything. So addictive, so corrosive, that ancient magic . . ."

He runs a still-sensuous hand over the complicated metalwork.

SADRIC: "I had a warrior's body once, to match a warrior's heart. Now, my hands can barely hold such power."

He replaces the helmet.

SADRIC: "Who shall wear it? My strong, cruel nephew. Or my weakling son. To survive we have always been ruthless. It is our duty."

He inspects obscene-looking daggers, mysterious cutting weapons, odd armour.

Wearing his crown of iron plumes, Sadric is in the upper part of the tower. From this curve four apparent flying buttresses. These also house the great chambers, such as the Hall of Steel, off his main living quarters. Now he looks out across the forest of ancient towers which is Melniboné. Behind him stands the human girl Arisand.

ARISAND: "A human is neither as wise nor as well educated as a Melnibonéan, master. But it seems to me your son puts aside his youthful weaknesses and becomes increasingly what you would wish him to be."

SADRIC (*coolly*): "Deficient blood, my dear. That's the problem. The test will come on the dream couches. That is where one or the other will prove their fitness. Now . . ."

He waves her away and she leaves through a door.

SADRIC: " . . . I must return to my grimoires . . ."

Next we see her making an entrance, slipping through another curtain. She has removed her over-dress. She is more sensuously clad.

Yyrkoon's bed of concubines is not far from where she now seats herself in a great, baroque chair.

Yyrkoon has his back to us. He will be seen to be leaning towards the great port of Imrryr, with its cliffs surrounding the harbour not fronted by the city. The sea-maze swirls. Ships are still loading and unloading.

Without looking back at her, Yyrkoon speaks to Arisand:

YYRKOON: "So, madam."

YYRKOON: "A score of our finest merchantmen will sail with the evening tide when they should have been warships!"

He turns. She smiles.

YYRKOON: "Did you discover my uncle's wishes? Will he make *me* his heir over that weakling?"

ARISAND: "He cannot bring himself to choose. All will be decided on the couches. If Elric survives the four dream-quests, he will rule."

Yyrkoon takes this information thoughtfully. Then he grins as if to Arisand, but actually directly addressing us, like a knowing, Jacobean villain . . .

YYRKOON: "That is good news for me, I think. We can challenge destiny!"

Last panel will be a small one of Elric and Cymoril riding over open, if slightly weird, countryside. We read Yyrkoon's words over this panel . . .

YYRKOON: "In past times, many perished hideously on those dream couches. Soon Elric will be one mummy amongst many—in the burial vaults of our ancestors."

Chapter Two

The Vaults of our Ancestors

Out of sight of the city, Cymoril and Elric pull their horses up before a great slab of limestone, surrounded by shrubs and small trees, moss, a few small streams making tears in the massive face.

ELRIC: "Ha! Here's my chance to show you something I learned during my dream-quests."

CYMORIL: "Could we not ride around it, my lord?"

Elric shuts his eyes and his face contorts almost to Mr. Hyde transformation as his fingers stretch to Hogarthian proportions and he utters an unholy word in an alien language—Cymoril covers her ears.

ELRIC: "←←←←⇉⌅⇇↖↰⇅⇅↖↶‿ →⇉⇊↰↳^⇇←←←←←←←←←←←"

(check spelling)

With an enormous cracking noise, the rockface splits—and keeps on splitting until it is a great fissure, large enough to admit human bodies. The horses are not taking this well. They will go forward no more.

ELRIC (*dismounts*): "There are some practical skills to be learned from those dream-quests. Our horses will find their way home. Come!"

Cymoril is not a little uncertain about this venture . . . She holds back but he insists, holding out his hand. Trusting him, but uncertain still, she goes with him. Down into the dank depths of the earth. The horses turn and gallop away home.

And when we have seen the last of Elric's and Cymoril's heads, descending into the darkness, the slab closes again with a sense of finality.

Elric is not alarmed and comforts Cymoril. Dark and dank as it is, there are fires flaring intermittently below. Enough light to allow them to make their way down a rocky spiral road towards the bottom.

Then a huge shape goes past them with a PHUNK, almost knocking them from the ledge, but Elric is laughing up at the shape—

CYMORIL: "Elric!"

—which, as it spirals towards the ground, a tiny rider on its back, proves to be a young Phoorn. A young dragon . . . The fires themselves come from the combustible venom which drips from the fangs of the mature dragons who sleep or raise drowsy eyes and snort clouds of steam through their nostrils.

ELRIC: "Do not worry, my lady. These are the Dragon Caves of Imrryr."

As the young couple descend the path, another young Melnibonéan ascends it to greet them. He's the laughing rider of the dragon, and still wears his dragon leathers, holds part of a bridle. In the other hand is his great dragon lance—a long, leaf-shaped blade which is set in a red jewel from the other end of which comes the haft of the lance. This will show a distinct similarity of design with the Black Sword, but where the Black Sword will have a red actorios, this has a light blue sapphire. The bearer is Dyvim Tvar, Elric's best male friend.

DYVIM TVAR: "Dear cousins! How good of you to visit me in my murky lair."

ELRIC: "Well met, Dyvim Tvar."

Dyvim Tvar bows and displays the rows of dragons who sleep in orderly ranks around the rim of a bay which is almost a perfect oval, an underground sea beneath the stalactites.

DYVIM TVAR: "Forgive me for startling you. We watch for intruders these days. More than we used to."

DYVIM TVAR (*with a hospitable gesture*): "Come, meet the Phoorn, my family. The few who are presently awake!"

The Melnibonéans stand looking up at a massive snout from which pour, like drool, rivulets of venom. Some of this venom has scarred the rock on which the dragon sleeps. Some still flickers, for it becomes fire when it meets air . . . Fiery streams run on both sides of the figures as they regard the huge, sleepy, half-open eye which regards them. Dyvim Tvar speaks to the Phoorn in their own language.

DYVIM TVAR (*runes*): "!@@###$%)))(*&&^^^," etc,

DRAGON (*answers in the same language*): "++%%$$##@@"

ELRIC: "I envy your knowledge of the dragon tongue."

DYVIM TVAR: "Once, when our folk were the simple Mernii, we and the Phoorn shared a common language. Now it cannot be learned. It has to be remembered . . ."

He guides them up some rather more recently built stone stairs towards a door which he opens for them.

They look back at the great near-circle of resting and sleeping dragons. Dyvim Tvar puts his hand on Elric's shoulders.

DYVIM TVAR: "Prince Yyrkoon will never have help. My loyalty's to you, my dragons and to our traditions."

They are out on a long, straight staircase which leads upwards from the Dragon Caves. They are briefly in an underground passage. Then on a spiral staircase. Then they are entering a chamber at the base of the Imperial Tower.

But these chambers are spare. A craftsman's rooms. Various heavy, ornate bits of dragon bridle hang on the walls. The furniture is sturdy but not ornate. Dyvim Tvar provides food, which they do not eat, and wine, which they drink. Elric tilts his chair back, enjoying this simple pleasure.

ELRIC: "What I would not give, dear friend, to be a simple Dragon Master . . ."

DYVIM TVAR (*smiles at this*): "Well, I must say I don't envy you your sorcerous learning . . . nor the means by which it's gathered. I am content. The dragons sleep. Only a few need tending."

He looks almost dreamy as he adds:

DYVIM TVAR: "Perhaps one day the Phoorn will again fly in a phalanx blotting out the sun—a final, mighty flight . . ."

He claps his hand on Elric's shoulder.

DYVIM TVAR: "And you'll be with me. Riding side by side on twin dragons. Flying above our empire."

Elric embraces Cymoril.

ELRIC: "Where shall we go now?"

CYMORIL: "To our beds. And tomorrow, my lord, to your studies. I shall not see you until you begin the first of your most important dreams . . ."

A montage of Elric studying, being taught by old Tanglebones—to fence, learn an incantation, summoning a small demon, sleep in exhausted slumber. Until Doctor Tanglebones wakes him before dawn and, carrying a lantern, leads the way. Washed by slaves, Elric next ascends the dream couch with its hard, marble head-rest, its decorated stonework and woodwork.

And so begins the first long dream: the Dream of Earth . . .

Chapter Three

Talking in Silence

Observed by the raven Sepiriz, which flies from Tanglebones's shoulder into the dream sequence, Elric's astral body leaves the couch and becomes this very good physical body—his own in its best possible condition. His hair is braided. He is stripped to the waist, wearing only a short jacket. He has a quiver of arrows, an unstrung bow, a long knife, leggings, breach-clout, deerskin boots. And he is entering what seems to be an amphitheatre—Pueblo-style dwellings, with ladders and cave entrances at every level. Some short, squat, sturdy dwarfish Mayan types (Puk Wa D'Jee, Pukwadji) stare out at Elric. Elric is now White Crow. Throughout this sequence the huge black raven is evident. White Crow greets the Pukwadji cheerfully.

WHITE CROW/ELRIC: "Hey, little allies. Have the Pukwadji no welcome for White Crow?"

Suddenly Elric has more friends than he needs. They are jumping on him, hitting him with clubs, holding him wherever they can. He attempts to fight them and sends several flying, but eventually they overwhelm him.

ELRIC: "I gather we're no longer allies. The last I knew, our peoples neared agreement . . ."

He is trussed in rawhide.

PUKWADJI LEADER: "Your folk betray us. We'll never return their ships now. They have no right to keep the black blade when it threatens our very existence."

PUKWADJI SHAMAN: "King Grome will destroy us if we do not return the black blade. But your folk will not trade it back. So Grome keeps your ships. and we feed him the few of your folk we catch—to placate him in his terrible distress."

ELRIC: "You attacked us, dragging our ships underground, stranding us, making our journey impossible to finish."

SHAMAN: "We used our last great pact with Grome to take those ships. We have little left to fight with. We'll keep the ships until we get the blade."

SHAMAN: "Meanwhile—we sacrifice you to King Grome, the earth-lord . . ."

Shaman holds up a skull with a crown of metal feathers stuck on it.

They carry the tied Elric deep, deep underground, down tunnels, passages, through chambers, through natural caverns, down and down until they come to where Grome awaits them, far below. Grome is gnarled and knotted, made of great tree roots, and clumps of earth and boulders and grass and moulds and fungus.

KING GROME: "A morsel to distract me from my pain? You fail to understand the importance of this matter. We are doomed unless you bring me the blade. You must bring me the blade! All are imperiled!"

FIRST PUKWADJI: "A morsel is all we can offer, great king of the earth. We are too weak to defeat the Mernii intruders. We are sorry we bartered the black blade."

GROME: "You will perish. I will punish you. King Grome still has his powers! And his pride."

Flashback of the Mernii ships breaking through dimensions onto a river. As the Mernii run for it, Grome buries all the ships, including the river, under huge mounds of earth . . .

But Grome is hungry, too . . .

GROME: "Oh, very well, give me the morsel . . ."

Elric is thrown down to Grome who catches him expertly with his strange, earthy, rooty hand.

GROME: "What bloodless thing is this?"

ELRIC: "I can assure you, your majesty, that I am better conversation than I am a canapé."

Grome continues to lift Elric towards his gaping maw.

GROME: "That blade brings doom upon the world. Unless I can put it back in the rock from which it was taken."

ELRIC: "I'll strike a bargain with you. Let me explain this to my people. Surely they purchased the black blade for a special reason."

GROME (*now hesitates and thinks*): "Mmmmmmmmmmmmmmmmmmmmm"

Grome returns Elric to the ground, releasing his bonds.

Puzzled Pukwadji return Elric's bow and arrows, etc. Set him on his way, scowling and unsure.

SHAMAN: "But if you fail to keep your bargain with him, King Grome will find you and eat you wherever you hide. *Go*!"

ELRIC: "I doubt my own folk will welcome me much more warmly."

Elric now approaches a mountain which those with sharp eyes might notice to resemble the contours of the Isle of Melniboné. On the side of this (where the harbour is now) stands a very elaborate and wealthy camp, protected by a tall, wooden fence. Within the compound are wigwam-style tents, very tall, with slender lodge poles and cowled tops. They are versions of the towers of Melniboné. A young Mernii guard looks at Elric with a mixture of humour and contempt.

GUARD: "Good afternoon, renegade. Have you received an order to return . . . ?"

ELRIC: "No, kinsman, but I come in some urgency."

Within the camp, which has a temporary quality to it, Elric is greeted by a group of aggressive young men.

LEADER (*of aggressive young men*): "Renegade! Our king is too lenient."

ELRIC: "A pleasant day, Tvarim Kha."

TVARIM KHA: "Both you and he deserve to die!"

But Elric pushes past them. They are glowering, reaching towards their swords.

Wearing the iron-feathered crown of kingship, King Varnik is still relatively young and fit. He is clearly White Crow's elder brother. He turns an unwelcoming gaze on Elric as he arrives in the big wigwam. The black blade (sans *runes) is laid on a sort of altar, guarded by tall, grim Mernii (Melnibonéans). It appears to be a lance-blade and there is a half-moon fitting at the top, supposedly for a shaft, but actually it is where the throbbing scarlet Actorios stone should sit.*

KING VARNIK: "You return early from your banishment, sir trickster . . ."

ELRIC: "Brother, I am hoping to end a war destroying both sides. How can we get our ships back and let them have the black blade?"

Varnik is interested.

ELRIC: "Grome will destroy the dwarves if they do not return the blade."

VARNIK: "Let him destroy them. Without the blade we'll have no means of pursuing our journey. The loss of the ships was terrible, but we can't give them back the blade."

ELRIC: "Destroying the dwarves, Grome will then begin killing us. Until he has the blade . . ."

VARNIK: "The blade has a special purpose. Our people will not survive without it. We must keep it."

ELRIC: "Will you still need it when it has performed this purpose?"

VARNIK: "Need it or not, it is ours by tradition. We'll never return it."

ELRIC: "So we'll never see our ships again, and yet the blade will be useless until we regain the Actorios stone. Would you bargain with Grome if I found you the stone?"

Varnik leans forward, laughing at Elric.

VARNIK: "You would have to bring back the Actorios in just over a year . . . For that is the time of the next great astral conjunction, when the sword is needed."

ELRIC: "Legend has it the Actorios was stolen from us before we owned the sword. The thief was a northern giant, too quick for any to follow, and not one of our warriors who sought him ever returned."

VARNIK: "Can you do what our greatest heroes failed to do? If so I give you my word—bring me the Actorios, the Dragon Stone . . . and Grome shall have his sword returned . . . after we have used it."

ELRIC: "Then clearly, my lord, I must find the Actorios for you . . . within the year!

The leader of the belligerent young men is cheered by what he overhears.

LEADER (*whispers*): "They'd trade away our birthright, but one will die on his quest, and the other's easily finished . . ."

Chapter Four

The Dragon Stone

And so White Crow journeyed north . . .

With the basic kit for a long journey on foot, White Crow sets off away from the tall lodges of his people. This page could be done like Indian pictograms.

Basically it will be four panels depicting the seasons, in which White Crow makes a journey across the North American continent from south to north.

(Summer)

. . . Risking death . . .

In this sequence White Crow is attacked by a white mountain lion and defeats it.

(Fall)

. . . Learning wisdom . . .

In this sequence White Crow sits with human people, passing the peace pipe and listening while wise oldsters read from long wampum belts.

(Winter)

. . . Controlling his powers . . .

Winter on prairie, White Crow uses his magic—to stop a charging white buffalo.

(Spring)

. . . Defending life . . .

We see White Crow binding the leg of a bear, helping a deer out of a ravine, setting a white beaver on its way . . .

BEAVER: "I am grateful, White Crow . . ."

BEAVER: " . . . But I will not accompany you. We shun the long house you seek. It lies due north. It is fairly well defended."

Beavers are famous for their understatement . . .

. . . and had good reason to shun the giants' "long house."

Elric arrives at last at the Giants' great long house—actually a massive ziggurat-shaped metropolis, with all kinds of city activity taking place in its galleries, between private windows and public walkways. But, save for a narrow, heavily defended causeway, there seems no way into the city, for the great lake around it boils with molten lava. Which does not concern those citizens. At the very top of the ziggurat is the Temple of the Actorios. You can see its red light burning, even in day. Giants have a distinctively Iroquois sort of look. Maybe we should save whole view of the ziggurat until next page . . .

ELRIC (*thinks*): "A lake of molten lava. With only one way to cross. Yet there's the Actorios they prize—atop their city's proudest point."

Elric's tiny in this picture, with the vast city dominating everything. Closer to foreground maybe is Sepiriz the raven—young Elric's mentor in these dreams. Sepiriz is, of course, an omen-ous bird.

ELRIC: "No mortal can cross that!"

SEPIRIZ: "With native skill and demon's lore

On supernatural wing's ye'll soar . . .

With sorcerous cunning and feline stealth . . .

A prince shall filch a giant's wealth . . .

Elric is almost amused by the appearance of his familiar.

ELRIC: "There you are, Master Sepiriz. Come to give me advice. As always. I'm glad to see you."

We see him beginning to puzzle out the spell—aha!—

ELRIC: "The flying demon! A recently learned spell . . ."

. . . and as he does so we fade to him actually doing the conjuring of the grumpy winged demon—

GRUMPY DEMON: "I do this because your spell grants you one wish of me."

—and forcing it to take him over to the long house.

Grumbling, yet triumphant, the demon flies off, leaving Elric on the dais up to the brazier which holds the Actorios Stone, the Dragon Stone. This has awakened a huge giant who looks up and sees Elric.

DEMON: "I said I'd carry you there. I said nothing of taking you back. My bargain's done!"

As the giant comes roaring up to defend the Actorios, Elric gets between himself and the glaring red crystal. Puts influence on giant, using the crystal as a sort of amplifier of his powers.

ELRIC: "*Through wizard's eyes and red stone's stare*

By Arioch's will and Arioch's glare . . .

By fiery crystal, blazing light . . .

Submit to me your giantly might!"

GIANT: "That is a powerful and dangerous spell, master. Hate thee as I do, I am bound to obey thee."

Elric clings to the giant's single scalp-lock as he poises on the edge of the city wall, like a diver ready to dive into a pool. Elric has the Actorios in his bag.

GIANT: "I have done you no wrong, Prince Elric. I shall die in agony but I can only obey . . .

Dives—

Elric on the giant's head, clinging to the scalp-lock, the giant swims through lava, his skin burning.

At edge of the lake of lava, White Crow jumps off the giant, who is dying, drowning as he is sucked back into the lava. White Crow begins to run, the raven flying overhead.

GIANT: "You will pay a price for your lack of mercy, Prince Elric. Mark my words . . ."

And then White Crow ran home.

Chapter Five

The Swearing of Oaths

White Crow is returning home, the sack over his back. It is summer.

The arrogant young rebel, Tvarim Kha, sees him approaching the camp and scowls in rage. He had expected White Crow to die on his quest.

TVARIM KHA: "So he survived the quest! We must end this prince's run of luck . . ."

Elsewhere—Yyrkoon puts an enchantment on Tanglebones so that his men can go in and finish off Elric—

YYRKOON: "There! The oldster's enchanted. Now do your work . . ."

Elric arrives at Varnik's wigwam. Varnik is almost as surprised to see him as Tvarim Kha.

VARNIK: "White Crow! You have it. And just in time!"

Elric holds the sack back from Varnik's eager fingers. In his other hand Varnik holds what looks like a lance-blade with a half-moon female joint for the haft. But the Actorios will actually fit there.

VARNIK: "Give me the Actorios. I know what to do!"

ELRIC: "Not until you have sworn the oath we agreed! After you have used it, you must return the blade to Grome."

VARNIK: "Quickly! Very well, I swear. I swear to do as you ask."

Enter Tvarim Kha.

TVARIM KHA: "There's no time left for the keeping of oaths. Your bloodline is about to end!"

At the same time, Yyrkoon's bravos push into the dream chamber, ready to kill Elric as he lies helpless.

And meanwhile Tvarim Kha's men follow him into the tent as White Crow yells urgently to Varnik:

ELRIC: "Brother—the blade—to me!"

A fraction of a second's hesitation and Varnik tosses the black blade to White Crow/Elric, while taking up another lance of his own.

The assassins press closer.

Elric fits the Actorios into the hilt. It still doesn't have a handle and crossbar, but he can wield the lance blade like a sword, two-handed.

And now a bizarre light burns in White Crow/Elric's crimson eyes. The Actorios brings red runes to the black iron. They ripple up and down its length, unstable and dangerous.

Black Sword in his hands, White Crow engages the bravos.

ELRIC/WHITE CROW: "By great Arioch, I'll take you all with me!"

In old-fashioned demonic glee, Elric lays about him with the sword and the wicked plotters go down like scythed wheat . . .

Weaponless, Varnik lies panting against the side of the tent as Elric finishes the last of the terrified attackers.

Elric finishes Tvarim Kha.

Meanwhile . . .

Tanglebones wakes from his enchantment to see with astonishment—

—the bodies of Yyrkoon's assassins, lying everywhere in the chamber.

And, in the prone Elric's right hand, the shadowy, fading shape of the Black Sword. Tanglebones reaches towards it, but it vanishes.

TANGLEBONES: "Wicked sorcery as I lay entranced—yet the danger's been averted! How—? Aha!"

Tanglebones stands over the sleeping Elric. The sword has gone, but there are splashes of blood on his body from those he has killed.

TANGLEBONES: "The sword! That damnable sword preserves its own existence . . ."

White Crow hands the sword to his brother, Prince Varnik, who has some very urgent business with it.

VARNIK: "Thanks, brother! The conjunction is almost over. There is so little time left if we're to bring our people through . . ."

Out of sight of their camp, Varnik hurries out to a great slab of rock the same as the one Elric encountered "earlier." Other members of his tribe stand *ready, uncertain, cheering as he holds up the black blade, with the Actorios in it, red runes rippling the length of that supernatural steel. Varnik takes a run at it and, calling out runes, brings the blade against the rock—which splits—***KRAK** *(because I know you'll put one in, Walter :)) . . . This rock goes on splitting—it splits upwards, then it splits the land, then the sky and through this sky, from the universe in which they have been trapped, fly the Phoorn—the great dragon brothers and sisters of the Mernii, who will one day be known as the Melnibonéans. It is DRAGONS, DRAGONS, DRAGONS . . . The human figures are thoroughly dwarfed by these huge beasts.*

VARNIK: "The Phoorn! Blood-kin to our folk!"

The dragons fly down—down towards the great underground cave-system revealed by the fissure in the rock. There we see the same underground lake around which the dragons were settled earlier.

As one dragon passes he speaks to White Crow. The dragon is Flamefang, one of the oldest of the Phoorn.

FLAMEFANG: "*Brother, in a million years . . . Flamefang will not have forgotten your help.*"

White Crow can only acknowledge the words, but not answer, he is so astonished at what has happened.

But White Crow has not forgotten his promise to King Grome. As the dragons continue to come through, Elric reaches his hand for the black blade.

ELRIC: "Now give me the blade. We must keep our promise to Grome!"

With the dwarves at his back, Elric gives the sword into Grome's keeping.

GROME: "You have done well, young silverskin. You can rely upon my help whenever your need is great."

GROME: "And I'll return this burdensome blade to the black rock which birthed it. It is cursed and would doom us all."

GROME: "Ready your folk. I will give them back their ships!"

Elric and Varnik are standing on the flanks of the hill, just below the tent town of Elric's people. A great gathering. Some distance off, pulling himself up out of the ground, comes King Grome, hating the sunlight. He has two ships—one under each huge earthy arm.

GROME: "Here're the first two. Hmmm. Ye'll need something to float 'em on . . . Best get to higher ground."

Now we see King Grome at full strength—raising the Mernii ships from deep underground where he had dragged them—so that they come bursting up through the earth—while creating an island out of the camp and the mountain it sits on, so that sea runs around it and the ships are floated, like so many toys, by his huge, earthy hands . . .

GROME: "So now Pukwadji and Mernii will live in peace by my decree! I have rewarded you well for keeping your bargain with me. Let us all prosper."

And so began the history of Melniboné . . .

White Crow fades discreetly back into the frame which shows Elric asleep on the dream couch.

Tanglebones and Cymoril greet Elric as Tanglebones gives Elric the potion as usual.

Tanglebones watches helplessly as Elric tosses the cup aside, puts his arm around Cymoril's shoulders and strides away.

TANGLEBONES: "You must rest, study . . ."

ELRIC: "Farewell, Master Tanglebones. We have old friends to visit . . ."

Main picture is Elric, Cymoril and Dyvim Tvar in Dragon Caves. Elric is communicating in runic with the old dragon we saw earlier. Cymoril and Dyvim Tvar (holding dragon lance which resembles the black blade in length and style but is fashioned into a tall spear, with a blue stone glowing where the haft meets the blade).

ELRIC: "*()^^&&)))" (*in runic*).

FLAMEFANG: "%%%^^^^^&&**(()(" (*also in runic*).

CYMORIL: "Now he speaks the language of the Phoorn!"

DYVIM TVAR: "I told you. Phoorn is not learned—it's remembered . . ."

Inset has King Sadric with Tanglebones:

SADRIC: "He's passed the first great test. But does he have the character to pass the next?"

Then final inset is Yyrkoon with Arisand, whose expression is unreadable.

YYRKOON (*glowering*): "I was too crude. Strong sorcery protects my puny cousin. Now I know how and where to defeat him!"

BOOK TWO

THE DREAM OF TWO YEARS: THE DREAM OF WATER

THE SEA-KING'S SISTER

CHAPTER ONE

Return of the Prince

NOW IMRRYR, the Dreaming City, stands at a node of the moonbeam roads.

Here the roads cross and re-cross the multiverse, taking travelers to worlds of every kind, all versions of our own.

Some worlds are substantial, others barely formed, the ghosts of realms unborn, of dying worlds and worlds who owe their existence only to our dreams.

Back and forth go the travelers on the moonbeam roads, making and destroying worlds, inhabiting dreams and desires, making real that which was unreal. Powerful dreams. Dreams of power. Of deep longing and wild desire.

Would one of these worlds, including our own, exist beyond our dreams? If we stopped dreaming would they fade into nothing? Would we fade with them?

Even old Tanglebones, administering the dream couch of his young master, the Sorcerer Prince Elric, dare not ask that question . . .

Meanwhile, Elric embarks on the second of his great dream-quests whose outcome will bring him enormous power and decide the fate of the multiverse, should, that is, it exist at all . . .

A panorama of Melniboné at the centre of a criss-crossing network of the roads between the worlds. A sort of reprise of the moonbeam road sequence in Michael Moorcock's Multiverse. *Elric, on his dream couch, sleeps and there is a suggestion that this is what he dreams . . . The black crow we have seen in the first book flies between Elric and the dream roads . . .*

Tanglebones and Cymoril walk together in a hanging garden overlooking the harbour of Melniboné.

CYMORIL: "He's changing, Master Tanglebones. The dreams are changing him . . ."

TANGLEBONES: "That's the nature of his education, my dear. Just pray that he is changed to your liking . . ."

Sadric and the human girl, Arisand, stand on a balcony looking down on Tanglebones and Cymoril.

SADRIC: "I'll wager that, like us, old Tanglebones and Lady Cymoril are contemplating my son's fate. Well, what do *you* say, girl? Does my son become the stuff of emperors? Or should his cousin Yyrkoon be given the throne?"

ARISAND: "He matures, my lord Sadric. Prince Elric grows in character if not in physical energy. Master Tanglebones's potions keep him strong."

Elsewhere, deep within the tower, Prince Yyrkoon prepares to lie down on his own dream couch.

His servant, gaunt and Heepish, readies the potion.

SERVANT: "Where would you go in your sleep, master?"

YYRKOON: "I'll follow my weakling cousin, of course. I have business with him there in the Dream Realms . . ."

The dream roads. Elric already walks them. In the dream chamber, Tanglebones looks down on Elric's troubled, dreaming face. Cymoril rushes in, concerned. She's just learned of Yyrkoon's decision.

TANGLEBONES (*muses*): "Now you dream the Dream of Two Years . . . the Dream of Water. You carry a great burden already, my lord, and it can only grow heavier on your journey."

CYMORIL: "Master Tanglebones! My brother Yyrkoon—he's taken to the dream couches. He can mean Elric only harm!"

TANGLEBONES (*sadly*): "Then Elric's test will be all the harder. He must fend for himself in those dangerous realms . . ."

In his dreams, Elric has come to a less magnificent but rather beautiful Melniboné. While he still sports braids and a vaguely Indian look, he is dressed in

much more sophisticated clothing. The city itself has yet to grow in might or splendour but is a long way on from the wigwam dwellings we saw in the first book. Beached ships indicate low tides, however, as he walks on to be greeted, again, as White Crow, by the sailors hauling their ships up the beach.

FIRST SAILOR: "Why 'tis White Crow himself come back to us. The queen will be glad to see you."

SECOND SAILOR: "Perhaps not. They say she was furious at his leaving. He claimed to be plotting against our enemies, the Falkryn."

ELRIC: "The tide's so low. What's the cause?"

SECOND SAILOR: "You have not heard? Our oceans shrink almost by the month. Some say a thirsty beast of Chaos is drinking all the world's water. Others blame the Falkryn.

ELRIC (*frowning*): "My memory deserts me. Best take me to the queen. Her name?"

SECOND SAILOR (*laughing*): "Ho, ho! You pretend not to know Queen Shyrix'x? You who were betrothed to her! You'd be advised to find your memory before you see her again! Come."

He's taken to Queen Shyrix'x IX—and she remembers him as a lover. He finds it hard to respond to her. She's angry, believing herself betrayed by him.

QUEEN SHYRIX'X: "Back from your quest, White Crow? Did you find the Falkryn sorcerer you sought?"

ELRIC: "I have no memory of my past, madam, forgive me . . ."

SHYRIX'X: "No memory? A lame excuse. You left to sulk because our love had died and I am due to wed Dyvim Mar!"

ELRIC: "I fear that past is gone from me, madam . . . I was astonished to find the tide so low . . ."

She responds angrily.

SHYRIX'X: "Rumour says some Chaos beast drinks the oceans. Caravans now cross where seas once were. You pretend not to know this, too?"

ELRIC: "You must believe me, Queen Shyrix'x . . . I—I think I was under a sleeping charm . . ."

SHYRIX'X: "No longer under *my* charm, that's evident! I refused your love—and you schemed against me, eh?"

She whirls pettishly, but she is half won over. A little puzzled by this attitude, which she had not expected. But she's beginning to believe him.

ELRIC: "Madam—I assure you . . ."

Elric and Queen Shyrix'x stand together looking out over the harbour. She puts a friendly hand on his shoulder.

SHYRIX'X: "Well, our cooled love and Imrryr's rebuilding must both wait. You know the sea levels fall—"

A caravan of odd beasts of burden crosses a desert, once an ocean.

SHYRIX'X: "—but our capital grows vulnerable to barbarian attack!"

The sea-maze. Waters grow very low, exposing rocks and stranded sea creatures.

SHYRIX'X: "Our sea defenses no longer protect us against our Falkryn foes. You are our nation's champion, White Crow. How will you help us?"

ELRIC: "I see my task, sweet lady. As to its solution . . . how can I see what is happening in the world at large?"

SHYRIX'X: "We must ask the Dragon Master . . . your rival, Dyvim Mar."

The Dragon Caves. Queen and Elric stand together observing the sleeping dragons. They are clearly in a very deep sleep, save for one younger dragon, who raises a sleepy eye to regard them. Dyvim Mar, the Dragon Master, greets them cheerfully. He wears a version, a little more primitive, of the clothing worn by the first Dragon Master Elric and Cymoril encountered when they visited the caves in Book One. He embraces Elric.

DYVIM MAR: "Ah, cousin! Our champion returns! Our need for you is great. You know of the seas receding?"

ELRIC: "Aye, but not why. We must wake a dragon, cousin. Is that possible?"

DYVIM MAR: "You'll recall we used all the Phoorn only some nine years past to defend ourselves against the Falkryn, who have long coveted us our power. But we held one back, as we always do. Snaptail! She's ready. And eager for the skies. Where would you go?"

ELRIC: "Across the world, so that we can observe all the oceans. If some natural dam has raised itself, perhaps we can destroy it."

DYVIM MAR: "Good thinking, cousin. She'll be ready by morning . . ."

Back at the palace, Queen Shyrix'x holds up her hands, believing that Elric means to follow her into the bedchamber . . .

SHYRIX'X: "If by feigning memory loss you hope to revive our love . . ."

ELRIC (*concerned*): "Believe me, madam, I intend to serve you and Melniboné only as your champion."

A little disappointed, the queen accepts his refusal. She claps her hands. Servants enter. She gives orders:

SHYRIX'X: "Prepare our champion's quarters. Sleep well, White Crow. And may your memory soon be restored."

And shortly after daybreak . . .

Queen and some warriors stand by while Elric and Dyvim Mar get ready to mount the huge dragon which now crouches on the side of the harbour. Further away stands a crowd of Melnibonéans. Others hang from balconies to watch. She embraces Dyvim Mar.

SHYRIX'X: "May the gods of Melniboné go with you, and may you find the solution you seek."

Elric and his cousin Dyvim Mar bow.

They climb into the high dragon saddles:

DYVIM MAR: "I trust you do not hate me for what happened, cousin. You were betrothed, 'tis true. But we could not resist our love . . ."

ELRIC: "Believe me, Dyvim Mar, I hold no ill will whatsoever . . ."

The dragon is airborne. She flies on vast wings away from the city across an evidently dying ocean. Strange islands emerge where none should exist. The two men fly towards the sun, shielding their eyes as they scan the landscape and the sea below.

DYVIM MAR: "As you know, cousin, dragons sleep for years and then have a few days of activity at most. We must be careful not to tire our steed or she'll be unable to fly back home!"

They are now flying over a butte-studded desert not unlike the Painted Desert. Great worn limestone cliffs emerge from glinting pools of water—the only water there is. Wild animals lap hungrily at the stuff, glancing up as the great shape of the dragon flies by overhead.

ELRIC: "These are not old deserts, but new-made. What sorcery could rob the world of her water?"

DYVIM: "There's a small lake below. While we have the chance we'd best land and let Mistress Snaptail drink."

They head towards the small lake where many other animals are already drinking, rearing away in panic when the shadow of the dragon passes over them. As they do so Elric spots something in the distance. It will prove to be a vast horde of warriors. Elric points.

ELRIC: "What's that?"

The two have landed and, while worried animals watch from a safe distance, Snaptail drinks. Meanwhile Elric and Dyvim Mar climb a great slab of rock so that they can look without being seen at a great army riding and marching towards them. At the head of the army are two men. One of them is Yyrkoon, though we can't quite make that out yet, maybe. The other is a rider who is almost too big for his mount, armoured in spikes and scales, like a lizard. Try for a Vin Diesel look. This is Agras Ti, sorcerer of the Falkryn and partner to Yyrkoon, who here takes on another persona, unaware of his life in Melniboné . . .

ELRIC: "The Falkryn horde! Without doubt they ride toward Melniboné!!"

DYVIM MAR: "When Snaptail's drunk her fill, we'll fly home to warn them . . ."

ELRIC: "First we'll take their measure, cousin."

It is sunset. The light casts long shadows, but the horde is closer now and we can make out the leading figures. This time it's obvious that the mounted warrior is Melnibonéan. And, of course, it's Prince Yyrkoon.

DYVIM MAR: "Do you know him?"

ELRIC: "Something in the back of my brain does. He means us no good, that's for certain . . ."

Close-up of Prince Yyrkoon, smirking with triumph.

Behind, at the lake, the dragon looks with surprise as something surfaces at the centre of the water—it is the angry eyes of what will be one of Straasha the Sea-King's people . . .

Chapter Two

A Thirsty Chaos Lord

An angry thrashing of the waters of the lake. Elric and Dyvim Mar turn to see Snaptail in a struggle with a huge water-creature. His fishy face identifies him as a water elemental.

The two beings wrestle each other while Elric and Dyvim Mar look helplessly from the shore.

DYVIM MAR: "A water elemental! Snaptail—break free!"

ELRIC: "She's not strong enough! We've lost our steed, cousin!"

But the dragon breaks free at last, beating up into the air as the elemental turns into a great water-spout, using up all the water in the lake, trying to reach the escaping monster.

ELRIC: "She's free!"

DYVIM MAR: "Aye. But at what cost?"

The water elemental falls back into the lake. But the dragon is falling, too. She's barely able to keep her height. Falling back to earth in a great spiral, she lands utterly exhausted far out across the wasteland.

Elric and Dyvim Mar race towards their fallen steed, reaching her at last. She is weary, barely able to keep her great eyes open.

DYVIM MAR: "She's exhausted. The fight took all her power. It will be days or weeks before she'll fly again!"

Elric whirls—hearing a sound behind him. And here come a whole host of barbarians, of the same kind as Yyrkoon led . . .

ELRIC: "Barbarians. Look to your sword, cousin!"

Elric and Dyvim Mar are swiftly embroiled in a heavy fight. Their swordsmanship is superior to that of the barbarians but there are a lot more barbarians . . .

Slowly but surely the barbarians get the upper hand.

Elric and Dyvim Mar are dragged before the two leaders of the barbarians—Yyrkoon and Agras Ti.

AGRAS TI: "Melnibonéans! Spying on us. Do you know them, Wild Dog?"

YYRKOON/WILD DOG: "I've told you. My memory fails me in some ways. But that's a silver warrior—like me, he's of noble birth—perhaps a prince of the line—only certain emperors and their blood have that pallour and those ruby eyes. We have a fine prize, Agras Ti."

Elric and Dyvim Mar, chained and thrown into a glass-sided cage on wheels, become part of the barbarians' advance as a seashore comes in sight. Again, there are beached boats far up above the waterline, indicating that the ocean has receded. Wild Dog and Agras Ti bring their troops to a halt and rest on their saddle pommels looking away to sea.

WILD DOG: "Beyond that ocean lies Melniboné. Once the sea was her friend and she was impregnable. Now she'll fall like a ripe apple into our hands. All we must do is wait a little for the sea to recede. Then we attack."

AGRAS TI: "You're sure her dragons sleep and cannot harm us?"

WILD DOG: "We have over a year before they can wake the mass of dragons. By that time we shall control both the city and, through me, the dragons, for we speak a common tongue. And through Melniboné's dragons—the whole world shall be ours!"

A raven appears and flies towards the cage of transparent obsidian where Elric and Dyvim Mar are imprisoned.

It comes to perch on a tree, watching the sun set.

In the firelight, the raven hops down from the tree to where a guard relaxes, his keys on the ground beside him.

Miraculously the raven manages to separate a key from the ring and fly off with it.

The raven flies to the cage where a miserable Elric and Dyvim Mar sit talking in their cage.

DYVIM MAR: "So that's their plan. They must know why the waters are falling so quickly. Perhaps their sorcery is the cause? But if we cannot warn our people, they lack the resources to resist such a powerful army. The sea has always been our best defense . . ."

Elric notices the raven hopping through the bars, the key in its beak. He frowns.

ELRIC: "Sorcery, you say? And what's this?"

RAVEN: "This is all I can do for you now. Later, perhaps, I will be able to help more. But Chaos rules this whole realm and my magic's not yet strong enough to fight it. A boat awaits you on the shore. Use it to warn your people of their danger."

DYVIM MAR: "A loquacious bird. And a useful one. Is he yours, White Crow? Or merely some relative?"

Elric is already unlocking his manacles.

He completes the job and passes the key to Dyvim Mar.

ELRIC: "Perhaps he is my totem, I do not know. Let's not question our fortune. Let's find that boat and warn the queen."

They make it to the shore and see the little skiff waiting for them.

They sail into the sunrise. The raven watches from his perch on a rock.

Elric and Dyvim Mar have a good wind behind them and they can see the slender buildings of Melniboné in the distance.

DYVIM MAR: "There! Imrryr's in sight! Now at last we can ready ourselves for the barbarian attack!"

But now the sea begins to swirl and tremble. Soon it turns into strange, half-recognizable shapes. The two men stare around them in dismay as the sea around the boat forms itself into a giant watery hand and begins to lift them—

—then the massive, fishy face of King Straasha, the king of the water elementals, materializes above them. He holds the boat in the palm of his hand. His other hand holds a great fishing spear. He is in poor temper and glares down at the two tiny mortals and their boat. But he is also sad. He is reluctant to interfere. It seems something might even control him . . .

KING STRAASHA: "Little mortals, I have no argument with thee. But if you interfere with your enemy's plans, 'tis I who shall suffer. I have no choice but to do what I must do."

Elric attempts to persuade the sea-king.

ELRIC: "King Straasha! Lord of the Waters. We mean you no ill. We seek to discover why your realm is vanishing so rapidly . . ."

STRAASHA: "Well, little mortal, I believe you. I can show you the source of our mutual danger. But I cannot let you fight it . . ."

King Straasha speeds with his mortal captives through the waters. He needs water to take shape so he can't go too far into the shallows.

STRAASHA: "This is the closest I can take you . . ."

He lifts his hand so that they can see further . . .

Standing in King Straasha's watery palm the two men look into the distance to where a monstrous form can be seen. He is Artigkern, Lord of Chaos—bloated and disgusting. He has taken the form of a gigantic toad and is sucking up water through a great hollow tree.

STRAASHA: "He is Artigkern of Chaos. He has already sucked the fourth planet dry of all its water and he will do the same to us. Agras Ti of the Falkryn brought him here through sorcery and I fear to stop him. He is too powerful—and—and . . .

ELRIC: "Great lord of elementals. You fear nothing. He must have some other hold over you."

Straasha frowns, almost ashamed.

STRAASHA: "What if he does? I must do what he demands or he will take *all* the water. Through this bargain, he leaves me a little hope . . . But as the water drains, so does my power. Even if he died, he says he will spit all the water into the sun first. There is nothing I can do against him . . ."

Elric is horrified, remonstrates with the great king of elementals.

ELRIC: "But, my lord king—this world will die as the last one did. Would you not help us to fight against him?"

STRAASHA (*truly shamefaced now*): "I cannot."

STRAASHA: "He holds my sister hostage. If I resist him, she dies. Come now, I have kept my promise . . ."

We see a cut of a beautiful merwoman, Straasha's sister, held in a gigantic semi-transparent clam shell.

ELRIC: "Upon my oath, King Straasha, if you take us to Melniboné I promise you I shall do all I can to save your sister."

STRAASHA: "What can a little mortal do? But I thank thee for thy good intent. For that I'll not return thee to Agras Ti, but take thee to thy destination."

Straasha transports the two men back to Melniboné.

He deposits them on the shores near their home island, which is visible far away across the glistening mud-flats—all kinds of abandoned ships, sea-creatures and so forth.

STRAASHA: "Thy heart is a good one, mortal. If only thou knew some way of saving my sister, I would be in thy debt for ever."

ELRIC: "I will think on it, sire. All our interests depend on defeating this Chaos creature!"

The two men are exhausted by the time they get to Imrryr. They stagger through the streets, issuing warnings to any who pause to listen—

ELRIC: "Arm yourselves! The Falkryn march upon Melniboné!"

DYVIM MAR: "They drain the sea—to remove our defenses!"

They come into the throne room where the queen sits on the traditional Ruby Throne of Melniboné. She scowls, scarcely believing what they have to say.

ELRIC: "Scarcely three days, your majesty, and the Falkryn horde's upon us! The dragons sleep. We have no walls against them!"

QUEEN SHYRIX'X: "You clearly have no faith in the courage and skill of our warriors, White Crow. Melniboné can beat any barbarian horde, no matter how large!"

DYVIM MAR: "A renegade Melnibonéan is with them, madam! They call him Wild Dog."

SHYRIX'X: "I know of no 'Wild Dog.' What I'd rather hear is how you came to lose one of our Phoorn. Where is the dragon on which you rode?"

Dyvim Mar is embarrassed. He explains and we hear him at the end of his explanation . . .

DYVIM MAR: " . . . then she was seized by a water elemental and exhausted. We were forced to abandon her in the drained lake. At that point we were captured by the Falkryn horde . . ."

SHYRIX'X: "Cowards! You concoct a fantasy to explain your own incompetence. White Crow, you're no true champion, but a fraud. And you, of all people, Dyvim Mar, have lied to me!"

SHYRIX'X: "Guards—to the oubliette with them!"

The pair are taken and thrown down into the oubliette—a deep pit with steep sides from which there is no apparent escape. A grille is placed over the top.

At the bottom, Elric and Dyvim Mar are disconsolate to say the least . . .

DYVIM MAR: "Well, cousin, it's an old adage but a true one—the bringer of bad news is never welcome at court. But I fear she believes herself betrayed by us. With luck she'll let us linger here for a few weeks and then forgive us."

ELRIC: "There'll be worse news soon. We must get out of here."

DYVIM MAR: "You know a spell to grant us wings?"

ELRIC: "There's one thing we can try . . ."

The two men have braced their backs against the walls of the oubliette, across from one another. They have twisted their legs together so that they create a kind of bridge between them. So long as they maintain this tension they can 'chimney' up the oubliette.

They are sweating by the time they get to the top and, using a narrow ridge for their toes, push up the grille.

Guards spot them and come running towards them.

Elric and Dyvim Mar take on the guards and, with superior fighting skills, disarm them and use their own weapons against them.

Then they go running through the tunnels.

DYVIM MAR: "This way. An old tunnel's a secret way to the Dragon Caves!"

They hide in the maze of caverns while the guards fail to find them.

They arrive in the secret Dragon Caves where all the dragons sleep solidly.

DYVIM MAR: "If only we had not awakened all but Snaptail. It will be a full year before we can use them again."

ELRIC: "Is there no sorcery which will wake them sooner?"

DYVIM MAR: "Sleep's the secret of their power. They restore their bodies and their venom. Even if they could fly, they would have no weapons against their enemies. They rely on our people to guard them while they sleep . . . All we can do is wait—and fight our enemies as best we can . . .

CHAPTER THREE

The Year of the Barbarian

Then the Falkryn came . . .

A massive battle scene as the Falkryn attack the Melnibonéans, driving them back into their own streets. At the forefront is the demonic Yyrkoon/Wild Dog while the sorcerer Agras Ti does not fight, but watches from safety, smirking to himself. In an inset he slips into the throne room.

Elric and Dyvim Mar have followed Agras Ti into the throne room as he attempts to kill the queen.

AGRAS TI: "Aha! The queen!"

While Dyvim Mar tries to get the queen to leave, Elric engages Agras Ti.

DYVIM MAR: "My lady! 'Tis the Falkryn chief. Beware his sorcery!"

ELRIC: "In his eagerness, he's left his bodyguards behind."

Under pressure, Agras Ti calls upon his protector, Lord Arioch of Chaos.

AGRAS TI: "*Arioch! My lord Arioch aid me now!*"

ELRIC: "So that foul duke of hell protects you! I should have guessed that's who helped you bring the drinker of oceans to this realm!"

As Dyvim Mar helps the queen out of danger, they look in horror as Arioch of Chaos begins to manifest himself.

He first appears as a hideous creature of smoke and flame but slowly manifests himself as a gigantic golden youth of impossible beauty, wearing cloth-

ing exactly the same style as that worn by the Melnibonéans. A way of flattering them and putting them at their ease.

Agras Ti runs towards his master, begging for help as Elric recoils.

AGRAS TI: "Master! Save me. They mean to kill me!"

Arioch smiles almost benignly down on his creature, Agras Ti. He reaches out one slender-fingered hand towards the sorcerer.

ARIOCH: " 'Twas thy sorcery brought me to this realm, Agras Ti. For that I repaid thee by inviting my brother Lord Artigkern, the drinker of oceans, to join us, even do thy bidding. But now he has what he wants and, indeed, I have exactly what I want. Thy purpose is fulfilled, mortal."

AGRAS TI: "P-purpose, lord?"

ARIOCH: "I have a destiny to carry out, as have we all. There is a mortal here more important to my plans than ever you could be. Elric—Silverskin—do you know me? White Crow, is it?"

As he speaks he casually raises the writhing, horrified Agras Ti towards his beautiful lips . . .

ELRIC: "I know thee not, Chaos Lord. Begone from this realm. We want none of your folk in Melniboné!"

Agras Ti is screaming in terror, unnoticed by Arioch, who now parts his lips a little, preparing to eat him . . .

ARIOCH: "But I come to help thee. I could destroy all these foolish humans, if you will let me . . ."

ELRIC: "Melniboné never makes bargains with Chaos. My destiny and thine have nothing in common!"

ARIOCH: "Ah, my friend, but we could do so much for each other, thee and I . . ."

Elric recoils as Arioch munches on half of the Falkryn sorcerer. The rest of him is still in his hands.

ELRIC: "Cruel monster! I'd rather die than make a compact with corrupted Chaos . . ."

ARIOCH: "Well, I inhabit thy realm now, young mortal. I suspect the time will come when thou'll find it convenient to strike a bargain . . ."

The golden youth begins to become the monster of smoke and flame again.

ARIOCH: "For the moment, farewell. To summon me, thou hast only to call for me by name. And all I'll ask for my help is a little blood, a few worthless souls . . ."

Elric leads Dyvim Mar and the queen behind the throne and down a flight of secret steps as the Falkryn barbarians, led by Yyrkoon, all of them covered with blood and bearing booty, burst into the throne room.

ELRIC: "Quickly! We have only seconds!"

YYRKOON: "Ha! She's fled. And left me the Ruby Throne. I'm Emperor of Melniboné now!"

He seats himself on the throne, brooding.

YYRKOON: "But until that silverskin is dead, I shall not know peace of mind."

Wild Dog spoke truth. Though he controlled Melniboné, he had poor control of the Falkryn, whose leader was now mysteriously vanished . . .

. . . and he maintained even less authority over his own people.

A montage of guerilla fighting. The occupying Falkryn, though cruel and vicious, have a poor time controlling the streets.

They are harassed, within Melniboné and in the Imrryrian countryside, by small bands of Melnibonéans led by Elric, Queen Shyrix'x and Dyvim Mar.

Death comes to the conquerors by secret arrows, sudden strangulation, sword thrusts and spear casts.

Artigkern has the sea-king's sister in the giant clam shell, semi-transparent. His horrible hands open the shell wide enough to reach in and caress her face . . . She recoils in horror.

Yyrkoon is riding out at night on a secret mission of his own.

YYRKOON: "Another few months . . . then the power of the dragons will be mine. Meanwhile those rebels shall be tamed . . ."

Yyrkoon meets Artigkern, grown even fatter, slimier and grosser than ever, still sucking the oceans and leaving fish, ships and all stranded . . . Yyrkoon addresses him angrily.

YYRKOON: "Must you drink it all? I helped summon thee to this realm."

ARTIGKERN: "I leave a realm when there is nothing left to drink. The time will come when I'll spit all this water into the sun and set off to find new worlds with fresh seas for me to sup . . ."

YYRKOON: "Then give up the sea-king's sister. He has no more power over you."

ARTIGKERN (*grinning*): "Give up my darling. Did I not tell thee, mortal? I'm in love. I'll take her with me when I go. Bring me a bride as beautiful and perhaps I'll give thee her and a little of thy water back . . ."

Months passed. The morale of the conquered people was maintained only by the activities of Elric and his companions.

While the rebels were free, the future held freedom . . .

Montage of Elric, Dyvim Mar and the queen. They lead small parties of warriors on secret raids. They attack Falkryn in the streets. They steal from rich carpetbaggers. They are applauded by the Melnibonéans. They disappear down alleys. And Queen Shyrix'x and Dyvim Mar grow closer, become lovers with Elric's blessing.

A deputation of Falkryn knights stands before Yyrkoon. They and their soldiers are leaving.

FALKRYN LEADER: "You promised us booty and booty we have. You promised us power over the world, and that we do *not* have. Water grows scarce here. The people thirst."

FALKRYN LEADER: "We leave to find the fabled 'lost ocean.' "

Now Wild Dog's grip on the throne grew weaker . . .

Yyrkoon/Wild Dog, surrounded by Melnibonéan guards who have a somewhat decadent look, sits brooding on the Ruby Throne.

YYRKOON (*thinks*): "I must consolidate my power or my plans come to nothing. Once the dragons wake, I rule the world. But until then . . ."

MELNIBONÉAN GUARD: "Our water runs low, Lord King. I understood you had a compact with Duke Artigkern . . ."

YYRKOON (*scowling*): "So I do. He'll keep his bargain. I'll see to that! But these rebels must be tricked into submission . . ."

ANOTHER GUARD (*whispers in his ear*): "Then, sire . . ."

A newly dry approach to Imrryr . . .

We see a caravan coming in from the drained sea bottoms. The beasts have giant water jars and skins strapped over them. Queen Shyrix'x and Dyvim Mar lie hidden in wait with a small band of men, ready to raid it.

. . . *now a caravan route for that most precious of commodities* . . .

SHYRIX'X: "The people grow thirsty. This water will ease their misery . . ."

She leads her men in an attack on the caravan.

The canyons echo with battle cries . . .

. . . followed by an abrupt silence!

SHYRIX'X: "*It's a trap!*"

From hiding all around them comes a large force of warriors. The queen fights bravely, but it's clear the soldiers want only her. Their men lie dead all around them. Dyvim Mar is badly wounded. She cries to him to escape:

SHYRIX'X: "Flee, Dyvim Mar! Warn White Crow and the others!"

She's dragged before Yyrkoon who grins in pleasure.

YYRKOON: "You're mine now, lady."

They then drag in the wounded Dyvim Mar.

YYRKOON: "Become my queen and consolidate my power over Melniboné—or your paramour dies in exquisite agony!"

Elric watches from cover as . . .

The great ceremonial procession winds its way through the streets of Melniboné.

Yyrkoon is very smug, but clearly Queen Shyrix'x is deeply miserable.

The watching crowd is not exactly overjoyed, but they bow low before the passing parade, accepting the inevitable.

ELRIC (*thinks*): "He has achieved some legitimacy. And soon the dragons will begin to wake. Wild Dog's power will be complete."

Elric sneaks into the royal apartments to keep an assignation with Shyrix'x.

She fears Yyrkoon but risks all to speak to Elric.

SHYRIX'X: "Dyvim Mar is thrown into the oubliette. His life ensures my good behaviour—but the people grow unruly. Water is too scarce. They thirst."

Elric gets into the dungeons and sees Dyvim Mar, still wounded, down at the bottom of the oubliette. As Elric speaks he breaks a dagger trying to undo the padlock holding the grille in place.

ELRIC: "Hsssst! Dyvim Mar!"

DYVIM MAR: "Cousin! Risk not your own liberty here. I'm too valuable. They'll not let me get free again."

DYVIM MAR: "While I'm his prisoner the queen will do whatever he orders. Yet she's right—thirst will madden them enough to rise up and overthrow him . . ."

In the dragon caverns . . .

Elric looks down on the sleeping dragons, some of whom are indeed stirring. He is thoughtful, trying to work out a plan.

Out of nowhere a black raven comes to settle on his shoulder. He addresses it.

ELRIC: "Ha, old friend. You saved my life once. But how can we save the folk of Melniboné from tyranny and the world from drought . . . ?"

VOICE (*from outside the frame [it's Arioch]*): "There's one way, my friend."

Chapter Four

Dealing with Darkness

A figure of smoke and flame gradually materializes into the golden youth who is Duke Arioch of Chaos.

ARIOCH: "I wish only to help you, young mortal . . ."

ELRIC (*reacts angrily*): "Before I make bargains with Chaos I'll risk everything!!!"

ARIOCH: "A few more weeks and the dragons wake. The emperor will control them. He will have the power to set the whole world on fire. But if he were thwarted and Artigkern were dead, Melniboné would thrive again as a force for good . . ."

ELRIC: "Good? What does Chaos know of good?"

ARIOCH: "You simplify the multiverse. Neither Law nor Chaos are forces for good or evil in themselves. It is the use to which they are put by mortals that determines those qualities . . ."

ELRIC (*buries his head in his hands. He is baffled, tormented*): "I don't know!"

We cut to the dream couch in contemporary Melniboné. Elric lies on it clearly in the grip of a terrible nightmare. Cymoril looks at him and is alarmed, turning to Tanglebones.

CYMORIL: "See how tormented he is! What is happening to him? You *must* let me go to him, Master Tanglebones!"

TANGLEBONES: "You would have no memory of this world and would be a stranger in his. You'd hinder rather than help him, I assure you, Lady Cymoril . . ."

CYMORIL: "But . . . !"

TANGLEBONES (*also deeply concerned as he stares out of the panel at us*): "Though I share your frustration, he must solve this problem for himself, risking life and mind . . . or defeat the point of his dream-quest . . ."

Elric is back at the oubliette, trying to get Dyvim Mar out again.

ELRIC: "No good. It won't budge."

DYVIM MAR: "Forget me. He means to trade Shyrix'x for water. She's served her turn and he knows she plots against him . . . Save her, White Crow! For my sake!"

ELRIC: "But how? I possess no power. No allies left . . ."

Yyrkoon/Wild Dog appears snarling at the top of the steps:

YYRKOON: "So true, White Crow! And now I have all three of you! I baited my trap well."

YYRKOON: "As the dragons fly again, the world shall know Melniboné's might, and you two will not live long enough to see me trade my beautiful queen. Tomorrow she'll became Artigkern's bride and the people will thank me for restoring their water to them again! They'll follow me, and the dragons will grant us imperial power!"

YYRKOON: "I outwit thee at every turn!"

Elric is up against it, fighting off dozens of well-armed warriors who are bound to beat him. Yyrkoon snarls with triumph.

YYRKOON: "*Kill him*! I would be rid of that vermin once and for all!"

And now the young albino made a decision which was to determine his fate and that of his people until the end of time . . .

ELRIC (*thinks*): "I have no choice. Either we perish, or I betray my own principles—and can I let my friends die and my nation become a tyranny because I have a few scruples?"

As the guards close around him Elric lifts back his head and cries out:

ELRIC: "*ARIOCH! ARIOCH! BLOOD AND SOULS FOR MY LORD ARIOCH!*"

And the thing of smoke and flame begins to materialize in the darkness of the dungeon . . .

Clobbering time, Walter. You draw it. I'll go hide. Sound effects to taste.

Arioch remains in demonic form for this moment, rending and tearing, scattering body parts, and sending guards left and right before reaching for Yyrkoon, who runs for it.

Arioch tears off the grille of the oubliette. Elric throws Yyrkoon down into it. He survives by crawling away into a hole to hide.

As Arioch does his deadly work, Elric secures the grille, then helps Dyvim Mar towards the upper regions of the palace, fighting as he goes.

ELRIC: "Quickly, the queen . . ."

Dyvim Mar finds Queen Shyrix'x already tied up ready for the trade with Artigkern. He releases her. They embrace.

The fighting's over in the dungeon. Elric looks sick as he reviews the carnage in the dungeon. Now Arioch has assumed the likeness of a golden youth, but he is grinning demoniacally, wiping the blood from his mouth. His hands, too, are bloody.

ARIOCH: "See, Elric. I keep my promises. What other help can I offer thee?"

ELRIC: "None, demon. I have no stomach for this bargain. Thou hast thy blood and souls. Now begone . . ."

ARIOCH (*bows*): "Very well, sweet mortal. But remember I am part of this plane from this day on—and always at thy service . . ."

The black raven settles on Elric's shoulder as the Lord of Hell fades again into smouldering smoke. Elric scowls at the bird, which flaps up into the gloom of the cavern. Elric looks at it suspiciously, unable to work out what its function is.

ELRIC: "I have a premonition. Nothing but darkness and bloodshed can come of this bargain . . ."

The day is won. The nobles of Melniboné bend the knee to Queen Shyrix'x and her consort Dyvim Mar.

Shortly, in the queen's restored court . . .

Elric comes hurrying into the chamber.

ELRIC: "The dragons begin to wake. But how do we restore the oceans?"

SHYRIX'X: "Wild Dog planned to trade me not only for water, but for the sea-king's sister, whom Artigkern holds captive."

ELRIC: "If Artigkern sees us coming in force, he'll know we plan to trick him. He'll spit the world's water into the sun and we'll all die of thirst . . ."

DYVIM MAR: "And no doubt kill the sea-king's sister."

ELRIC: "Then here's what we must risk . . ."

Artigkern, as large as a large island, glistening and bulging with all the water he has drunk, still keeps the sea-king's sister in the shell he has created for her.

ARTIGKERN: "The mortal's a fool if he thinks I'll give up satisfying my thirst for a fresh bride, no matter how beautiful. I'll take the new woman he offers, but if I give up the sea-king's sister he'll take his vengeance on me if he can . . ."

Elric, dressed like Yyrkoon, comes riding a deep-sided wagon over the drained ocean floor escorting an apparently bound and gagged Queen Shyrix'x. It's the same wagon he and Dyvim Mar were trapped in earlier.

ELRIC: "My Lord of Chaos! I come to keep our bargain. You will give me a ration of water and the sea-king's sister, and I'll give thee this mortal woman."

ARTIGKERN: "'Tis a bargain. Bring her closer."

Elric, driving the wagon, approaches the impossibly huge bulk of the Chaos Lord.

As he gets close to where the sea-king's sister wallows in melancholy in her half-open shell, he whips up the horses!

ELRIC: "Faster, faster! Ha! Ya!"

The draperies on the wagon fall back to reveal a near-transparent obsidian tank of water and Queen Shyrix'x throws back her cloak to reveal she's not bound. With a war-axe she smashes the clam shell, releasing the sea-king's sister and then half-hauls her into the tank of water the wagon is drawing.

SHYRIX'X: "Quickly, my lady—we must not hesitate!"

Artigkern makes to reach towards them to stop them—then looks to the horizon.

ARTIGKERN: "What's this?"

Over the horizon pours a huge flight of Phoorn dragons. (Inset is Dyvim Mar, with his long dragon-goad in his hand, riding the leading Phoorn.)

Suddenly the sky is black with dragons.

As the wagon hauls away, the first dragons dive on Artigkern, their venom striking his swollen body—and piercing the skin . . . bursting him so that water erupts from every wound . . .

. . . and Elric and Queen Shyrix'x, hauling the sea-king's sister, are pursued by a vast tidal wave of water released from Artigkern . . .

. . . which overwhelms them so it seems they must drown . . . The horses fight for their lives. Elric slashes their harness . . .

. . . until Dyvim Mar swoops down on the dragon to rescue Queen Shyrix'x . . .

. . . and the sea-king's sister, in open water now, catches up Elric and the horses, swimming with them to a high hill which is swiftly becoming an island . . .

. . . whereupon Straasha the Sea-King, clearly delighting in his watery kingdom again, comes swimming towards them to embrace his sister . . .

STRAASHA: "Against all odds you've kept your promise, mortal—henceforth thy people and mine shall be allied and I shall be forever in thy debt! Your nation shall prosper and become the strongest in the world!"

In the distance, heading for Melniboné, Dyvim Mar and Queen Shyrix'x wave farewell from the back of the dragon.

ELRIC: "And sweet Melniboné shall know peace and security again . . ."

In the dream chamber Elric stirs and wakes. He looks pretty wasted, but he's smiling as he's greeted with relief by Tanglebones and Cymoril, who hands him his reviving potion.

CYMORIL: "Thank Arioch! You survived!"

TANGLEBONES: "Another dream-quest accomplished. Another lesson learned. Welcome back, young master!"

Elric swings off the couch and begins to stride for the door. They follow him, puzzled.

He enters another dream chamber where Yyrkoon is also coming to. But Yyrkoon does not look at all happy. He glares at his cousin. He strikes away the offered potion.

YYRKOON: "So you wake, cousin. You still live . . . I recall—I recall—it was not a pleasant dream . . ."

ELRIC: "For my part, cousin, I'm feeling all the better for my long slumber. Yours, it seems, has not entirely agreed with you!"

Yyrkoon staggers away on the arm of his slave, snarling. Cymoril moves to embrace Elric.

YYRKOON: "There'll be other opportunities, I'm sure . . ."

Meanwhile the brooding Sadric frowns as he looks down on the scene from a gallery high above the room . . . The mysterious Arisand stands beside him.

SADRIC: "So once again my enfeebled son survives. But for how long? How long? The crown's not yet decided . . ."

BOOK THREE

THE DREAM OF FIVE YEARS: THE DREAM OF AIR

THE SOUTH WIND'S SOUL

Chapter One

Death from Above

SUNRISE IN MELNIBONÉ . . .

Three small panels across the top of a large panel:

Yyrkoon is getting up from his bed, donning his robe and talking to the human woman Arisand.

Prince Yyrkoon, Elric's rival, rises . . .

YYRKOON: "The dream's done! Two more still to dream . . . And that weakling dog lives on. How to destroy my feeble cousin and make myself old Sadric's heir?"

Sadric, brooding as always, stares into the rising sun from his balcony.

. . . while Elric's father Sadric broods on . . .

SADRIC: "Two dreams, two powerful allies gained. My son does well, but can his success be sustained?"

Elric is about to mount the dream couch and is sipping a concoction handed him by Cymoril as he addresses Tanglebones.

TANGLEBONES: "You'll sleep, Lord Elric, for twenty hours. Each four hours represents a year in the dream lands of our common past."

ELRIC: "Thanks, Master Tanglebones." *(Addresses Cymoril:)* "Shall I find your brother lying in wait to murder me again, my dear Cymoril?"

CYMORIL: "No doubt, in some guise. You can be killed as readily in your dream reality as you can here. You must take care, my love."

And so the fresh dream begins.

It is some eight thousand years earlier, when Melniboné had achieved economic ascendancy over the peoples of the "Old Kingdoms" but had not yet begun to build her empire . . .

From the viewpoint of Melnibonéan King Feneric and his teenage son, Silverskin (Elric in this dream), we look out across a stylized map of the Old Kingdoms (which, believe it or not, preceded the Young Kingdoms). The map can be based on the Cawthorn map in the White Wolf editions, but many of the names will be different. I'll do a rough drawing of the map and send it to Walter and Joey [Cavalieri, editor of the book at DC]. It will show, among other things, the distant Mountains of the Myyrrhn, the port city (across the sea from Melniboné) of Port Norvaknol in the Kingdom of Forin'Shen and so on. The outlines of the main continent will be the same, of course, but many of the names will be different. These are the "Old Kingdoms" which will disappear with the rise of Melniboné, replaced with the "Young Kingdoms."

KING FENERIC: "Our island nation grows in power and influence. We trade across the wide world. My son, you must learn diplomacy if you would rule in Melniboné's interest. You must ever respect the Old Kingdoms who were here before us . . ."

ELRIC/SILVERSKIN: "You teach me my duty, Father, and my responsibilities. Respect, I think, is at the heart of all."

FENERIC: "Trade is the source of our power. If we are fair and honourable, our power is well earned and will never be threatened . . ."

Feneric is taking his son through a market where Melnibonéans trade with strange-looking people from all over the Old Kingdoms, including the Pukwadji we saw in the first story. All are humanoid, but some are distinctly alien.

FENERIC: "But should we seek to maintain that power by the sword, Melniboné shall inevitably fall. That is the fate of all who would force their will upon the world. Our ancestors knew that and passed their wisdom down to us."

ELRIC: "I have learned that much, at least. If we remain adaptable, we remain strong. If we force others to accept our traditions and values, we ultimately grow weak . . ."

FENERIC (*smiles*): "How well you learn the statecraft of Melniboné. You will make a great king one day . . ."

His brother Ederic strides up, all arrogance and swaggering power.

EDERIC: "My lord Feneric!"

FENERIC: "Ah, Ederic, brother! Well met!"

EDERIC (*laughs in a somewhat sinister way*): "Kings are judged by the firmness of their fists, brother, not the sweetness of their tongues. Greedy hands reach for our wealth, young Silverskin. Greedy eyes burn with envy."

Young Silverskin scowls, finding this advice unpalatable.

Weeks went by while the young Silverskin studied, oblivious of the rivalry between his father and his uncle. But then, one morning—

Elric/Silverskin is at his lessons when he hears a shout from the street. Going to the window he sees people pointing skyward and out to sea. There is a great armada—ships sailing across the sky as they might sail across the sea. The ships are single-sailed, rather like Viking ships, with ugly carvings as figureheads and green-skinned, hairless men crowding their rails and rigging, as hideous a group of raiders as we've ever seen. Their sails billow with a mysterious wind as they approach the island of Melniboné and the city of Imrryr. Flying alongside these ships are a different breed—the Winged Men of Myyrrhn—who have appeared in the Elric books. They are armed with long spears and bows and arrows. They are handsome and strong and have huge, downy wings which make them resemble stereotypical angels . . .

FIRST CITIZEN: "Raiders! The green men of Karasim!"

SECOND CITIZEN: "And the winged men of Myyrrhn are with them!"

ELRIC (*thinks*): "The Karasim have long hated our power. And now they come to challenge it. But what sorcery drives those ships?"

FENERIC (*bursting into the room*): "Lad, we must to arms. But whoever aids the Karasim and their allies cannot be defeated by swords alone . . ."

ELRIC: "I'll seek Ivram Tvar, the Dragon Master . . ."

Elric speeds off through the corridors of the palace, down the steps which lead to the secret passages in turn leading to the Dragon Caves . . .

A Melnibonéan captain has already reached the caves and addresses Ivram Tvar, the Dragon Master. Ivram Tvar spreads his hands helplessly:

IVRAM TVAR: "Their time to strike is well chosen. All the Phoorn sleep and cannot be wakened. Powerful sorcery aids the Karasim. I suspect Chaos itself has a hand in this!"

ELRIC: "If the dragons cannot save us, what can?"

IVRAM TVAR: "Only our courage and our weapons, young prince . . ."

A sword in his hand, Elric emerges into the Imrryrian street, to find towers burning as skins of Greek Fire are dropped from the ships above and green warriors slip down ropes dropped over the sides of the hovering ships.

ELRIC: "The winged men of Myyrrhn have never been our enemies. What makes them attack Melniboné now?"

Attacked by several Karasim at once Elric defends himself well. From overhead his father sees him and cries encouragement. Elric shows considerable skill and ferocity in the fight.

FENERIC: "You fight well, my son!"

ELRIC (*to the raiders*): "We have no quarrel with you! Why do you attack us?"

A Karasim captain sees Elric fighting outside a burning building and calls from where he swings by a rope from his ship, pointing at Elric.

CAPTAIN: "He's the one! Capture him alive!"

Elric fights well but is eventually captured. A winged man of Myyrrhn swoops down and carries him up towards the Karasim ship. Elric is bopped on the head and passes out.

Scene from the ground. The Karasim ships are swinging around to leave. Laden with booty, the green men climb back up into their ships. The Myyrrhn have no booty. They carry their dead or wounded with them in the air, disdaining the Karasim ships. It is as if they wish to have little to do with their green allies. Ederic watches, sweating in his armour. Could he be glad of what's happening?

MELNIBONÉAN (*in burning ruin*): "They retreat! We've driven them off."

FENERIC: "They've taken young Silverskin! They've stolen my son!"

IVRAM TVAR: "They've gone beyond the Edge of the World. As soon as I can rouse a dragon, I'll follow."

FENERIC: "We'll need an army—and who knows what will have become of him by the time we get there . . ."

Bowed with grief but looking grim Feneric turns back to his gutted palace.

FENERIC: "But we must do whatever we can to find him. Rally my captains. Harsh sorcery's at work here and I know not how to fight it."

EDERIC: "Go, brother, and good luck!"

Chapter Two

Into the Middle March

In less than an hour Melniboné was far behind and the young Silverskin grew tired of struggling . . .

They invaders are now over the ocean, with Melniboné out of sight behind.

Elric is weary. He is now tied up and lying on the deck of one of the ships whose sails fill with a mysterious wind, blown by scarcely seen supernatural creatures.

ELRIC (*thinks*): "Wind spirits aid them and no doubt keep their ships airborne. How do the Karasim make allies of such supernaturals? If I escaped now I'd have an ocean to swim before I could reach home . . ."

The Karasim captain stands over Elric as his men lift him up off the deck.

CAPTAIN: "He's served his turn. We've no further use for him. Throw him overboard!"

Elric is thrown overboard, falling down into the clouds below.

Elric is plunging helplessly through the clouds.

A handsome Myyrrhn warrior swoops in and snatches him up.

Flying with him away from the Karasim fleet.

Towards an horizon on which bleak, spiky mountains can be seen. This is the land of the Myyrrhn and others are flying towards the mountains.

ELRIC: "You saved me. Why?"

Prince Vashntni offers Elric a grim smile.

PRINCE VASHNTNI: "I am Vashntni, Prince of the Myyrrhn. We are warriors, not murderers."

They have reached the vast, high, spiky mountains in which the Myyrrhn make their homes. On these peaks are built houses which bear some resemblance to eagles' nests. Prince Vashntni drops down towards an elaborate house of this kind and deposits Elric on a balcony.

VASHNTNI: "You are now my guest."

ELRIC: "I must return to Melniboné at once. My father . . ."

VASHNTNI: "You will remain with us. I cannot anger the Karasim . . ."

ELRIC: "Why would a people as honourable as yours ally themselves with corrupt thieves like the Karasim?"

VASHNTNI (*scowling*): "We had no choice. Ask no further questions, young Silverskin. You are welcome to remain here, to move as freely as possible. Our famous libraries are yours. It is the best I can offer you."

And so the Melnibonéan prince became an exiled prisoner, pining for his homeland, but determined to continue his studies—especially in the arts of sorcery . . .

Time passes as Elric wanders the strange labyrinthine "nests" of the Myyrrhn, befriended by young winged women in particular. He studies old manuscripts, stares yearningly over the mountains, and generally pines for his home . . .

ELRIC (*thinks*): "I yearn to know how my father fares. If I could get even a message to him . . . For now, I'll study what sorcery I can."

Meanwhile, there were diversions . . .

The Myyrrhn girls and youths befriend Elric. High in the air they toss him from one to another, bearing him for miles over the wild peaks of the mountains.

Elric dallies with one of the winged girls. He asks her a question:

ELRIC: "I wonder why folk as fine as yours should aid the Karasim?"

Girl drops her eyes, telling him a secret she shouldn't really tell.

GIRL: "The Karasim hold Vashntni's daughter hostage. We had no choice . . ."

Then, late one night, a visitor . . .

Elric wearily pores over old scrolls in the library. Then through the window flies the black raven (Sepiriz) which perches on one of the old books and looks at him with wise, ancient eyes.

ELRIC: "The raven! It seems I recognize you . . . What book would you have me read?"

Elric has discovered a spell in one of the old books. A breakthrough!

ELRIC (*thinks*): "Here's a means of creating a portal to return me home. If only I can remember all I learned in Melniboné, there could be a way. 'Tis dangerous magic . . ."

Referring to the scroll, Elric begins to make strange passes in the air and speaks in "runic" . . .

He is blown back by a blast which effectively blows black light into the chamber. You can see from his face that the spell has gone wrong.

ELRIC: "*NO!* The spell failed! This is disaster!"

A portal had been created—now it dragged the young albino into horrible darkness . . .

Elric is dragged, screaming, into a black hole. He falls backwards, deeper and deeper into darkness . . .

. . . to arrive not in Melniboné, but a chill landscape, grim and near-lightless . . .

Elric has landed on a black featureless plain. A little pale light comes down from a tiny moon high overhead. There are some distant stars, but unfamiliar.

ELRIC: "Those stars! They are like no constellations I've ever seen. This place—what have I done? Where am I?"

VOICE (*from outside the frame*): "Welcome, young Silverskin. Welcome to limbo—the place some call 'The Middle March'—the lands between the worlds."

Elric turns—and there stands the one we know as Arioch, who here calls himself The Unknown. His own light emanates from him. He is a golden, gorgeous youth. A dandy in strange, alien clothes. At his hip is a scabbarded black sword and in his right hand is a golden staff. He himself is of stunning appearance. He smiles a little sardonically.

ARIOCH: "Have you forgotten who I am, Silverskin?"

ELRIC: "We've never met before!"

ARIOCH: "Oh, we've met before and we'll meet again, for I am your supernatural mentor. Your interests and mine are the same. And shall be to the end of time . . ."

ELRIC: "I've never seen you before, sir!"

ARIOCH: "Perhaps you don't recognize me. I'll forgive your poor manners. After all, you are not very old."

Elric recovers himself and makes a short bow to the newcomer.

ELRIC: "Excuse me, my lord. Perhaps my memory has been affected by my fall . . ."

ARIOCH: "I can tell I'm unwelcome. Call for me should you need my help. Farewell."

And Arioch vanishes in a golden flash, leaving nothing but the dark, bleak, moonlit landscape.

ELRIC: "I suspect that creature. But I need a guide if I'm to return to Melniboné. What's that slithering, unwholesome sound?"

He whirls at a sound behind him and catches a glimpse of a Night Worm. The Night Worms are huge, blind white worms. They crawl at the edge of the darkness, scenting for Elric's blood. They have vampire mouth-parts.

Another voice whispers out of the darkness:

FENKI: "Heh, heh, heh—the Night Worms are sniffing for your blood, little Silverskin . . . They hunger so for such sweet, fresh sustenance . . ."

ELRIC: "Who's that?"

Fenki is sitting on a high rock looking down at Elric. The Night Worms slither in closer.

FENKI: "Only old Fenki, master. Just another poor lost soul like yourself . . . exiled to the Middle March through his own bad sorcery . . ."

ELRIC: "Come down, sir, and declare yourself!"

FENKI: "It would be rude to interrupt the Night Worms when they feast on your tasty blood . . ."

Elric has no weapon, no means of defending himself. The worms slither in closer. He tries to scramble for the rocks and slips. Fenki capers above, enjoying Elric's predicament. Elric kicks futilely at the Night Worms.

ELRIC: "Filthy creatures . . . *Aarkkk!*"

FENKI: "Hee, hee! You must learn to scramble faster than that, Silver-skin!"

There comes a blast from out of the darkness which sends Fenki hopping away in terror.

FENKI: "*Eek!* No offense, my lord! Forgive me . . ."

Arioch has reappeared. He is grinning at Fenki's discomfort and also at Elric's disgust. He throws Elric a black sword (it's Stormbringer).

ARIOCH: "Here, take this blade. See if you can use it!"

Then the Night Worms have closed in on Elric and he is fighting for his life.

ELRIC: "This sword! It seems to lend me strength!"

Slicing and stabbing around him.

Elric becomes demonic as he fights the Night Worms. Scores of them attack him, but he succeeds in fighting them off while Arioch, smiling with satisfaction, watches him beat them off. Fenki sits on his own bit of rock nearby, scared both of Arioch and Elric's sword.

ARIOCH: "He fights well, eh, Master Fenki?"

FENKI: "Oh, aye, master—very well. But who could not, with that damned blade?"

Arioch claps his hand on Fenki's shoulder.

ARIOCH: "Oh, come now, Master Fenki. You don't give the lad enough credit . . ."

FENKI (*shuddering*): "Whatever you say, my lord."

Elric rests panting as the remaining Night Worms slither away to safety. He looks down at the bloody sword in his hands. He is somewhat aghast at the havoc he has been able to cause.

ELRIC: "How—? How could I have killed so many?"

Arioch jumps down from the rock and approaches him.

ARIOCH: "See. You're more skilled than you thought, Master Silverskin, eh?"

In revulsion, Elric flings the sword down.

ELRIC: "No! Some foul sorcery has aided me. That blade's enchanted!"

ARIOCH: "Possibly. But you owe it your life, do you not?"

ELRIC: "I thank you for your aid, sir. I fear that weapon. It seems alive . . ."

Arioch stoops and picks up the sword.

ARIOCH: "I must admit, it has its sentient moments. Do you still resist my help?"

Elric remains highly suspicious of Arioch.

ELRIC: "I suspect there are conditions to that help, my lord. Where is this place and how did you know when to expect me?"

Arioch shrugs and spreads his hands, making a pantomime of his innocence. He sheathes the Black Sword in his own scabbard.

ARIOCH: "Merely a traveler between the worlds, like yourself, Sir Silverskin. Perhaps I'm a little more familiar with these marches. I could help you save your father and return to Melniboné . . . Meanwhile . . .

He makes a passage in the air and we see a shadowy table and chairs appear.

ARIOCH: " . . . let's eat! You must be tired of Myyrrhn's simple fare and long for the luxury of the life you left behind."

Arioch has conjured a table and two chairs. While Fenki looks on from a safe perch, Arioch produces delicious food for the table, a jug of wine. Fenki is hungry. As Arioch eats, he throws the creature scraps.

Elric is hungry and sets to. But he is still deeply suspicious.

ELRIC: "You are a sorcerer, that's plain. Can you get me back to my father in Melniboné?"

ARIOCH: "Regrettably, your father is not in Melniboné. For the past two years he has been crossing the world to its very edge!"

Arioch makes a passage in the air to show a scene of Elric's father's expedition. He heads a weary, battered army on bony horses in ragged armour.

ARIOCH: "Naturally he saw the Karasim steal you. And it is to the Abyss of Karasim that he ventured. It has been a long, hard journey with many dangers on the way . . ."

ELRIC (*half-rising from the table*): "Then I must go to his aid! I had no idea so many lives were at risk!"

ARIOCH (*lifts his goblet in a toast*): "Sit down, young man. We are in limbo. Time has stopped here. But you must make up your mind. Would you return home—or aid your father? Your uncle Ederic sits on his throne, ruling in his stead. If you were in Melniboné now, I could help you seize that power back . . ."

ELRIC (*puzzled*): "Why should I do that? I'm sure my uncle rules well in my father's absence . . ."

Arioch spirits them up from the ground to a rocky ledge where he throws scraps of food down to the Night Worms while Fenki hovers in fear below him.

ARIOCH (*amused*) "Ah, such innocence! Know you not that your uncle aided the Karasim raid just so that you could be captured, knowing your father would mount an expedition to find you?"

ELRIC (*angry*): "Why would my uncle plot such infamy?"

ARIOCH: "He believes with me that Melniboné will only maintain her power through strong magic and force of arms."

ELRIC: "My father sees such thinking as the ruin of all we stand for! If you share Ederic's opinion, why not aid *him*?"

ARIOCH: "Because I cultivate the larger picture."

ELRIC (*angry*): "What mean you by that?"

ARIOCH: "A few thousand years, and you'll learn my purpose. Never fear . . ."

Elric reaches towards Arioch who backs away with a smile.

ELRIC: "Take me to my father! I'll thwart you yet, Sir Demon!"

Arioch is amused and still dandified, unhurried. He smiles down at the sniveling Fenki.

ARIOCH: "Well, Fenki? Would you lead our young Silverskin out of here to join his father in defeat?"

FENKI (*grins in anticipation*): "Oh, gladly, master. Gladly!"

Arioch puts his hand on Elric's shoulder. The young albino scowls at him.

ARIOCH: "Then so be it!"

ELRIC: "What cunning is this? Why would you help me?"

Arioch smiles insouciantly.

ARIOCH: "Why? Because you asked! But now I grow tired of your callow rudeness. I'll leave you in Master Fenki's good hands . . ."

Again Arioch vanishes.

FENKI: "Come, then, young master, let's be on our way before the Night Worms sense you're weaponless again . . ."

Fenki leads Elric across a glinting peat bog from which sinister mist rises and in which sinister shapes shift and shamble . . .

And then, suddenly, the sun begins to rise over the bog until Elric sees figures in the distance. Fenki points and grins. The ruined, weary army of King Feneric can be seen trailing its way over the wasteland.

FENKI: "There. You are back in your own world. And there's your wretched father. Join him in his misery!"

Elric begins to run towards the distant warriors.

ELRIC: "*FATHER!*"

Chapter Three

To the World's Edge

Elric runs towards the ribbon of soldiery on the horizon, but as he draws closer he realizes that this is a defeated army. Their armour is dented, their clothes in rags, their mounts and the horses which draw their chariots are exhausted, as are the soldiers themselves. They look up as Elric approaches and there is only misery in their faces. Elric's father is not among them.

ELRIC: "Melnibonéans, yes . . . But where's my father?"

SOLDIER: "My prince! You live still! But you are too late!"

A captain conveys the terrible news to Elric.

CAPTAIN: "Great Feneric fought heroically as a true king of Melniboné. All around him were killed and he, too, could be dead. We had no choice but to retreat . . ."

SOLDIER: "They have wind demons to aid them, and they hide deep in an abyss. Feneric's courage and skills were not enough."

Elric scowls and clenches his fists.

ELRIC: "You abandoned my father! Well I shall not."

He reaches towards the soldier.

ELRIC: "Give me weapons and I'll return to the Karasim Abyss alone!

Equipped with armour and weapons, mounted on a horse, Elric sets off in the opposite direction to the battered army. One warrior shouts after him—

WARRIOR: "Prince, your courage is not doubted. But they have sorcerous help."

Elric flings back over his shoulder:

ELRIC: "As I have, captain. As I have!"

Weeks later . . .

Elric reins in his horse on a ridge, looking out across a wide plain. The plain ends at the edge of a vast abyss. The other side of the abyss is invisible. Great dark clouds obscure the far side, giving the impression, indeed, that we have reached the edge of the world.

The other strange sight is that of the Karasim fleet, at rest on the edge of the abyss as if they were beached in harbour. Their sails are furled and their oars shipped. These are the same ships which attacked Melniboné, but are not moored on water. They are not moored at all.

ELRIC (*thinks*): "That can only be the Karasim Abyss. I recognize their ships. And they appear to have no guards. Doubtless they take confidence from the defeat of our soldiers."

Elric leaves his horse and weapons, and approaches the ships, using what cover he can.

There is no sign of the Karasim.

ELRIC (*thinks*): "They say the Karasim favour darkness to daylight. Could they all be down below the Edge of the World?"

Under cover of darkness, Elric sneaks amongst the Karasim warships. There are a few of the green men sleeping on the decks but it is easy for him to reach the "edge of the world" and lying on his belly peer down into the gorge.

What he sees there astonishes him. A long stairway, occasionally becoming steps, which winds down the side of the abyss. There are brands guttering in holders every few feet. Unsuspecting Karasim come and go. But there is no sign of his father.

ELRIC (*thinks*): "I've no choice but to go down there. If my father's alive, I must find him . . ."

Elric begins to descend into the abyss.

ELRIC (*thinks*): " . . . and save him . . ."

Soon the young Silverskin was deep into the abyss . . .

ELRIC (*thinks*): "Their city is carved into the living rock. Somewhere here they'll have my father, if he still lives."

Elric sneaks past a group of Karasim warriors. They seem very cheerful, having just won a great victory and captured some important prisoners.

The city is huge and gloomy, full of ancient carved obsidian pillars and walls. Carved stairways, galleries and halls. Elric sneaks through these, avoiding green Karasim warriors and womenfolk at every turn. Great brands flare everywhere and he uses the shadows to conceal himself.

ELRIC (*thinks*): "The Karasim celebrate their victory. But where in this vast warren . . . ?"

He finds himself in a huge hall where clearly the Karasim are celebrating. On his carved obsidian throne sits King Minak, chief of the Karasim. He drinks from an upturned Melnibonéan helmet and two dead Melnibonéans hang in chains on the wall beside him. A scene of barbaric horror and cruelty.

ELRIC (*thinks*): "If I only had a weapon . . ."

Suddenly an old woman hisses and points at him. He tries to turn and flee but he is surrounded by Karasim warriors. He knocks one out and grabs his sword and puts up a good fight but—

—he's overwhelmed and dragged before the gleeful King Minak.

KING MINAK: "Ha! One we overlooked. Like the silverskin we killed, he's pale enough to resemble those creatures who live in our city's depths. We'll skin him when we're done with our entertainment. Put him with the others!"

ELRIC (*thinks*): "At least he doesn't recognize me . . ."

Elric is dragged through more corridors, deeper into the city, into a chamber which is a kind of wide pit. Around the edges are a number of iron cages, fancifully worked. In the centre of the pit is a block of rock and on the rock is perched a sealed wine jug. Most of these cages are filled with Melnibonéan prisoners, some of them wounded. A sorry sight. Elric's father is in one of these and stifles an exclamation as Elric is thrown into the cage next to his.

The green warriors depart.

FENERIC: "My son! We are reunited in sorry circumstance. Where did they keep you?"

ELRIC: "I was saved from death by a prince of the Myyrrhn. He told me by what infamy the Karasim employed his people . . ."

FENERIC: "I know. His daughter is here with us . . ."

Elric looks around in surprise. A voice comes from overhead.

PRINCESS: "I am Dela-Fwaar. You have seen my father?"

Elric looks up and sees a beautiful winged girl clinging to the roof of a nearby cage. She flies down towards him and clings to the bars of the cage.

ELRIC: "He saved my life. But could not let me go. I escaped with supernatural help."

FENERIC: "How so?"

Elric turns to his father.

ELRIC: "By a poorly cast spell and then with the aid of a Lord of Chaos . . ."

FENERIC (*brow clouds*): "Help from Chaos always has a price."

ELRIC (*skeptically*): "Well, his seemed low enough."

FENERIC: "Our legends tell how Chaos has sought to trick us in the past."

ELRIC: "Without that help I'd not be here with you, Father. Have you considered a means of escape?"

MELNIBONÉAN: "Even if we could get out of their city, they'd hunt us down with those flying ships of theirs."

Elric turns to the princess:

ELRIC: "I owe my life to your father, lady. And my escape I owe to his library. How did you come to be captured?"

We see a flashback scene. The princess is flying with some of her maidens when wind elementals seize them.

PRINCESS: "I was flying one day with my maidens when we were ambushed by wind sprites. They have always been our friends in the past."

The wind elementals carry the struggling princess to the Karasim Abyss.

PRINCESS: "They brought me here and I've been a prisoner ever since."

Elric's father is deep in thought.

FENERIC (*broodingly*): "I cannot work out the logic behind these plots."

ELRIC (*points to wine jar*): "It's simple, Father. Uncle Ederic seeks to rule in your stead. Secretly he's studied sorcery."

ELRIC: "'Twas he who captured the South Wind's soul and imprisoned it in yonder jar. That gave him control over the wind elementals who in turn helped the Karasim, who were commissioned to kidnap me so that you would take those loyal to you and try to rescue me."

FENERIC: "But why would my brother go to such lengths?"

ELRIC: "No doubt he believes you are too soft. That Melniboné should rule the world, attacking all potential enemies before they attack us."

FENERIC: "That goes against all our traditions."

ELRIC: "Which is why he'd be rid of all those who support those traditions . . ."

FENERIC (*slumps in despair*): "So 'tis not merely our own deaths we anticipate, but the death of everything we hold dear."

ELRIC: "Aye, I heard their plans for us. Our torture will be their entertainment."

FENERIC: "We have no hope of escape."

ELRIC: "There is one hope, Father. All I have to do to summon the Chaos Lord is call his name."

FENERIC: "No! Better a few of us die than the whole world be tormented by unchecked Chaos!"

Feneric is horrified. He reaches through the bars to grab at Elric's clothing.

FENERIC: "Chaos Lords can enter our world only if we invite them. That's his trick to ensnare you—and put Melniboné in his power. Believe me, my son, I have read the old books. More than once they have tried, but we have resisted. Best we perish than make alliances with Chaos!"

ELRIC (*angry*): "Let me decide! I'll not watch my own father tortured and killed, knowing I could have helped him!"

King Minak and some of his nobles appear on the steps above the cages. Minak is gloating with his power.

MINAK: "What's this? Quarreling amongst yourselves? Well, your shouts will be louder still tonight, when our entertainments begin."

Minak caresses the wine jug in which is kept the soul of the South Wind.

MINAK: "You upstart Melnibonéans thought you could lord it over the Old Kingdoms, but now you know how foolish you were to challenge us."

ELRIC: "So you make alliances with our traitors and expect them to be less of a threat? You don't deserve to survive."

Minak is angry. He pokes at Elric through the bars with his cutlass.

MINAK: "That tongue will beg me for mercy before it's torn from your mouth!" *(He turns to his guards:)* "Take the old king first. We'll show our guests what torments to expect tonight!"

ELRIC (*in rage*): "*No! Leave him or I'll—*"

MINAK (*grins*): "You'll do what? Beg me for mercy?"

In desperation Elric throws back his head and shouts for the help of the Chaos Lord—

ELRIC: "*ARIOCH! AID ME NOW, I BEG THEE! ARIOCH! BLOOD AND SOULS! BLOOD AND SOULS!*"

MINAK (*laughs at him*): "You pray to your useless gods. They'll not help you here."

But already a thick, black smoke is beginning to roil over in one corner of the cage. Minak and his men look startled.

ELRIC: "Arioch! Bring me the Black Sword!"

Elric's father shouts out in one last attempt to stop his son.

FENERIC: "My son! No! Please do not do this!"

But the black roiling smoke is forming a demonic, hideous shape. Already Minak is retreating up the stairs leaving his men to deal with it.

MINAK: "Some conjuring trick. Deal with it, men. I have business elsewhere . . ."

The hideous shape gradually becomes the beautiful youth, the form Arioch always prefers on Earth. Soon he stands there, smiling, drawing the Black Sword from his scabbard.

FENERIC: "That sword was banished from our world centuries ago. Only evil can come of its return."

ELRIC: "And only evil will befall us if I do not use it now!"

And with a single mighty blow he has cut through the bars of the cage and is already advancing upon the Karasim who ready their weapons.

Watched by an elegant Arioch, twice the size of a normal man, who leans against a wall, applauding, Elric takes on the whole pack of Karasim warriors who come at him from all sides. They are no match for the black blade, nor with Elric's demonic energy as he moves about the prison pit killing man after man.

ELRIC: "So . . . are you still entertained by the sight of dying men, my friends?"

The work done, he hacks away the bars of the cages. Arioch grins in cynical delight at all this mayhem.

ELRIC: "There, my countrymen! You are free. Take what weapons are here and follow me."

Still perturbed, Feneric stoops to pick up a fallen sword then helps the princess through the mangled bars of her cage.

ARIOCH: "Well, Feneric, would you rather be martyred or free to be avenged on your brother?"

FENERIC: "Why help us when Ederic serves your cause better than I ever could?"

ARIOCH: "Ah, I am a patient demon, you see. I look to the long term. Well, I have done all I can for you here and I'll say farewell."

Arioch turns into fading smoke, only his cynical smile remaining for a moment. Scowling back at him, Feneric helps one of the wounded Melnibonéans up the steps of the pit. Elric, too, helps a wounded man, while the princess hovers in the air overhead.

In the passage outside, King Minak has assembled more warriors, but he has taken care not to be in the forefront.

MINAK: "That demon's abandoned them. Slay them all. Don't let one escape!"

Elric, his father and the Melnibonéans fight their way to the outside and eventually make it to the top of the abyss, no longer pursued by the Karasim. Elric pauses on the edge of the abyss and looks down. The battle light is still in his eyes and he laughs almost like a demon himself.

ELRIC: "The cowards have had enough. They're reluctant to pursue us now."

Elric looks around but can't see the Princess Dela-Fwaar.

ELRIC: "Where's the princess?"

MELNIBONÉAN: "There—there she goes—flying home!"

They see Princess Dela-Fwaar in outline against the sky as she heads for home.

FENERIC: "Get rid of that blade now, my son, I beg thee. The thing's addictive. Abandon it before it's too late!"

Elric finds this amusing but is prepared to humour his father.

ELRIC: "I'll not become so easily dependent on a mere sword, however powerful . . ." *(He looks at his father's frightened eyes.)* "But if it pleases you, father—"

He hurls the black blade out over the abyss. It falls, turning and twisting, down into the clouded darkness.

ELRIC: "There! It's gone. It will never perturb you again."

ELRIC: "And now . . ."

He signs to his men. Using the "firebags" which the Karasim had used against Melniboné, they ignite brands and start setting fire to the ships.

ELRIC: "They'll never use these ships to pursue us."

His father is looking back, still perturbed, but says nothing of his thoughts.

The Melnibonéans, with their worst wounded on the back of Elric's horse, are now leaving the World's Edge. The ships are all blazing and they are not pursued by the Karasim.

Elric grins as he turns his eyes away from the scene.

ELRIC: "Let's for home, Father—to confront your ambitious brother."

Chapter Four

The Long Way Home

The dream couches. Cymoril and Tanglebones look down on a disturbed Elric who frowns and moans in his sleep.

TANGLEBONES: "I fear his dream-quest does not go easily for him."

CYMORIL: "Does he know that he is one person in this life and another in his dream?"

TANGLEBONES: "He is almost certainly unconscious of his two lives—just the same as your brother Yyrkoon . . . But some instinct drives them both to fulfill a destiny which mirrors the life they inhabit in this world."

They walk through the dream chambers until they find Arisand, the human girl, together with Sadric, looking down on Yyrkoon who, in contrast to Elric, has a satisfied smirk on his sleeping features.

TANGLEBONES: "Your brother's dream persona seems to be somewhat happier than your cousin's, Lady Cymoril."

They leave Yyrkoon's chamber.

CYMORIL: "Is there nothing we can do to help Elric?"

TANGLEBONES: "Nothing. That, after all, is the point of dream-quests."

He pauses, drawing his brows together.

TANGLEBONES: "We can only pray to the powers of fate that Prince Elric has the resources to defeat what dangers and temptations wait for him in his dreams . . ."

Though there was no immediate threat from the Karasim, the Melnibonéans had fled without provisions or mounts and the march home was to be long and grueling, while King Minak was eventually to overcome his caution as well as the loss of his sky ships and raise an army of pursuit . . .

By the following winter, King Feneric, his son and his warriors had reached the Melmane Marshes and Minak had their scent . . .

Elric and the Melnibonéans are hiding in a forest of peculiar trees on the edge of a desolate peat bog criss-crossed by waterways. The Melnibonéans are watching the far horizon where King Minak and a large army of Karasim, mounted on ugly, white hippopotamus-like beasts, ride in pursuit.

Elric turns to his father.

ELRIC: "Father, they're catching up with us. Another few days and there will be no more than half a mile between us."

FENERIC: "At least our wounded are in better condition and we need fear no attack from above . . ."

FENERIC: " . . . but I agree our chances of staying ahead of them are slim unless we can lose them in the marshes ahead."

ELRIC: "I'm beginning to wish I had not given up that sword so readily."

Feneric becomes intense. He seizes his son by the shoulder and turns him round so that they are face to face . . .

FENERIC: "Believe me, my son, that blade is cursed, and cursed is any man who makes a compact with Chaos. As it is, Lord Arioch now inhabits our world by your invitation. And that can only mean disaster for some, if not for Melniboné.

ELRIC (*grins*): "Then let's hope it is for King Minak and the Karasim who reap Chaos."

The little band is now in the wide marshland. Marsh birds fly overhead and the place has a desolate beauty. The tiny figures of the Melnibonéans make their difficult way from one piece of relatively dry land to another and, very close behind, with tracker beasts of a reptilian appearance, who can swim easily through the swamps as well as run over dry land, comes Minak and his great army of Karasim.

ELRIC: "Perhaps I was hasty in ridding myself of that sword, Father. After all, you said yourself the damage is done and Arioch already in our world."

FENERIC: "No need to compound the folly, my son. We can only hope—and press on . . ."

MINAK: "There! Ahead! They'll soon be paying the price of inconveniencing the Karasim . . ."

Soon there was nothing for it but to make a stand and prepare to fight.

The grim-faced band of Melnibonéans has found some relatively high ground surrounded by a natural moat with only a narrow causeway leading to it. Here they will make their stand against the whole Karasim army.

FENERIC: "Here's a natural fort we can defend. At least we'll take a good many of our enemies with us!"

A full scale battle scene as the Karasim attack from all sides, wading or swimming through the water, using the corpses of their own slain men and animals to get to the mound on which the Melnibonéans stand. Elric, Feneric and their men give good account of themselves, through the course of the day.

But as night falls . . .

MINAK: "Fall back! The darkness only aids them. We'll attack again at dawn!"

The Karasim fall back, leaving the battle-weary men of Melniboné to count their losses—four dead and twelve wounded—and be rallied by Elric's praise.

ELRIC: "Well, done, warriors of Melniboné! Each of you has sent at least a score of Karasim down to hell!"

FENERIC: "But can we last another night, my son?"

ELRIC: "Only by calling on supernatural aid, Father."

Close up of a weary, angry Feneric clutching at Elric.

FENERIC: "No! Future generations will curse us if we rely on the aid of Arioch of Chaos and that damned black blade!"

ELRIC: "And I will curse myself if, by not summoning Chaos, I see my father die under Karasim steel!"

FIRST MELNIBONÉAN SOLDIER (*points*): "Dawn is almost upon us and the Karasim advance!"

Elric, scowling, backs away from where his father stands, sword in hand, rallying the weary remnants of his army.

FENERIC: "Stand ready!"

ELRIC (*slips down behind a rock*): "Arioch! Bring me back the black blade, I beg thee!"

We get a glimpse of a triumphantly smiling face as Arioch causes the Black Sword to materialize.

ARIOCH: "There, little mortal. Do your worst with it."

The Melnibonéan soldiers are forced into a tighter and tighter knot as the Karasim gain the islet and close in on them.

FENERIC: "They close for the kill! Where's my son? Dead already?"

Elric, his face a mask of terrible vengeful glee, the Black Sword in both hands, suddenly appears to deal death to the astonished Karasim.

MINAK: "No! He wields the Chaos sword again! But he still cannot defeat so many of us. Destroy him and make the sword our own!"

Feneric looks over his shoulder at Elric and is horrified:

FENERIC: "Foolish youth! You have no idea what monstrous terror that blade will bring upon the world!"

SECOND MELNIBONÉAN SOLDIER (*points into the rising sun. Out of it comes a swarm of flying soldiers. The men of Myyrrhn, led by their prince*): "We're finished. Those are the warriors of Myyrrhn, come to join their allies!"

But the Prince of Myyrrhn was no longer in King Minak's power—and brought him not help but revenge . . .

The flying warriors of Myyrrhn descend upon the Karasim with wild ferocity, so the Karasim and their king are now trapped between two groups of warriors.

FENERIC: "They side with us! We are saved! And you, foolish son, summoned the sword too soon!"

Elric's crimson eyes still glow with berserk blood-lust and the sword in his hands gives off a black glow.

ELRIC: "You call me foolish, yet I have saved thee once, Father!"

Then, to his astonishment, the sword twists in his hand and, against Elric's will, attempts to stab Feneric . . .

FENERIC: "What? You'd kill your own father now?"

ELRIC: "No! The sword moves by itself! *No!*"

With all his strength, the young Silverskin was barely able to stop the sword's movement . . .

In horror at what he had almost done, Elric hurled the Black Sword far into the marsh . . .

ELRIC: "Oh, Father! You are right! I should never have called on Chaos. I almost killed you! There, damned sword, go—never again will I seek the aid of Chaos!

Almost sobbing, he falls into his father's arms. The old man still looks grim as he comforts his son.

FENERIC: "My son, you have learned a good lesson. But even now it could be too late . . ."

ELRIC: "I promise you, Father, not even at my moments of greatest trial will I summon either Arioch or the sword. From now on I will listen to your wisdom and obey . . ."

FENERIC: "I hope so, my boy. There are many great trials still ahead of you. And we have yet to face the usurper who sits on my throne."

The winged men of Myyrrhn have routed the Karasim. King Minak is dead, his body, still with a spear in its side, is being carried off by the ragged remnants of the Karasim army. They are thoroughly defeated and getting away as fast as they can. Prince Vashntni is smiling as he puts his hand on young Elric's shoulder.

PRINCE VASHNTNI: "I am glad to see thee again, young Silverskin. And my daughter sends you her affectionate greetings. What now? Do you return to Melniboné to claim the throne from that traitor Ederic?"

ELRIC: "That is for my father to decide, but I hope he will decide to go back to our homeland."

FENERIC: "It will be dangerous, but we must make the journey. I cannot allow Ederic to corrupt the heart of our great nation. But knowing he has studied sorcery, I am unsure if we will be successful."

VASHNTNI: "We can help—"

FENERIC: "Thanks, great prince, but we Melnibonéans alone should be present when we confront my brother. Soon we'll reach Port Ishagd, where our friends the Pukwadji rule. They will lend us a ship. When we reach Melniboné we can only hope the people will rise to place me back upon my throne."

VASHNTNI: "You are a man of wisdom and faith, King Feneric, and I honour your decision. However, it is possible my daughter will want to visit your son. Will you permit that?"

FENERIC: "Of course, she will always be welcome at our court." *(He turns his head towards the north. It is time to think of the last stage of their journey.)* "But many weeks will pass before we get there . . ."

Chapter Five

A Gift from the Heavens

The dream couches again. Cymoril and Tanglebones look down on Elric with considerable pity and frustration as he writhes in his sleep.

CYMORIL: "Still he is in torment. What can be happening to him, Master Tanglebones?"

TANGLEBONES: "An inner conflict fills him, clearly. We can only hope he has the sense and the resources to save himself."

They look in on the next chamber. Sadric is leaving Yyrkoon's dream chamber but the human girl remains at his side. Yyrkoon looks decidedly happy.

SADRIC: "By the look of satisfaction on his face, my nephew has been thoroughly successful in his ambitions. Does this mean my son is dead?"

TANGLEBONES: "No, sire. But clearly Prince Yyrkoon feels no threat from Prince Elric . . ."

Sadric takes Tanglebones aside.

SADRIC: "I would not have my son die—is there nothing you can do to ensure he lives on?"

TANGLEBONES: "I fear not, sire. For it is his soul which travels the Dream Realms, if his memory and his body do not . . ."

SADRIC: "Soul and memory? Are they not the same?"

TANGLEBONES: "The soul's memory is not the same as the mind's, my emperor . . ."

Sadric walks sadly up the stairs towards his own apartments. Cymoril and Tanglebones watch him leave.

CYMORIL: "He would deny it, I know. But I think there is something in that old man which loves the son he claims to spurn."

TANGLEBONES: "He puts his nation first, however. And that is his duty . . ."

The Melnibonéans are on a ship about to leave the harbour. They are saying farewell to their Pukwadji friends (see Book One) who have also attained a much greater level of sophistication than when we first met them. Feneric has his hand on his son's shoulders.

FENERIC: "Farewell, friend. We thank thee for the loan of this ship. It will be returned when we get to Melniboné."

PUKWADJI MERCHANT: "May your brother give up the throne with good grace, sire."

ELRIC: "I suspect Uncle Ederic will not be so generous, Father. After all, he must think us dead these many moons!"

FENERIC (*looks up at the filling sail*): "It will be his duty to give the throne back to me, my son. And most Melnibonéans will support us in that."

The ship makes good speed.

In a few days, the towers of Melniboné came in sight . . .

From the deck of the ship we see the towers of Melniboné in the distance. Some are still burned out, some are restored, many have scaffolding still around them. There is a bleak, dark mood about the city.

ELRIC: "There she is, Father. After almost five years she seems like a different city. So bleak and ravaged."

FENERIC: "Yet there must have been treasure aplenty in the public coffers to rebuild her."

ELRIC: "Unless Uncle Ederic keeps that treasure for himself and his cronies."

In the great throne room of Melniboné there is a dark, brooding, atrophied air to all. The throne is surrounded by harsh-faced, cruel men and women, some of whom are slaves, wearing neck rings and other manacles. There is a barbaric feel about the place.

A soldier comes running in and prostrates himself before King Ederic, who half-starts from his throne, scowling . . .

SOLDIER: "My lord! My lord, the king! The rumours are true. I have come from the harbour. Your brother, his son and their warriors have just disembarked. They are returned from the quest to rescue young Silverskin!"

EDERIC: "By Chaos! This cannot be!"

We switch to the dockside. Feneric and Elric are waving to the cheering crowds who throng the harbour. There is no doubt that they are popular with the people.

FIRST MELNIBONÉAN ON QUAYSIDE: "Hurrah! The king and his son return!"

SECOND MELNIBONÉAN: "Now prosperity, peace and justice will be restored and Ederic deposed!!!"

The returning Melnibonéans are embraced by their friends and fellow nobles. One noble speaks to Feneric:

NOBLE: "Oh, lord king, you are most welcome. Your brother has taxed and tyrannized us almost since the day you left!"

FENERIC: "Fear not, my friend, we are here to re-establish the gravity and dignity of the State."

News spreads throughout the city . . .

. . . while, back at the palace . . .

EDERIC (*murmurs to one of his minions*): "The two must die. We shall do it with poison at the welcoming feast tonight. Put out the word that they brought a disease with them from foreign parts . . ."

As Elric and Feneric enter the throne room, Ederic rushes down the steps of his throne, arms spread to greet them.

EDERIC: "My brother! My nephew! We heard you were dead, that you had contracted a foreign disease while fighting abroad."

He grins a sinister welcome:

EDERIC: "How good it is to see you. You look as if your hardships have wearied you. Please rest. Tonight we hold a feast in your honour, to celebrate your safe return. Slaves! Take the king and the prince to their apartments!"

Cringing slaves take Feneric and Elric through gloomy passages to their own rooms, which are dusty and poorly maintained. They pause in Feneric's apartments first . . .

FENERIC: "These rooms are so badly kept. Slaves? We had naught to do with such barbarism. An air of terror hangs over the whole palace. There is much work to be done here, my son, though I fear we'll prove little if we accuse my brother."

ELRIC: "First we must begin rebuilding. Justice for Uncle Ederic must wait, Father."

Back in the throne room, Ederic whispers to another minion:

EDERIC: "Ensure every dish they eat is thoroughly poisoned. Meanwhile, spread the rumour that they are sickly, fearing death . . ."

Later, freshly dressed, Feneric and Elric and the surviving Melnibonéan warriors come down the stairs into the great banqueting hall where again Ederic greets them, ushering Feneric to his place at the top of the table. Elric will sit on his father's right side, Ederic on the left.

The dinner hour, in the great banqueting hall . . .

EDERIC: "Returning heroes, all! You are doubtless famished. Our chefs have prepared their best for you, dear relatives."

The returned heroes seat themselves at the table. They are just about to be served with the first course when the doors of the hall fly open and through them flies a newcomer. It is Princess Dela-Fwaar and she carries a sack in her hands. Ederic rises, startled from his chair, eyes wide—

EDERIC: "What? A new attack from the air? Guards! To arms!"

Feneric stays Ederic with his hand, smiling.

FENERIC: "No, no, brother! She is our friend. The Myyrrhn aided us. Without them we should not be sitting down to meat with you tonight!"

ELRIC: "Greetings, princess. This is unexpected but a welcome honour. Will you dine with us?"

The princess alights on a nearby plinth, reaching into the sack as she does so.

PRINCESS: "Thank you, Prince Silverskin. I should be glad to accept your hospitality. But first I have a gift for your uncle . . . which I have carried all the way from the Edge of the World!"

She pulls out of the sack the simple wine jar in which Ederic had imprisoned the South Wind's soul!

EDERIC (*starts backward in terror*): "No! It cannot be! That jar's in safe-keeping with King Minak!"

PRINCESS: "King Minak's dead and most of his warriors with him. I took this from his prison when Silverskin rescued us from the Karasim who had captured us at your instigation!"

EDERIC: "No! Kill her. The Myyrrhn bitch lies!"

FENERIC: "Do not harm our guest. She tells the truth."

King Feneric rises from the table, pointing at Ederic:

FENERIC: "My brother condemns himself. That whole attack on Imrryr was his contrivance! He has enslaved you while pretending to protect you!"

EDERIC: "This is just another trick by those who would bring terror and grief to Melniboné. Guards! Obey me. I am your true king!"

The guards look uncertainly from one to another. Around Elric and Feneric their old guard assemble. None of them has swords or other weapons, however, whereas Ederic's guards are heavily armed.

EDERIC (*grins in his certain power*): "Seize them at once. They are traitors!"

ELRIC: "We are not the traitors! It must be plain to anyone that my uncle planned this disaster! He had his own folk killed and imprisoned so he could take the throne!"

As the armed guards close in on the little band of Melnibonéans, the winged princess flies up and hovers above them, the wine jar held over her head.

PRINCESS: "Fear not, friend Silverskin. I know exactly how to settle this dispute!"

And she flings down the wine jar . . .

. . . which shatters on the flagstones of the hall . . .

EDERIC: "*NOOOOOO!*"

. . . and from it begins to pour a dense, white cloud . . .

It is Shaarnasaa, Queen of the South Wind, her soul released from the wine jar where Ederic's sorcery had kept it . . .

PRINCESS: "I free Shaarnasaa, Queen of the South Wind, whose soul was imprisoned by King Ederic's foul sorcery!"

The cloud grows and grows until it becomes the outline of a huge and lovely creature, whose hair curls around her like trees streaming in a powerful wind. Everything about her is reminiscent of the South Wind of which she is ruler.

SHAARNASAA: "So there is my captor, who by his bleak enchantments did trap me in a jar! I was foolish to trust him, as I had learned to trust the folk of Melniboné. But he tricked me as no doubt he has tricked you all. My imprisonment meant my servants were forced to obey him and his allies. But now I am free and shall not be tricked again!"

Shaarnasaa moves towards the terrified Ederic, who cringes backwards.

EDERIC: "Men! Protect me. I command thee!"

But the looks on the faces of his guards are hard and their eyes are like ice.

Shaarnasaa picks up Ederic who begins to beg her for his life.

EDERIC: "Spare me, I beg thee! Do not kill me, gentle queen!"

SHAARNASAA: "It is not the habit of the South Wind's queen to kill. I am sworn to bless and to heal. But you, little mortal, are an evil thing which pollutes the earth and stains it with every breath you take."

EDERIC: "Th-then have mercy, gentle queen!"

SHAARNASAA: "Oh, I am not always gentle, as you shall discover. I will carry you off to the tall peaks of the world where you can never harm immortal or mortal again!"

FENERIC: "It is just he should be banished."

SHAARNASAA (*looks down at Elric*): "And you, young Silverskin, shall be remembered by all the spirits of the air. When you or your descendants need our aid, you must call on us and we shall come."

With this the Queen of the South Wind leaves the hall. Elric and Feneric and the winged princess all watch from the steps of the palace as she goes up into the air, bearing the shrieking Ederic with her. Black clouds boil high on the horizon . . .

SHAARNASAA: "Farewell, mortals. I go to fulfill this creature's punishment!"

They watch as she disappears out over the water. King Feneric embraces his son, then turns to take the princess's hand:

FENERIC: "Princess, I thank thee most gladly for all thine aid . . ."

PRINCESS: "'Tis your brave son you should thank, o king. Without him, all our lives would be ended bloodily and dark villainy a shadow on our worlds and souls."

FENERIC: "Now, instead, this island city shall rise again in glory and beauty, to shine her light upon our lives and harmonize our destinies." *(He turns again to Elric:)* "And you, my son, shall continue that work when I am gone, making Melniboné's name a synonym for justice and integrity . . ."

ELRIC (*smiling with joy, thinks*): "Aye, but in future I shall trust fewer mortals or immortals and bring a sterner hand to our rule, lest our nation be threatened again with the doom we've so narrowly avoided."

The sun suddenly breaks through the black clouds on the horizon, sending deep shadows across the scene as the three all turn to go back into the tower and continue the feast.

FENERIC: "Let's continue our celebration feast, content in knowing our enemy has met his just deserts!"

ELRIC: "Father, with respect to Uncle Ederic's feast, perhaps we should give his chefs the first taste. Of everything."

We see a close-up of Silverskin as he frowns, turning away from his father and looking out towards the harbour where Melniboné's ships are at anchor.

ELRIC (*thinks*): "While my father lives, I'll honour my vow to him. But the time might come when I shall need the help of Chaos and that black blade. It's helped us once, and saved us, too. Mayhap it will save us again in years to come."

We make a transition now from Elric in the palace to Elric lying on the dream couch. Cymoril points at his face and Tanglebones is astonished:

CYMORIL: "Master Tanglebones! Look! His face!"

TANGLEBONES: "The gods bless us!"

We see Elric's face. The torment has gone from it and now he smiles.

While in the nearby chamber . . .

Sadric is bending over Yyrkoon's dream couch and the human maiden is herself deeply concerned with something, though she seems to nurse a small, secret smile . . .

SADRIC: "What ails my nephew? His expression changes!"

ARISAND: "It seems, my lord emperor, that Prince Yyrkoon has met with an unexpected reversal in the other life."

Yyrkoon sits up on his bench, frowning and cursing and reaching for a goblet Arisand holds out for him.

YYRKOON: "*Aark*! I have a miserable headache. My dream fades, as they always do. What's happened to my cousin? Did he die?"

Tanglebones appears in the doorway, bowing to emperor and prince.

TANGLEBONES: "Good news, my lord. The young Prince Elric lives and is well."

YYRKOON: "What! How is it that he survives every dream-quest? Everyone knows how full of danger they are."

SADRIC: "He's well, you say. I must congratulate him on his success . . ."

TANGLEBONES: "He has left already, lord emperor."

SADRIC: "What? Where does he go?"

TANGLEBONES: "He told me he planned to take the Princess Cymoril—sailing . . ."

Elric is steering a small boat out of the harbour. He has already passed through the great sea-maze. He has his other arm around Cymoril and she is laughing with delight—for the wind elementals are puffing the sails and making the boat scud across the harbour, leaving the great warships of Melniboné's secret harbour far behind.

CYMORIL: "And what did you learn in your dream, my lord?"

ELRIC: "As usual, I don't remember. But now I command the *h'Haarshann,* so I must have learned something, eh? More sorcerous wisdom to help me carry the burden of my destiny on the day when I become Emperor of Melniboné."

Yyrkoon glowers in his apartments eating voraciously from a plate of food.

YYRKOON: "Today my cousin delights in his survival and goes out to play, but the powerful poison of my ambition shall destroy him yet. I swear . . ."

The boat is caught by a shaft of sunlight piercing the clouds and Elric laughs in his delight as the h'Haarshann *continue to fill his sail with air and Cymoril trails her hand in the water.*

ELRIC: "Meanwhile, sweet Cymoril, let's enjoy the remains of the evening while we may."

BOOK FOUR

THE DREAM OF TEN YEARS: THE DREAM OF FIRE

DRAGON LORD'S DESTINY

Chapter One

Two Ways to Forge an Empire

THE GREAT THRONE room of Melniboné. Ancient, brooding Sadric sits slumped in the great Ruby Throne, staring with melancholy eyes down at his son and nephew who stand, at odds, before him. Elric on one side, Yyrkoon on the other. By Yyrkoon's side stands Arisand, the human woman; by Elric's side stand Cymoril and Tanglebones. On Tanglebones's shoulder sits the black raven, our old friend. Elric and Yyrkoon have almost come to blows and their companions touch their sleeves, hoping to restrain them.

ELRIC: "We must settle this soon, cousin Yyrkoon. I challenge you to confront me here, and not in the shadows of the Dream Realms!"

YYRKOON: "Your physical weakness now infects your mind, cousin Elric. Surely my uncle Sadric notices how his son grows daily less fit for power? 'Tis I who own all the qualities demanded of an emperor."

SADRIC: "Silence, nephew. You, too, my son. I am still Emperor and not yet dead. My concern is for Melniboné and what is best for the nation. You are tested now on the dream couches. That is where your destinies will be resolved."

Sadric rises from his throne.

As he speaks we see a panorama of Melnibonéan history. Kings and emperors in the battle armour of their calling lead men and demons to victory over human fighters.

We see the golden battle-barges, the flying dragons. With both of these Melniboné established her great empire.

SADRIC: "Our ancestors fought to establish this empire. They made the pacts with Chaos allowing us to rule for ten thousand years. For too long have the Chaos Lords been absent from that compact."

SADRIC: "The one who'll rule best is he who revives our power—who proves the best sorcerer!"

Sadric sweeps from the throne room, summoning Arisand to come with him. With a backward look at Yyrkoon, she follows. Tanglebones plucks at Elric's urgent sleeve.

TANGLEBONES: "Come, young master. Your father is right. Your destiny will be determined on the dream couches. It is time for your last dream—your most crucial dream—the Dream of Ten Years . . ."

CYMORIL: "Master Tanglebones speaks wisely, dear Elric."

Yyrkoon is already striding, grim-faced, from the throne room. He snarls one last retort behind him as he leaves.

YYRKOON: "You all disgust me. You stink of weakness and compromise. Aye, to the dream couches—and battle!!!"

ELRIC: "Very well. I am ready."

It had become obvious to all now that a kind of duel was being fought on the dream couches of Melniboné. Each party went to its own chamber. A crucial battle was about to commence, while the two chief combatants lay asleep . . .

In Elric's chamber, the black crow flies from Tanglebones's shoulder to Elric's.

ELRIC: "So our destiny truly does lie in our dreams, Master Tanglebones?"

TANGLEBONES: "So it seems, my lord. But your education will be accomplished there, also."

CYMORIL: "I fear you are in great danger, dear Elric . . . !"

ELRIC: "Aye, I smell it in the air, Cymoril. But we must do what conscience and circumstance demands . . ."

While, in Yyrkoon's chamber . . .

The mysterious human girl, Arisand, is diffidently suggesting something to Yyrkoon, who listens with haughty interest.

YYRKOON: "Bah! The weakling has so far engineered his victories by tricks and luck. How am I to ensure his defeat in this, the final dream of his initiation?"

ARISAND: "If I can offer some simple human magic to aid you, my lord . . ."

YYRKOON: "Human magic? Unsophisticated and crude compared with ours. How can that help me?"

ARISAND: "Sometimes, my lord, the simpler spell can be more effective . . ."

YYRKOON (*coming round to the idea*): "I take your meaning. What do you suggest?"

ARISAND: "I know a way which will not make you vulnerable to dying with your avatar. And I can accompany you, if you will permit . . ."

Yyrkoon drinks his potion and lies down on his couch as Arisand lays herself down beside him.

YYRKOON: "After all, what do I risk?"

Meanwhile Elric's limp hand falls from Cymoril's. She looks up, her eyes filled with fear.

CYMORIL: "Be lucky, my lord. For I suspect luck is all you'll have on your side in this long dream . . ."

Then the dream roads of the multiverse opened before them . . .

Both Elric and Yyrkoon set their feet on the dream roads of the multiverse. A ghostly Arisand is with Yyrkoon as both set off.

ARISAND: "Stay close with me, Lord Yyrkoon. I'll help your soul occupy a perfect vessel, while you yourself will be invulnerable. And be patient . . . for we must stay a little behind Elric if we're to be successful anon . . ."

They pass along the great roads, with Elric a little ahead of Yyrkoon and Arisand, unaware that they are behind him. And behind them all flies the black crow.

Thus all three walked the moonbeam roads, with Elric unaware of Yyrkoon and his companion, until at last the towers of ancient Melniboné lay ahead, thousands of years in their past . . .

These Melnibonéan towers are not so high nor as elaborate as the ones we've left. But they are still pretty impressive.

. . . when the power of the Bright Empire had reached a peak of magnificent strength.

Then Elric's dreaming soul had occupied that of his avatar, King Elrik, brother to his beautiful "silverskin" Queen Asrid, joint ruler of this other, ancient Melniboné . . .

Elric merges into King Elrik who stands hand in hand with his sister Queen Asrid, observing a great golden sailing quireme being built. These are the early types of the battle-barges which, with the dragons, form the basis of "modern" Melniboné's power.

ASRID: "Another ship is added to our fleet, brother Elrik. Her holds will carry our goods far abroad, and bring back the wealth of all the world!"

ELRIK: "Aye, dear sister Asrid. Melniboné grows rich on her trade. We have much to be grateful for. Though I once chose a more direct route to power, I know you will rule with gentle and effective wisdom while I am gone."

Asrid turns to Elrik/Elric embracing him with sisterly concern. The golden barge is still behind them, still being worked on.

ASRID: "You seek to educate yourself abroad, learning all you can from the emerging humans of the new, civilized tribes . . . But I cannot help fear for you, sweet brother. There are so many unknown dangers . . ."

ELRIK: "The new tribes still remain wary of us. They see us as alien interlopers. Not only will I learn their customs and condition, sister . . . but I will act as ambassador, making friends and creating new trade for Melniboné. Such knowledge and diplomacy is worth gold in Melniboné's coffers. We shall be rich in wisdom as well as money!"

ASRID: "I myself persuaded you to this idea, I know. The new tribes covet our wealth. We must always be ready to defend against any attack. But it is far better for our security to be liked than feared. By venturing abroad on this exploratory journey, you will forge alliances and friendships. You'll secure our strength at every point . . ."

An interior chamber.

ELRIK (*in close up, indicates a map*): "I leave in the morning for Pukwadji, our old ally. From there I head inland. We all know the rumours of entire civilizations to be found there, some more ancient than our own. While I am gone, you must rule here alone, wisely . . . as you have always done. Together we will lay the foundations of a great, peaceful trading empire . . ."

The map is of the same land area as other maps we've seen, but it shows the worlds of The "New Tribes," mostly mountains, forests, rivers and plains, with large parts marked as unknown territory. Pukwadji is plainly marked, as a territory on the coast nearest to Melniboné.

ASRID: "Farewell, dear Elrik. When you return, our whole fleet will be complete . . ."

And so the young king went forth . . .

. . . to complete his education . . .

. . . in the lands of the new tribes . . .

. . . the people who one day would emerge . . .

. . . as "the Young Kingdoms" . . .

Elric/Elrik aboard a Melnibonéan ship. He stares forward, dreaming of the adventures he is likely to have.

The ship docks. Elrik rides his horse off the ship onto a dock where Pukwadji people greet him with pleasure, as an old friend.

We see him leaving the Pukwadji city and heading off into the interior. The black crow follows him.

He meets friendly tribespeople (some black, some white) in simple villages and towns. He sees strange animals, some of them gigantic mammals (such as riding giraffes with black warriors on their backs), some transporting people. In one village, he sits down with a Wise Woman. Black crow perches in distant tree.

WISE WOMAN: "There is an ancient city, far from here, which has the same name in every human tongue. Tanelorn is a city of peace . . ."

WISE WOMAN (*voice*): " . . . there all peoples can meet and know tranquility. There is no fighting there. Few own weapons. She has no king, but is administered by a council known as the Grey Lords . . . They say past, present and future come together there . . ."

ELRIK: "I think I'll search out this city and see what I can learn from it . . ."

And so, some four years later . . .

Elrik rides out over a verdant plain. It's sunrise.

Next panel and it's sunset. Black crow flies against the setting sun.

ELRIK (thinks): "It's time I found a good place to camp."

Suddenly the earth begins to rise and bulge under his horse's hoofs. Elrik fights to control his horse.

ELRIK: "? The earth! It's moving beneath me!"

Chapter Two

The Heart of Creation

Massive movement of earth as King Grome (from Book One) bursts up out of the ground.

GROME: "Aha! Ho, little mortal! It has been a few thousand years since we last met!"

ELRIK: "Wha—?"

The horse throws Elric and gallops off. Elrik picks himself up as Grome reaches towards him. He draws his sword, backing away. Grome looks puzzled.

GROME: "Do you not recognize me, mortal? We have a compact, you and I!"

Elrik frowns, his hand going to his brow.

ELRIK: "I—I—remember something—a dream, perhaps . . ."

GROME: "I am Grome, king of all that is of the earth and below it. You once did me a service . . ."

ELRIK: "Not I, King Grome . . ."

GROME (*suddenly realizing he's made a mistake*): "Ah! What a fool I am. I forget how short-lived your folk are. No doubt I made the pact with your ancestor! Still, that pact remains . . ."

Grome bears Elric/Elrik down into a great wonderful cave, full of glinting jewels.

He frowns trustingly down at the albino.

GROME: "The Black Sword has been stolen again. Uprooted from the rock in which I secured it. I suspect grave sorcery was involved. I need you to find it again . . ."

ELRIK: "Again? Why should I know where it is?"

Grome places a vast finger against Elrik's chest and smiles—

GROME: "Because you have an affinity for the blade. Among mortals, only a 'silverskin' of your blood can handle it. If it is not returned to me, then great harm will fall upon our world."

ELRIK: "Doubtless, 'tis my duty to seek it. Yet how could I begin . . . ?"

GROME: "You must go to the city of Tanelorn and ask the Grey Lords. They will help you."

ELRIK: "Very well, sire. That's the city I seek, even now. Tell me how to find Tanelorn."

GROME: "'Tis hard to find, mortal. Best I take you there myself."

Grome picks up Elric and starts off through the night, but now the black crow flies ahead of them. Grome pauses at one point when he sees Elric's horse.

GROME: "Hmm. You'll be needing him . . ."

Grome picks up the startled horse and tucks it under his other arm.

Next morning . . .

Elrik is astonished by what Grome reveals to him. It is an incredibly beautiful city, with a somewhat mediaeval appearance, the sun rising behind it. It is Tanelorn, the beautiful. The mythical city where all warriors are said to find peace, where there is no conflict and which exists on every plane of the multiverse, perhaps in every person's heart. The black crow flies away into the city.

GROME: "Not all can find Tanelorn. I am blessed. And now you are also blessed."

GROME: "Go in peace, young mortal. Discover what you need in holy Tanelorn . . ."

Grome lopes away over the horizon.

GROME: "Farewell. Find the Black Sword and return it to where it belongs."

Elric/Elrik walks through the peaceful streets of Tanelorn, leading his horse.

ELRIK: "I've never known a more beautiful, nor more civilized place. A man could settle here and know peace for ever . . ."

A big, hearty fellow, clearly a warrior, but without weapons, grins down at Elric as the albino asks him a question.

HEARTY: "How can I help you, friend?"

ELRIK: "Where shall I find the Grey Lords?"

HEARTY: "Ho! Ho! You'll not find them! But they'll find you, friend."

HEARTY: "Go to any tavern and ask."

We see Elric entering a tavern and speaking to the landlord, who also smiles in reply, pointing behind him to a bench at which sit five old, grey men, playing chess and drinking porter.

Elric approaches the table and politely addresses the five old men.

ELRIK: "Pardon me, gentlemen. I gather you are the rulers of this city . . ."

FIRST GREY MAN: "Not us, young sir. We rule nothing and no-one. In Tanelorn, citizens rule themselves."

ELRIK: "I'm sorry. I understood you were the Grey Lords . . ."

SECOND GREY MAN: "So we are, young sir. So we are."

THIRD GREY MAN: "But we merely counsel—to maintain the peace of Tanelorn."

FOURTH GREY MAN: "Whatever is necessary, my boy. That's our only calling—to be called . . ."

FIFTH GREY MAN: "How can we help you?"

ELRIK: "I seek the Black Sword."

FIRST GREY MAN: "In the one place it's least likely to exist?"

FOURTH GREY MAN: "A pretty irony. Who sent you, my boy?"

ELRIK: "King Grome."

FIRST: "Our old friend."

SECOND: "If he trusts you, then so shall we."

THIRD: "You must look for the Chasm of Nihrain, far, far from here."

FOURTH: "Then ask the black crow . . ."

FIFTH: "Only he will know . . ."

ELRIK: "How will I find this place?"

LANDLORD: "I have a map. But it is on the world's farthest edge."

More years were to pass until . . .

. . . on the far side of the world . . .

Elrik is riding through black mountains, whose peaks rise to spikes all around him.

A dreary, morbid place, with no apparent life. He is weary, battered and no longer has his horse. There are no arrows left in his quiver and it is clear he has been through the wars in order to get here. He has only a drop of water left in his flask.

ELRIK (*thinks*): "Food gone. Horse gone. Water almost gone. I've followed the map to the letter . . . Those grey ones joked with me. They sent me to my death."

As he thinks this, he looks up and there, perched on a rock, staring at him with what appears to be amusement, is the black crow.

CROW/SEPIRIZ: "Good evening, Lord Elrik. And welcome to the land of Nihrain."

Elrik is astonished.

ELRIK: "You speak! Has my weariness turned my brain?"

The crow begins to change before him—

—and becomes a huge black man—Sepiriz, leader of the ten Nihrainian brothers. And while you should do your best, Walter, to make him look as different from the guy in The Matrix *as possible, it's not my fault that I thought Sepiriz up looking like this in 1963 or whenever it was. OK. Give him long hair. He was bald in the original. He's wearing a simple yellow toga. He's smiling.*

SEPIRIZ: "I have awaited this moment for a thousand years. I am Sepiriz, leader of the ten Nihrainian brothers and the servant of the Balance. Welcome, young silverskin."

Sepiriz claps his hands, and around the great black rock comes a chariot pulled by a single black horse, whose hoofs do not quite touch the ground. This is one of the famous stallions of Nihrain, whose hoofs tread the space of another time and place, and can thus traverse almost any terrain in this world.

Helping the astonished young man into the chariot beside him, Sepiriz sets off at a wild gallop through the mountains—to the Chasm of Nihrain—

which lies at the heart of the mountains and from which, from time to time, bursts flame and smoke.

SEPIRIZ: "Behold! My home. The great Chasm of Nihrain!"

Elrik sits drinking wine, a finished plate of food pushed back, as he begins to tell Sepiriz why he is here. But Sepiriz raises a hand.

SEPIRIZ: "You need tell me nothing, young man. I know why you are here. You seek the Black Sword which Lord Arioch stole."

ELRIK: "It's true, Lord Sepiriz. Do you know where I can find it?"

SEPIRIZ: "First you must come with me . . . to the heart of creation . . ."

Sepiriz rises and leads Elrik from the cave room, out into a vaster cave, which is black glassy rock reflecting the fires which are burning far below. A series of steps and walkways leading deeper and deeper downwards.

SEPIRIZ: " . . . where the Fire Elders await us."

The two tiny figures are dwarfed by the vast walls of the dark cavern.

SEPIRIZ: "The entire multiverse is ruled by Law and Chaos, the two forces held in check by the power of the Cosmic Balance . . . and those who serve it."

They have descended until they stand before a great roaring wall of fire. Elric/Elrik looks wonderingly at his flesh and clothing.

ELRIK: "I do not burn. Why?"

SEPIRIZ: "This is the fire which creates life . . . but does not take it—look—!!!"

The flames part to show a vision of the Cosmic Balance. It is shadowy, clearly only a representation. The shaft of the balance consists of a black sword. The crosspiece supports a long, slender staff, imbedded with every kind of jewel. This is the Runestaff. From the jeweled ends of the Runestaff depend the two cups of the Balance.

SEPIRIZ: "The Balance consists of the Black Sword and the Runestaff. One is a negation of life. The other is the essence of life. Yet neither can exist without the other. The two cups of the Balance represent Law and Chaos. If one tips too far we shall have nothing but sterile Law. Too far the other way and we have unchecked Chaos. It is your destiny and the destiny of all those we call 'The Champion' to fight not for Law or Chaos, but for the Balance itself."

ELRIK: "So one is good and the other evil?"

SEPIRIZ: "No. The uses to which mortals and immortals put them determine whether they are used in the service of good or evil. Just as it is not possible to have life without death, so one can only exist if the other exists. It is the eternal paradox. The eternal truth."

ELRIK: "Why burden me with this weighty secret?"

Suddenly a beautiful flame elemental appears in the fire, speaking to Elrik.

FLAME ELEMENTAL: "Because it is your destiny to serve both. You, or your descendants, will learn more in the course of the next few thousand years, but now you must find the sword which Arioch of Chaos stole from King Grome . . . and which we, with Grome's compliance, will place on another plane, where it will be safe for as long as need be . . ."

ELRIK: "I don't understand . . ."

ELEMENTAL: "You are not asked to understand. You must make the journey back towards Melniboné. There you will find the rest of your destiny and the Black Sword. When you hold the sword, a word we have placed in your mind will summon us. If you need our help, you'll receive it . . ."

The flame elemental begins to fade back into the common fire. Elrik turns to Sepiriz—

ELRIK: "My destiny? The Black Sword? I want only to be a good and wise ruler of Melniboné . . ."

Sepiriz turns away, half smiling, half in grief.

SEPIRIZ: "That will become a matter of opinion, King Elrik . . ."

They are back in Sepiriz's chamber. Elrik looks a bit scared and distinctly puzzled.

ELRIK: "I did not ask you to make me a servant of the Balance, Lord Sepiriz!"

SEPIRIZ: "None of us asks that, young king. It is fate which selects us, in spite of our wishes."

He raises an arm to show Elrik out of the chamber.

They return to Sepiriz's quarters.

ELRIK: "How am I supposed to seize a sword from a Chaos Lord?"

SEPIRIZ: "You must take it from the one Arioch has given it to. Come. I'll set you on your way home."

Sepiriz drives his great chariot. He and Elrik occupy the chariot, which goes at a great pace, not quite touching the ground. Tethered to it is a great Nihrainian stallion, the match of the horse which pulls the chariot.

ELRIK: "Tell me, Lord Sepiriz. To whom did Arioch give the Black Sword?"

SEPIRIZ: "The one who even now brings the power of your kingdom against the new tribes."

Elrik is astonished as Sepiriz drags on the reins to bring the chariot to a halt.

ELRIK: "*What??*"

Sepiriz hands the reins of the stallion to Elrik who stands bewildered beside the chariot now.

SEPIRIZ: "Go home. You'll discover what I mean. I can tell you no more."

Elrik, still baffled, mounts the stallion.

Sepiriz looks at him in sympathy and sadness.

SEPIRIZ: "Farewell, Elrik. Forgive me. I do not envy you your destiny . . ."

Chapter Three

Changing Destinies

Back through the lands of the new tribes rode King Elrik, his mind heavy with questions, his heart full of uncertainty . . .

People in the fields look up in surprise as the haunted figure rides past on the great black Nihrain steed. He is a driven creature, his red eyes blazing as he stares ahead of him.

PEASANT: "Greetings, master—where dost thou—? *Miggea*! He rides as if hell's horde pursues him!"

Elrik reins in his horse as he comes upon the town where he spoke to the Wise Woman. The place has been burned to the ground.

The Wise Woman, wounded and half-burned herself, comes hobbling out of cover to confront him.

WISE WOMAN: "*You*! You're the Melnibonéan! May you and your kind be cursed for ten thousand years!"

ELRIK: "Believe me, mother, I know nothing of what you speak!"

WISE WOMAN: "You lie! You came scouting here all those years ago. Your aim was to discover our defenses. Then your war-dogs and their flying allies came upon us, taking all we owned! Kill me, if you will, whiteface. I have nothing left to love and no loved one left to mourn me!"

Elrik rode on while the old woman hurled curses at his back.

He is deeply troubled.

ELRIK (*thinks*): "How can Melnibonéans have done this? My gentle sister would never have permitted it."

The hills above Pukwadji Port, where the young king first came ashore so many years before . . .

Elrik reins in the great Nihrain horse in the hills above the port town where he came ashore on [page eight]. The whole place has been razed to the ground. All are dead.

He is even more horrified. On these ruins squat the weary dragons of Imrryr, the Phoorn. They look sleepy, sated. A little venom drips from the mouths of one or two of them. From gibbets hang the bodies of Pukwadji men and women. In the harbour are golden Melnibonéan barges onto which Melnibonéan soldiers are loading their loot.

ELRIK (*thinks*): "So, it's the same here, as it has been across all their lands. Every Pukwadji dead. Every city razed and looted. I left Melniboné with my sister sworn to pursue the peace she persuaded me of. Now I find nothing but death. It can only mean she has been usurped, perhaps killed, and another ruling in her place."

ELRIK (*thinks*): "But how?"

Elrik has waited until night. He sneaks past the roving Melnibonéan soldiers and the dragons and reaches the water, remounting his stallion on the beach.

ELRIK (*thinks*): "Now to see if this steed can gallop over the ocean, as Sepiriz promised—"

He rides the great black stallion over the moonlit water. The towers of Melniboné can be seen in the distance.

ELRIK (*thinks*): "Soon I'll reach my home and confront the destiny I was warned I'd find."

Elric/Elrik has dismounted from the horse and with the reins in his hands creeps towards the towers of Melniboné.

ELRIK (*thinks*): "What possesses my Melniboné? Even here it stinks of blood and fire."

He leaves the horse and sneaks into the city. Melnibonéan soldiers are dragging slaves ashore from ships and carrying bundles of booty home. Melnibonéans triumph in their victories, all quite mad with their filthy glory.

ELRIK (*thinks*): "The hidden passage will bring me out in the Tower of Kings where I last saw Asrid."

Elrik sneaks up towards the Tower of Kings, where he last left his sister. He sneaks into the tower and into the great throne room. Here is a figure in black armour, face hidden by a wonderfully elaborate visor which resembles the face of a snarling dragon. It lounges in the throne, a massive black sword held in its gauntleted hands. Beside the throne is none other than the figure of Arisand, the beautiful human woman who accompanied Yyrkoon here. She is smiling in evil pleasure. A tribal king is dragged before the figure.

FIGURE: "So, little chief. You've seen the power of Melniboné. Swear loyalty to us. Promise the empire half your wealth, or die at the point of my blade!"

CHIEF: "Melnibonéans were once fair and honourable people. We traded with you because we chose to. Now you are naught but thieves and murderers, using your dragons and your ships against weaker foes. I'll promise you nothing!"

Figure rises from the throne and holds the great black battle-blade out by the blade, offering the hilt to the barbarian.

BLACK ARMOUR: "Would you kill me, little mortal? I offer you the opportunity . . ."

Hesitantly, knowing he is being tricked, but feeling he has nothing to lose, the mortal stretches his hand towards the hilt of the blade . . .

He grasps the hilt and then yells in pain and terror.

CHIEF: "Aaaaaaaaaaaah! Oh, no, the thing sucks my very soul from my body. Aahhh. P-please-n-no . . . !"

He writhes, unable to release his hand from the sword as the blade sucks his soul from him.

BLACK ARMOUR: "Ha! Ha! Only I can handle that black blade and live! You shall die, little mortal! Your body will feed my dogs. Your soul will feed my sword!"

Chief sobs as the sword drinks his soul. Not every Melnibonéan can stand watching this. Some, who seemed hardened, now turn away.

CHIEF: "Aach! My soul—n-not my s-soul . . ."

BLACK ARMOUR: "Ha! Ha! Ha! The reality's worse than you could imagine, eh? It always was!"

And Elrik, horrified, sneaks away, back into the shadows.

ELRIK: "I can do nothing against such evil sorcery. I must discover what has happened to my sister . . . surely Dyvim Karm, Lord of the Dragons, will know . . ."

Melnibonéan guards spot Elrik. He begins to run.

GUARD: "Who's that? Some spy?"

ELRIK: "If they've killed my sister, then I'll share her fate."

Elrik is pursued through the corridors by the soldiers. At one point he's surrounded by guards and fights them. He gets to his horse and rides as fast as the great Nihrain stallion will carry him, the pursuing guards in disarray.

GUARD: "*STOP HIM!*"

He's riding across the island when he looks back and sees a great shape rise into the sky behind him. It is one of the Melnibonéan dragons.

ELRIK: "And now they send a dragon against me! This is a nightmare!"

He lies flat across his horse's neck as overhead one of the huge Melnibonéan dragons flies in rapid pursuit. He's riding over the ocean again, the dragon getting closer and closer.

They have reached land. The horse rears up as the dragon lands in front of it.

It opens its maw, poison and fiery venom bubbling from it and falling with a fiery splash to the ground.

ELRIK: "I cannot defeat a dragon. But I can die like a Melnibonéan king!"

The dragon pauses, surprised.

DRAGON: "*You speak the language of the Phoorn? You are our kin?*"

ELRIK: "Aye. I expect no mercy from you. I have seen what you have done to the mainland tribes . . ."

DRAGON: "*You are the Silverskin. We have a bond, you and I. I am Flamefang, oldest of the Phoorn.*"

Elrik dismounts and reaches a hand to Flamefang's snout.

ELRIK: "Bond?"

FLAMEFANG: "*The silverskins saved us from limbo. Our loyalty is to you first. Many Phoorn now sleep in our caves. They are weary of their work. But I have slept longest and am ready to serve my brother. How can Flamefang help?*"

ELRIK: "I do not yet know. Return to your cave. I will call you if you are needed. Now I go to seek allies amongst the new tribes . . ."

The dragon turns to leave, but Elrik stays it for a moment—

ELRIK: "Stay, brother. Tell me what has become of my sister Asrid. Less than ten years ago I left her ruling a peaceful kingdom—and now that black-armoured creature rules in her place . . ."

Flamefang pauses.

FLAMEFANG: "*I cannot help you, brother. I know nothing of the court politics. We merely serve whoever rules—unless, like me, we remember certain loyalties . . .*"

ELRIK: "Is Dyvim Karm still Lord of the Dragon Caves?"

FLAMEFANG: "*He fled when he refused to lead us against the new tribes. His brother Dyvim Nir now commands us. But most already sleep. We have become weary with all this warfare. And now—farewell! Call me when you need me!*"

The great shape of the dragon ascends into the dawn sky, leaving Elrik puzzled, confused and dismayed.

Only a few days later . . .

Elrik comes upon a Mèlnibonéan, ragged and starving, and greets him with joy.

ELRIK: "*Dyvim Karm*! I've sought you everywhere. I feared you killed."

The two men embrace with some joy.

We next see them sitting beside a fire while Dyvim Karm eats part of a rabbit with some gusto.

DYVIM KARM: "It happened so swiftly. One moment your sweet sister enjoined us all to peace. The next, this creature in black armour, wielding that filthy sword, was on the throne. Those who refused to serve the Black Armour lost their souls to the sword. Your sister, I fear, is murdered. All I could rescue in my flight was my Dragon Horn . . ."

ELRIK: "We must find allies to attack and reconquer Melniboné. What's more, I am sworn to take that black sword back to its rightful keepers."

Through the coming months, King Elrik sought the remnants of the mainland tribes, trying to create an alliance powerful enough to defeat the usurper . . .

Elrik is in the mountains again. He is meeting with the remnants of various barbarian tribes who have been attacked and defeated by the Melnibonéan forces.

One of the tribal leaders, the most striking and forceful, is Queen Bisrana, who is Queen of the Shazaars. She steps forward to confront Elrik.

QUEEN BISRANA: "I am Bisrana, Queen of the Shazaar. Why should we trust one of your blood?"

ELRIK: "Because we have common cause. My cousin, Dyvim Karm, has told you how Melnibonéan power was stolen from my sister."

Chief Thokor of the Jharks now springs up.

THOKOR: "I, Thokor of the Jharks, would know what you offer us."

ELRIK: "A pact between our nations. I played no part in my people's attack on yours."

King Ralyn of the Dhar tribe now speaks:

KING RALYN: "I am Ralyn of the Dhars. You promise us loot, which will repay us for what has been stolen."

ELRIK: "I want none of my people needlessly killed. He who wears the black armour is responsible for what has happened. I do not believe he is of my blood."

The chiefs are in conference, talking amongst themselves while Elrik waits to one side.

Eventually Queen Bisrana steps forward from the gathering and addresses Elrik.

BISRANA: "We'll join you in this attack. But we want our fair share of the booty."

ELRIK: "You promise you'll leave the population and the buildings unscathed?"

BISRANA: "Only those who threaten us will be harmed."

Elrik embraces Queen Bisrana.

ELRIK: "Then we are agreed. One dragon at least will aid us in the attack. We must strike suddenly and soon, before word of our plans gets back to Imrryr."

Chapter Four

Bitter Vengeance

Elrik, Bisrana and the other leaders of the barbarians look down on a secret bay as the ships assemble. It is a large fleet of miscellaneous ships, including a captured golden battle-barge.

BISRANA: "We are ready. Let us take our revenge!"

ELRIK: "The majority of the dragons now sleep, exhausted. It is the best time to strike. We'll have one dragon to aid us—whom Dyvim Karm here will summon with his horn."

BISRANA: "This captured battle-barge will lead our fleet. We'll deceive their watchmen long enough to breach their defenses."

DYVIM KARM: "The last thing they'll be expecting is a counter-attack."

Elrik turns to Queen Bisrana and addresses her fiercely—

ELRIK: "But remember—I will confront the thing in black armour. I have a strange instinct . . . I believe I know who he is."

The ships sail out to sea towards the distant towers of Melniboné. Inset of Elrik on the deck of the golden battle-barge, staring fiercely towards the towers.

From the POV of Melnibonéans. In astonishment they watch the ragged navy approach (this is in the years before the sea-maze). Hastily they scramble to defensive positions, some rubbing sleep-filled eyes, some buckling on bits of armour.

A Melnibonéan soldier runs into the throne room where Black Armour sits, his black sword still with him.

SOLDIER: "*Sire! A fleet attacks us!*"

BLACK ARMOUR: "What? I thought those savages had learned their lesson."

FIRST CAPTAIN: "It's too late to ready the battle-barges. We must fight them as they come ashore."

SECOND CAPTAIN: "We expected no attack. We have no defenses ready."

BLACK ARMOUR: "We'll defeat them easily enough . . ."

And then the barbarian invaders are pouring ashore, led by Queen Bisrana and the other chieftains . . .

Behind them, offshore, the golden barge lies at anchor.

On it, Dyvim Karm raises the Dragon Horn to his lips. Elrik beside him speaks grimly.

ELRIK: "Now, Dyvim Karm. Blow the note to summon my brother Flamefang!"

The barbarians clash with the startled Melnibonéans. They pursue them into their towers. Black Armour has sneaked away into the highest tower while his men are fighting.

BLACK ARMOUR: "NO!"

He climbs the steps to the throne room, where Arisand stands, smiling slightly.

BLACK ARMOUR: "You promised me triumph! Now we face defeat."

ARISAND: "Come now, mortal—you must keep your nerve. I made you the gift of the Black Sword. You know how to use it best."

BLACK ARMOUR: "If this body is killed, then I die also!"

ARISAND: "I promised you I would save you from that fate. I keep my promises."

A great shadow passes against the window outside. Black Armour turns when he sees it.

BLACK ARMOUR: "What's that?"

Outside, flying around the Tower of Kings is Flamefang, with Elric on his back.

Black Armour runs out to the balcony and looks down. In the streets the barbarians are driving the Melnibonéans back into the tower. One of the chieftains flourishes a brand.

FIRST CHIEFTAIN: "*Burn the cursed city to the ground!*"

BISRANA: "We swore we'd not fire Imrryr."

SECOND CHIEFTAIN: "You think he'll keep his word to us? Burn the whole foul place and every Melnibonéan with it!"

Queen Bisrana makes an effort to stop the chieftain but she's held by some of his men as he and other warriors throw burning brands through windows where women and children can be seen drawing back in terror.

Elrik sees this from the back of his dragon and is horrified.

ELRIK: "The barbarians break their word!"

He sees Black Armour staring up at him from the balcony and, in a wild leap, sword in hand, jumps from the back of the dragon to the balcony.

ELRIK: "*Flamefang*! *Go*! Aid my people! *Go*! Help them drive off the barbarians if you can!"

BARBARIANS: "KILL!"

"Kill them all!"

"Above us! Look to your lives!"

Flamefang swoops down on the barbarians and their fleet, his fiery venom destroying everything it touches.

BARBARIANS: "He circles again!"

"Fly, brothers! To the ships while we can!"

"The monster comes too late to save their precious city, anyway!"

Meanwhile, back on the balcony of the Tower of Kings, Elrik confronts Black Armour . . .

ELRIK: "*You*! One thing I can do—and that is kill the one who has betrayed everything Melniboné stood for!"

So fierce is Elrik's attack that he drives the black-armoured figure back into the throne room where Arisand still watches, her face full of nervous glee.

Black Armour pauses at the throne.

BLACK ARMOUR: "You are more powerful than I guessed."

He flings the sword at Elrik's feet.

BLACK ARMOUR: "There. The sword is yours. Kill me if you will . . ."

ELRIK (*thinks*): "I know this trick—and yet . . ."

He stoops to pick up the sword.

ELRIK (*thinks*): "I have no choice but to take the risk and kill this foul being who has brought my sister and my kingdom to disgrace!"

His hand reaches towards the sword.

Elrik's hand closes on the grip.

He is astonished. The sword does not harm him.

ELRIK: "The sword. It does not harm me!"

BLACK ARMOUR: *"What??"*

Black Armour's head whirls to where Arisand still stands.

BLACK ARMOUR: "Arioch! You swore only I could handle the sword!"

Arisand smiles quietly, her great eyes full of malice and a kind of triumph.

ARISAND: "No, mortal—I swore only that one of *your blood* could handle the sword."

Then Elrik lunges forward, driving the sword towards the heart of Black Armour.

ARISAND: "But fear not. It suits my plan to save you before this vessel dies . . ."

We see a ghostly human form pulled out of the armoured figure by Arisand, who shows enormous, supernatural strength as she does so.

Just as Elrik plunges the blade deep into the armour. To terrible effect.

As the ghostly form escapes, a great scream comes from the black helmet.

ELRIK: "There, usurper! Die as you deserve!"

He lets his grip on the sword fall away as he stands listening in astonishment.

ELRIK: "That scream! It was a woman's scream. What's this? More sorcery?"

The figure in black armour collapses, the black blade still sticking into the breastplate where its heart should be.

Unnoticed, Arisand opens a path to the moonbeam roads, all of which are ghostly.

Leading her ghostly charge, she steps out onto one of the roads. Elrik kneels beside the fallen figure, pulling off the helmet.

ELRIK: "Let's see the face of this filthy creature!"

Arisand and the other figure disappear out onto the moonbeam roads.

Elrik pulls off the helmet.

There is the sweet face of his sister. Her eyes are full of tears and she is clearly dying.

ELRIK: "Asrid! My sister! This cannot be!"

ASRID: "The sword takes my soul, brother. I was possessed by a demon. It was not I did those terrible deeds . . . Aaah. My soul! My soul!"

ELRIK (*in rage and agony*): "*No! No!!!*"

ELRIK: "I have killed my beloved sister! I have murdered my kin!"

Dyvim Karm comes running up the steps into the throne room.

DYVIM KARM: "My lord Elrik! The barbarians have fired the city. They have broken their oath to you!"

Elrik is in tears. He pulls the sword from his sister's body. She is dead.

ELRIK: "I have killed my sister. What care I if oaths are made and broken? They are meaningless sounds in the empty void . . ."

DYVIM KARM: "Imrryr burns, my lord. There are women and children in those buildings."

Elrik looks up, his eyes full of grief.

ELRIK: "I want this black blade gone. I wish it banished forever from this realm. Where are the Fire Elders? They said they would come when I held the Black Sword!"

ELRIK: "Well here it is! Now, Fire Elders, keep your word! Abolish this filthy thing to where no mortal hand can ever find it again!"

Dyvim Karm backs away in awe as the Fire Elders, creatures of pure flame, manifest themselves in the room, reaching out to take the blade from Elrik.

FIRE ELDER: "Here we are, King Elrik. You have done us a great service which we shall not forget."

Elrik hands a Fire Elder the black blade.

ELRIK: "Take it. Make sure it is never again seen in Melniboné."

FIRE ELDER: "As long as one of your blood never holds it, it will do no further harm in this realm."

ELRIK: "None of mine will ever touch such a filthy thing, I swear! But this, too, I swear—that I shall keep no bargains with humans. Henceforth I shall rule by blood and fire, making Arioch and the Dukes of Hell my allies! All others shall all bow the knee in vassalage to Melniboné!"

Dyvim Karm speaks urgently:

DYVIM KARM: "My lord! The towers still burn. Is there nothing these allies can do against those flames?"

The Flame Elder turns to look at Dyvim Karm.

FLAME ELDER: "Fear not, mortal. We shall gather the flames to our own bodies and take them with us when we leave." *(He turns to Elrik:)* "Farewell, young King Elrik. We sorrow for your lost sister. But I fear your own destiny is not a happy one . . ."

Elrik's face screws up with pain and anger as he watches the Flame Elders fade and leave.

ELRIK: "Happiness? That's no longer a quality we of Melniboné shall seek. I'll keep the compact made with Arioch. He shall have his share of blood and souls! Henceforth we shall be strong and merciless and our pleasures will be of the cruelest kind!"

Dyvim Karm goes to the balcony and looks down. He turns with astonishment to address King Elrik—

DYVIM KARM: "My lord king! The fires are out. The barbarians retreat. Imrryr is saved!"

We see a close up as Dyvim Karm's face goes from astonished delight to horrified surprise—

DYVIM KARM: "Elrik? My lord?"

Elrik has collapsed on the flagstones of the throne room, beside his sister.

A black crow perches on the throne itself, looking down at them.

Then it spreads its wings and flies out of the window.

Dyvim Karm looks up as Melnibonéan soldiers rush into the throne room.

DYVIM KARM: "Quickly . . . our king has fainted from exhaustion . . . !"

MELNIBONÉAN SOLDIER: "And our queen?"

DYVIM KARM: "She's dead. And her soul, I fear, is forever in limbo. This is the end of the Melniboné she hoped to create. From this day on, our history darkens . . ."

Dyvim Karm returns to the window and looks out across the blackened streets towards the harbour where the battle-barges lie at anchor.

DYVIM KARM: ". . . from this day on, we begin the making of an empire."

Epilogue

The dream has ended, but the dreamers have yet to wake . . .

We are back at the dream couches. Tanglebones is distraught. He tries to lift Elric's head. He takes a cup from Cymoril's hand.

TANGLEBONES: "This is what I feared, Lady Cymoril."

CYMORIL: "What is it, Sir Tanglebones?"

Tanglebones can't get the still-sleeping Elric to take the potion.

TANGLEBONES: "If he was killed in the dream, the chances are he is dead—or at least in limbo. Yet this is strange."

TANGLEBONES (*looks up, frowning*): "He still breathes. It's as if he refuses to wake. As if something happened in his dream adventure which was so terrible, he has no will to come back to life!"

Cymoril turns as a shout comes from the nearby dream chamber, where Yyrkoon went at about the same time as Elric.

UNSEEN VOICE: "Dead! No question of it!"

CYMORIL: "Yyrkoon—dead? But—"

Cymoril leaves Elric's chamber—and enters Yyrkoon's.

Her eyes widen in astonishment. Yyrkoon has a goblet in one hand and is leaning heavily on his elbow, clearly groggy, but definitely not dead.

YYRKOON: "He—she—Arioch can't be . . ."

But it is Arisand who lies sprawled on the flagstones.

And Yyrkoon rises weakly, in horror.

YYRKOON: "He promised me triumph—"

Yyrkoon sits on the bench, his hand to his chest, exactly on the spot where Elrik plunged the Black Sword into Black Armour's body.

YYRKOON: "—and brought me death . . ."

Yyrkoon puts his hand to his head.

YYRKOON: "Ah. Memory fades. The dream—I no longer recall it . . ."

CYMORIL: "Whatever scheme you and this human woman concocted, brother, it clearly failed again."

Cymoril hurries from the room, back to Elric's chamber.

Where Tanglebones is reviving a very faint, weak Elric, whose eyes will scarcely open.

TANGLEBONES: "He revives—but barely . . ."

ELRIC: "Arioch. He possessed my sister. No—two beings possessed her—who was the other . . . ?"

Tanglebones tries to soothe his master.

TANGLEBONES: "My lord, you must not tax yourself. It was but a bad dream."

Elric glares up at Tanglebones.

ELRIC: "No! It was all too real. All too dark and terrible. It was how we let ourselves become what we are today. Creatures bereft of mercy or real happiness . . ."

Cymoril speaks soothingly to him:

CYMORIL: "Some of us feel it is a mercy you are saved from oblivion, my lord. And some of us are happy that you live."

Elric softens as he takes Cymoril's hand.

ELRIC: "Oh, sweet love. Yet you and I are still Melnibonéans. Still what our history has made of us . . ."

CYMORIL: "Cannot our will overcome such things, my lord?"

ELRIC: "I do not know. That terrible dream. It fades now. Yet I seem to have learned lessons which permeate my very bones. No matter what our will, we must always be thwarted by dark destiny."

CYMORIL: "No, Elric. No, my lord. Our love will overcome any so-called 'destiny'. We can carve a new fate for ourselves. One that allows our love to flourish."

ELRIC: "I hope so, sweet Cymoril. I hope so."

But when we look into his face, into his brooding eyes, it is clear he holds no such hope.

There is a step in the corridor. We catch a glimpse of Sadric as he comes towards the dream chambers.

Emperor Sadric stared at his son without speaking.

He seemed to be reading something there.

It was as if he understood what had happened in that dream . . .

Sadric enters, pausing at the entrance to the dream chamber.

Pausing for only a moment, he made his way to the next dream chamber, occupied by his nephew . . .

Sadric looks down at Yyrkoon, who is snarling, though still very groggy. He looks at the body of Arisand still sprawled there.

SADRIC: "What happened here?"

YYRKOON: "The bitch—or whatever the creature was—betrayed me. She said she'd aid me against that bloodless weakling. Instead, she died. I—I cannot remember how . . ."

SADRIC: "You killed her? You killed my only consolation?"

Yyrkoon simply cannot remember what happened. He tries to explain himself to Sadric, but cannot.

YYRKOON: "N-no, my lord—at least, I d-do not think so . . ."

Wordlessly, the emperor turned his back on his nephew and returned to where his son still tried to rid himself of his last, long dream . . .

Sadric looks down on Elric. He is not smiling. It is almost as if he is reluctant to voice the words he speaks. But speak them he does . . .

SADRIC: "The tests are complete. The duel is done. You have won, my son. Though it will bring you scant satisfaction, you will be the next emperor of Melniboné."

There was no more to be said. Sadric returned to his books and his solitary misery.

Elric's eyes still carried the shadows of that terrible dream.

He felt no triumph in his father's decision. Yet there was some comfort in the embrace of the beautiful young woman beside him . . .

Cymoril embraces Elric, who is now pretty much recovered, though there are still shadows in his eyes as he tries to forget, rather than recall, the dream he has emerged from.

CYMORIL: "It means we can be wed, my lord. As emperor and empress we shall bring a new era of prosperity and power to Melniboné. We'll learn, as you say, to live with the humans of the Young Kingdoms, to win their friendship and offer them ours . . ."

ELRIC: "Yet we shall still be Melnibonéans, my darling. We shall still be what we are. For Chaos remains our ally."

Tanglebones turns his head suddenly, for he thinks he sees something behind him.

There, hanging like smoke in the far corner of the chamber, is a triumphantly smiling face. It is the face of Arioch, but what we can see of the body seems to bear the clothes of Arisand.

Tanglebones frowns, lost in his own thoughts, and a black raven comes to perch again on his shoulder.

Elric turns to look at the old seer.

ELRIC: "But I brood too much, eh, Master Tanglebones?"

Then the young prince was on his feet, shrugging off his melancholy as the dreams of doom faded from his memory.

Elric is smiling again. He has risen and has his arm around the delighted Cymoril.

ELRIC: "Come, my dear Cymoril. Let's to our horses and the clean sweet air again. I have a fancy to taste the simple pleasures."

He and Cymoril leave the room, laughing joyfully.

Leaving Tanglebones who, in his thoughtful wisdom, watches them go.

TANGLEBONES: "Aye, my lord. Taste them while you may. And pray they last—as I shall also pray."

For the old man feared that tragedy and death would soon fall upon Melniboné, and when they came, they must surely signify . . .

The End

A PORTRAIT IN IVORY

A PORTRAIT IN IVORY

(2005)

Chapter One

An Encounter with a Lady

Elric, who had slept well and revived himself with fresh-brewed herbs, was in improved humour as he mixed honey and water into his glass of green breakfast wine. Typically, his night had been filled with distressing dreams, but any observer would see only a tall, insouciant "silverskin" with high cheekbones, slightly sloping eyes and tapering ears, revealing nothing of his inner thoughts.

He had found a quiet hostelry away from the noisy centre of Séred-Öma, this city of tall palms. Here, merchants from all over the Young Kingdoms gathered to trade their goods in return for the region's most valuable produce. This was not the dates or livestock, on which Séred-Öma's original wealth had been founded, but the extraordinary creations of artists famed everywhere in the lands bordering the Sighing Desert. Their carvings, especially of animals and human portraits, were coveted by kings and princes. It was the reputation of these works of art which brought the crimson-eyed albino out of his way to see them for himself. Even in Melniboné, where barbarian art for the most part was regarded with distaste, the sculptors of Séred-Öma had been admired.

Though Elric had left the scabbarded runesword and black armour of his new calling in his chamber and wore the simple chequered clothing of a regional traveler, his fellow guests tended to keep a certain distance from him. Those who had heard little of Melniboné's fall had celebrated the Bright Empire's destruction with great glee until the implications of that sudden defeat were understood. Certainly, Melniboné no longer controlled the world's trade and could no longer demand ransom from the Young Kingdoms, but the world was these days in confusion as upstart nations vied to seize the power for themselves. And meanwhile, Melnibonéan mercenaries found employment in the armies of rival countries. Without being certain of his identity, they could tell at once that Elric was one of those misplaced unhuman warriors, infamous for their cold good manners and edgy pride.

Rather than find themselves in a quarrel with him, the customers of the Rolling Pig kept their distance. The haughty albino too seemed indisposed to open a conversation. Instead, he sat at his corner table staring into his morning wine, brooding on what could not be forgotten. His history was written on handsome features which would have been youthful were it not for his thoughts. He reflected on an unsettled past and an uneasy future. Even had someone dared approach him, however sympathetically, to ask what concerned him, he would have answered lightly and coldly, for, save in his nightmares, he refused to confront most of those concerns. Thus, he did not look up when a woman, wearing the conical russet hat and dark veil of her caste, approached him through the crowd of busy dealers.

"Sir?" Her voice was a dying melody. "Master Melnibonéan, could you tolerate my presence at your table?" Falling rose petals, sweet and brittle from the sun.

'Lady," said Elric, in the courteous tone his people reserved for their own high-born kin, "I am at my breakfast. But I will gladly order more wine . . ."

"Thank you, sir. I did not come here to share your hospitality. I came to ask a favour." Behind the veil her eyes were grey-green. Her skin had the golden bloom of the Na'äne, who had once ruled here and were said to be a race as ancient as Elric's own. "A favour you have every reason to refuse."

The albino seemed almost amused, perhaps because, as he looked into her eyes, he detected beauty behind the veil, an unexpected intelligence he had not encountered since he had left Imrryr's burning ruins

behind him. How he had longed to hear the swift wit of his own people, the eloquent argument, the careless insults. All that and more had been denied him for too long. To himself he had become sluggish, almost as dull as the conniving princelings and self-important merchants to whom he sold his sword. Now, there was something in the music of her speech, something in the lilt of irony colouring each phrase she uttered, that spoke to his own sleeping intellect. "You know me too well, lady. Clearly, my fate is in your hands, for you're able to anticipate my every attitude and response. I have good reason not to grant you a favour, yet you still come to ask one, so either you are prescient or I am already your servant."

"I would serve you, sir," she said gently. Her half-hidden lips curved in a narrow smile. She shrugged. "And, in so doing, serve myself."

"I thought my curiosity atrophied," he answered. "My imagination a petrified knot. Here you pick at threads to bring it back to life. This loosening is unlikely to be pleasant. Should I fear you?" He lifted a dented pewter cup to his lips and tasted the remains of his wine. "You are a witch, perhaps? Do you seek to revive the dead? I am not sure . . ."

"I am not sure, either," she told him. "Will you trust me enough to come with me to my house?"

"I regret madam, I am only lately bereaved—"

"I'm no sensation-seeker, sir, but an honest woman with an honest ambition. I do not tempt you with the pleasures of the flesh, but of the soul. Something which might engage you for a while, even ease your mind a little. I can more readily convince you of this if you come to my house. I live there alone, save for servants. You may bring your sword, if you wish. Indeed, if you have fellows, bring them also. Thus, I offer you every advantage."

The albino rose slowly from his bench and placed the empty goblet carefully on the well-worn wood. His own smile reflected hers. He bowed. "Lead on, madam." And he followed her through a crowd which parted like corn before the reaper and he left a momentary silence behind him.

Chapter Two

The Material

She had brought him to the depth of the city's oldest quarter, where artists of every skill, she told him, were licensed to work unhindered by landlord or, save in the gravest cases, the law. This ancient sanctuary was created by time-honoured tradition and the granting of certain guarantees by the clerics whose great university had once been the centre of the settlement. These guarantees had been strengthened during the reign of the great King Alo'ofd, an accomplished player of the nine-stringed *murmerlan,* who loved all the arts and struggled with a desire to throw off the burdens of his office and become a musician. King Alo'ofd's decrees had been law for the past millennium and his successors had never dared challenge them.

"Thus, this quarter harbours not only artists of great talent," she told him, "but many who have only the minimum of talent. Enough to allow them to live according to our ancient freedoms. Sadly, sir, there is as much forgery practised here, of every kind, as there is originality."

"Yours is not the only such quarter." He spoke absently, his eyes inspecting the colourful paintings, sculptures and manuscripts displayed on every side. They were of varied quality, but only a few showed genuine inspiration and beauty. Yet the accomplishment was generally higher than Elric had usually observed in the Young Kingdoms. "Even in Melniboné we had these districts. Two of my cousins, for instance, were calligraphers. Another composed for the flute."

"I have heard of Melnibonéan arts," she said. "But we are too distant from your island home to have seen many examples. There are stories, of course." She smiled. "Some of them are decidedly sinister . . ."

"Oh, they are doubtless true. We had no trouble if audiences, for instance, died for an artist's work. Many great composers would experiment, for instance, with the human voice." His eyes again clouded, remembering not a crime but his lost passion.

It seemed she misinterpreted him. "I feel for you, sir. I am not one of those who celebrated the fall of the Dreaming City."

"You could not know its influence, so far away," he murmured, picking up a remarkable little pot and studying its design. "But those who were our neighbours were glad to see us humiliated. I do not blame them. Our time was over." His expression was again one of cultivated insouciance. She turned her own gaze towards a house which leaned like an amiable drunkard on the buttressed walls of two neighbours, giving the impression that if it fell, then all would fall together. The house was of wood and sandy brick, of many floors, each at an angle to the rest, covered by a waved roof.

"This is the residence," she told him, "where my forefathers and myself have lived and worked. It is the House of the Th'ee and I am Rai-u Th'ee, last of my line. It is my ambition to leave a single great work of art behind, carved in a material which has been in our possession for centuries, yet until now always considered too valuable to use. It is a rare material, at least to us, and possessed of a number of qualities, some of which our ancestors only hinted at."

"My curiosity grows," said Elric, though now he found himself wishing that he had accepted her offer and brought his sword. "What is this material?"

"It is a kind of ivory," she said, leading him into the ramshackle house which, for all its age and decrepitude, had clearly once been rich.

Even the wall-hangings, now in rags, revealed traces of their former quality. There were paintings from floor to ceiling which, Elric knew, would have commanded magnificent prices at any market. The furniture was carved by genuine artists and showed the passing of a hundred fashions, from the plain, somewhat austere style of the city's secular period, to the ornate enrichments of her pagan age. Some were inset with jewels, as were the many mirrors, framed with exquisite and elaborate ornament. Elric was surprised, given what she had told him of the quarter, that the House of Th'ee had never been robbed.

Apparently reading his thoughts, she said: "This place has been afforded certain protections down the years." She led him into a tall studio, lit by a single, unpapered window through which a great deal of light entered, illuminating the scrolls and boxed books lining the walls. Crowded on tables and shelves stood sculptures in every conceivable material. They were in bone and granite and hardwood and limestone. They were in clay and bronze, in iron and sea-green basalt. Bright, glinting whites, deep, swirling blacks. Colours of every possible shade from darkest blue to the lightest pinks and yellows. There was gold, silver and delicate porphyry. There were heads and torsos and reclining figures, beasts of every kind, some believed extinct. There were representations of the Lords and Ladies of Chaos and of Law, every supernatural aristocrat who had ever ruled in heaven, hell or limbo. Elementals. Animal-bodied men, birds in flight, leaping deer, men and women at rest, historical subjects, group subjects and half-finished subjects which hinted at something still to be discovered in the stone. They were the work of genius, decided the albino, and his respect for this bold woman grew. "Yes." Again she anticipated a question, speaking with firm pride. "They are all mine. I love to work. Many of these are taken from life . . ."

He thought it impolitic to ask which.

"But you will note," she added, "that I have never had the pleasure of sculpting the head of a Melnibonéan. This could be my only opportunity."

"Ah," he began regretfully, but with great grace she silenced him,

drawing him to a table on which sat a tall, shrouded object. She took away the cloth. "This is the material we have owned down the generations but for which we had never yet found an appropriate subject."

He recognized the material. He reached to run his hand over its warm smoothness. He had seen more than one of these in the old caves of the Phoorn, to whom his folk were related. He had seen them in living creatures who even now slept in Melniboné, wearied by their work of destruction, their old master made an exile, with no-one to care for them save a few mad old men who knew how to do nothing else.

"Yes," she whispered, "it is what you know it is. It cost my forefathers a great fortune for, as you can imagine, your folk were not readily forthcoming with such things. It was smuggled from Melniboné and traded through many nations before it reached us, some two and a half centuries ago."

Elric found himself almost singing to the thing as he caressed it. He felt a mixture of nostalgia and deep sadness.

"It is dragon ivory, of course." Her hand joined his on the hard, brilliant surface of the great curved tusk. Few Phoorn had owned such fangs. Only the greatest of the patriarchs, legendary creatures of astonishing ferocity and wisdom, who had come from their old world to this, following their kin, the humanlike folk of Melniboné. The Phoorn, too, had not been native to this world, but had fled another. They, too, had always been alien and cruel, impossibly beautiful, impossibly strange. Elric felt kinship even now for this piece of bone. It was perhaps all that remained of the first generation to settle on this plane.

"It is a holy thing." His voice was growing cold again. Inexplicable pain forced him to withdraw from her. "It is my own kin. Blood for blood, the Phoorn and the folk of Melniboné are one. It was our power. It was our strength. It was our continuity. This is ancestral bone. Stolen bone. It would be sacrilege . . ."

"No, Prince Elric, in my hands it would be a unification. A resolution. A completion. You know why I have brought you here."

"Yes." His hand fell to his side. He swayed, as if faint. He felt a need for the herbs he carried with him. "But it is still sacrilege . . ."

"Not if I am the one to give it life." Her veil was drawn back now and he saw how impossibly young she was, what beauty she had: a beauty mirrored in all the things she had carved and moulded. Her desire was, he was sure, an honest one. Two very different emotions warred within him. Part of him felt she was right, that she could unite the two kinsfolk in a single image and bring honour to all his ancestors, a kind of resolution to their mutual history. Part of him feared what she might create. In honouring his past, would she be destroying the future? Then some fundamental part of him made him gather himself up and turn to her. She gasped at what she saw burning in those terrible, ruby eyes.

"Life?"

"Yes," she said. "A new life honouring the old. Will you sit for me?" She too was caught up in his mood, for she too was endangering everything she valued, possibly her own soul, to make what might be her very last great work. "Will you allow me to create your memorial? Will you help me redeem that destruction whose burden is so heavy upon you? A symbol for everything that was Melniboné?"

He let go of his caution but felt no responsive glee. The fire dulled in his eyes. His mask returned. "I will need you to help me brew certain herbs, madam. They will sustain me while I sit for you."

Her step was light as she led him into a room where she had lit a stove and on which water already boiled, but his own face still resembled the stone of her carvings. His gaze was turned inward, his eyes alternately flared and faded like a dying candle. His chest moved with deep, almost dying breaths as he gave himself up to her art.

Chapter Three

The Sitting

How many hours did he sit, still and silent in the chair? At one time she remarked on the fact that he scarcely moved. He said that he had developed the habit over several hundred years and, when she voiced surprise, permitted himself a smile. "You have not heard of Melniboné's dream couches? They are doubtless destroyed with the rest. It is how we learn so much when young. The couches let us dream for a year, even centuries, while the time passing for those awake was but minutes. I appear to you as a relatively young man, lady. But actually I have lived for centuries. It took me that time to pursue my dream-quests, which in turn taught me my craft and prepared me for . . ." And then he stopped speaking, his pale lids falling over his troubled, unlikely eyes.

She drew breath, as if to ask a further question, then thought better of it. She brewed him cup after cup of invigorating herbs and she continued to work, her delicate chisels fashioning an extraordinary likeness. She had genius in her hands. Every line of the albino's head was rapidly reproduced. And Elric, almost dreaming again, stared into the middle distance. His thoughts were far away and in the past, where he had left the corpse of his beloved Cymoril to burn on the pyre he had made of his own ancient home, the great and beautiful Imrryr, the Dreaming City, the dreamer's city, which many had considered indestructible, had believed to be more conjuring than reality, created by the Melnibonéan Sorcerer Kings into a delicate reality, whose towers, so tall they disappeared amongst clouds, were actually the result of supernatural will rather than the creation of architects and masons.

Yet Elric had proven such theories false when Melniboné burned. Now all knew him for a traitor and none trusted him, even those whose ambition he had served. They said he was twice a traitor, once to his own folk, second to those he had led on the raid which had razed Imrryr and upon whom he had turned. But in his own mind he was thrice a traitor, for he had slain his beloved Cymoril, beautiful sister of cousin Yyrkoon, who had tricked Elric into killing her with that terrible black blade whose energy both sustained and drained him.

It was for Cymoril, more than Imrryr, that Elric mourned. But he showed none of this to the world and never spoke of it. Only in his dreams, those terrible, troubled dreams, did he see her again, which is why he almost always slept alone and presented a carefully cultivated air of insouciance to the world at large.

Had he agreed to the sculptress's request because she reminded him of his cousin?

Hour upon tireless hour she worked with her exquisitely made instruments until at last she had finished. She sighed and it seemed her breath was a gentle witch-wind, filling the head with vitality. She turned the portrait for his inspection.

It was as if he stared into a mirror. For a moment he thought he saw movement in the bust, as if his own essence had been absorbed by it. Save for the blank eyes, the carving might have been himself. Even the hair had been carved to add to the portrait's lifelike qualities.

She looked to him for his approval and received the faintest of smiles. "You have made the likeness of a monster," he murmured. "I congratulate you. Now history will know the face of the man they call Elric Kinslayer."

"Ah," she said, "you curse yourself too much, my lord. Do you look into the face of one who bears a guilt-weighted conscience?"

And of course, he did. She had captured exactly that quality of melancholy and self-hatred behind the mask of insouciance which characterized the albino in repose.

"Whoever looks on this will not say you were careless of your crimes." Her voice was so soft it was almost a whisper now.

At this he rose suddenly, putting down his cup. "I need no sentimental forgiveness," he said coldly. "There is no forgiveness, no understanding, of that crime. History will be right to curse me for a coward, a traitor, a killer of women and of his own blood. You have done well, madam, to brew me those herbs, for I now feel strong enough to put all this and your city behind me!"

She watched him leave, walking a little unsteadily like a man carrying a heavy burden, through the busy night, back to the inn where he had left his sword and armour. She knew that by morning he would be gone, riding out of Séred-Öma, never to return. Her hands caressed the likeness she had made, the blind, staring eyes, the mouth which was set in a grimace of self-mocking carelessness.

And she knew he would always wonder, even as he put a thousand leagues between them, if he had not left at least a little of his yearning, desperate soul behind him.

ASPECTS OF FANTASY
(PART 3)

In this third article concerning the undercurrents in much of our gothic and weird-story history, Michael Moorcock covers the good-and-evil hero-villain aspects of many classic writers and their works.

—John Carnell, SCIENCE FANTASY No. 63, February 1964

ASPECTS OF FANTASY
(1964)

3. Figures of Faust

Cut is the branch that might have grown full straight,
And burnèd is Apollo's laurel-bough,
That sometime grew within this learnèd man.
Faustus is gone: regard his hellish fall,
Whose fiendful fortune may exhort the wise,
Only to wonder at unlawful things,
Whose deepness doth entice such forward wits
To practise more than heavenly power permits.

—The Tragical History of Doctor Faustus
by Christopher Marlowe

A FITTING EPITAPH for the majority of hero-villains whose appearance in fantasy is the subject of this article. It helps, also, to illustrate why horror stories relying on the Christian idea of good and evil no longer convince us so much as they used to. Most modern readers can't believe in the existence of rewards and punishments for the good or evil man. Yet Faust, and heroes like him, continue to convince in spite of this. There is no denying that even to a wicked old atheist like me, the pathos and tragedy of Marlowe's closing chorus is moving (even though I suspect him of tacking it on as a sop to the Elizabethan censor).

I intend to make my "Faust-figure" category rather a broad one, partly for reasons of space, partly because Faust is marvelously interpretable. So here the Faust theme will mean roughly the tragedy of the curious and brilliant man destroyed by his own curiosity and brilliance.

In my last article, I described the device of using natural and architectural scenes to induce a mood of terror, strangeness or sublimation. Often this device could dominate the entire novel and characters were very much in second-place, not a serious defect in the terror tale or tale of wonder, but the best fantasies contain a complementary balance of marvel and characterization. The characters need not always be subtly drawn, but they are always archetypes.

The Faustian character-type appears again and again in fantasy tales. He has appeared, in various guises, more than any other type and his development in fantasy fiction is still going on. Ignoring his ancestors (including the magician-alchemist Dr. Johannes Faustus of German legend) we can begin with Marlowe's rather bitty play about him which was first published in 1604. The play is memorable for some of its passages, but is clumsily constructed and does not have the impact on present-day readers which it obviously had on its Elizabethan and Jacobean audiences.

Basically the story is of brilliant Doctor John Faustus who is a dabbler in alchemy and magic. He contacts Mephistophilis the Devil's agent, who tempts him to sell his soul. Friends and good angels urge him to desist, but he finally gives in on the following conditions:

> First, that Faustus may be a spirit in form and substance. Secondly, that Mephistophilis shall be his servant, and at his command. Thirdly, that Mephistophilis shall do for him, and bring him whatsoever (he desires) . . . I, John Faustus, of Wittenburg, Doctor, by these presents, do give both body and soul to Lucifer prince of the east, and his Minister Mephistophilis; and furthermore grant unto them that, twenty-four years being expired, the articles

> above written inviolate, full power to fetch or carry the said John Faustus, body and soul, flesh, blood, or goods, into their habitation wheresoever.

After this businesslike document is prepared, Faustus asks Mephistophilis "Where is the place that men call hell?" Mephistophilis tells him that "Hell hath no limits, nor is circumscrib'd in one self place; for where we are is hell, and where hell is, there must we ever be; and, to conclude, when all the world dissolves, and every creature shall be purified, all places shall be hell that are not heaven." To which Faustus replies: "Come, I think hell's a fable."

Mephistophilis has an ominous answer: "Aye, think so still, till experience change thy mind."

Faustus then embarks on a series of rather disconnected adventures ranging from tragedy to farce and finally gets his come-uppance in a dramatic last scene where he repents too late. In other versions of the story Faust is saved in the nick of time by his repentance. In the Gothic tales particularly, the Faustian hero-villain has no such luck.

The basic Faust plot involves an intelligent man whose experiments lead him—and often others—to a sticky end. In religious terms this is a man who is attracted to evil, who succumbs to it and is finally ruined by it. In scientific terms it is a man who conducts a dangerous experiment which gets out of control and overcomes him.

Probably it was the influence of Goethe's more complex *Faust* and Milton's Satan of *Paradise Lost* on the German Schauer-Romantik ("Horror Romance") school of the late eighteenth century which, by *their* influence, produced the superfluity of Faustian heroes in the English Gothic novel and its progeny. Mrs. Radcliffe's monk Schedoni of *The Italian* (1797) is the villain of her finest novel which concentrates on the Satanically attractive Schedoni, with his cowl which "threw a shade over the livid paleness of his face" which "bore the traces of many passions, which seemed to have fixed the features they no longer animated."

M.G. Lewis was influenced by Radcliffe (though not by Schedoni) when he wrote his very readable *The Monk* (1796—Bestseller Library,

3/6). Here, a lustful woman, Matilda, takes the place of Mephistophilis and uses sex to bring down her prey, but the pact with Satan soon follows:

> Ambrosio started, and expected the demon with terror . . . The thunder ceasing to roll, a full strain of melodious music sounded in the air! At the same time the cloud disappeared, and he beheld a figure more beautiful than fancy's pencil ever drew. It was a youth seemingly scarce eighteen, the perfection of whose form and face was unrivalled. He was perfectly naked, a bright star sparkled on his forehead, two crimson wings extended themselves from his shoulders, and his silken locks were confined by a band of many-coloured fires, which shone with a brilliancy far surpassing that of precious stones. Circlets of diamonds were fastened around his arms and ankles, and in his right hand he bore a silver branch imitating myrtle. His form shone with dazzling glory: he was surrounded by clouds of rose-coloured light, and at the moment that he appeared a refreshing air breathed perfumes throughout the cavern. Ambrosio gazed upon the spirit with delight and wonder.

The Monk had its mysterious ruins, crypts and labyrinths and virtuous imperiled heroines, but was unusual in that the main narrative was told from the villain's viewpoint and not from the heroine's. It was also unusual for its overt eroticism. As in many other Gothic novels, the shadow of Lovelace, demon-lover of Richardson's *Clarissa Harlowe* (1748) is observed here.

In Mary Shelley's *Frankenstein* (1817) the downfall of the hero comes about because of his basically-alchemical dabbling. Frankenstein continues in the Faust tradition. His evil takes on independence in the tragic monster (really the hero of the tale) and he struggles with an evil he is no longer able to control and which, in the end, is his doom. Frankenstein's monster is, of course, really an aspect of Frankenstein himself and his frantic attempts to destroy his creation, his long conversations with it, can be seen as an ever-weakening effort to control his own "bad" self. In *Frankenstein* we see the early development of one of fantasy fiction's largest sub-genres—science fiction. Dabbling in magic is replaced by dabbling in science—but the basic theme and result is the same. Here is the first anti-science science fiction tale in which the elements of fantasy blend with an interest in scientific theory to create a theme which is today commonplace in SF—particularly English SF in the hands of Wyndham, Ballard, Aldiss and Brunner for instance.

The last of the great Gothic hero-villains was Charles Maturin's *Melmoth the Wanderer* (University of Nebraska Press, 15/- or $1.70). Melmoth (a combination of Faust and Mephistophilis) is doomed to virtual immortality, wandering the world as an agent of the Devil, seeking to purchase another's soul in order to get his own out of pawn. One of the best Gothics, thought by some to be the form's culmination, it is spoiled by lengthy and largely boring sub-plots in the form of whole tales embedded in the main narrative—tales which don't serve any noticeable purpose in furthering the basic story. This is about Melmoth, a tragic, menacing and mysterious figure who always arrives on the scene when someone is about to suffer a nasty fate—he then tries to tempt them to barter their souls to Satan for an easier lot. He never succeeds.

The book was published in 1820 and Maturin's development of the Faust theme helped later writers to produce even subtler workings of the basic story. Technically, it relies on a mystery element involving the reader's curiosity about Melmoth's motives, which are only very gradually made clear—a device used to good effect by Wilkie Collins and more recent mystery writers, as well as authors of less sensational novels. At the end of 150 years, having failed to find one person who would agree to his proposition, Melmoth knows he must perish: "No one has ever exchanged destinies with Melmoth the Wanderer. *I have traversed the world in the search, and no one, to gain the world, would lose his own soul!*" He then dreams of his fate:

> His last despairing reverted glance was fixed on the clock of eternity—the upraised black arm seemed to push forward the hand—it arrived at its period—he fell—he sunk—he blazed—he shrieked! The burning waves boomed over his sinking head, and the clock of eternity rung out its awful chime—"Room for the soul of the wandered!"—and the waves of the burning ocean answered, as they lashed the adamantine rock—"There is room for more!"—The Wanderer awoke.

Having wakened, the Wanderer discovers he has aged hideously and tells his visitors, "I am summoned, and must obey the summons—my master has other work for me! When a meteor blazes in your atmosphere—when a comet pursues its burning path towards the sun—look up, and perhaps you may think of the spirit condemned to guide the blazing and erratic orb."

He warns them that if they watch him leave the house "your lives will be the forfeit of your desperate curiosity. For the same stake I risked more than life—and lost it!" He leaves and terrible shrieks are heard from the nearby cliffs overlooking the sea, indescribable sounds are heard all night over the surrounding countryside. In the morning there is only one trace of the Wanderer on the rocks above the sea—his handkerchief.

Robert Spector in his introduction to *Seven Masterpieces of Gothic Horror* (Bantam Books, 95¢) says that "*Melmoth the Wanderer* is a Faust story that begins in contemporary Ireland but re-creates the adventures of John Melmoth, who has lived since the seventeenth century through a pact with the devil. Through six episodes of terror, Maturin creates the experiences of modern anguish. Maturin combines the myths of Faust and the Wandering Jew with all the horrible episodes of the Gothic romances, and yet he never depends on blood and gore for his effects. What Maturin does is to probe the psychological depths of fear, and in doing so, he was a little ahead of his audience. Although *Melmoth* has come to be regarded by many as the masterpiece of terror fiction, it attracted little attention until psychological Gothicists like Poe and the French Romantics resurrected it some years later."

Throughout this long book, Melmoth can also be seen as the Faceless Man of our dreams, the unknown aspect of ourselves which is symbolized, as well, in the figure of the cowled monk, his face shaded and half-seen, or the shadowy, omniscient spectre. He appears in many modern fantasy tales—Leiber's Sheelba of the Eyeless Face in the Grey Mouser yarns, Tolkien's faceless protagonist in the Rings trilogy, Anderson's Odin in *The Broken Sword*—even Bester's Burning Man in *Tiger! Tiger!* There's a link, too, perhaps, between the unknown aspect and the "evil" aspect of ourselves in that we sense the presence of the unknown aspect and fear it, therefore judging it "evil."

Robert Louis Stevenson might have experienced such a process and in his *Dr. Jekyll and Mr. Hyde* (1886), which was inspired by fever-dreams and nightmares during a bad illness, produced a new variant on the Faust-character in Jekyll slowly becoming dominated by Hyde. We see also our bestial origins, still within us, in the frightful Mr. Hyde. *Dorian Gray* (1891) for all its artificiality, is another development of the Faust theme.

The doomed hero, bound to destroy himself and those he loves, is one of the oldest character-types in literature. Byron saw himself in this role, to the discomfort of his friends and family, and by acting it out helped to foster it in Romantic literature. Recent hero-villains of this type have been Peake's Steerpike in the Titus Groan trilogy, Poul Anderson's Scafloc in *The Broken Sword,* T.H. White's Lancelot in *The Once and Future King,* Jane Gaskell's Zerd in *The Serpent* and my own Elric in *The Stealer of Souls.*

Bram Stoker's *Dracula* (1897) is another variation. Here, of course, vampirism is the strongest element in the story, but Count Dracula's lust for blood is almost identical with the lust for virtuous women which marked his predecessors. Faust desired to have and corrupt Margaret, just as dozens of later "demon-lovers" like Schedoni, Ambrosio and, in real life, Byron and de Sade pursued innocence solely to destroy it. Whether witting or unwitting, the hero-villains of fantasy fiction are usually marked by their ability to destroy qualities in others, and this somehow makes *them* attractive to women readers who are fascinated by them and men readers who identify with them. There is no doubting their appeal, and they are not likely to lose it.

Byron himself wrote an early vampire tale (*A Fragment,* 1819) and Goethe's contribution to vampire literature was *Braut von Korinth* (1797). Mario Praz in his *Romantic Agony,* the standard work on the Romantic Movement, says:

> The hero of Polidori's *Vampire* is a young libertine, Lord Ruthven, who is killed in Greece and becomes a vampire, seduces the sister of his friend Aubrey and suffocates her during the night which follows their wedding. A love-crime becomes an integral part of vampirism, though often in forms so far removed as to obscure the inner sense of the gruesome legend—Thus in *Melmoth the Wanderer,* the hero, who is a kind of Wandering Jew crossed with Byronic vampire, interrupts a wedding and terrifies everybody with the horrible fascination of his preternatural glare: soon after the bride dies and the bridegroom goes mad.

Byron and other Romantics took the crude Middle European legend of the vampire and transformed it. Praz remarks that Byron was largely responsible for the fashion of vampirism in literature. The desire to steal something valuable from his victims, whether it be blood, innocence or souls, is intrinsic to the Faustian/Byronic hero-villain. In later stories the hero-villain was transformed into a heroine-villainess—such as Le Fanu's *Carmilla* (1871), the female vampire—who has since found her way into American popular literature to an unhealthy extent—remember her on the covers of *Planet Stories* or, whip in hand, on the more recent "magazines for men" whose covers are beginning to brighten London bookstalls now?

Since the psychoanalysis of character-types is liable to produce dozens of different theories, I leave the reader to decide what all this means in sexual terms. Many young fantasy fans often share their enthusiasm for the genre with a taste for the erotic fantasies of Henry Miller, Jean Genet, William Burroughs and others. Certainly the link is obvious in Burroughs's *Naked Lunch, Ticket that Exploded* and *Soft Machine* which are works of sheer science fiction and the most brilliant ever to appear. *His* Faust is the whole human race rolled into one.

An interesting light on the classic hero-villain comes in J.G. Ballard's *Drowned World,* one of the best novels to appear since the War. Ballard's hero-villain Strangman is not the central character of the book, but he tends to dominate the scenes he appears in.

> His handsome saturnine face regarding them with a mixture of suspicion and amused contempt, Strangman lounged back under the cool awning that shaded the poop deck of the depot ship . . .
>
> "The trouble with you people is that you've been here for thirty million years and your perspectives are all wrong. You miss so much of the transitory beauty of life. I'm fascinated by the immediate past—the treasures of the Triassic compare pretty unfavourably with those of the closing years of the Second Millennium."

Strangman's studied interest in things which seem to the other characters mere trivia shows us the Byronic hero-villain for what he probably is (if he exists in real-life at all today) a brilliant, but bewildered man rebelling against the entire order of things, destroying them because they baffle him, fighting a lonely, hopeless battle against forces which are sure, in the end, to destroy him—even courting that destruction as Oscar Wilde did. Wilde, incidentally, changed his name to Sebastian Melmoth after his release from prison, seeing himself as the character created by Maturin, his kinsman. They all seem to have this quality—Marlowe's Faust, Milton's Satan, the Gothic villains—and Byron himself. We admire them because of it.

EARL AUBEC OF MALADOR

EARL AUBEC OF MALADOR

Outline for a series
of four fantasy novels
(1966)

EARL AUBEC, CHAMPION of Lormyr, Earl of Malador, first appeared in the [attached] story "Master of Chaos" (originally called "Earl Aubec and the Golem") in *Fantastic,* May 1964.

"Master of Chaos" will not be incorporated into the novels, but is [enclosed] to give some idea of the character and background etc., of the projected series.

Background

The world of Earl Aubec is The Age of the Bright Empire—the same as the world of Elric, only set some time earlier than the Elric stories. The Bright Empire is flourishing. It is the most powerful on Earth and the influence of the Dragon Princes of Imrryr is felt everywhere (though whenever possible they disdain contact with the race of true human beings of the Young Kingdoms). Elric's ancestor, Gadric the Eleventh, moody son of Terhali, the Green Empress, sits on the Dragon Throne, close consort, it is rumoured, of the Dukes of Hell, particularly Arioch.

The Lords of Chaos, in fact, still have the greater part of the power over Earth. At the edges of the world, Chaos Unbound still exists (in "Master of Chaos," Earl Aubec's task was to make a little of that Chaos-matter stable).

The cosmology, therefore, is the same as the cosmology of the Elric stories, as is the basic geography [see attached map], but the Young

Kingdoms have not yet risen to power and the Dreaming City of Imrryr dominates the world by virtue of her sorcery, her Dragon Masters, her golden battle-barges and her pact with Chaos.

Central Character

Earl Aubec of Malador is a big, powerful warrior in middle years, his sole companion his cat, who travels everywhere with him and has a great sense for danger when it threatens.

Aubec's patron gods are the Lords of Law, and he has something of an ally in the sorceress Micella of Kaneloon whom he loves secretly and hopelessly, hardly daring to admit it to himself, for his loyalty, according to tradition, must be to the dead Queen Eloarde of Lormyr. (These characters also originally appear in "Master of Chaos.")

Events

Earl Aubec, deprived of his lands by the machinations of Queen Eloarde's half-brother Aradard, is an exile, roaming the world, sought by Aradard's assassins (only Aubec witnessed the murder of Eloarde by her half-brother's men), selling his sword, ready for a chance to win the fortune that will enable him to finance an army that he can lead back to Lormyr. His one abiding hope is that he will be able to wreak vengeance on Aradard, restore the throne to Eloarde's young son Prince Haminak (who is, in fact, Aubec's son, too) whom Aubec believes is still alive, having smuggled him from the palace himself before Aradard's men found the boy.

All Aubec's motivations, therefore, involve his need to raise an army to attack Aradard, his willingness to rob, murder or in other ways destroy or discomfort Aradard's men, his wish to find his lost son Haminak.

But Micella has other motivations. She knows that Aubec has a particular quality of character which makes him an able champion against the Lords of Chaos and their efforts to retain control of the Earth as their domain. While she can never convince Aubec of the fact that he is a somewhat extraordinary kind of man, she can sometimes help him in his ambitions concerning Aradard and Haminak and therefore where her interests and his self-interest combine, she can sway him to work on behalf of her masters, the Lords of Law.

The first book, therefore, deals with these main events and concerns.

Aubec arrives in Tanelorn (also described in an earlier story about Rackhir the Red Archer, "To Rescue Tanelorn . . . " in *Science Fantasy* No. 56) which is a city on the edge of the Sighing Desert. Tanelorn shelters many outcasts and has a peculiar nature, in that neither the forces of Law nor Chaos have any influence over the inhabitants. Here Aubec learns from a man who has come to recruit mercenaries that an army is being raised in Hikach, capital city of Argimiliar (a near neighbour of Lormyr), with a view to attacking Kachor, chief port of Lormyr. Aubec himself, as a much respected tactician and leader of warriors, is offered a fifth share of all loot if he will come in with the Argimilites.

Aubec has no love for the folk of Argimiliar, for they are the Lormyrians' traditional foes, but the prospect of striking a blow at Aradard and raising money for his own army convinces him that he will throw in with the Argimilites.

In two weeks a boat will be leaving the port of Shad in Ilmiora. All the warriors must arrive by that time. The boat will take them to Hikach.

Several days later, as he readies himself for the journey, Aubec is approached by Micella the sorceress of Kaneloon. She tells him that the Melnibonéans, under the direction of the Lords of Chaos, are fomenting civil war amongst the Young Kingdoms. The raid on Kachor will spark this off and soon all the Young Kingdoms will be at war, threatening the development of the power of true human beings and enabling the Lords of Chaos to increase their power. Aubec must not help the Argimilites. He must, instead, try to stop the raid.

Aubec will have none of this. He is wary of the sorceress, knowing that her professed motives and her actual motives are not always the same. He sets off for Shad, arrives and boards the ship.

Their voyage takes them across the Dragon Sea, close to the Isle of the Dragon, Melniboné.

A storm—evidently of supernatural origin—blows up. The ship is wrecked on the dreadful coast of the Dragon Isle where no true human being would willingly set foot. Aubec and a small party of warriors survive. Everyone, including Aubec, is extremely fearful. Aubec sets them to building a raft, hoping that he will be able to get off the Dragon Isle before the inhuman Melnibonéans discover the intruders.

But it is too late. Dragon riders appear in the sky. Some of the warriors run and are destroyed by the flaming venom. Aubec stands his ground. The dragons land. Dyvim Kang, Dragon Prince, dismounts and haughtily approaches the little band, questioning them.

"Likely meat to feed our lord Arioch," smiles one of the inhumanly handsome Melnibonéans. "Or perhaps they will furnish some more elaborate form of entertainment to lighten King Gadric's gloom."

Dyvim Kang silences the man. He is interested in Aubec. Perhaps he recognizes in Aubec that peculiar quality of character already noted by Micella. "Are you a sorcerer?" he asks. "You have not the sorcerer's manner?"

"I disdain sorcery," answers Aubec, "just as I disdain all that Melniboné stands for. But my quarrel is not with the Bright Empire. Let me go on about my own business and you concern yourselves with yours. A small skiff's all I need to get me to Hikach."

"We are not in the habit of dispensing gifts to human folk," Dyvim Kang says. "Why do you journey to Hikach?"

Aubec briefly tells him of the projected raid. Dyvim Kang nods. He already appears to know something of the Argimilites' plans. He seems half-prepared to let Aubec have his skiff, but then thinks better of it and orders that the few remaining warriors be used for sport and Aubec be brought before the Dragon Throne.

There follows Aubec's first confrontation with King Gadric the Eleventh, whose deep green pupilless eyes are a reminder that his mother was the near-immortal Terhali, the Green Empress. Gadric, too, is impressed with Aubec and summons a "friend." The friend appears—actually Lord Balan of Chaos—a youth of frightening beauty. Balan knows of Aubec, knows that the earl serves Donblas of Law (though Aubec is not aware of this). They ascertain that Aubec really is bent on aiding the Argimilites and this amuses them greatly. It dawns on Aubec that Micella was right—this raid is the creation of Melniboné and her gods. But Aubec, always obstinate, refuses to consider the implications. He will continue with his original plans.

Aubec, by sorcerous means that he finds distasteful, is transported to Hikach. Here he prepares to sail against Kachor. The fleet sets sail. Micella appears with evidence that his son is held by King Ronon of Argimiliar—to ensure Aubec's good faith should he change his mind en route.

Aubec is in a quandary. He doesn't know whether to trust Micella's word or not, whether to continue with the raid or rescue his son.

"Even if I did turn back now," he tells Micella, "Ronon would have word of my coming and Haminak would be put to the sword—"

"—or worse," agrees Micella. But she then tells him that he has an ally in a "certain person possessed of considerable power."

"Why should this person aid me?"

"Because you aid him," she replies.

Aubec is more than ordinarily suspicious as she hands him a bracelet of oddly glowing metal and tells him to wear it. Instead he casually places it as a collar around the neck of his cat. "Whose bracelet is this?" he asks. "Yours?"

"No." She smiles mysteriously. "Where would you wish to be now?"

"Naturally, I would wish to be in Hikach, madam!" he replies pettishly.

The ship fades. He is in the streets of Hikach, his cat looking as startled as he feels. He is furious, convinced he has been duped by Micella. The cat runs off in fright. Aubec decides to investigate Ronon's castle and manages to sneak in. Searching the castle at night he can find no trace of his son and is doubly convinced of Micella's treachery.

Seized suddenly by Ronon's guards, Aubec fights his way free. But then he is trapped by Ronan's tame Pan Tang sorcerer. Ronon is furious. Aubec's son is not in the castle—the sorcerer has seen to that. He is in the city of Nieva, in the Argimilian hinterland, bound by spells. Now the boy will perish!

Ronon has Aubec chained in his armour over a slow fire. "We are going to cook you in your own shell."

The sorcerer leaves for Nieva to deal with the boy.

Ronon glowers. Aubec's turncoat trick might well have lost him the spoils of Kachor.

Aubec roasts. He is half-dead when his cat arrives, somewhat sheepishly, having found his master at last. Aubec decides to try out the bracelet and orders himself free. The chains drop off him. He uses the brazier as a weapon to fight Ronon's guards, gets his own great sword back, mounts a horse, the cat clinging to his shoulder, and rides for Nieva.

But in Nieva the sorcerer has gone, taking Aubec's son with him, for the sorcerer has plans to use the boy for his own purposes, as a pawn in a plot to rob Ronon of the Treasure of the Pikaraydians, which Ronon himself stole from his neighbouring monarch in the last great border battle on the banks of the River Jepchak. By holding the Pikaraydian Treasure (which has a mystical significance as well as a material value) Ronon ensures that he keeps Pikarayd in thrall. The sorcerer knows that with the Treasure he will have power over both Ronon and Pikarayd. But he needs Aubec's help in his scheme and has thus kidnapped the boy with a view to ensuring that Aubec will work for him (he has heard that Aubec was on his way).

Aubec meets the sorcerer and reluctantly agrees to aid him.

The Pikarayd Treasure lies in Ronon's secret vaults hidden in the caverns of the Shivering Cliffs that flank the River Marr far to the south of Nieva.

Aubec and his cat set off for the Shivering Cliffs, Aubec unreasonably blaming his present plight on Micella, for he suspects her hand in the plot since Kaneloon is not far from the Shivering Cliffs.

He reaches the Shivering Cliffs and enters battle with the various sorcerous and semi-sorcerous guardians (the Pan Tang sorcerer has given him a couple of protective runes), eventually reaching the Treasure. Lashing the treasure chests to the backs of the strange half-human creatures he has released at the same time, Aubec begins the slow journey back to Nieva. Soon he will be reunited with his son. He is also considering a scheme whereby, once he has his son, he can turn the tables on the sorcerer and get the Treasure for himself, thus enabling him to raise an army against Aradard.

On the second night of his journey back, he stops at the walled town of Oonak-Rass.

Unbeknownst to Aubec, Count Palag Fhak and his men have been trailing him. Palag Fhak is the cleverest and most courageous of Aradard's assassins. He had heard that Aubec was in the Southlands and has at last tracked him down.

In a tavern Aubec's cat warns him of the danger. Aubec is set upon by Palag Fhak's men. There is a brutal fight. Wounded, Aubec manages to escape from Oonak-Rass with the best part of the treasure train, running into the night.

Count Palag Fhak pursues him, but he manages to keep ahead of the assassins, eventually getting back to the tower where he has agreed to meet the sorcerer.

To ensure that the sorcerer keeps his part of the bargain, Aubec has left his treasure train hidden in a forest. He will tell the sorcerer where the Treasure is when he sees his son free. The sorcerer is disconcerted. Palag Fhak's men attack the tower.

There is a big battle, involving the assassins in fighting the sorcerer and the minions he summons from the nether regions. Aubec uses the confusion to get to the room where his son is kept.

He embraces the boy and then lets out a shout of horror.

The sorcerer has duped him. The boy is nothing more than a changeling—a creature created by sorcery—a simulacrum of the actual child. Aubec weeps and returns to have his vengeance on the sorcerer, who tells him that there was no real child. Ronon had him create the mindless and soulless changeling. Aubec destroys the sorcerer and leaves Palag Fhak to be devoured by the last and mightiest of the sorcerer's creatures. Aubec wants only vengeance on Ronon now, for the terrible trick played on him.

He returns to Hikach just as the defeated fleet is docking. Ronon is furious. Aubec is again captured on the quayside but notes that there are several Pikaraydian ships there, full of evil-tempered Pikaraydian sailors who have joined the venture only because Ronon has forced them to. Aubec tells them that the Treasure of Pikarayd is no longer in Ronon's keeping. If they aid him, he will tell them where it is.

A battle begins, with most of the mercenaries siding with Aubec and the Pikaraydians against Ronon.

Ronon is slain and his city is sacked.

Micella appears, telling Aubec that Ronon was the chief threat to the uneasy stability of the Southern Young Kingdoms. Now Ronon is dead, the main threat is over. But the Lords of Chaos are still scheming to create more trouble.

Aubec is sour. He has been cheated of a reconciliation with his son. He has lost the Treasure of Pikarayd. He has been duped and used as a pawn by half a score of different interests. All he has is his cat and the ridiculous bracelet, which he mistrusts.

Micella begs him to join forces with her, telling Aubec that it is in his own interest. But Aubec will have none of her.

Completely unimpressed that he has been the means of stopping a destructive war, Aubec rides off with his cat on his shoulder, still bent on finding his lost son and the means of having his vengeance on his old enemy Aradard.

As he goes, Micella smiles to herself as she sees the sun glint on the collar that the cat still wears.

Rest of the Series

Through three further books—*The Chronicle of Earl Aubec*—we will trace Aubec's adventures, his quest for his son and his attempts to avenge Eloarde. Gradually the issues will build until the final book where he is responsible for exiling the Lords of Chaos from Earth and sowing the seeds that will eventually lead to the decline of Melnibonéan power: The formation of the Lormyrian Confederacy which throws off the shackles of the Bright Empire.

This will also leave room for further tales concerning The Age of the Bright Empire, gradually, perhaps, leading up to The Age of the Young Kingdoms and the earlier adventures of Elric of Melniboné.

INTRODUCTION TO THE TAIWAN EDITION OF ELRIC

INTRODUCTION TO THE TAIWAN EDITION OF **ELRIC**

(2007)

I HAVE TO say that it is a great pleasure for my Elric books to be appearing in Taiwan after so many years. Chinese-language editions of my work have been rare and the only major language in which Elric has not appeared, so I feel honoured that they can at last be read by people whose culture I have always held in considerable esteem.

While Elric was never influenced by the few Chinese stories available to me as a child and young man, I have always felt that they have something in common with many of the legends and folk-tales I have since read and which have appeared, in various forms, on the screen or in graphic novels. My chief influence for the stories were the Norse and Celtic epics which I enjoyed as a child, before I discovered the supernatural adventure fiction of writers like Edgar Rice Burroughs, Robert E. Howard, Fritz Leiber and others. I had begun writing such stories long before I had heard, for instance, of J.R.R. Tolkien who began to publish his great trilogy around the time when I was fourteen and fifteen and editing my fantasy fanzine *Burroughsania,* originally based on my youthful enthusiasm for the fantasy stories of Edgar Rice Burroughs (most famous as the author of *Tarzan*), but I am probably one of the few surviving writers of fantasy who was *not* influenced by *The Lord of the Rings.* Instead my influences in fantasy were writers like Lord Dunsany, T. H. White and Mervyn Peake, as well as Poul Anderson, whose novel *The Broken Sword* had the same tragic elements I found in the great Icelandic tales.

By the time I was asked to write a series of fantasy novellas for the magazine *Science Fantasy,* which prided itself on the literary qualities of its fiction, I was reading very little fantasy fiction at all, but had developed an enthusiasm for modernists like Conrad, Proust, Woolf and contemporaries such as Elizabeth Bowen and Angus Wilson. However, I suspect my exposure to French existentialism coloured much of what I was writing around the age of nineteen, when I first began to develop the Elric character. I was a huge Camus and Sartre fan at twenty when I wrote those early short stories and by the time I was twenty-three I had, I believed, killed my hero off and had no plans to write more stories.

The demand for more stories from editors and readers—as well as a continuing love for my character—meant, of course, that I came to write another ten volumes over the years and though I write mostly non-fantasy fiction, these days, I still find myself moved to write further short stories about Elric. During the forty years or so in which I have depicted his adventures I have seen my hero's influence grow, as he has appeared in almost every media, including radio, games and comics, but I resisted, until very recently, allowing him to appear in a movie, largely because I had already seen other work of mine translated to the screen and had been unhappy with the translation. Recently, however, Universal purchased the film rights on behalf of the Weitz brothers, whom I believe could probably do justice to the character, and as I write a movie is in production. In some ways my ambiguous albino has already appeared on the screen because he has influenced many similar characters (for instance in Japanese animé) but I have no reason to complain of that "borrowing," since Elric himself was an homage to a character who helped me while away my boyhood with such pleasure. That character appeared in a long-running series of Sexton Blake detective stories which were published before the Second World War and whose name was Zenith the Albino, a villain who plagued the existence of Sexton Blake from 1918 until 1940. I found them late, needless to say, and bought second-hand all the copies I could find. I have not only given credit to Zenith's influence, I have in later Elric stories, and my series of Metatemporal Detective tales, done my best to show that they are actually one and the same character!

Zenith, of course, did not have either the power nor the heritage of Elric but I am glad that I have kept him alive, at least in some form, being instrumental in republishing his only adventure in novel form in a recent edition by Savoy Books, who are a firm dedicated to publishing only work about which they feel enthusiastic, irrespective of cost. So strong has Elric's influence been, some readers believed that I had invented Zenith as well as Elric! Many authors have been good enough to tell me how their own wish to write was encouraged by the Elric stories, so it feels good to pass on a torch which Anthony Skene (Zenith's creator) first passed to me.

Of course, when I began writing Elric, there was no defined genre of "fantasy" and publishers did not know really what to call the kind of stories I was writing. Even Tolkien was seen by critics as creating some sort of post-nuclear disaster world because they were used to "serious" science fiction by the mid-1950s but could not conceive of a world set in a mythical alternative place like "Middle-earth." Indeed, none of us could imagine the popularity of what became known as epic fantasy (my choice of term) or "sword and sorcery" (Fritz Leiber's choice) which was why I happily allowed games companies and others to use my characters and world, to the point when two companies (Dungeons & Dragons being one) used them in their gaming scenarios. Later those companies would go to law over who owned rights to material which I had freely given away and only then did I begin to realize that, from being the enthusiasm of a few, fantasy fiction was growing into "big business." As a result I was forced to formalize by own work and institute trademarks and copyrights which, in those early days, had seemed both unnecessary and against the spirit of what I was trying to create. For many years Tolkien and myself were, in the public mind, the only writers of our kind and it would not be until the 1970s, with a new generation of authors, that we began to see the creation of what is, in most respects, a fresh genre. I had originally been attracted to writing supernatural fantasy fiction because it was, like certain kinds of science fiction, a "clean canvas" on which I could create work that was unlike anything I had previously read. I did the same with my Jerry Cornelius stories.

Cornelius, initially, was an attempt to produce a kind of myth-hero for modern times and his first novel, *The Final Programme* (sometimes known by its strange film title of *The Last Days of Man on Earth*!) actually paralleled Elric's first adventures. Again, the stories were an attempt to write a new kind of fiction, this time one that engaged with the present without calling on the methods of "modernism" which, in my view, had become merely generic, having very little to say to me, at least. Jerry was the epitome (with Ballard's "condensed fiction") of what others called the New Wave in SF, where we tried to use science fiction in subtler, more complex ways than before, to confront rather than avoid the issues of the modern world. The authors who gathered around my magazine *New Worlds* shared my feelings that through literary SF we could regenerate Anglophone fiction. I am glad to say that this experiment largely succeeded, so that most of our best-known literary writers employ techniques which we were responsible for developing. The latest Thomas Pynchon novel, *Against the Day,* as well as work by Martin Amis, Salman Rushdie, Don DeLillo, Brett Easton Ellis and many, many other writers contains methods first developed in *New Worlds.* We were all, of course, part of the general zeitgeist which was also influenced by non-European fiction and created what some came to call "magic realism."

Elric, of course, contains more magic than realism, but I do hope there is enough realism in his stories to help you suspend disbelief long enough to enjoy them as they were intended—a way of passing a few hours in an agreeable "other world" where the big issues are a matter of sorcery and battle, rather than mortgages and politics! These stories were first and foremost intended as escapism in the manner of the great romances and folk-stories of the world—and so I wish you "a happy escape."

With best wishes to all my new Chinese readers.

Sincerely,
Michael Moorcock
Lost Pines, Texas
January 2007

ONE LIFE, FURNISHED IN EARLY MOORCOCK

ONE LIFE, FURNISHED IN EARLY MOORCOCK

(1994)

by Neil Gaiman

The Pale albino prince lofted on high his great black sword "This is Stormbringer" he said "and it will suck your soul right out."

The Princess sihged. "Very well!" she said. "If that is what you need to get the energy you need to fight the Dragon Warriors, then you must kill me and let your broad sword feed on my soul."

"I do not want to do this" he said to her.

"That's okay" said the princess and with that she ripped her flimsy gown and beared her chest to him. "That is my heart" she said, pointing with her finger. "and that is where you must plunge."

HE HAD NEVER got any further than that. That had been the day he had been told he was being moved up a year, and there hadn't been much point after that. He'd learned not to try and continue stories from one year to another. Now, he was twelve.

It was a pity, though.

The essay title had been *Meeting My Favourite Literary Character,* and he'd picked Elric. He'd toyed with Corum, or Jerry Cornelius, or

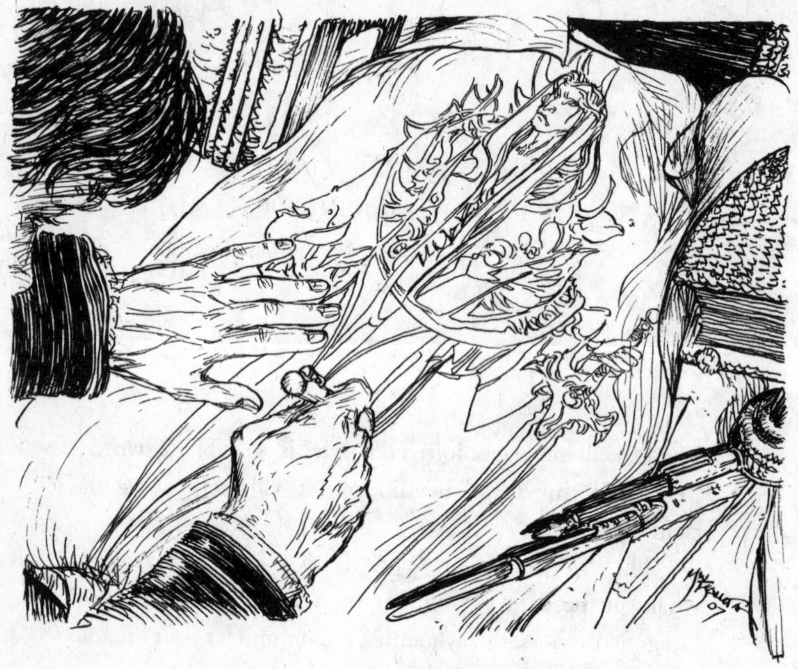

even Conan The Barbarian, but Elric of Melniboné won, hands down, just like he always did.

Richard had first read *Stormbringer* three years ago, at the age of nine. He'd saved up for a copy of *The Singing Citadel* (something of a cheat, he decided, on finishing: only one Elric story), and then borrowed the money from his father to buy *The Sleeping Sorceress,* found in a spin-rack while they were on holiday in Scotland last summer. In *The Sleeping Sorceress* Elric met Erekosë and Corum, two other aspects of the Eternal Champion, and they all got together.

Which meant, he realized, when he finished the book, that the Corum books and the Erekosë books, and even the Dorian Hawkmoon books were really Elric books too, so he began buying them, and he enjoyed them.

They weren't as good as Elric, though. Elric was the best.

Sometimes he'd sit and draw Elric, trying to get him right. None of the paintings of Elric on the covers of the books looked like the Elric that lived in his head. He drew the Elrics with a fountain pen in empty school exercise books he had obtained by deceit. On the front cover he'd write his name: *Richard Grey, Do Not Steal.*

Sometimes he thought he ought to go back and finish writing his Elric story. Maybe he could even sell it to a magazine. But then, what if Moorcock found out? What if he got into trouble?

The classroom was large, filled with wooden desks. Each desk was carved and scored and ink-stained by its occupant, an important process. There was a blackboard on the wall, with a chalk-drawing on it: a fairly accurate representation of a male penis, heading towards a Y shape, intended to represent the female genitalia.

The door downstairs banged, and someone ran up the stairs. "Grey, you spazmo, what're you doing up here? We're meant to be down on the Lower Acre. You're playing football today."

"We are? I am?"

"It was announced at assembly this morning. And the list is up on the games notice board." J.B.C. MacBride was sandy-haired, bespectacled, only marginally more organized than Richard Grey. There were two J. MacBrides, which was how he ranked a full set of initials.

"Oh."

Grey picked up a book (*Tarzan at the Earth's Core*) and headed off after him. The clouds were dark grey, promising rain or snow.

People were forever announcing things he didn't notice. He would arrive in empty classes, miss organized games, arrive at school on days when everyone else had gone home. Sometimes he felt as if he lived in a different world to everyone else.

He went off to play football, *Tarzan at the Earth's Core* shoved down the back of his scratchy blue football shorts.

He hated the showers and the baths. He couldn't understand why they had to use both, but that was just the way it was.

He was freezing, and no good at games. It was beginning to become a matter of perverse pride with him that in his years at the school so far, he hadn't scored a goal, or hit a run, or bowled anyone out, or done anything much except be the last person to be picked when choosing sides.

Elric, proud, pale prince of the Melnibonéans, would never have had to stand around on a football pitch in the middle of winter, wishing the game would be over.

Steam from the shower room, and his inner thighs were chapped and red. The boys stood naked and shivering in a line, waiting to get under the showers, and then to get into the baths.

Mr. Murchison, eyes wild and face leathery and wrinkled, old and almost bald, stood in the changing rooms directing naked boys into the shower, then out of the shower and into the baths. "You, boy. Silly little boy. Jamieson. Into the shower, Jamieson. Atkinson, you baby, get under it properly. Smiggins, into the bath, Goring, take his place in the shower . . ."

The showers were too hot. The baths were freezing cold and muddy.

When Mr. Murchison wasn't around boys would flick each other with towels, joke about each others' penises, about who had pubic hair, who didn't.

"Don't be an idiot," hissed someone near Richard. "What if the Murch comes back. He'll kill you!" There was some nervous giggling.

Richard turned and looked. An older boy had an erection, was rubbing his hand up and down it, slowly, under the shower, displaying it proudly to the room.

Richard turned away.

Forgery was too easy.

Richard could do a passable imitation of the Murch's signature, for example, and an excellent version of his housemaster's handwriting and signature. His housemaster was a tall, bald, dry man, named Trellis. They had disliked each other for years.

Richard used the signatures to get blank exercise books from the stationery office, which dispensed paper, pencils, pens, and rulers on the production of a note signed by a teacher.

Richard wrote stories and poems and drew pictures in the exercise books.

After the bath Richard toweled himself off, and dressed hurriedly; he had a book to get back to, a lost world to return to.

He walked out of the building slowly, tie askew, shirt-tail flapping, reading about Lord Greystoke, wondering whether there really was a world inside the world where dinosaurs flew and it was never night.

The daylight was beginning to go, but there were still a number of boys outside the school, playing with tennis balls: a couple played conkers by the bench. Richard leaned against the red-brick wall and read, the outside world closed off, the indignities of changing rooms forgotten.

"You're a disgrace, Grey."

Me?

"Look at you. Your tie's all crooked. You're a disgrace to the school. That's what you are."

The boy's name was Lindfield, two school years above him, but already as big as an adult. "Look at your tie. I mean, *look* at it." Lindfield pulled at Richard's green tie, pulled it tight, into a hard little knot. "Pathetic."

Lindfield and his friends wandered off.

Elric of Melniboné was standing by the red-brick walls of the school building, staring at him. Richard pulled at the knot in his tie, trying to loosen it. It was cutting into his throat.

His hands fumbled around his neck.

He couldn't breathe; but he was not concerned about breathing. He was worried about standing. Richard had suddenly forgotten how to stand. It was a relief to discover how soft the brick path he was standing on had become, as it slowly came up to embrace him.

They were standing together under a night sky hung with a thousand huge stars, by the ruins of what might once have been an ancient temple.

Elric's ruby eyes stared down at him. They looked, Richard

thought, like the eyes of a particularly vicious white rabbit that Richard had once had, before it gnawed through the wire of the cage and fled into the Sussex countryside to terrify innocent foxes. His skin was perfectly white; his armour, ornate and elegant, traced with intricate patterns, perfectly black. His fine white hair blew about his shoulders, as if in a breeze, but the air was still.

—*So you want to be a companion to heroes?* he asked. His voice was gentler than Richard had imagined it would be.

Richard nodded.

Elric put one long finger beneath Richard's chin, lifted his face up. Blood-eyes, thought Richard. Blood-eyes.

—*You're no companion, boy,* he said, in the High Speech of Melniboné.

Richard had always known he would understand the High Speech when he heard it, even if his Latin and French had always been weak.

—*Well, what* am *I, then?* he asked. *Please tell me. Please?*

Elric made no response. He walked away from Richard, into the ruined temple.

Richard ran after him.

Inside the temple, Richard found a life waiting for him, all ready to be worn and lived, and inside that life, another. Each life he tried on, he slipped into, and it pulled him further in, further away from the world he came from; one by one, existence following existence, rivers of dreams and fields of stars, a hawk with a sparrow clutched in its talons flies low above the grass, and here are tiny intricate people waiting for him to fill their heads with life, and thousands of years pass and he is engaged in strange work of great importance and sharp beauty, and he is loved, and he is honoured, and then a pull, a sharp tug and it's . . .

. . . it was like coming up from the bottom of the deep end of a swimming pool. Stars appeared above him and dropped away and dissolved into blues and greens, and it was with a deep sense of disappointment that he became Richard Grey, and came to himself once more, filled with an unfamiliar emotion. The emotion was a specific one, so specific that he was surprised, later, to realize that it did not have its own name: a feeling of disgust and regret at having to return to something he had thought long since done with and abandoned and forgotten and dead.

Richard was lying on the ground, and Lindfield was pulling at the tiny knot of his tie. There were other boys around, faces staring down at him, worried, concerned, scared.

Lindfield pulled the tie loose. Richard struggled to pull air, he gulped it, clawed it into his lungs.

"We thought you were faking. You just went over." Someone said that.

"Shut up," said Lindfield. "Are you all right? I'm sorry. I'm really sorry. Christ. I'm sorry."

For one moment, Richard thought he was apologizing for having called him back from the world beyond the temple.

Lindfield was terrified, solicitous, desperately worried. He had obviously never almost killed anyone before. As he walked Richard up the stone steps to the matron's office, Lindfield explained that he had returned from the school tuck-shop, found Richard unconscious on the path, surrounded by curious boys, and had realized what was wrong. Richard rested for a little in the matron's office, where he was given a bitter soluble aspirin, from a huge jar, in a plastic tumbler of water, then was shown in to the Headmaster's study.

"God! But you look scruffy, Grey," said the Headmaster, puffing irritably on his pipe. "I don't blame young Lindfield at all. Anyway, he saved your life. I don't want to hear another word about it."

"I'm sorry," said Grey.

"That will be all," said the Headmaster, in his cloud of scented smoke.

"Have you picked a religion, yet?" asked the school chaplain, Mr. Aliquid.

Richard shook his head. "I've got quite a few to choose from," he admitted.

The school chaplain was also Richard's biology teacher. He had once taken Richard's biology class, fifteen thirteen-year-old boys and Richard, just twelve, across the road, to his little house opposite the school. In the garden Mr. Aliquid had killed, skinned and dismembered a rabbit, with a small, sharp knife. Then he'd taken a footpump and blown up the rabbit's bladder like a balloon, until it had popped, spattering the boys with blood. Richard threw up, but he was the only one who did.

"Hmm," said the chaplain.

The chaplain's study was lined with books. It was one of the few masters' studies that was in any way comfortable.

"What about masturbation. Are you masturbating excessively?" Mr. Aliquid's eyes gleamed.

"What's excessively?"

"Oh. More than three or four times a day, I suppose."

"No," said Richard. "Not excessively."

He was a year younger than anyone else in his class; people forgot about that sometimes.

Every weekend he traveled to North London to stay with his cousins, for barmitzvah lessons taught by a thin, ascetic cantor, *frummer* than *frum,* a cabbalist and keeper of hidden mysteries onto which he could be diverted with a well-placed question. Richard was an expert at well-placed questions.

Frum was orthodox, hardline Jewish. No milk with meat, and two washing machines for the two sets of plates and cutlery.

Thou shalt not seethe a kid in its mother's milk.

Richard's cousins in North London were *frum,* although the boys would secretly buy cheeseburgers after school and brag about it to each other.

Richard suspected his body was hopelessly polluted already. He drew the line at eating rabbit, though. He had eaten rabbit, and disliked it, for years before he figured out what it was. Every Thursday there was what he believed to be a rather unpleasant chicken stew for school lunch. One Thursday he found a rabbit's paw floating in his

stew, and the penny dropped. After that on Thursdays he filled up on bread and butter.

On the underground train to North London he'd scan the faces of the other passengers, wondering if any of them were Michael Moorcock.

If he met Moorcock he'd ask him how to get back to the ruined temple.

If he met Moorcock he'd be too embarrassed to speak.

Some nights, when his parents were out, he'd try to phone Michael Moorcock.

He'd phone directory enquiries, and ask for Moorcock's number.

"Can't give it to you, love. It's ex-directory."

He'd wheedle and cajole, and always fail, to his relief. He didn't know what he would say to Moorcock if he succeeded.

He put ticks in the front of his Moorcock novels, on the By The Same Author page, for the books he read.

That year there seemed to be a new Moorcock book every week. He'd pick them up at Victoria station, on the way to barmitzvah lessons.

There were a few he simply couldn't find—*The Stealer of Souls, Breakfast in the Ruins,*—and eventually, nervously, he ordered them from the address in the back of the books. He got his father to write him a cheque.

When the books arrived they contained a bill for twenty-five pence: the prices of the books were higher than originally listed. But still, he now had a copy of *The Stealer of Souls,* and a copy of *Breakfast in the Ruins.*

At the back of *Breakfast in the Ruins* was a biography of Moorcock that said he'd died of lung cancer the year before.

Richard was upset for weeks. That meant there wouldn't be any more books, ever.

"That fucking biography. Shortly after it came out I was at a Hawkwind gig, stoned out of my brain, and these people kept coming up to me, and I thought I was dead. They kept saying 'You're dead, you're dead.' Later I realised that they were saying, 'But we thought you were dead'."

—Michael Moorcock, in conversation. Notting Hill, 1976

There was the Eternal Champion, and then there was the Companion to Champions. Moonglum was Elric's companion, always cheerful, the perfect foil to the pale prince, who was prey to moods and depressions.

There was a multiverse out there, glittering and magic. There were the agents of balance, the Gods of Chaos, and the Lords of Order. There were the older races, tall, pale and elfin, and the Young Kingdoms, filled with people like him. Stupid, boring, normal people.

Sometimes he hoped that Elric could find peace, away from the Black Sword. But it didn't work that way. There had to be the both of them—the white prince and the black sword.

Once the sword was unsheathed it lusted for blood, needed to be plunged into quivering flesh. Then it would drain the soul from the victim, feed his or her energy into Elric's feeble frame.

Richard was becoming obsessed with sex; he had even had a dream in which he was having sex with a girl. Just before waking he dreamed what it must be like to have an orgasm—it was an intense and magical feeling of love, centred on your heart; that was what it was, in his dream.

A feeling of deep, transcendent, spiritual bliss.

Nothing he experienced ever matched up to that dream.

Nothing even came close.

The Karl Glogauer in *Behold the Man* was not the Karl Glogauer of *Breakfast in the Ruins,* Richard decided; still, it gave him an odd, blasphemous pride to read *Breakfast in the Ruins* in the school chapel, in the choir stalls. As long as he was discreet no-one seemed to care.

He was the boy with the book. Always and forever.

His head swam with religions: the weekend was now given to the intricate patterns and language of Judaism; each week-day morning to the wood-scented, stained-glass solemnities of the Church of England; and the nights belonged to his own religion, the one he made up for himself, a strange, multicoloured pantheon in which the Lords of Chaos (Arioch, Xiombarg and the rest) rubbed shoulders with the Phantom Stranger from the DC Comics and Sam the trickster-Buddha from Zelazny's *Lord of Light,* and vampires and talking cats and ogres, and all the things from the Lang coloured Fairy books: in which all mythologies existed simultaneously, in a magnificent anarchy of belief.

Richard had, however, finally given up (with, it must be admitted, a little regret), his belief in Narnia. From the age of six—for half his life—he had believed devoutly in all things Narnian; until, last year, rereading *The Voyage of the Dawn Treader* for perhaps the hundredth time, it had occurred to him that the transformation of the unpleasant Eustace Scrub into a dragon, and his subsequent conversion to belief in Aslan the lion, was terribly similar to the conversion of St. Paul, on the road to Damascus; if his blindness were a dragon . . .

This having occurred to him, Richard found correspondences everywhere, too many to be simple coincidence.

Richard put away the Narnia books, convinced, sadly, that they were allegory; that an author (whom he had trusted) had been attempting to slip something past him. He had had the same disgust with the Professor Challenger stories, when the bull-necked old professor became a convert to Spiritualism; it was not that Richard had any problems with believing in ghosts—Richard believed, with no problems or contradictions, in *everything*—but Conan Doyle was preaching, and it showed through the words. Richard was young, and innocent in his fashion, and believed that authors should be trusted, and that there should be nothing hidden beneath the surface of a story.

At least the Elric stories were honest. There was nothing going on beneath the surface there: Elric was the etiolated prince of a dead race, burning with self-pity, clutching Stormbringer, his dark-bladed broadsword—a blade which sang for lives, which ate human souls and which gave their strength to the doomed and weakened albino.

Richard read and re-read the Elric stories, and he felt pleasure each time Stormbringer plunged into an enemy's chest, somehow felt a sympathetic satisfaction as Elric drew his strength from the soul-sword, like a heroin addict in a paperback thriller with a fresh supply of smack.

Richard was convinced that one day the people from Mayflower Books would come after him for their twenty-five pence. He never dared buy any more books through the mail.

J.B.C. MacBride had a secret.

"You mustn't tell anyone."

"Okay."

Richard had no problem with the idea of keeping secrets. In later years he realized that he was a walking repository of old secrets, secrets that his original confidantes had probably long forgotten.

They were walking, with their arms over each other's shoulders, up to the woods at the back of the school.

Richard had, unasked, been gifted with another secret in these woods: it is here that three of Richard's schoolfriends have meetings with girls from the village, and where, he has been told, they display to each other their genitalia.

"I can't tell you who told me any of this."

"Okay," said Richard.

"I mean, it's true. And it's a deadly secret."

"Fine."

MacBride had been spending a lot of time recently with Mr. Aliquid, the school chaplain.

"Well, everybody has two angels. God gives them one and Satan gives them one. So when you get hypnotized, Satan's angel takes control. And that's how Ouija boards work. It's Satan's angel. And you can implore your God's angel to talk through you. But real enlightenment only occurs when you can talk to your angel. He tells you secrets."

This was the first time that it had occurred to Grey that the Church of England might have its own esoterica, its own hidden caballah.

The other boy blinked owlishly. "You mustn't tell anyone that. I'd get into trouble if they knew I'd told you."

"Fine."

There was a pause.

"Have you ever wanked off a grown-up?" asked MacBride.

"No." Richard's own secret was that he had not yet begun to masturbate. All of his friends masturbated, continually, alone and in pairs or groups. He was a year younger than them, and couldn't understand what the fuss was about; the whole idea made him uncomfortable.

"Spunk everywhere. It's thick and oozy. They try to get you to put their cocks in your mouth when they shoot off."

"Eugh."

"It's not that bad." There was a pause. "You know, Mr. Aliquid thinks you're very clever. If you wanted to join his private religious discussion group, he might say yes."

The private discussion group met at Mr. Aliquid's small bachelor house, across the road from the school, in the evenings, twice a week after prep.

"I'm not Christian."

"So? You still come top of the class in Divinity, jewboy."

"No thanks. Hey, I got a new Moorcock. One you haven't read. It's an Elric book."

"You haven't. There isn't a new one."

"Is. It's called *The Jade Man's Eyes.* It's printed in green ink. I found it in a bookshop in Brighton."

"Can I borrow it after you?"

"Course."

It was getting chilly, and they walked back, arm in arm. Like Elric and Moonglum, thought Richard to himself, and it made as much sense as MacBride's angels.

Richard had daydreams in which he would kidnap Michael Moorcock, and make him tell Richard the secret.

If pushed, Richard would be unable to tell you what kind of thing the secret was. It was something to do with writing; something to do with gods.

Richard wondered where Moorcock got his ideas from.

Probably from the ruined temple, he decided, in the end, although he could no longer remember what the temple looked like. He remembered a shadow, and stars, and the feeling of pain at returning to something he thought long finished.

He wondered if that was where all authors got their ideas from, or just Michael Moorcock.

If you had told him that they just made it all up, out of their heads, he would never have believed you. There had to be a place the magic came from.

Didn't there?

"This bloke phoned me up from America the other night, he said,
'Listen man, I have to talk to you about your religion.'
I said, 'I don't know what you're talking about.
I haven't got any fucking religion.' "

—Michael Moorcock, in conversation, Notting Hill, 1976

It was six months later. Richard had been barmitzvahed, and would be changing schools soon. He and J.B.C. MacBride were sitting on the grass outside the school, in the early evening, reading books. Richard's parents were late picking him up from school.

Richard was reading *The English Assassin.* MacBride was engrossed in *The Devil Rides Out.*

Richard found himself squinting at the page. It wasn't properly dark yet, but he couldn't read any more. Everything was turning into greys.

"Mac? What do you want to be when you grow up?"

The evening was warm, and the grass was dry and comfortable.

"I don't know. A writer, maybe. Like Michael Moorcock. Or T. H. White. How about you?"

Richard sat and thought. The sky was a violet-grey, and a ghost-moon hung high in it, like a sliver of a dream. He pulled up a blade of grass, and slowly shredded it between his fingers, bit by bit. He couldn't say "*a writer*" as well, now. It would seem like he was copying. And he didn't want to be a writer. Not really. There were other things to be.

"When I grow up," he said, pensively, eventually, "I want to be a wolf."

"It'll never happen," said MacBride.

"Maybe not," said Richard. "We'll see."

The lights went on in the school windows, one by one, making the violet sky seem darker than it was before, and the summer evening was gentle and quiet. At that time of year the day lasts forever, and the night never really comes.

"I'd like to be a wolf. Not all the time. Just sometimes. In the dark. I would run through the forests as a wolf, at night," said Richard, mostly to himself. "I'd never hurt anyone. Not that kind of wolf. I'd just run and run forever in the moonlight, through the trees, and never get tired or out of breath, and never have to stop. That's what I want to be when I grow up . . ."

He pulled up another long stalk of grass, expertly stripped the blades from it, and, slowly, began to chew the stem.

And the two children sat alone in the grey twilight, side by side, and waited for the future to start.

Neil Gaiman
January 1994

ORIGINS

Early artwork associated with Elric's first appearances in magazines and books

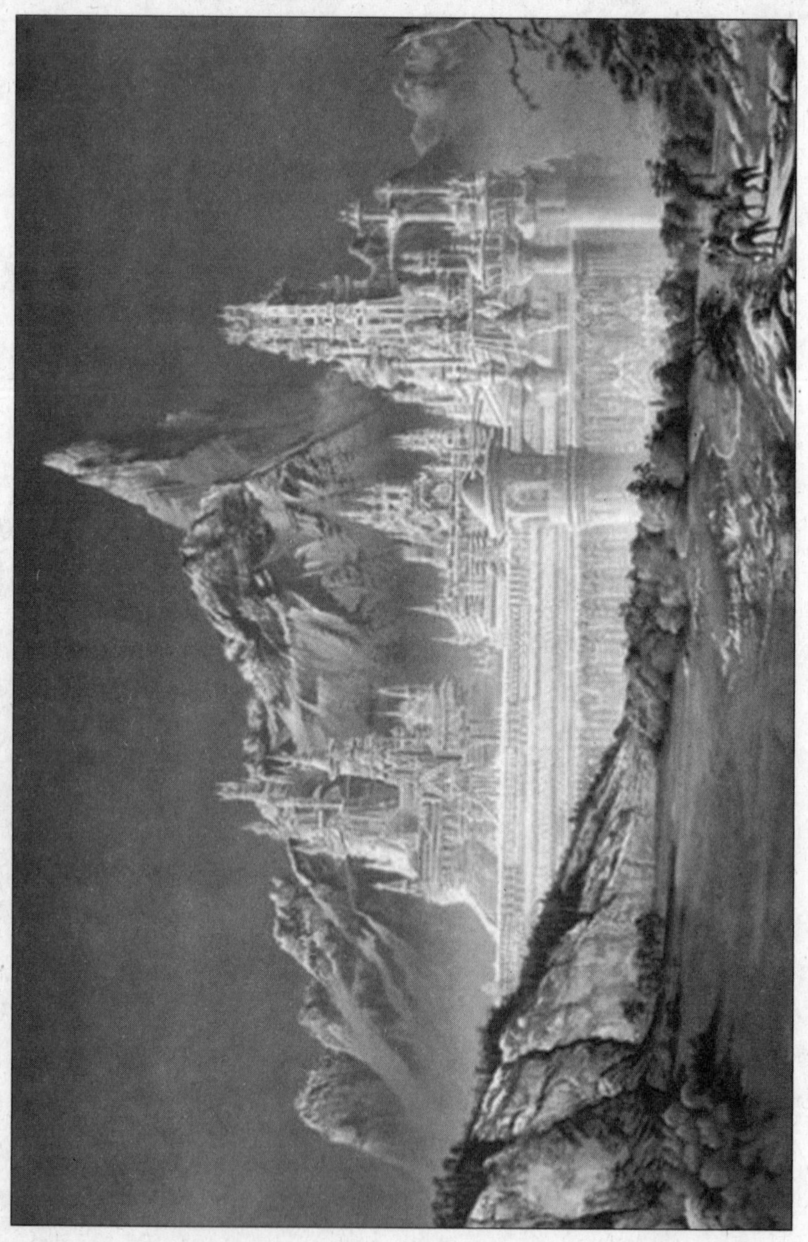

Original artwork by Geoff Taylor, used for the cover of *The Fortress of the Pearl,* first edition, Victor Gollancz, 1989.

Elric thumbnail illustration (enlarged here), by James Cawthorn, used for chapter headings in *The Fortress of the Pearl,* first edition, Gollancz, 1989.

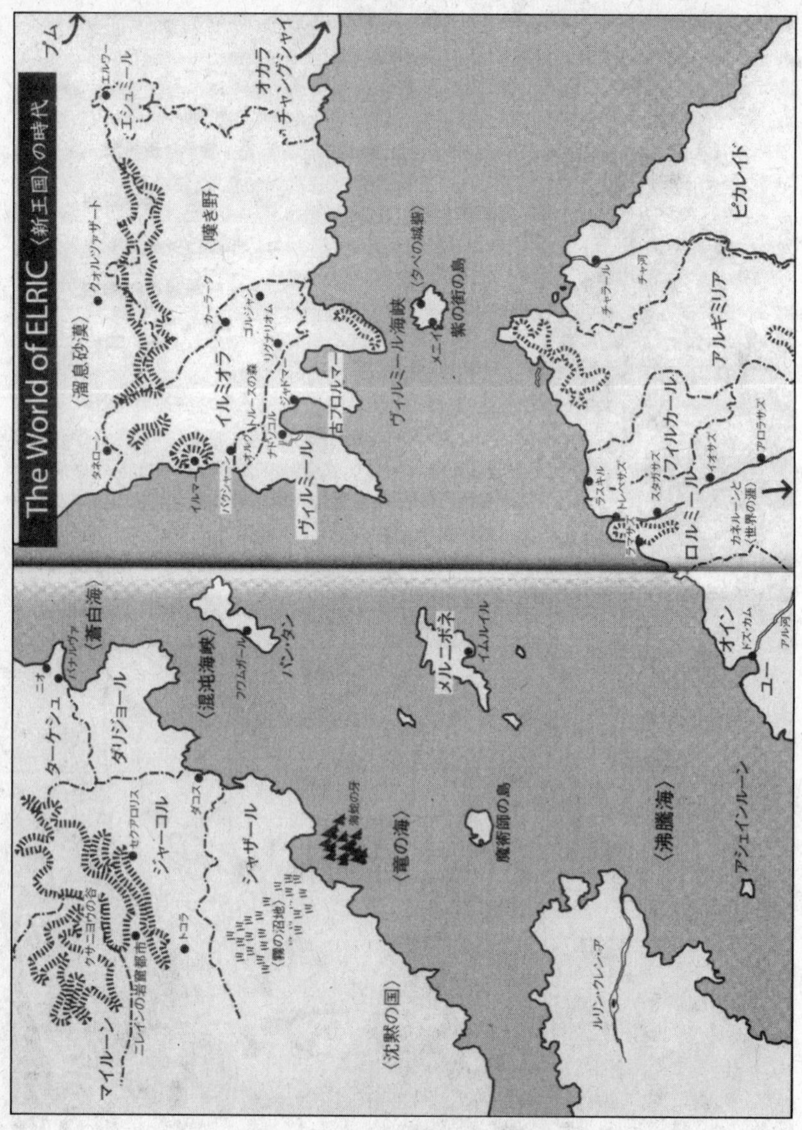

"The World of Elric" map, appeared in *Elric of Melniboné/The Fortress of the Pearl,* Japanese edition, © Hayakawa Publishing, Inc., 2006.

「只要對奇幻小說有興趣，就不能不讀麥克・摩考克。他一手改變了這個文類的風貌，是奇幻文學界的巨人。」——泰德・威廉斯（Tad Williams；紐約時報暢銷排行榜奇幻／科幻作者）

BEST 嚴選

永恆戰士

The Eternal Champion

梅尼波內的艾爾瑞克

Elric of Melniboné

麥克・摩考克（Michael Moorcock）◎著

嚴韻◎譯

這是個悲劇故事，龍之島梅尼波內的故事。

故事裡有激越的情緒和高遠的野心；有法術、背叛、崇高的理想；

有苦痛和可怕的歡愉，有苦澀的愛和甜美的恨。

這是梅尼波內的艾爾瑞克的故事。其中許多情節，日後艾爾瑞克將只在夢魘中記起。

Cover artwork by "Hugo," for *Elric of Melniboné,* Taiwanese edition, Fantasy Foundation Publishing, 2007.

「只要對奇幻小說有興趣，就不能不讀麥克・摩考克。他一手改變了這個文類的風貌，是奇幻文學界的巨人。」——泰德・威廉斯（Tad Williams，紐約時報暢銷排行榜奇幻／科幻作者）

BEST 嚴選

永恆戰士

The Eternal Champion

珍珠堡壘

The Fortress of the Pearl

麥克・摩考克（Michael Moorcock）◎著

嚴韻◎譯

文爾瑞克對未婚妻席芙蕊說了三個謊，

讓野心勃勃的表親奕爾昆以攝政身分坐上紅寶石王座，

前往未知的國度追尋知識。

但是，是在夸札撒這個沙漠城，他展開了那段將影響之後多年命運的冒險……

Cover artwork by "Hugo," for *The Fortress of the Pearl,* Taiwanese edition, Fantasy Foundation Publishing, 2007.

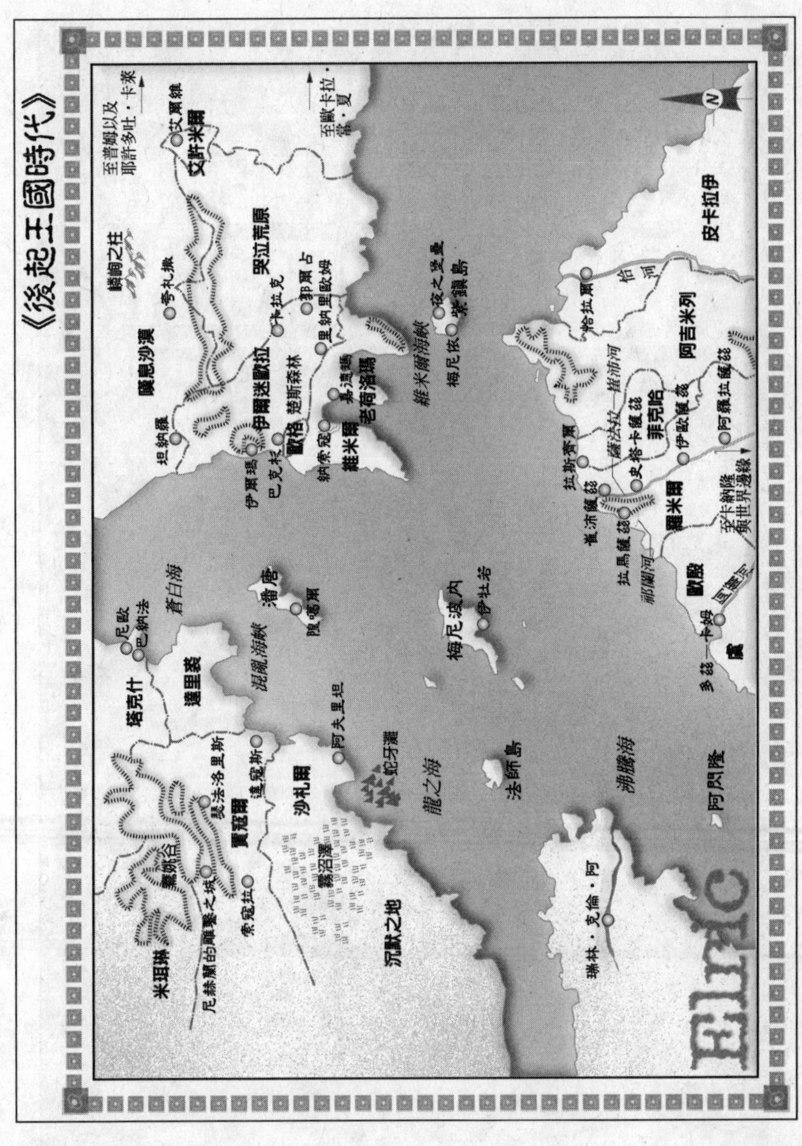

"Elric" map by Li-Chin Zhang, appeared in *Elric of Melniboné,* Taiwanese edition, Fantasy Foundation Publishing, 2007.

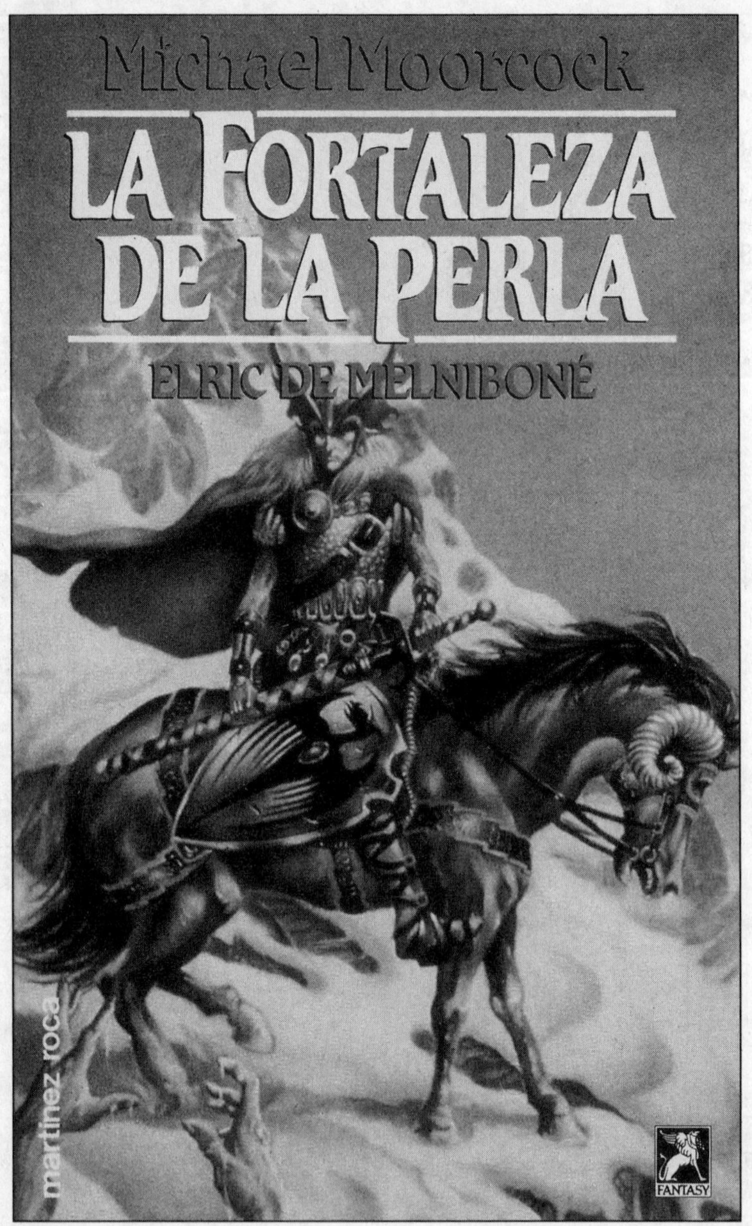

"Elric Stormbringer," by Frank Brunner, used as cover artwork for *La Fortaleza de la Perla,* Spanish edition, Martínez Roca, 1982.

Cover artwork by Walter Simonson, for *Elric: The Making of a Sorcerer,* issue No. 1 (of 4), DC Comics, 2004. *Michael Moorcock's Elric: The Making of a Sorcerer* published by DC Comics.

A double-page spread, by Walter Simonson (written by Moorcock), from *Elric: The Making of a Sorcerer,* issue No. 4 (of 4), DC Comics, 2006. *Michael Moorcock's Elric: The Making of a Sorcerer* published by DC Comics.

WHY BURDEN ME WITH THIS WEIGHTY SECRET?
BECAUSE IT IS YOUR DESTINY TO SERVE BOTH.
YOU...OR YOUR DESCENDANTS...WILL LEARN MORE IN THE COURSE OF THE NEXT TEN THOUSAND YEARS, BUT NOW YOU MUST FIND THE SWORD THAT ARIOCH OF CHAOS STOLE FROM KING GROME...
...AND WHICH WE, WITH GROME'S COMPLIANCE, WILL PLACE ON ANOTHER PLANE, WHERE IT WILL BE SAFE FOR AS LONG AS NEED BE...
I DON'T UNDER-STAND...
YOU ARE NOT ASKED TO UNDERSTAND. YOU MUST MAKE THE JOURNEY BACK TOWARDS MELNIBONÉ. THERE, YOU WILL FIND THE REST OF YOUR DESTINY AND THE BLACK SWORD.
WHEN YOU HOLD THE SWORD, A WORD WE HAVE PLACED IN YOUR MIND WILL SUMMON US.
IF YOU NEED OUR HELP, YOU'LL RECEIVE IT...
MY DESTINY? THE BLACK SWORD? I WANT ONLY TO BE A GOOD AND WISE RULER OF MELNIBONÉ...
THAT WILL BECOME A MATTER OF OPINION, KING ELRIK...

Cover artwork by Dawn Wilson, for *The Fortress of the Pearl,* first American paperback edition, Ace Books, 1990.

For further information about Michael Moorcock and his work, please send a stamped, self-addressed envelope to:

The Nomads of the Time Streams
P.O. Box 385716
Waikoloa, HI 96738

ABOUT THE AUTHOR

MICHAEL JOHN MOORCOCK is the author of a number of science fiction, fantasy, and literary novels, including the Elric novels, the Cornelius Quartet, *Gloriana, King of the City,* and many more. As editor of the controversial British science fiction magazine *New Worlds,* Moorcock fostered the development of the New Wave in the U.K. and indirectly in the U.S. He won the Nebula Award for his novella *Behold the Man.* He has also won the World Fantasy Award, the British Fantasy Award, and many others.

ABOUT THE ILLUSTRATOR

MICHAEL WM. KALUTA studied art at the Richmond Professional Institute (now Virginia Commonwealth University). Arriving in New York in 1969, he was hired by DC Comics and eventually assigned to what is now a classic stint: the creation of *The Shadow* comic book. In the mid-seventies he, Jeffrey Jones, Barry Windsor-Smith, and Bernie Wrightson formed The Studio; he later collaborated with Elaine Lee in adapting her play *Starstruck* to comics. He is inspired by Frank Frazetta, Roy Krenkel, and Al Williamson.